Europe Has Fallen

Andrew Gouriet

February 21,1879

To Brigadier Steiner

We have had no news from Unghvar for almost a month. I have dispatched several letters requesting an update and have received no response. We have not even heard of our riders' welfare, and due to the weather, we cannot leave the fort until spring.

I must implore you: do we know if we are at war with Russia? Should we be ready for an attack?
The men are ready and fresh but are concerned about the lack of contact from the garrison.

Finally, there have been strange happenings here over the past week. I cannot fully describe them in a letter, but hopefully, they are nothing more than winter occurrences.

I await your response with due haste.

I remain your faithful servant,

General Von Bloch.

Chapter 1

The larch trees had lost their colour, and the mountainous landscape was a feast of white. The silence was hypnotic and soothing, maybe even a little sinister.

Sergeant Butcher and a group of four soldiers were making their way back to the fort. The idea of being in the Carpathian Mountains over the winter did not appeal to these Royal Engineers. England was a great distance away, and spending time without their loved ones and families was hard. Their original British military winter clothes were not really adequate for the conditions they found themselves in. The Austrian army had been very forthcoming with better winter coats, and the British detachment embraced this and vowed to continue their support for sharing knowledge of modern improvements in structural engineering. It turned out to be more of an exchange of ideas, but it was useful, nonetheless.

Snowflakes struck their faces as they walked down a narrow path. The aromas of cooking meat wafted through the air. Each of them hastened their step as their stomachs dictated their newfound speed. Sergeant Butcher raised his left hand, and the four soldiers stopped. They tried to see what was causing him to make them wait, but the heavy falling snow reduced their range of vision. All they could make out were silhouettes of each other.

A deep, trembling growl rose up around them, seeping through the darkness. It was sharp and menacing.

One of the soldiers raised his Martini-Henry rifle. His vision was impaired, but he looked for movement in the whiteness that surrounded them.

Within a flash, Sergeant Butcher was toppled by something whistling past him, and a shriek rang out as one of the soldiers in the patrol was dragged at speed away from the group. In the confusion that followed, shots were fired aimlessly in all directions. It took a few seconds for the remaining men to gain their composure.

Blood patches stained the freshly fallen snow. The sergeant wasted no time. "Quickly, we must follow the trail."

There was a young soldier amongst the group, Private John Brown. This was his first posting to Europe, and his heart pumped with excitement and nerves. The man who had been taken was not well known to him, but he was one of their own, something that had been drummed into every British soldier.

It was hard to move fast in the deep snow; their legs were tiring, and their senses were jaded. The fort was now maybe a ten-minute walk away, which made the sergeant wary.

John looked up at a ridge and raised his rifle.

"Hold your fire, son."

Sergeant Butcher pointed to the hundreds of piercing eyes now staring at them. At the bottom of the ridge was the dismembered body of the dead soldier. All of them were aghast at what they saw, even the battle-hardened sergeant.

There was no time to retrieve what was left of the body. It was now about retreating and getting back to the fort as quickly as possible.

The sergeant turned to his men.

"When I say run, you move as fast as you can to the fort. I'll bring up the rear."

No one had to ask any more questions. The sight of teeth snarling was enough to make every man's neck hair stand on end.

"Run!"

John turned and moved as fast as he could through the deep snow. A chorus of howls echoed around him; it was deafening.

His heart was racing, eyes pulsating, and sweat was streaming from his helmet and running down his cheeks. He did not want to turn around, so he just kept on moving.

A shot rang out, and a yelp followed, but there was still a steady sound of movement as if a thousand tiny feet were on the march. Even in the snow, there was a constant, muffled advance.

John stumbled several times but managed to keep his feet. He could see the old fort and the gateway which led inside.

In the rush to escape, he had been separated from the group and was anxious to know if they were okay. He afforded himself one glance over his shoulder. His eyes widened to what he saw.

He snapped his head back and doubled his speed, which, in the deep snow, forced him to almost jump in and out of his stride as if he were doing hurdles. A scream crept up from behind him, and a collection of growling and ripping sounds followed. A soft mumbling and gurgling noise superseded this.

John let his rifle slip, causing him to fall forward. The moment his face hit the ice-cold snow was almost refreshing until a motion of weightlessness followed it. He was startled for a split second or two, not knowing what was happening. Then, the sergeant's familiar voice came into his ear loud and clear.

"No time for a bloody rest, boy."

John was lifted to his feet in one motion and was almost running again without a pause for breath.

"My rifle, Sarge."

"Not now, Brown."

The sergeant led them to the gate, where the sentry was waiting, looking panicked. The other soldiers followed swiftly behind.

"I tried to save Weaver, but he was overwhelmed. I couldn't do anything. There were too many, too many," said the soldier who had been with him.

Private Brown almost collapsed inside the fort gateway but was held up by his comrades.

A young officer ran over to them and ordered the gate to be shut immediately. He then signalled for the alarm, and a Bugler belted out a rising call to arms.

Within seconds, the fort was buzzing with life. Austrian and British soldiers moved quickly about, gathering their weapons and making their way to the walls and gun emplacements.

The general of the Austrian soldiers was a man named Von Bloch. He was a seasoned campaigner who had mellowed with age and enjoyed the slower life of engineering compared to the domestic issues surrounding Europe at that moment in time. He went straight to Major Harry Richmond and demanded an update.

Captain Hayward was at the gate as they slammed it shut. He wanted to check with Sergeant Butcher about what had just happened.

The sentry called out. "Sir, they're dragging a man to the front of the fort."

"Who's dragging a man to the front?" Captain Hayward responded, puzzled.

"Wolves, sir."

No one could believe their eyes; four enormous wolves were dragging a half-eaten Private Weaver to the front of the fort. His torso had been ripped open, but he was still managing to reach up to his fellow men. The wolves around him had larger bodies than his, with teeth more appropriate in a sabre-toothed tiger. They circled the man and sniffed and grunted at each other.

Major Richmond, Captain Hayward, and Von Bloch were looking down from the battlements. They were all taken aback by what was happening. A wolf with a white streak across its face seemed to growl and hiss at the other three, making them snap into line.

The other men on the battlements looked at the officers for orders. The Austrian and British soldiers raised rifles. They wanted to open fire upon these creatures, but they waited for a command, nonetheless.

The dominant wolf lifted itself onto its hind legs as though showing off its size. Three Austrian soldiers aimed a cannon in its direction.

Von Bloch didn't want to waste any time and ordered a unit of men to scare off the wolves and collect the body. Just as he did so, Sergeant Butcher came to the battlements with an anxious look.

"Sir, if I may, I believe this could be a mistake. There is something about this I do not like... There were –"

The front gates were opened as he was about to explain how they had seen an army of growling teeth. Ten Austrian soldiers went out with bayonets attached to their rifles. The gates were half-closed behind them.

The dominant wolf looked in their direction and waited.

Once the men were about twenty metres away, their captain gave the order to fire over the wolves' heads. They all did so in unison. Not one wolf moved; they just looked at the Austrians with cold, black eyes.

The snow trembled as if it were melting.

An Austrian soldier shouted to the small group: "Get back to the fort!" The larger wolves then started ripping into Private Weaver. Von Bloch took the rifle and, with one clean shot, hit him in the head.

"He shouldn't suffer any more."

Von Bloch called for every man to go to the walls.

Within seconds, a massive pack of wolves charged towards the small group of Austrian soldiers. They tried to retreat but could not move quickly enough. The only option left was to fight off the wolves that had descended on them.

British and Austrian soldiers lined up together and started firing from the battlements. Cannons were also being used, but the speed and movement of the wolves made it hard for them to gain good targets. They were not static infantry lines; these were mobile creatures and distinctively quick.

Captain Hayward looked for the wolf with the white stripe on its face, but it had gone. One of the other larger wolves attacked a soldier outside the fort, picking him up and slinging him against the wall. The soldier's leg had been severed off in the process. The sheer force of wolf numbers was overpowering the other soldiers outside the fort.

Sergeant Butcher took aim with his rifle, breathed in once and pulled the trigger, hitting a large wolf in the hind quarters. It gave out a yelp and looked up at him. It was then hit by several other bullets, recoiling as the bullets impacted its body, but it was able to keep attacking. Wolves' bodies lay strewn outside the fort walls.

In a small cluster of trees, the men could see a silhouette of someone in dark clothing carrying what looked like an upside-down cross. Next to this shadowy figure was an enormous wolf. It came forward and started to howl, echoing around the valley.

The wolves broke off the attack and scuttled back into the surrounding forests from all angles. The ten Austrian soldiers who had gone outside to retrieve Private Weaver were in a bad way; some had lost limbs, and others had received bite wounds. It was not until a few minutes had passed that a relief group was sent to retrieve them, but during that time, six had died from blood loss and flesh wounds. The four remaining men needed medical help and would have to be worked on by the fort surgeon immediately.

It took a moment before Captain Hayward could comprehend what had just happened. It had all been so surreal.

Was it a lack of food in the forests or something else that had brought the wolves out in such force?

There was an air of uncertainty as the heavy flakes began to fall again. They fell hard and soon covered the blood-soaked snow. The dead soldiers were carried to the barn within the fort.

General Von Bloch called for a meeting in his quarters. The word was spread that all officers and sergeants should join him in ten minutes.

The fort consisted of around two hundred soldiers, roughly a fifty-fifty split between the Royal Engineers and the Austrian Engineers. Around fifty civilians also stayed with them, helping out over the winter months with the livestock and general upkeep of the outpost.

Captain Hayward made his way to the general's office across an open courtyard but stopped when his senior officer and friend approached him. Both were very concerned about recent events and what their future actions should entail.

"We have lost two British soldiers today and six Austrians," said Major Richmond.

Captain Hayward shook his head in disbelief. "Why would wolves attack in such numbers?"

Major Richmond paused. "Frankly, I'm unsure." Still deep in thought, he continued. "I've always been a keen hunter, and yes, you may come up against an alpha male occasionally, but these were four to five times that size."

Captain Hayward nodded in agreement, but the conversation had to stop there as it was time to go to Von Bloch's quarters.

"One last thing, Harry, did you see the larger wolf being hit by bullets and not dying?"

Major Richmond just stood and stared into the whiteness around them. "We must join the other officers now."

Von Bloch cleared his desk and laid out a map of the mountain terrain surrounding them. He wanted everyone to see the scale of their situation. "Gentlemen, this could be the Russians."

Two young Austrian officers agreed with their commander. Captain Hayward looked at Major Richmond.

Von Bloch continued: "We should send another message to the local garrison and request reinforcements immediately."

Major Richmond piped up: "With all due respect, General, we have sent two messengers in the last two months, and we've not had a single reply."

The general turned his head to one side, scratched his left earlobe, and then tweaked his long grey moustache. "Maybe you're right, but we will still send someone, nonetheless. We face a difficult situation, gentlemen; make no bones about it. The weather is such that moving down from the mountains until March at the earliest would be impossible."

They took time to consider the maps. The general's concerns were centred on what sort of enemy they were up against: why the wolves attacked as they did and whether a sizeable military force would soon attack the fort.

A staff sergeant brought in coffee and quickly updated the general on what was happening outside. So far, everything was clear; there was not a sound from anywhere. The snow was slowly covering the dead wolves, and soon, it would be as if nothing had happened.

Private Brown was busy cleaning his bayonet. They had alerted the fort but told half the soldiers to stand down. In this case, they thought it would be easier to have the Royal Engineers take one shift and the Austrian Engineers the other.

Some of the Austrian soldiers had a good command of English and would try to use it whenever possible. Even though the Austrians had the second watch, there were plenty of chores to be done around the fort. The dead bodies, most lying in pieces but some still intact with open wounds, were being kept in the barn, and, due to the temperature, they were not being put into the ground straight away.

Their comrades gathered near the barn and prayed together. Corporal Erin didn't want the men to dwell too long, as the attack had shaken morale.

Private John Brown spoke to his friend William about what had happened. They were all on edge, but they had also been told to keep their wits about them and not just focus on the wolves.

"William, are you scared?"

"No, are you?"

"If you saw them up close like I did, you would be." John looked a little pale as he said this.

They both gripped their rifles slightly tighter. The discussion then turned to one of the milkmaids in the fort, a young Austrian girl whom John had had his eyes on. She was tall and cute, with long blonde hair and a full figure.

"I saw the way you've been looking at Heidi."

John looked to the sky and watched snowflakes fall effortlessly down. He blushed a little, but the cold hid this. It wasn't really the time for him to be thinking about a girl, but somehow, it helped relax him.

A call went up for dinner, and soon, the cook and his assistant brought along a large soup cauldron with a hunk of bread for each man. The heat from the broth was marvellous to watch, and their mouths started to salivate.

They held out their mess tins and asked for them to be filled to the brim, which caused the cook to look disconcerted.

William and John began tucking into the soup and dipping the bread into the tin. Even in these torrid conditions, having a hearty meal in their stomachs made it more bearable.

Captain Hayward left the general's office to visit the men. The fort wasn't a straightforward square shape; it was more hexagonal. It had been modernised since the Crimean War days and enlarged to allow more civilian use in later years.

Corporal Smith was waiting at the top to guide the captain through the defences. An hour had passed since the wolves had attacked en masse. It had been totally silent since then.

The men moved along the walls to keep warm. They wore long winter coats and thick caps to keep out the icy wind. Due to the wintry conditions, it was hard to maintain this surveillance on the horizon.

He decided to get some of the men to stand down and return to regular duties. No one was allowed to leave the fort without permission from the commanding officer. They would have to maintain a high readiness level, which meant all men were briefed about future action. The majority of the British and Austrian engineers had not seen conflict and were more suited to mending and providing support to the regular armies.

Major Richmond spoke with his officers about reassuring the men. Losing eight soldiers so rapidly would unnerve any army unit.

Captain Hayward called Sergeant Butcher and Corporal Smith over. He spoke about General Von Bloch's decision to send two riders to reach the main garrison in the nearest town. He had expressed his concerns over this, but the general insisted they must try something. It had been decided the riders would be Austrians, as they knew the quickest route to the town.

The British soldiers agreed they were glad to be staying in the fort for now.

Von Bloch spoke privately with his second-in-command, Captain Egger. He had heard rumours of someone standing in the forest; this figure seemed to have something in its hand. Some believed a large wolf was by its side.

The old general did not want idle chat to spread amongst the soldiers. He suggested it was their imagination running away with them. He admitted that a large wolf attack on this scale was rare, if not unique, but he also believed that even animals could form large packs and search for food in times of hunger. He hoped the wolf attack was a one-off incident and would pass quickly. One of his nagging thoughts, though, was that the Russians could be preparing to attack, and he wanted to be ready should that happen. He had to write a report of the day's events and, unfortunately, inform the families of the fallen men. The riders could take this information with them when they set out. Major Richmond was also busy working on his summary of the attack and how he had lost two soldiers. Both commanders kept their personal thoughts about the day's events to themselves for now.

The hours passed with no sign of movement anywhere. Darkness fell, and the Austrians took the night watch. Captain Egger kept the lookouts to a minimum. The men would huddle in the fort's corners around small fires burning in iron caskets.

The Austrians were more acclimatised to these conditions, but that did not mean they enjoyed them. There were now just ten men patrolling the walls as they went into the graveyard shift.

Private Clegg and Private Brown were fast asleep in their quarters. Cannons had been loaded and rifles cleaned; Von Bloch was pleased with the soldiers' response to the situation. Every man was told he should be ready for combat in minutes should they hear the call to arms.

While everyone slept, the two riders were dispatched to carry out news of their plight in the mountains. Von Bloch saw them off and wished them Godspeed for the journey that lay ahead.

General Von Bloch took time to visit the wounded soldiers and then went onto the bodies of the fallen men, pausing to reflect on the day's events. It was late and cold, but he was an old soldier who knew the cost of life. He didn't notice one of the bodies had gone.

Captain Hayward bumped his head as the Bugler let rip with the call to arms. He grabbed his trousers and socks.

His throat was dry. He was sure he had hardly slept at all, and now he hurriedly dressed himself. Gunshots started to ring out, which only made the captain stumble about as he quickened his speed.

He attached his sword and revolver and grabbed his thick winter overcoat and helmet. Outside his quarters, the staff sergeant was waiting to greet him and update him on what was happening.

The staff sergeant was flustered and clearly out of breath.

"We're under attack, sir. We think they're in the fort."

"Their numbers, Sergeant?"

"Hard to tell, sir. The morning has not fully broken yet."

Captain Hayward finished buttoning his coat and followed the staff sergeant out of the barracks. He was handed a rifle and an ammunition belt. He took a second to fix his bayonet.

The scene outside was frantic. Soldiers were moving to the battlements, and even civilians were taking pitchforks and weapons in a bid to help.

Major Richmond was taking command of one side of the fort. Von Bloch was taking the other. Captain Hayward sprang up the stone steps to witness the attack for himself.

His eyes fell upon a mass of grey coats flowing from side to side. It was early morning, and the sun was just about to break. Thousands of tiny eyes were everywhere, lit up by the burning torches. The wolves made up a sea of movement as far as the eye could see.

There was a more significant increase in the number of larger wolves than previously, and again; the larger wolves seemed to be barking and snarling to control the smaller ones. Bullets were hitting these larger wolves, but this did not seem to have much effect on them.

Major Richmond knelt and began firing. Captain Hayward joined him, crouching down by his side.

"Charles, this is not good. We believe some have climbed over. I've sent a small detachment to intercept them. We must keep communication lines open with the Austrians on the other side of the fort."

Captain Hayward nodded and suggested that he and the staff sergeant would help attend to the wolves that had breached the fort.

Privates Brown and Clegg were part of the detachment of four searching for the wolves that had broken in. Both soldiers felt the adrenaline pumping through their veins.

Rifle shots came from all directions, and thunderous bangs and muzzle smoke filled the air. They slowly moved along, passing each wooden outbuilding, looking for movement. It was decided that the barn and livestock were a good place to check. The two other soldiers with them went cautiously into the barn, each step slow and ponderous. The rifle fire going on around them disorientated their senses and made it hard to pinpoint exactly where each sound was coming from.

The barn was a fair size, and hay was stacked on both sides, creating little corridors everywhere. It was dark and musty, with farm ploughs and other machinery scattered around.

Grain was piled against a wall, creating a small hill because of the amount needed through the winter.

They pushed on to where the animals were penned. The cows were grouped together, bellowing out calls. Each man had his bayonet attached in anticipation. In the corner where the goats were penned lay a dead carcass – it had been ripped to pieces. The other goats were missing.

Gunfire occasionally lit the darkness, making each soldier twitch a little. They were ready to shoot at anything that moved. John caught William's attention and then pointed to the corner of a haystack. A single wolf was feeding on a dead goat. It was preoccupied with its feast and did not see John raise his Martini-Henry rifle and slowly and quietly load the bullet into the chamber.

The roar of the rifle sent vibrations around the barn. It was a clean shot, and the wolf slumped to the side of a hay bale before falling uncoordinatedly. John smiled at William; he was happy with his shot. It wasn't just the distance but the lack of clear light that impressed him.

The other two soldiers came over to Privates Brown and Clegg. They patted John on the back but kept quiet as they suspected this was not the only wolf in the barn. They split up into two groups.

Captain Hayward and the staff sergeant entered the barn after hearing the gunshot. The fighting on the outside had died down, and there were no more reports of breaches to the fort defences.

Charles drew out his Adams revolver and put his rifle over his shoulder. He was an army Engineer, but he had a good hand on him and would practise shooting with the revolver whenever possible.

The staff sergeant followed behind him with his bayonet attached.

One of the two soldiers had found an alley created by supply boxes stacked in a way that fashioned a tunnel. He knelt down, wondering if he should look inside.

His companion was not too sure; it was dark and dusty. The soldiers could see their breath as they waited for a decision. They hurriedly scanned the area with their eyes to see if Private Clegg or Brown were in close proximity, but unfortunately, they were alone.

With that, the first soldier bent down and crawled inside the tunnel. The darkness made it hard to see the sides. Halfway in, something felt wet under his hands. It felt as if the ground was moving. Something wriggled. He looked down to see a half-eaten goat. It was still alive and moving around, and there was sheer panic in the animal's eyes.

It now felt like a bad idea to be enclosed in a small space. As he turned, he caught something moving in the alley and out of the tunnel. He could not raise his rifle in time as the thing turned and moved towards him, its teeth gleaming as they came at him. This was not a normal-sized creature; it was bigger than a lion, and when it got close, it was able to bite at his body, almost breaking him in half.

He had tried to move, but the beast was fast and direct. It pushed him into the boxes, causing him to scream out as the teeth pierced his body. The other soldier started to enter the alleyway and was unsighted when he felt a sharp pain in his calf muscles. He turned in horror to see three wolves clamping down on him. "Help me!" he screamed.

Private Brown took aim, and the roar from the Martini-Henry rifle filled the area. One of the wolves was blown into the hay bales. Its nearest companion looked up, snarled and then made a beeline for Private Brown.

He fumbled briefly as he attempted to load his rifle under pressure. It was time for the basic training to take over.

Private Clegg stuck out his bayonet and skewed the charging animal as the wolf was upon Private Brown. It thrashed around and tried to nip and bite the rifle. He quickly withdrew the blade and then lunged forward again with it. He almost enjoyed exacting revenge for the men who had already perished in this animal's attack.

He finished it off with the butt of his rifle, then, helping John to his feet, they made their way to the other soldier, who was being bitten and pulled around.

Captain Hayward and the staff sergeant had arrived at the chaotic scene and promptly opened fire on the attacking wolves. It needed a steady hand and mind to ensure the wounded soldier was not shot instead.

They came over to the man and checked over his injuries. The staff sergeant ordered Privates Clegg and Brown to take the man to the infirmary.

Charles then looked down the tunnel to see if anyone was moving. The gunfire had ceased outside.

The air in the barn had turned from a musty animal smell to a gunpowder-like aroma. Charles looked around and thought about getting reinforcements. With that, he loaded his Adams revolver and whispered to the staff sergeant that it would be best if they sought help. They had been warned that something was lurking in the alley and that four dead wolves were now scattered in the barn.

The two men slowly got up and moved backwards from the bales and animal pens. They would have turned around fully if not for the throaty, hissing snort that caught their ears. There, on top of the bales, was a colossal wolf looking down on them. It had at its feet a half-dismembered body.

It looked each man up and down and then leapt forward. Captain Hayward fired his Adams revolver directly at the large wolf but to no avail; the bullets pierced the fur but had no effect on the animal. It was quickly on top of the captain, forcing him to fall backwards under its powerful body weight. It lowered its nose to his forehead before opening its mouth to reveal sharp, pointed teeth.

As it went to strike, the staff sergeant who had been knocked back in the initial attack took aim with his rifle and hit the wolf directly in the head. Its eyes rolled for a second, and then it began to fall. The animal's paws slipped onto his shoulders, and its body slumped directly on top of the captain.

The weight was crushing, and he was grateful for help as it was slowly pulled off him.

"Captain, what is this?"

"I don't know. The bullets had no effect – it was only the headshot that killed it."

Both of them took a short moment to examine the animal. Its size was surely not normal, even if it did turn out to be an alpha male.

Charles asked for the animal to be covered and for the staff sergeant to get several more soldiers to check through the barn and ensure there were no more hidden wolves.

He intended to report this to the other officers but was anxious to find out what was happening outside the fort. He knew the guns had fallen silent and wanted to be kept informed of the situation.

The soldiers were scanning the landscape for movement. The number of dead animals lying around had lifted their spirits, and they now felt that the situation would return to normal due to the fort's firepower.

Captain Hayward joined Major Harry Richmond on the battlements. He debriefed him on the situation about the wolves that had broken in. The message had also been sent to the Austrian side of the fort. It was essential to keep communication alive at all times.

A detachment of twelve men searched the rest of the barn, but no more wolves were reported. As rapidly as the wolves had attacked, they disappeared into the forests again. General Von Bloch joined the officers on the British side. He stroked his moustache and sighed, offering his sympathy for the fallen British soldiers, his face blank with concern and puzzlement.

They all agreed that this was a freak occurrence. The predators would have learnt that this meal would come at too high a price, and this huge pack would move off into the mountains in search of other food. No one wanted to think past this being the end of it all.

Chapter 2

Three weeks passed. Patrols of fifty men were sent out at a time, but the area was clear. The dead carcasses had been burnt, and the fallen soldiers were being kept in the barn. Each soldier was temporarily stored in a box filled with ice; it was still cold enough for them not to decompose. When the weather improved, they would be given a military burial.

No news had arrived from the nearby garrison, and the civilians in the fort were anxious to hear about their loved ones.

General Von Bloch had realised it might be time to leave the fort as soon as the good weather arrived. It was approaching mid-March, and if they were lucky, it might only be a few weeks before they could set off.

The order for the evacuation was given. Every able man, woman, and child would take enough food and water to make the trip to the nearest town. Von Bloch was wary because they could be cut off from the main Austrian army if war broke out.

The Royal Engineers helped with all the preparations. They were good at logistics and used their skills to pack food and materials needed. Some livestock would be allowed to go free into the wild, as they could not herd every animal down through the mountains.

Private Brown had used his spare time to speak to Heidi, and they had even agreed to go on a picnic together once the drama had died down. They had occasionally looked into each other's eyes, and John was sure he was falling for her. He hoped she had the same feelings he had.

As the snow melted away, the dead soldiers were given a full military burial outside the fort. It was still hard digging in the ground as the cold had made it rock solid, but the comrades of these men knew no difference and would have wanted the same for themselves if they had perished in the mountains as well.

Captain Hayward and the staff sergeant listened to the short address by the major and the general. They both focused on the hard work the men had put in and their services to their countries and the Army Engineers. A sombre mood descended over the barracks and fort.

While the focus was on survival, no one had much time to dwell on anything else. In the evening, the general decided to hold a celebration in memory of the fallen men. It was the best they could do to raise spirits before the march down through the mountains.

Letters to the soldiers' families, both Austrian and British, would travel down with the convoy from the fort as no more messengers' lives would be risked.

As night began to fall, the head cook slaughtered some pigs and began a feast of roast pork and vegetables. Ale was brought in from the cellars, and the soldiers were allowed to enjoy themselves.

The celebration continued into the early morning. The few soldiers who remained on guard were promised extra leave to compensate them for missing the festivities.

It was another three weeks before the snow completely disappeared. The old general wanted to give everything enough time to ensure the safety of everyone in his command, including his foreign guests.

Heidi and Private Brown took the opportunity to go to a secluded spot that Heidi had spoken about. They had a large picnic with them. The weather was mild for April, and only the wind carried a slight chill.

The odd bud had started to peak through, but the landscape was mostly clear of new life. Vast forests covered much of the terrain. The spot they chose for their rug overlooked the valley. They had not travelled too far from the fort but far enough to feel detached from it.

Sitting in the spring sun, they felt relaxed and slightly giddy from the excitement. It was nice to be away from the hustle and bustle of the fort. They had some bread and cheese and dried fruit from the barrack stores. John had saved some money and had acquired some wine.

They ate their feast and gazed into each other's eyes. It wasn't long before they kissed and made love on the rug. John had not intended for it to go this fast, but recent events allowed them to release tensions in each other. Time passed with ease, and as the day passed, they fell asleep in each other's arms.

A sharp horn sound brought the tranquillity to an abrupt end. It filled the forests and valleys, and the mountains came alive with the piercing noise. John awoke semi-naked next to Heidi, grabbed his tunic and stood up. It wasn't the usual bugle call to arms, so he looked around for where the sound could be coming from.

Heidi started to dress herself quickly. John stroked the back of her hair, and she looked up and smiled at him.

The following noise to fill the spring air was howling. It was so loud it almost made the ground shake. Heidi's eyes searched for contact with John's. He ran over to a ridge which overlooked a deep valley. Heidi could feel his fear before she joined him and stood beside him.

The valley was moving. It was like watching an army of ants swarm. Unfortunately, these were no ants; this was an army of wolves. John grabbed Heidi's arm and started to run, and she was pulled along with his motion. He didn't stop to pick up the rug or other items they had with them.

His heart was thumping, and his mind was racing about what was going to happen. Heidi had no shoes on and was having to sprint barefoot. She looked over her shoulder and let out a yelp as her ankle gave way underneath her. It brought both of them to the ground. John looked around. The howling had stopped, and the ground was shaking. He put his left hand under her buttocks and his right under her arms. "Sorry, Heidi, I need to pick you up." As he turned, he saw a terrifying sight: wolves streaming from everywhere. The forests were bursting with them.

He held her close and started to run. Though she was telling him to leave her, he would do no such thing as it meant certain death. As they closed in on safety, the beasts closed in on them.

A shout went out for them to run to the walls instead of the gates. Ropes had been lowered down for them. John reached the wall, exhausted, and got Heidi to hold on to the rope.

She was speedily hoisted up and carried over the battlements. John grabbed the other rope but felt the rush of air around him. What followed was pain: teeth were biting him from every angle. He shouted out but held firm as the soldiers pulled him up. He heard words of encouragement from Sergeant Butcher and a volley of bullets whistling over his head.

As he was pulled up, the soldiers jabbed at the wolves, still holding onto him. One of them fell straight off, and Sergeant Butcher shot the other with a clean hit. Heidi and John were swiftly taken for medical treatment.

Captain Hayward was on the battlements with his men. The sight that greeted him was a sea of wolves as far as the eye could see. They were running around the fort, trying to find weaknesses. It was noted that there were even more giant wolves than before.

The word was spread that only headshots would suffice for the larger wolves. The cannons were rapidly swung into action. Not enough soldiers were present to man all of them, though, so their firepower was rendered less effective.

The civilians in the fort were tasked with bringing ammunition and water to the soldiers on the walls. They were also formed into teams to help any wounded men to the orderlies to be treated.

The wolves' attacks seemed futile, as hundreds were dying right next to the battlements. The mounting pile of wolves' bodies gave the animals a chance to clamber up their dead pack members and leap at the walls. The giant wolves were massing in the distance, and the general felt it was only a matter of time before they would try to ascend the outer defences.

Major Richmond ordered the barracks secured should the fort fall. Captain Hayward took three men and made his way to the building. En route, they gathered the blacksmith and two carpenters. He explained the task they had in mind: for it to work, the barracks had to be secure.

Everything was done at speed as the situation was unclear.

The general made his way around the fort, looking for any openings through which they could make a break for it. He reflected on whether they should have left a week earlier but then pondered over them being attacked in the open with so many animals on the loose.

His mind was thrown back to the Austrian side of the fort as the wolves were starting to come over the top. Captain Egger was given the order to retreat as they poured onto the eastern side. The head pack members were tearing and biting at all the soldiers around them. One man was flung in the air and almost eaten whole as the wolf caught him again. They knew headshots would kill these beasts, but their movement and speed made it hard to hit their targets.

The Austrian side had sent a message to retreat, and the British were starting to report wolf breaches on the fort's Western side. There were chaotic scenes: orderlies struggled to open the ammunition boxes; some had been nailed shut, which meant there was a shortage of bullets.

Captain Hayward gave the order to take as much ammunition to the barracks as possible. As he did this, a grey flash sprang from the wall above him and landed on top of him. He held back its head as it tried to bite his face. It was not one of the larger wolves, but it was still a handful. His Adams revolver came to the rescue; with difficulty, he drew it out of his gun holster and shot the animal in the head.

He rolled the dead animal off. The bugler gave the sound of the retreat, and everyone began to fall back to the barracks. There was still an army of wolves outside the fort trying to get in. Some of the larger ones were running at the gates, crunching their bodies against the wood and then starting the whole process over again. Hundreds, maybe even thousands of wolves, lay dead outside, but this did not affect their numbers.

As they retreated, hand-to-hand fighting spread everywhere: men versus wolves. Major Richmond was with Corporal Smith and several other men manning an Armstrong cannon on the battlements. Sergeant Butcher tried to get word to them to leave the cannon as the fort was being overrun, and the last place to retreat was the barracks.

Major Richmond and three soldiers kept on firing from a fixed turret at the corner of the defences. The cannon was having some success with the large wolves, blowing them to smithereens when hit. The problem they were having with the Armstrong gun was that it was a breech-loading cannon, and the design was not quick enough for their situation. If it had been a muzzle-loading cannon, it would have meant a more rapid rate of fire, but the cannon was at least allowing soldiers and civilians to fall back to the barracks. As they re-loaded, a giant wolf leapt onto the turret and lashed out at a gunner's back. He managed to push the wolf back but did not deter it.

Major Richmond stepped forward and plunged his sword into the wolf's chest. It sank to the ground, but its eyes were still wild and full of life. He was quick to react, pulling out his revolver and shooting the animal in the head.

More wolves were pouring onto the turret, and it was starting to be swamped. The wounded gunner lay on the floor and tried to help the other men load the cannon. The major gave the signal to start using their rifles as it was time to retreat to the barracks.

They fixed bayonets and made haste towards the stone steps leading down to the courtyard. The fort was teeming with animals now, and some men had been forced into cabins and storage huts as the onslaught increased.

The civilian quarters were not that well protected, but some people had still made their way in there. Corporal Smith had reacted to this and tried to persuade everyone to follow the soldiers to the barracks, but unfortunately, that moment had passed, and now he was trapped in the building with ten bullets and his Snider Enfield rifle.

He had found three men and two women holding a small child inside the building. His spoken German was limited, but it was enough to take them upstairs and barricade themselves into a room. Corporal Smith put down his rifle as they grabbed what they could to block the entrance. There was a steady sound of something coming up the stairs. It took just seconds before it was pounding at the door. The ferocity of the attack was astonishing; bits of wood started to split and break from the door frame.

The three men and the corporal pushed back against it while one of the women picked up the rifle and shot through the door. She said, in broken English, "Farmer's daughter."

The noise on the other side stopped, and she passed back the rifle for Corporal Smith to reload.

The sound on the other side differed from a wolf panting or growling. It was more of a groaning sound and a shuffling scrape. They moved a large wardrobe in front of the broken panels and then anything else that was free. The banging stopped.

The small child had seen and pointed to an attic hatch. The men seized upon this and set about trying to open it. When they paused, all they could hear was their own heartbeat.

The barrack doors were shut hard as wolves tried to break in. They began to scratch at the doors with such vigour and determination that all eyes followed the sound. The general tried to assess their situation. The barn had horses in it, but the rest were in the stables. He had sent some soldiers to hold out in both places.

Every window and door in the barracks was being reinforced from within. Snipers were going out onto the roof to shoot down on the attacking force, but this could offer an element of risk as there were opportunities for the wolves to get across from adjacent buildings.

Unfortunately, there were many soldiers and civilians still stranded outside the barracks. They were either trying to get into the nearest building or fighting their ground. One problem with this was the lack of numbers, as even the strongest man could not hold back so many. The bigger problem was the larger wolves, which were more powerful than a bear and twice as deadly as a lion. These larger creatures had got themselves into key positions around the fort. From there, they howled and grunted. It was almost as if they were controlling the beasts around them.

Major Richmond knew they had to move fast. The fort was awash with the enemy, and they were gaining the upper hand over anyone left in the open. An Austrian soldier saw that they were leaving the cannon and made a break for it. He dropped his rifle and sprinted to the blacksmith's workshop. Halfway there, three wolves brought him down; the screams and the tearing of flesh could be heard inside every building. There was nothing anyone could do. Within seconds, three wolves soon became twenty to thirty.

In the barracks, women and children started to become upset. Captain Egger tried to control their wavering emotions, but anxiety levels were high, and nerves had become frayed.

Major Richmond and his men were too far away to join the others, so they decided to get to the stables. They knew a contingency plan had been put in place for some Austrian Engineers to guard the horses and protect them as long as possible.

He grabbed the wounded gunner and asked if he could make it across the open square towards the stables. He nodded and was helped to his feet by his fellow soldiers. The major loaded his Adams revolver and grabbed what ammunition he could, instructing the others to do the same. A second or two was used to gain composure, and then they moved down the stone steps leading from the turret with speed. A soldier was helping the wounded man to keep their speed up as they did not want to attract any attention until they were in full flight.

When they hit the main square, wolves started to come at them. The Adams revolver came in handy as the major was able to pick off several creatures before they got close enough to attack. Then he ordered two soldiers to shoot and then reload as they made their way to the stables while he covered them.

He thought the gods were smiling in their favour as this pattern gave them time to reach the stable doors and shout for them to be opened. At first, when no one came, panic set in as the wolves started to home in on them like buzzards on a dead carcass.

"Make every round count, men," said Major Richmond.

Even the wounded soldier had raised himself up and was given his rifle. All four of them were firing in turns: two fired, two reloaded, which maintained a constant rate of fire. Wolves were appearing from rooftops and over the walls, and the main gates had started to split as giant wolves burst through.

"Private Jones should smash them in if no one opens the doors. We will die very quickly out here in the open."

Major Richmond's assessment was based on the sheer number of wolves now flowing towards them. Their eyes were stone-cold black, and their canine teeth looked sharp and intimidating. Several wolves started to back up around the men and were only kept back by bayonets. Each wolf studied its victim and searched for a weakness before launching itself at the soldiers.

Their grey fur coats looked in good condition, so food had not been much of a problem recently. The fur on their backs stood up, and the sound of mass growling made everyone focus that little bit more.

It was only then that the doors behind them opened. "Come in quickly," an Austrian soldier told them. Two other soldiers stood behind him, and they fired at the wolves as the men retreated into the stable.

They explained that some wolves were trying to dig underneath the stable from the other side, so they had been busy trying to secure this area. One of them thought he had heard shouts and banging on the door, so they came as soon as possible.

Once inside, the wounded soldier was helped onto some bails to rest. They had to stop the bleeding and clean his wounds the best they could with limited medical supplies. An Austrian came forward and introduced himself and Corporal Heinz. He was in charge of holding out the stables for as long as he could. The general had said the horses might be the only chance they would all have of escaping this nightmare.

The building was fair-sized and contained many spooked animals. The horses were stirring and restless in their boxes, and you felt tension. Some of the soldiers tried to calm them the best they could, but it was a losing battle. The wolves were howling again outside, and this time, every man, woman, and child knew the fort now belonged to the wolves.

"If we can make it through the night, we might have a chance."

"You could be right, Corporal Heinz." Major Richmond said whilst stroking his chin.

They had some food and water in the stables but only limited ammunition.

Outside, the wolves were running amok. Some were eating the carcasses of dead soldiers and anything else that was not a wolf. The noise of animals fighting over food and feeding was unsettling.

Captain Hayward was perplexed that they had all split up around the different buildings. No one was sure of casualties, and it was going to take a massive effort to stop sheer desperation from taking over. The wolves had not given up and were moving around like rats outside, biting, pawing and banging at the doors, windows and walls. The real problem lay with the giant wolves. These creatures had the size and weight to cause real problems if they repeatedly threw themselves at the entrances.

The hospital wing within the barracks was filling up fast with bite victims. It was being run by one Austrian military doctor who was assisting the wounded with the help of some nurses.

The general had arranged that everyone who could fire a rifle would get one should the building start to fall. It was going to be the only way – fight to the last. He summoned the captains and sergeants to meet briefly in his quarters.

"Gentlemen, we are facing something extraordinary. We must devise a plan to get the women and children to the stables, onto the wagons, and away from here."

Captain Hayward nodded in agreement. He was concerned for Major Richmond and his men but knew he was a good officer and would do his utmost to get them to safety.

"General, how long do you think we can hold out?"

There was a pause.

"Not long, my friend."

With that, they quickly drew a map of the inside of the fort and where each building lay. The best way to get people out would be a distraction that would more than likely involve men shooting from the rooftops and a group going out, leading the families to the stables.

It was a risky plan, but at that moment in time, it was all they had.

A tremendous thump was heard at a side entrance as soon as the ink had dried. The general turned to the officers and sergeants and shook their hands.

"It's starting."

General Von Bloch left his quarters to join the others. The soldiers were split into groups of four. Two soldiers would fire, and two would load. This way, they could lay down a constant barrage of bullets should the wolves break in.

Orderlies were handing out ammunition to everyone with a gun. Different bangs and crunching sounds could be heard all over the building. The wolves' attack was spread out, not concentrated in one place.

The general put on his favourite parade coat. It was ceremonial and covered in medals, but he wanted to go out in full glory.

Corporal Smith was still with the civilians. Most of them had reached the attic, but he was the last to climb up. He was waiting for a surge from the wolves on the door, but it never came, just a shuffling outside and the odd murmur. This kept him from going up into the attic. It puzzled him: Why weren't they trying to break in?

He lowered his rifle. The Austrians were calling him to come up quickly as they wanted to shut the hatch. Corporal Smith ignored them for the time being and even had the nerve to lean the rifle against the wall.

He slowly made his way over to the small hole in the door, the same hole the women had shot through. He waited for a second or two. His tunic was half unbuttoned, so he patiently did it up. Sweat started running from his helmet, and his hands felt clammy. He took a deep breath and leaned forward, his eyes taking a second to adjust to the darkness on the other side. There was nothing: no wolves, no movement, just emptiness. He took his head away and lifted his helmet.

What followed was a snapping sound and a roar. Then, a long tongue came through the hole and licked around it feverishly. The wood was then hit hard and continuously. It was a crazed assault. He stood there, frozen to the spot. The door started to shake, and the furniture moved under the pressure being exerted on it.

A hand smashed through the hole. It had long nails, and the flesh was decaying. The smell hit him; it was rotten as if something had died, and its odour was then released. A mouth with broken teeth came to the opening, snapping and biting in a manic way, the tongue almost tasting the air.

Corporal Smith could not move; he was still in shock. When a hand touched him on the shoulder, he jumped and fell forward to grab his rifle. It was an elderly man who looked worried about the bayonet, which was now pointing at his chest.

They wasted no time by looking at what was trying to come through the door and instead made their way up through the hatch.

The corporal did not say anything to the others as he wasn't sure himself what was trying to come in. The old man was happy to be back with the group and led the Royal Engineer to the other side of the attic. They had seen a way to climb into a storeroom and maybe reach the stables.

One of the women was carrying a lantern and had her child tucked under her arm. She led the way when she slipped through a rotten panel in the attic. The woman automatically grabbed for her small boy. In doing so, the lantern slipped from her grasp, rolled and smashed into a corner beam. Flames instantly started to shoot up. The others tried to put it out, but the dry wood and ceiling did not need an excuse to combust.

The fire spread rapidly all around them, but the smoke was more dangerous. They continued out of the attic and onto the roof. The building was starting to burn, and the fire was jumping from room to room.

The storeroom was close enough for them to take a good stride and be on top of it. They helped the old man and the children get across. Corporal Smith quickly scanned the fort; it was still inundated with wolves. They were getting excited about the fire, howling and biting at each other.

The fire had turned out to be the perfect distraction. The smoke was drifting away from them, but also creating a shield from the main body of wolves attacking the barracks. With this in mind, the group rapidly planned a quick burst to the stables.

It was vital that they picked the moment, except they had the growing heat behind them. Led by Corporal Smith, they made their way down from the storeroom. He got everyone to focus on the door at the side of the stables. This was their goal. Not everyone in the group understood English, but their fellow Austrians who did updated them.

Seconds later, they were all running to the door. Corporal Smith hung back a little as he had the rifle and wanted to guard against animals or anything else that might be out there.

The old man who had rescued him was doing well until two wolves came from the back of the storeroom and made a beeline for him. Corporal Smith went down onto one knee and took aim. He was not the best shot in the regiment, but he was steady. With a thunderous bang, the first charging wolf buckled and collapsed on the ground. The second launched itself at the old man, who fell backwards. Just as it tried to sink its teeth into him, the corporal stepped forward and smashed it with the butt of his rifle, knocking it over. Then, before it could regain its senses, a bayonet was rammed into its chest. Its tongue slipped out of the side of its mouth, and its eyes rolled.

"Bang on the door so they can hear us," shouted Corporal Smith.

One of the Austrians who understood English better than the rest went straight to the door and started shouting and hammering on it. He called for help in English and Austrian.

A soldier standing by the door quickly opened it and was surprised to see this group of people wanting to come in. Within moments, wolves were starting to flow in from everywhere – the shouting had attracted their attention. A large wolf appeared on the scene and made its way towards Corporal Smith. He was in no mood to fight this beast and backed into the stable. They closed the door and started to barricade it. The large wolf started the onslaught on the entrance and rallied the others to keep attacking everywhere around the stables.

Major Richmond appeared with several more soldiers to help reinforce the entrance. He shook Corporal Smith's hand. He almost wanted to pat his shoulder but felt it would have been inappropriate for a major to do that.

"Do you have any more news on the barracks, Corporal?"

"No, sir. We could only see the animals swarming all around it. It's under intense pressure from the wolves, sir."

The major scratched his head. "Are there any more pockets of people trapped around the fort?"

"I am not too sure about that, sir. The civilian building is now on fire, but there are storerooms, the blacksmith's, the barn…"

Both agreed that it was possible that some were lying low. The next thing was to plan what to do should the barracks or stables start to fall. The numbers of wolves outside were still immense, and they even conceived that more could arrive by nightfall.

The number of casualties and the reason behind this continued assault had not been discussed; for now, it was all about survival. Corporal Smith thought about bringing up the subject of the thing behind the door. The trouble was that he was not too sure about what was lurking there himself. He was sure it was not a wolf, but that was as far as his assessment went.

Major Richmond started devising a plan for the survivors in the stables and their journey to the barracks. He tried to think of a distraction they could use. The problem was—what?

An hour passed slowly, the sound of digging and chewing constant and threatening.

The stables were starting to buckle under the sheer number of paws and bodies smashing into the wooden doors. A small opening had emerged near the back of the stables, and wolves were desperately trying to squeeze in. Each time a wolf would just about make it, a soldier was there to bayonet or shoot it in the head.

They had been advised to save bullets where possible, but if they had to fire, as Major Richmond had said: "Remember to shoot the larger animals in the head for a clean kill".

Von Bloch was discussing ideas for escaping the barracks, but the situation outside looked grim: the wolves were out there in their thousands. It was an unbelievable sight; nature was winning this battle, and the driving force behind it seemed to be annihilation.

The barracks were split into a main entrance, a social room, a dinner hall, sleeping quarters upstairs, and officers' quarters at the back end of the building. There was also a small hospital wing, which was now full of wounded soldiers. The main entrance had to hold firm; otherwise, the whole building would be lost.

Shouts went out for more ammunition and reinforcements as windows broke under pressure from the outside attackers.

Sergeant Butcher came into the main entrance with a lance in one hand and a revolver in the other.

"The officers' quarters have fallen, sir. The wolves are in the building."

Captain Hayward drew his sword and checked his Adams revolver. Captain Egger knew this was a critical development: they only had upstairs to fall back to.

"Evacuate the hospital and move the wounded upstairs." Captain Hayward then took Captain Egger with him and requested the Austrians hold the corridor linking to the main entrance.

Most of the soldiers were dressed in their spring clothes, while some were in blue shirts and blue trousers.

A cry went out to signal that wolves were on the roof. Shortly after, the officers' quarters and dinner hall fell. Women and children were ushered upstairs as more soldiers fell back into the main entrance. Screams and cries for help rang out.

The gunshots were more intense as the animals ran amok in the building. Von Bloch prepared himself for the last stand. He had wanted to get the civilians and soldiers into the stables, but sheer numbers had forced them to sit tight and eventually succumb to being trapped. Nervous tension hung heavily in the air, but most of the seasoned soldiers kept calm and awaited orders.

The sound of a horn, strong and drawn out, pierced through the broken wood and smashed glass. Its tone, sinister and direct, caused the fighting to stop immediately, as the wolves broke off the attack without even flinching. It was as if someone had turned off a tap, and the water had stopped flowing.

Within a blink of an eye, they were gone.

Sergeant Butcher approached the officers and stood there for a second or two. They could see the puzzled look on his face. It was obvious to them that he was trying to make sense of it all. They were all a little astonished and confused by what had just happened. He reported that the building was now secure again. He had bloodstains on his helmet, and his red tunic was slightly torn.

"Excellent, Sergeant. Please take some men and check the fort for survivors and any signs of wolves." Captain Hayward said, nodding his head.

Captain Hayward then went to General Von Bloch, who was talking to his captain. He wanted to waste no time and move everyone out of the fort and to the nearest town as soon as possible.

"We must load the wounded into the carts and wagons and leave here now."

"General, should we see if they are waiting in the forests first? It could be a trap."

He smiled at them.

"It could very well be a trap, but if we stay here and they attack again, we will all die. This is our only opportunity to leave."

They all agreed, and the evacuation started immediately. There was a sense of urgency with everything now. People buzzed around, getting supplies and water for the journey. A detachment of men searched the fort for survivors. The dead, or what was left of the bodies, were also checked over. Records had to be made of missing soldiers or those killed in action.

Major Richmond was relieved to come out to find the wolves had dispersed. He sent a scout to link up with the barracks and inform them they were still alive. The relief on the women's and children's faces at seeing the other Austrians told a story. However, the atmosphere was still agitated, and there was no time to hang around.

Bite wounds and open flesh were cleaned as carefully as possible. Doctor Brown was the Royal Engineers' military surgeon. He was a modern-thinking doctor who liked to learn new techniques in the field. The Austrian doctor was older and did this by the book, but they still managed to treat people with speed and efficiency.

While all the loading took place, sentries were placed on the walls again, and lookouts stood by the gates. If there were any sign of wolves, they would all have to make a dash for it.

Chapter 3

About half an hour before, the soldiers and civilians were ready to leave. They had around thirty mounted soldiers to escort them whilst the rest would follow behind.

Once the wagons and carts were fully loaded, Sergeant Butcher took a horse and two mounted soldiers to scout the track down from the fort. This was done with haste as the fear of another attack loomed.

Smoke from the fort fire drifted across the parade square and over the barn. Flames were licking out of the shattered windows, and due to the extreme heat, part of the building had collapsed.

When Sergeant Butcher returned, his horse was agitated and nervy; the other two mounted soldiers stayed by the road.

"As far as we can see, the path is clear, sir."

Von Bloch was standing next to the other officers. He barked out the orders for the convoy to start moving. The nearest town was Unghvar, a hard slog down from the mountains.

Captain Hayward offered to bring up the column's rear with several mounted men. Some of the Austrian soldiers were of Hungarian descent. They had excellent riding skills, which were useful considering their current situation. They hoped to get to the garrison in Unghvar in two days.

Major Richmond wished he had a cavalry detachment with them. He would have fancied their chances more over the plains and forests which lay ahead. Fortunately, they had only lost twenty men in this latest engagement. Their numbers were few, but they had food and ammunition.

The officers had spoken about the protection needed for the women and children. There were not too many soldiers to spare, but some were ordered to ride with them on the wagons and carts. Civilians were now carrying rifles, too. This would help fill the casualties lost at the fort.

Von Bloch sat high on his horse, allowing the last cart to trundle past him. Listening to the creaking wheels and the clatter of hoofs of the stony path, he surveyed the horizon. The noise was a concern, as was their exposure to an open attack. His mind rolled over this for a moment or two. Captain Hayward waited for him with four soldiers, but he waved them on. He spent another minute looking at the fort and the smoke rising from it.

He had lost a battle before, but this one had a strange feel to it. Nature had beaten him, and they had only been saved by sound. The sound from the horn played on his mind: Was it the Russians pulling the strings, or was someone else involved?

With one last look, his eyes danced over the closest forests, then he dug his heels into the horse's flanks and joined the others.

The spring air was fresh and welcoming. The trees were coming into leaf, and the valleys were full of life. The odd animals were scampering around, but the distinct lack of birds was a concern.

The British soldiers stood out in this incredible landscape in their red tunics, blue trousers, and dark blue helmets with spikes on top. The Austrians were less imposing in their dark blue tunics and light blue trousers.

After an hour on the dusty track, there were still no signs of wolves. Captain Egger rode ahead with a scout; it was essential to always keep on guard. The men and women started to relax more and chatted amongst themselves. The children were not so sure, though. None of them had lost parents in the attacks, but the sight of injured or dead soldiers was enough to take the edge off them wanting to play.

The tracks were narrow, and the convoy had to go at a snail's pace to ensure no wheels were lost from the carts or wagons. The wagons had canvas covers to keep the passengers warm and sheltered.

The wounded were resting the best they could; being escorted along on a stony track was not easy. The doctors had worked hard to clean their wounds and keep the dressings sterile.

General Von Bloch called a halt to the group after six solid hours of travelling. Everyone was tired and hungry, but he wanted to put as much distance between them and the fort as possible. They found a place with an open field and a small farmhouse. Two Austrian soldiers went over to speak to the farmer and request water. They came back with blank expressions on their faces.

Corporal Heinz spoke to them and then returned to Captain Egger. They discussed, in German, what they had found on the farm. General Von Bloch was updated and then immediately ordered them to move on.

A groan went out as everyone wanted to know why they could not stop.

Captain Hayward spoke to Major Richmond, and he, in turn, rode on to be next to the general.

"We must have water, sir, and the animals need to rest."

"I fully understand that, but something is very wrong here at the moment. There is a small river half an hour away. We can rest there."

Major Richmond returned to reassure the British contingent. It was late afternoon, and nightfall would soon be upon them.

A soft breeze brought a slight chill as dusk settled in the valley. The wagons and carts were formed into a defensive circle, and scouts were sent to scour the area for anything dangerous.

Corporal Heinz took several men to collect water for the group and horses. After a long journey, this travelling caravan needed to rest and feed.

The river was slightly swollen from the melting snow in the mountains and some spring showers. The soldiers knelt down by a small stream, cupped their hands, and drank thirstily for a moment or two. The ice-cold water was very refreshing; it helped ease their dry throats and gave them a moment of solace.

Corporal Heinz then instructed the men to fill the barrels and any flasks they had with water. Back at the camp, the horses were rounded up and led to the river for a well-earned drink.

Fire pits were dug to keep their position as secret as possible, and stones were added to the sides to minimise the escaping light. The cook insisted on taking some livestock with them, mainly chickens and rabbits. Two pigs were also in a cart, which were butchered that evening for the meal.

Bread and cheese, vegetables, dried meat, and anything the storeroom had spare were among their supplies.

Captain Egger was confident of picking up extra supplies along the way. He knew there would be small villages on the way that would help them out with food.

Major Richmond took out his pipe and loaded it with tobacco. He used his thumb to press it in and then lit a match to ignite it. He puffed away and let the smoke filter out of his mouth. This was heaven to him, a moment to relax and take in their situation. Captain Hayward joined him. He had a mug of wine and looked relaxed himself.

"Bloody nightmare, eh?"

"Not the most fun I've had, no."

Both of them stood looking into the darkness.

"What was wrong with the farmhouse, Major?"

"Something is wrong with this whole area. I can feel it in my bones."

Von Bloch wanted everyone to rest before they pressed on to Unghvar. He nodded at the major as he approached the head cook.

The roll call had been completed now. They had made quick notes at the fort, but it was time to check who was left. Out of the combined Austrian and British forces, thirty soldiers had died; out of the fifty civilians, though, thankfully, no one had been killed.

Von Bloch wanted it to stay that way and ensured they had enough sentries on watch that evening. He had not spoken to his British counterpart regarding what had been seen at the farmhouse. His mind was still working through everything that had happened recently. He wanted to digest it and come up with a reasonable explanation.

Everyone tucked into the food as if they had never eaten before. It was a feast; the cook had made sure there was more than enough food to go around, and it was just a case of people tucking in. Wine was available for the adults and children were happy with fresh water.

That evening, Captain Hayward lowered his weary body into his blanket, using his kit bag as a pillow. It wasn't perfect, but it was dry and warm. The weather was reasonable for that time of year, and, importantly, there was no rain.

His mind did not take long to drift towards his family. They were staying in Paris with his wife and two children. It gave him great solace to think of them there and not experiencing this remarkable event surrounding him.

He had seen the children playing with their families in the fort and was glad none had suffered during the attacks. He spared a thought for the soldiers who had perished. He was fairly new to the detachment but had struck up a great bond with his men. Major Richmond had been in command and was due to hand that over to him, but the unforeseen change of events prevented that.

Letters would have to be written to the fallen soldiers' families. Often, government payments for death whilst serving for queen and country were not good enough.

It did not take long for everyone to get settled and fall into a gentle sleep. Ten guards would be doing the late watch; no chances would be taken. They had drunk coffee and were allowed tobacco to help pass the time. Bayonets were fixed, and a Bugler was also on watch should his alarm call be needed.

The night passed, and the sun began to rise. The change of guard allowed the night watch to sleep on and get some well-earned rest. Everyone's spirits were high upon waking. Leftover food was hurriedly devoured for breakfast, and the camp was dismantled. Scouts were sent to survey the local vicinity.

Private John Brown was speaking to Heidi. They were happy to have survived the attacks at the fort and were now en route to Unghvar. Heidi leaned over and kissed John on the neck. John blushed. However, the other soldiers around him were too busy packing and preparing to leave to notice the show of affection.

"John, stay close to my wagon if you can," Heidi whispered.

He smiled and continued to help the others.

A raucous howl broke the moment of tranquillity. It was so loud and fierce that the sound vibrated off trees and almost shook the very ground they stood on.

Everyone stopped; it was as if a lever had been pulled, and time stood still. Faces were full of dread and concern. A scout returned but indicated he had seen nothing. Then another arrived with the same news. When a third scout, who had gone off along the road, came back at a normal pace, Von Bloch gave the order for them to move on.

The officers gathered around the old general, who insisted there could be a wolf or two in the valleys, but that did not mean the whole pack was with them. Nonetheless, speed was doubled, and they would press on for another long stretch to reach Unghvar.

As they made haste, scouts were sent out to get a broad view of the area around them. They wanted to make sure no hidden traps were waiting ahead. Several farms appeared along the way, but all of them seemed empty and disused. No one was allowed to check them over; the order had been given to keep pressing on. Eventually, Major Richmond spoke to Captain Hayward and asked him to hang back and search the next farm they passed. He wanted to know what was being kept from them.

The hours passed, and the convoy made good progress. There had been no more howls or sightings of anything. Something started to play on the major's mind: there had not been one single person en route, not one.

A farmhouse came into view in the distance, but the group continued, passing by the track leading to it. Captain Hayward spoke quietly to Sergeant Butcher. Both of them were on horseback and drifted to the back of the convoy before choosing an adequate moment to slope off.

Further down the track was an overturned cart that couldn't be seen from the main road. Sergeant Butcher pointed out the blood surrounding the cart. It was as if there had been an explosion, blowing something to pieces.

The horses stirred as they tried to lead them towards the farm entrance. The gate appeared to have been crushed under enormous pressure. They tied the horses to a fence thirty metres from the house.

Sergeant Butcher had a rifle strapped across his back, which he swung around and readied for what may lie ahead. Captain Hayward drew out his Adams revolver. It felt good to have his old trusty friend with him.

The area around the farmhouse had been crushed. There had been a struggle here at some point. They both looked at each other, but nothing was said. The look was more to tell the other to be ready for something.

The door to the farmhouse was broken, and there were bloodstains around the entrance. The smell hit them hard. It was pungent and made both men lose their breath for a moment.

Captain Hayward said, "We must press on. I'll go first; you cover me."

The captain used his shoulder to push open the door. It was daylight outside, but this farm cottage was old and didn't have too much light within. They walked along the hallway.

A side table contained a picture of a farmer and his wife. They passed it, giving the photograph only a quick glance.

The house was a wreck: chairs were broken, tables smashed. There were bullet holes in the walls. The smell was particularly strong from one corner of the house. It seemed to be coming from behind a closed door. Charles nodded in that direction, and both men made a slow, calculated approach towards it.

The door had chipped paintwork and large fractured pieces of wood missing. In a soft voice, Sergeant Butcher counted to three, and then they both hurled themselves at it. It flung open with some force. They were greeted with an even more pungent, putrid odour and could almost taste rotting flesh. The buzzing sound was unnerving. Millions of flies were in the room, making it hard to see at first.

Sitting in a chair, three-quarters eaten, was a human body. The "body" was, in truth, more of a skeleton. Maggots were spilling from where its eyes and lips had been. The room was covered in dried blood.

As they turned to leave, Sergeant Butcher pointed to the wall. Drawn in blood was an image of an upside-down cross and a figure holding its arm up.

Once outside again, both men took in huge gulps of air.

"Sir, what's going on?"

"I don't know, Sergeant. We'd better get back to the others."

Their horses were still tied to the fence, looking flighty and nervous. Captain Hayward mounted his first and helped steady the other for Sergeant Butcher. Then, they both took off at speed to rejoin the rest of the group. Neither man spoke of what he had seen.

Major Richmond needed to be informed, and Von Bloch confronted him about whether this was the same scene he had found in the other farmhouse. They quickly caught up with the rest of their party. Corporal Smith was walking at the back of the group, some hundred metres or so behind.

He raised his rifle at first as they approached but promptly lowered it as he realised it was the sergeant and captain. They nodded to each other as they passed. Captain Hayward went to the front of the column and brought his horse broadside to the majors.

He waited a while before indicating to the major that he had something to say. He did not want to be too obvious about what they had seen, so instead, he told the major that one of the wounded men wanted to see him. With that, they broke off from the front of the column and slowly trotted back along the line.

When Major Richmond was informed of what was in the farmhouse, he understood the need for the discovery to be kept under wraps, although he would have liked to have known a little more, being the second highest-ranking officer there. Morale was still high amongst the soldiers and civilians. The general had been wise to keep these findings secret.

It took several hours before they were on the outskirts of a small town called Uzhok. The lack of activity and life was a concern: no farm animals were in the fields, and no people could be seen anywhere.

Von Bloch hoped to find them all camped in the town, awaiting reinforcements, but he feared the wolves had been here too. He sent two scouts to check out the area. They would wait a safe distance before being given the all-clear.

Most people were ready for a break. The civilians in the carts and wagons were desperate to stretch their legs, and the wounded needed some peace and quiet. It was not easy to be injured and to travel on the bumpy roads.

The scouts chose a nearby hill to survey the town. It was covered in long, wild meadow grass, gently swaying in the spring breeze. From this vantage point, they looked down across the town. Even from there, they could see no movement. There was no one around at all. Both scouts then rode into Uzhok. Their initial assessment was that there seemed to have been signs of a struggle – there were some burnt-out buildings and patches of dried blood spread throughout the town. It was not long before they came back and confirmed as much.

It was decided that the convoy would go into the town and get what supplies it could before moving on to Unghvar. It was hoped that the city would still be under Austro–Hungarian control.

The conversation turned to what was happening. They wanted to know where everyone was and if they should expect another wolf attack. The corporals and sergeants kept the soldiers in line, and the captains spoke to the civilians. Soon enough, they were able to calm the mood down.

Captain Hayward led ten men into the town on a quick reconnaissance mission. They did not want to take any unnecessary risks. The bullet holes in the houses and broken windows did not bode well. Once the area was secured, a soldier rode back and led the convoy in.

Uzhok had a wooden church—Saint Archangel Michael— and a collection of other buildings. Von Bloch ordered some soldiers to find him a table. The old general was still convinced that the wolves had been here and that the town folk had fled to Unghvar.

The general laid out a rolled-up map once the table was set out in the street. He used his sword to weigh down one end and his pistol on the other. The wagons and carts were kept on the road. This was for everyone's safety should they need to leave in a hurry. Detachments were sent around the town to collect what useful items they could, such as water from the wells.

The wounded were unloaded, and the civilians got down to stretch and move about. There was an air of tension hanging over everyone. Lookouts were posted around the town.

Von Bloch did not waste time. He pointed out different routes and suggested they get to Unghvar as soon as possible, ideally via the Uzhok Pass, which had been used for many years as a transport highway through the Carpathian Mountains. He wanted to rendezvous with the nearest garrison.

While he reviewed details with the captains and the major, the soldiers searched the houses for food and supplies. Some came out looking shocked and puzzled at their findings. It was now becoming evident that the farmhouses were not the only ones holding dark secrets.

There had been some good finds: a hardware shop full of fresh blankets and tools, a butcher's shop with dried meat and supplies, and a grocery store with fresh fruit. This led them to believe the town had only recently fallen.

After an hour, the supplies were fully replenished. The cook had started preparing a meal and was helped by two Austrian women who didn't mind peeling potatoes. He was going to make some broth.

Major Richmond took the time to talk with Von Bloch. The day was drawing in, and both had second thoughts about setting off for Unghvar that evening. There had been no sightings of anything, no humans or wolves, which gave them enough comfort to decide to stay the night in the town.

Several houses were picked out, and some time was spent determining the best way to keep watch over the weary group. A couple of soldiers were sent to the church, which had a high bell tower and offered the best viewpoint over the village in daylight. In the evening, should an attack materialise, they would ring the bells to warn everyone.

Private Brown took time to chat with Heidi. He was happy to be near her. In all this darkness, she was his light. He was a young man and hadn't had these kinds of feelings for a girl before. It made him feel strange and light-headed. He had been with a girl back in England, but she was frequented by many of the soldiers before they went on their postings abroad. It all happened very quickly, and when it was over, she wanted payment for her services. John wished he hadn't been drunk. He wouldn't do it again.

Heidi stood outside the house she was to stay in for the night. John was on sentry duty, which gave them a moment of closeness. He gave her a quick kiss. She smiled at him and brushed the side of his face. Her chest brushed against his body, causing a rush of blood and excitement within him.

Just as things were going in the right direction, a call went out.

"Private Brown. On holiday, are we, son?"

He froze to the spot.

"Back to your post and let the young lady rest."

Sergeant Butcher had let him have more time with the girl than he knew. Even the battle-worn sergeant saw a moment of youthfulness filled with love and let them have that. Sadly, though, all the sentries had to be on full alert, and that meant Private Brown as well.

The evening passed without incident, and everyone welcomed the well-earned rest.

The general briefly considered sending a scout to check out Unghvar but then decided they could do that once the city was in sight.

Chapter 4

The weather had been kind to them over the past few days, and this morning was no different. The sun burst into life, and the clouds were few and far between. The convoy set off quite early. The track that led to the Uzhok Pass was narrow in places and crossed a large open plain. At one point, cattle and sheep would probably have grazed it. The shrubs and bushes were well maintained by foraging creatures, and the animal tracks led up and down some small foothills.

Sergeant Butcher was riding at the back of the convoy, which moved at a steady pace. The route was to take them through the Uzhok Pass and onto a bridge that crossed the River Uzh. From there, they would travel to Unghvar.

A cold breeze crept up over the hills and swept down the valley, carrying a strange odour with it. The long grass swayed side to side, like a sea on a stormy day.

A dust cloud started to gather on the horizon, stretching for miles in both directions. The weather had been dry, but there must have been some strong wind to cause such an enormous cloud. Captain Egger pointed this out to the officers riding at the front. He questioned whether they should get undercover and bed down until the storm passed.

Two scouts rode out to check on the storm that was coming. After twenty minutes, the convoy had almost reached the Uzhok Pass highway. Private Clegg, who was lagging behind and dreaming of drinking vodka in Unghvar, spotted the two scouts coming back across the plains at great speed.

An Austrian soldier who was also watching the riders returning took in the situation before riding on to the front of the convoy. The dust cloud was moving incredibly fast over the hills and onto the plains.

Captain Hayward raised his binoculars to the riders. They looked shell-shocked and were at full gallop. He then directed his binoculars towards what was coming out of the dust cloud. At first, he put the binoculars down and cleaned them, not believing what he saw. He looked again. His eyes fell upon thousands of faces, their eyes sunken, skin torn, and mouths stripped to the bone with teeth and gums showing.

Charles could barely take it all in. Some of the people looked human but had stretched bodies with long limbs. They had enlarged jaws with teeth protruding from their mouths like tusks.

He barked out to the Bugler without further ado to raise the alarm. He galloped to the general and the major and hurriedly explained what he saw. Without a second thought, everyone was given an order to get to the Uzhok Pass. The drivers of the wagons and carts snapped at their reins. Soldiers on foot started to run towards the pass.

Many were helped onto the carts and wagons. Most people did not realise what was happening, but the thought of a mass wolf attack spurred them all into action.

The human-like creatures descended onto all fours with their extra-long limbs and picked up speed. They started to let out shrieking sounds that pierced the airwaves. Their movement was gangly but quick.

Von Bloch was leading the wagons and carts towards Unghvar. He told Captain Egger to hang back with twenty Austrian soldiers, who were then ordered to bring up the rear of the last wagon.

Captain Hayward rode swiftly with Sergeant Butcher to the back of the convoy. He passed two more mounted British soldiers and took them with him. A minute later, they were the only ones left on the junction entering the pass.

The noise from this mass army of long-limbed creatures was thunderous, with groans, barks, grunts and snapping sounds. They would be upon the four of them within minutes. One of the soldiers lent forward on his horse.

"Er, excuse me, sir, for asking, but should we possibly leave now?"

"Don't worry. We're not going to charge this abomination, oh no. We're going to see if they'll follow us, " Captain Hayward said calmly.

The soldier sat back in his saddle, his face white with fear. This was probably not what he had in mind.

The soldiers looked on in amazement and with apprehension.

"What are they, sir?"

"God only knows."

Captain Hayward had seen enough.

"Follow me, men."

Sergeant Butcher gripped his reins tightly. He was a tough man, but what was coming at him was something he had never even seen or imagined possible. It was hell as he imagined it.

With that, Captain Hayward led the men off at an angle to the Uzhok Pass. He wanted to draw as many creatures as possible away from the main group. He knew that there was a bridge further up the highway before entering the road towards the city. He wanted to stay away from the dead forest if possible, too. Captain Egger warned him off it because of the number of dead pine trees there, making it very hard to manoeuvre through.

He also said that a large area of forest had suddenly died, and the locals had become superstitious about it and had never ventured in there again.

Captain Hayward did not let that cloud his mind. He was more interested in where the horses could gallop at speed.

The majority of the attacking horde followed them as planned, and the plains and woodlands were now crawling with movement.

Captain Hayward did not see several riders approaching the foothills amongst the horde. They were dressed in black robes and carried upside-down crosses. Nothing was attacking them; if anything, the creatures acted as their personal bodyguards.

With controlled riding, they galloped over the highway and up onto a ridge above it. The convoy had moved on swiftly but was still being pursued by a large group of creatures.

Chapter 5

The robed riders stopped in the distance.

A shadowy figure rode his horse in front of the men.

"I want them dead. There should be no one in this area now."

Another rider came forward.

"Sire, we let the flesh-eaters loose on the whole valley. They must have come from the fort in the Carpathian Mountains."

"Why wasn't that fort destroyed? Should I tell the Great Ruler that his plan has failed?"

The rider looked him in the eye.

"No, I shall call in the bears."

With that, he snapped his horse around and signalled to another rider, who brought a horn to his lips and belted out a high-pitched call.

Moments passed before a large bald man brought forward ten bears. These were no ordinary bears. They were the size of elephants and had two heads. Their fur was prickly, and their claws razor-sharp.

The priest in command rode over to the bald man and whispered something to him. The bald man shouted out in a strange dialect to the beasts and then unleashed them.

They sprang into life and raced after the main convoy at a frightening speed. Both heads roared together as they pursued their victims.

The main convoy was moving as fast as possible, but its pursuers were gaining ground. Soldiers on foot started to fall back, and carrying heavy rifles and backpacks was taking its toll. Major Richmond had a plan: if he sacrificed several wagons to block the pass, the others would have more time to escape. However, this would mean some soldiers staying at the barricade for as long as possible.

Major Richmond had to think quickly. He rode alongside Von Bloch and told him his idea, stressing that mounted soldiers had to be at the barricade as they would have the best chance of escape afterwards.

Most of the mounted men were Austrian, and Captain Egger volunteered to command them at the pass. This discussion was carried out quickly. They would have to pick three wagons to be sacrificed. Two of the earmarked wagons were semi-loaded with non-essential supplies; the other was full of chickens and a couple of goats.

Captain Egger rode to the front and stopped the convoy, and the order was shouted out in Austrian and English. The soldiers set about moving the wagons into place. The chickens and goats were set free. One of the Austrian soldiers led the horses further down the pass. Once the barrier could no longer hold the horde, they would have to run to them to escape.

A minute passed as the last of the convoy trundled out of sight. The Austrians pressed up against the wagons. Captain Egger gave the order to turn them over and use any loose debris to help fill any gaps. It was not the best barrier ever made, but it was something.

Two of the Austrian engineers had grenades. They had been instructed to use them wisely, as there were few to spare.

The soldiers settled down behind the overturned wagons, each raising their rifle and looking down the sights. At first, nothing came their way, but slowly, a sea of bodies appeared. They were moving with purpose and at a reasonable speed, groaning and snapping as they advanced.

One soldier started to move away from his position, but a short, rasping voice brought him back.

"Aim for the heads, just like the giant wolves," said Captain Egger.

They held fire until Captain Egger gave the order. At three hundred yards, he shouted out, "Fire!" The thunderous sound of nineteen soldiers firing at once was powerful. The others, travelling ahead in the convoy, looked at each other and hoped for the best.

The bullets ripped into the first row. Some hit cleanly into the oncoming horde, sending them smashing to the ground. Bits of flesh were flung out as the bullets blasted their intended victims. The beasts shot in the head did not get up, but the others rose again.

Captain Egger did not waste any time giving the order to light and throw two grenades. As the flesh-eaters closed in, the grenades had a devastating effect on their tightly packed ranks.

He then gave the order to fire at will, which was broken only when grenades were thrown. This was having a telling effect. The creatures had not attacked them en masse, and most had fallen for Captain Hayward's decoy.

For a split second, the soldiers almost felt guilty about shooting at these poor souls staggering towards them. They looked human to a degree, but rotting flesh and distorted features took away their natural human look.

The horde in front of them stopped.

Captain Egger told his men to keep firing and make the most of this stationary target. They had two grenades left. As they were firing and reloading, a powerful roar bellowed out— louder than the gunshots.

Then, bursting forward through the masses, the bears appeared. Even Captain Egger was taken aback by their size and shape. He imagined the people attacking them to be some sort of plague victims, but these giants with their two heads were monsters.

He was frozen to the spot, just like his men. The bears came forward at great speed and were upon the barrier within a blink of an eye. Some soldiers had started shooting at them, but it was difficult to get a headshot—and there were two heads to aim for.

Captain Egger gave the order to retreat as the animals smashed into the wagons, spinning them around with their sheer size and weight. One bear reared up and came down, smashing a wagon to pieces. It lashed out as a soldier reached forward and stuck his bayonet into the beast's chest. It recoiled, only to come round and grab the man with one of its mouths. The giant jaws crushed him, sending blood spraying out over his comrades.

Captain Egger grabbed the two grenades whilst his men fought the bears.

He had only one plan left.

With a quick strike of a match, he lit both grenades. He then shouted at his men to fall back. He took himself past the shattered wagon and dodged two bear heads as they snapped at him.

Three more bears moved around him, eyes focusing on their victim, mouths drawn wide open, revealing razor-sharp teeth. With seconds to spare, he ran into the side of one of the bears. The other two lunged at him, but it was too late.

Captain Egger looked up before being blown to smithereens. The explosion dramatically affected the three bears around him, taking off their legs and heads. The other bears bore some of the brunt of the blast but not enough to stop them from attacking the retreating soldiers.

The remaining bears continued to drive forward, snapping at anything in their way. The flesh-eaters started to flow through the broken barricade and join in the pursuit of the soldiers.

One soldier shot an advancing bear in the head with magnificent accuracy, but unfortunately, as he reloaded, the second head clamped down on his shoulders, biting through flesh and bone in one quick swoop. The bear's dead head slumped to the side of the animal. It did not hinder it in any way.

Some of the men were able to escape back to the horses and quickly mounted them. They turned and rode to help their fellow soldiers whom bears and flesh-eaters had set upon.

A soldier ducked as a huge claw came at him but then fell victim to a flesh-eaters bite to his leg, which sent him crashing to the ground. He tried to get back up, but another flesh-eater launched itself at him.

Two soldiers at his side opened fire, killing his attackers. The problem was that ten to fifteen more were now moving in on him. Their eyes were transfixed on their meal. They moved with a desperate hunger that totally controlled them. It did not take long before he was being swarmed over by flesh-eaters biting and clawing at his body with long nails and sharp teeth. These things had once been normal people, but something had changed them to make them hunger for human flesh.

The speed with which they ripped open his chest and gorged on his intestines was shocking to those around. Biting him all over, his face, hands, and legs, he was literally being eaten in front of his fellow men.

The mounted Austrians arrived with the spare horses and gathered those they could. This was a frantic situation as one of the bears was taking a man and a horse with each of his two mouths and flinging them into the bushes at the side of the highway.

A burly Austrian soldier with an adapted breech-loading Lorenzo rifle shot dead the bear with only one functioning head. As it hit the ground, a cloud of dust rose up, giving the fleeing Austrians extra time to mount up.

The creatures were tearing apart a couple of men. It was like ants defending their nest the way the horde streamed on top of them. The burly soldier did his best to help, shooting one in the head and bayoneting another in the face. He knocked over two with his rifle butt and crushed their skulls in two swift, downward strikes.

As he turned to hit it, another bear knocked his rifle out of his hand and sent him flying into the grass. A flesh-eater sprang forward to attack its victim as he lay stranded momentarily. The bear, though, got there first and with a quick swipe of its paw, the flesh-eater was sent off the track. The other flesh-eaters were knocked back; the bear had complete command. Both its heads bellowed at the horde, and it then moved its giant frame forward.

The soldier had got to his feet and saw an opportunity to retreat. A mounted soldier aimed and shot from his horse, hitting the giant bear in the neck. He had another horse and was holding it ready for the burly man, who managed to grab a rein and start moving without even saddling up.

The remaining bears charged after them with anger and pace, but the soldiers kept their speed and galloped away. While the bears were fast in short bursts, they could not maintain their speed over a long distance.

Ten men had perished in defending the highway. Captain Egger's sacrifice had given the others time to escape, and they all hoped their losses were not in vain.

The main group had reached the wooden bridge over the River Uzh. The highway was now streaming with flesh-eaters, who were making their way along it on the scent of the convoy. The remaining bears were also following this route towards their next meal.

The dead soldiers had, by now, been stripped to the bone by the bears and flesh-eaters.

Captain Hayward had not seen the collapse of the barricade. They still had a massive army of flesh-eaters on their tail. They also had the long-limbed creatures chasing them. They were faster due to the fact they could go on all fours.

He had taken his party of four to the edge of the dead forest. It was huge, and its thick fallen trees, mixed with dead-standing ones, created a spiked jungle. Captain Hayward had no other choice than to dismount with his men. They led the horses into the forest, with the flesh-eaters not too far behind. This route would take them longer to get to the bridge, but he had no other choice.

Von Bloch sat on his horse by the bridge. The defence of the pass had given them time to cross at a steady rate. He rode over to Major Richmond and had a brief discussion. An order went up for dynamite to be placed in the middle of the bridge and under any struts where possible. Time was of the essence.

The convoy waited on the other side. Heidi looked at John, who was helping unload barrels of gunpowder. The Engineers began setting up explosives and felt confident they could destroy the bridge.

It would certainly give them time to escape with the river swollen from the melting snow. This aside, their thoughts were with the soldiers still out there. They had no idea of what had happened on the pass or to Captain Hayward moving through the dead forest. The next crossing was fifteen miles further along the river.

The icy water licked at the banks, and the old wooden bridge creaked a little under the weight of people on it. Corporal Smith lined up twenty British soldiers. They did not fix bayonets to their Martini-Henry rifles; this would be covering fire. The other Engineers continued working to destroy the bridge.

In the distance, horses could be seen galloping towards them at speed. A mounted rider was on the pass to check on the incoming riders. He could see their numbers were reduced.

The men arrived at the bridge, with Corporal Heinz there to greet them. The sorry news broke that Captain Egger had sacrificed himself to save them. It was also pointed out that there was not much time as the horde was coming.

The horses were tired and needed to drink and rest. General Von Bloch rode up to the men and saluted their efforts.

"Take the horses to the other side and give them water."

He reflected on the dead Austrians. Captain Egger had been a promising young officer. His courage was what the Austrians needed. He thought back to the Austro–Prussian War and the men who had perished in that conflict.

In the distance, he could see a roaming dust cloud; they were coming, and they were hungry.

The general was the last man on the other side of the river. His thoughts were all about what to do next. Major Richmond joined him. Both horses snorted as they stood side by side. One scratched its hoof into the dusty road.

Von Bloch looked at the major.

"Your men are on the other side; it will decrease their chances of survival if we destroy the bridge."

"If we don't blow the bridge, those things will kill us in a blink of an eye."

General Von Bloch was glad it was Major Richmond making the decision about cutting his men off. He, too, knew it was their only chance.

As the rambling flesh-eaters came closer and closer, the giant bears appeared on the foothills to the side of the highway. Five bears had been slain, but that still left five more.

Amongst them rode a black-robed figure. They were too far away to shoot, but it gave the soldiers their first taste of who was leading this assault against them. Four more robed riders appeared next to the figure.

Chapter 6

"We must blow the bridge now," said Major Richmond.

He then rode onto the bridge, dismounted, and spoke to the engineers who were setting the charges.

General Von Bloch rode back to the other side and lined up a row of Austrian soldiers next to the British line.

The long-limbed creatures appeared, pushing through the walking dead and gathering pace as they closed in on the bridge. Their mouths were open, and their teeth gleaming in the sunlight. They made a whinnying, hissing sound as they moved forward. It was an eerie noise that unsettled everyone.

The speed with which they approached was enough to make Corporal Smith call out to his men to get ready and wait for his command to fire.

The distance of their approach slipped away as this terrible army of long limbs and flesh-eaters eventually descended onto the bridge.

"Wait..."

"Wait..."

"FIRE!"

The volley of bullets was accurate and unforgiving. The long-limbed creatures buckled under the piercing rounds. Heads exploded, limbs were blown off, and creatures crashed into each other. Then, the Austrians opened fire, which also had a devastating effect, scattering many of the attacking creatures.

The problem was that the numbers kept coming. Behind them followed the flesh-eaters, hundreds upon hundreds of them.

Major Richmond did not let too many get onto the bridge before allowing the fuses to be lit. The remaining soldiers were also firing from the banks, stopping the horde from fully crossing.

They had all moved back a fair distance from the crossing. It only took seconds before the burning fuses leapt into the dynamite, blowing the bridge into millions of pieces and sending debris hurtling into the air. The Austrians and British took cover as shards fell from the skies.

Once the smoke had settled down, the flesh-eaters were left hissing and groaning on the other side of the river. Some had tried to get across only to be swept away by ferocious water.

The soldiers started firing on them again. They were easy targets, stationary and trapped. The bullets found their targets with ease. Headshots were not always possible, though, and those that missed resulted in the flesh-eater getting back up on its feet.

General Von Bloch ordered a cease-fire to save bullets. The five-robed riders had disappeared from the hill, and the creatures started to move along the riverbank.

This was enough to convince the general they were heading for the other crossing, fifteen miles downriver.

With that, the convoy turned and headed down the highway towards Unghvar. The civilians had already started moving in that direction towards the garrison they hoped was waiting there to help fight this devilish army.

Captain Hayward was still leading his four men through the dead forest. It was so silent; every twig or branch snapping made them wary of an attack. They faced a situation where moving at speed would be difficult. They had all heard the loud explosion whilst passing through the forest. In the back of Ch's mind, he wondered whether they had destroyed the wooden bridge.

He ensured they kept to the outskirts of the forest as much as possible. He had a small map showing the forest and the pass. It also detailed the area around the river and the crossing points. If the bridge was gone, they would have to cross further down the highway.

The men talked quietly when a raucous roar smashed through the dense forest. It was followed by hundreds of cries and snarling. The forest felt alive behind them, and the breaking of branches and twigs became louder.

Captain Hayward looked at his men. The look was simple: "We must move faster or perish in this forest."

Sergeant Butcher stopped the group.

"Fire, sir. Why don't we burn the forest? It's incredibly dry, and we haven't had rain for weeks."

They all paused. It had been a freakishly dry period, and everything looked combustible.

"Excellent, let's see what we can do," said Captain Hayward.

None of them knew the distance between themselves and the horde, but it would give them time if the smoke or flames deterred the attackers.

Some of the soldiers had oil, which was usually reserved for the lamps. Charles thought this would be a start and got the men to spread out twenty metres apart. The dead wood lying around was too large, but there were enough small branches and twigs to gather and light. The oil would speed things up.

It did not take them long to light several fires. The floor matter, a mixture of twigs, branches, and dried long grass, quickly caught alight.

The fire spread along the ground faster than they anticipated. The smoke would be a problem if the wind changed in their direction. Captain Hayward made sure all four of them gathered together and then led their horses towards the highway. The creatures behind could be heard hissing and coughing as the smoke drifted their way.

Some sounds were stronger than others, some booming, some quiet. All of them filled the forest with life. The fire only added to this, crackling and popping away. They needed time, and this diversion gave them that.

It took an hour or two before they reached the forest's edge. They had not gone into the depths of this dried-up wilderness, and this now paid dividends as they came out into the daylight. The smoke had started to drift, allowing them more cover than anything else.

Once out, they mounted up and started to ride. Captain Hayward explained that the second bridge was further down the highway and hoped they would meet the others heading towards the city.

As they came down to the highway road, a rumbling sound came from behind the bushes to the side of the river. It then moved all around the water's edge. Five long-limbed creatures hurtled towards them as Charles gave the order to gallop.

They managed to get going. The distance between them and the long limbs became greater and greater. At this point, five more appeared to their right, sweeping down on them with great speed. Captain Hayward drew his Adams revolver and shot three times, hitting one in the body and legs.

This only slowed it down. A long limb dismounted one soldier as it swiped and hit him with its arm and claws.

The other five creatures were now catching up. Sergeant Butcher circled his horse as he tried to get to the fallen man, but they quickly responded and isolated their prey. The fallen soldier, with his Martini-Henry rifle and bayonet, managed to scramble up the banks to the edge of the dead forest.

The soldier was brave and shouted at them to ride. Captain Hayward did not want to leave him, but there were now ten long-limbed creatures between the three riders and the fallen soldier. To make matters worse, flesh-eaters started to emerge from the dead forest further back.

Captain Hayward tried to push through to him, but the long limbs reared up and forced him back. It did not take long before they were massing and advancing on the captain and the others. The fallen soldier went down onto one knee and raised his rifle. He looked down at the sight. A thunderclap rang out, coinciding with a long limb collapsing. It had been hit in the head, and death swiftly followed.

This signalled the others to turn and go after the soldier. His horse had panicked and tried to bolt away, drawing some of the flesh-eaters after it. The horse got caught in the thicket, thrashing around and kicking as creatures poured on top of it.

Soon, it was being swamped by hungry flesh-eaters. They were getting knocked over left, right and centre, but sheer numbers were making it hard for the horse to escape. It gave out a desperate groan as it was hauled over and then ripped apart whilst still alive.

The soldier did not wait around and moved back into the dead forest. He wanted to give his fellow comrades as long as possible. The forest was unforgiving as he moved through it at speed. The smoke drifted his way from time to time, creating a thick blanket but also making it hard to breathe.

He could hear something else entering the wooded area behind him, making a laughing sound, almost like a hyena. The sound was sharp and deep, troublesome and fierce.

With bayonet fixed, the soldier loaded his rifle and backed deeper and deeper into the forest. A long limb had caught sight of him and was now following his scent. It wanted to get closer before pouncing.

Captain Hayward was disheartened. He never liked having his hand forced in this manner. It took Sergeant Butcher several attempts to tell him they must ride or face being cut off from the other bridge. With a wistful look over his shoulder, he snapped at his reins and rode towards the bridge.

The soldier held his breath as a smoke cloud passed through and around him. When this had passed, the creature emerged from it.

Up close, it was larger. It had human characteristics but also a menacing look and feel. Its legs and arms were stretched, with sharp claws protruding at the ends. Its mouth had giant teeth and a tongue that rolled out and almost tasted the air like a snake.

It lowered its head, allowing its eyes to focus on the soldier. They were as dark as the night and carried such malice in them. It reared up onto two legs and then leaned back and made a barking sound. The soldier wanted a clean shot and waited for his moment. As it came back down to the ground, it refocused on him. The eyes were wide and hypnotic, making its prey stare into them. The soldier did just that, but he looked at it down the barrel of his rifle.

"Goodnight, darkness."

Boom.

It fell to the ground with its head split open.

The soldier smiled. He looked at the creature with its semi-human body and extra-long limbs.

The smoke wave came again. It was brief but blinding, nonetheless. He fumbled in his pouch to load another bullet into the rifle. As the smoke lifted, he noticed something moving around him. This distraction caused him to drop the bullet to the ground. It was at this moment that his eyes fell upon three more long limbs. The creature he had just shot had called in the others.

He slowly and calmly knelt down, taking a deep breath as they bared their teeth. Again, they snorted at each other, which seemed to be their way of talking. One stayed in the middle while the other two circled him.

He calmly placed the bullet, which had fallen to the ground, into the breech and cocked the rifle. There was a fallen tree behind him and a thicket of dead trees to his right. Waiting a second, he accepted his fate, even saying a quick prayer.

Another large smoke cloud rolled in, triggering the attack. Unbeknown to the long limbs, this soldier was a sniper; he had trained with the Marines and had seen some action in Africa.

With the fallen tree to his back, he stayed low as the front creature came straight at him. He was lightning-fast with his shot, killing it the instant it moved. In the same motion he rotated to his right and stuck his bayonet into other oncoming long-limb head. It squealed in agony and flipped its head back, taking the rifle and bayonet with it.

The third long limb slammed into the left-hand side of the soldier, its teeth puncturing his back. He twisted in agony as he tried to get a grip of his attacker, blacking out for a moment or two.

The soldier's father had always been a military man; "Was married to the army and Empire". He had followed suit and wanted to impress him. They'd had an awkward relationship since he was small. His father wanted him to have a senior position like himself and rise through the ranks. He had started well, going to Sandhurst and training as an officer. Then, he was assigned to the Marines.

Things were on the up until he fell in love with a lord's daughter whilst stationed down in Portsmouth. The soldier's father had worked hard to improve the family's social standing and wealth. She, however, was engaged to marry another officer who was on tour aboard. Even though she had only briefly met this man, both his and her family had agreed that it would be a suitable arrangement.

It was not the time for a scandal. When the news broke about the affair, it shook all parties involved. The father was threatened with demotion, and his son was stripped of his rank and sent overseas.

Before he left, his relationship with his father was heavily strained. He had expressed his love for this girl, and the pure fact that she was in love with him and not this stranger should have made a difference. His father reminded him that this was how it was, and rules and etiquette were to be adhered to at all times.

He explained how he once knew a fine young lady before meeting his mother at a military ball, but she was of another social standing, and it would have meant the same situation his son was now going through. His father told him to keep his head down for the next few years and work his way up through the ranks. He also advised him to live somewhere else in the Empire where his name would not be known amongst the chattering classes.

It was a sombre farewell. His family wanted the best for him, and it was only at the end that his father came forward and wished him well. He told him it would pass, and he would rise up the ranks and find a new love. Then he did something out of character and hugged him. As they released their embrace, he produced a gift wrapped in a cloth. The soldier took it and put it in his pack to open later.

Two years had passed since then. He was due to be made a Corporal and was awaiting his commission to come through via Paris. The Engineers had offered more chance of promotion than the Marines, as the officer who had been wronged had strong links to that regiment. Memories of this whole episode passed in front of him now, his mind racing over the girl he loved as if he were reliving it.

The moment passed as teeth sunk into his back, and a claw spun him around. He lay motionless on the floor with blood flowing from his wounds. The creature almost took pleasure from looking at him and examining its meal, wondering where best to start eating.

Its tongue came out of its mouth and licked at the blood covering its teeth. A squeal of delight erupted. It sniffed at the other three dead, long limbs and rose up on two feet to survey the horizon. The stench around the long limb filled the soldier's nostrils. He could hear the flesh-eaters making their way through the dead forest towards them.

The creature did not want to share its meal and knew it had to eat quickly. It went down onto all fours and pressed its body up against his. Its eyes narrowed, and its mouth started to open. The soldier felt at the cloth he had received from his father and was now sitting in his belt. The gift his father had given him that day in Portsmouth turned out to be his life.

As the long limb prepared to strike, the soldier undid the cloth with his right arm. He waited for the beast to come in even closer.

Its eyes reacted quicker than its body as his injured left arm grabbed its skull. His right arm swung round and stuck an Indian knife through its head, cracking skin and bone. Blood spurted as the creature recoiled and hissed in pain, falling sideways to the ground and shaking and writhing for a moment. The soldier gingerly got to his feet, pulled the knife out of the beast's skull, and then stabbed it repeatedly. Alexander Chamberlin was still alive. He did not know for how long, but for now, he was. There was no time to reflect; he gathered his rifle and staggered deeper into the dead forest.

Chapter 7

Captain Hayward could see the second bridge. The horses were tired and could not be pushed any harder, but he was wary of what was behind them.

As they reached it, they could hear the sound of drums; an intense, rhythmic beating surrounded the area. He did not wait to see where or what was causing it. They gingerly crossed the bridge. Luckily, it was still intact, and they were glad to reach the other side.

Once across, they started down a road signposted to Unghvar. Meanwhile, more flesh-eaters began to emerge from the dead forest. The sight of them, with their rotting flesh and razor-sharp teeth, never seemed to get easier on the eye. They were driven by hunger and controlled by the figures in black.

Questions were raised about why and how all of this had started, but Captain Hayward knew now was not the time to seek answers.

The rest of the horde travelled across the bridge in a steady procession. They did not have the speed to match the horses. They did have a second gear to their movement, but that only seemed to kick in if there was a specific guarantee of food.

Charles looked through his Porro prism binoculars and surveyed the road before them, not wanting any surprises along the way. Sergeant Butcher had his rifle on his hip and was ready for an ambush. All of them were thinking about Alexander and the sacrifice he had made. In war, soldiers were killed. It was an unfortunate part of battle and life in the army, but it never made it easy to expect death or lose the value of life. Captain Hayward was a soldier, but he was an Engineer at heart. He wanted to return with his family to Surrey and start his own business.

The Hayward family were mainly in India, where his father had gone with the railways. He had worked his way up to a position of power. Charles had wanted to stay and work out there, but schooling in England and the chance to see the world with the British army had proved too much of a temptation to turn down.

His wife Rebecca and two children, Arthur and Emily, were in Paris. He longed for their embrace. He missed being away from them. The children were in a French school, and Rebecca was helping a friend with a printing venture. He thought about Rebecca's long blonde hair and infectious laugh. She was an active woman and kept herself in good shape. She always made him feel alive, and her kiss sometimes made him feel giddy. Some joked that it was because they were not always with each other that they still enjoyed each other's company after seven years of marriage. Charles felt it had to do with love itself and how they made time for each other. They argued like any couple, but they did spend time enjoying life together when possible as well.

He prayed that that time would be coming soon. He had seen a dark threat rising here in Austria and hoped it could be snuffed out quickly.

"We can ride for an hour or two and then rest the horses. We must get some distance between us and them."

The other two agreed and trudged along.

The main convoy was far ahead. They had rested and fed the animals and themselves. Major Richmond and Von Bloch were discussing the best course of action. They both had reservations about Unghvar. With the army of creatures they had encountered flowing through this area, it could surely only mean one thing.

As they passed a dilapidated village, Major Richmond took the opportunity to pin a note to a tree describing how they would pass Unghvar and continue down the road. He did not want to put too much detail, as there would be followers who could intercept it first.

They had decided to press onto Tokay. Von Bloch explained they could hopefully get a train to Vienna and put this nightmare behind them. He wanted to get to the Austrian army headquarters and take command of a regiment. Then, he would return and destroy this invading army.

The old soldier in him wanted to fight; he did not like retreating. He had been around long enough to understand defeat, and the Prussians had handed Austria a good beating not that long ago. He had lost family and friends during that conflict.

This was different; the new aggressor was unearthly. It had one primary desire: to feed on its victims. Of the various types of creatures attacking them, some were half-human, half-demon. He also wanted to know more about the dark-robed riders and their role in this conflict.

Vienna hopefully held the answers.

They had lost three soldiers on the journey. The army surgeon and his team had done a remarkable job with the wounded, but some of the injuries inflicted by the wolves had meant they needed specialist help, something they did not have access to on the road.

Their supplies were doing well, but even now, the sergeants were telling everyone to ration their intake. They did not know when they could top up supplies or what lay ahead. Most people's mouths were dry from the dusty tracks and roads. They had not washed for several days. It was a very uncomfortable situation, but no one complained. If anything, the thought of being on the move made them feel at ease; escaping something that wanted to eat you felt good.

Chapter 8

Further back with the walking flesh-eaters, a group of robed riders gathered in a circle.

"Send a messenger to the high priest. It is time to step up the campaign."

"Shall we send in the riders of the North?"

A rider at the front of the group came forward.

"We have waited many years for this time. The High Priest has given his orders, and we shall follow them."

"Yes, my lord, but what about this convoy and the soldiers?"

"Destroy them. I will ride and join the main army. They will never know what's coming."

With that, three riders galloped off. The remaining two then spoke to the big bald man who had been in charge of the bears. He was given more instructions and was then joined by two soulless-looking individuals. Their faces looked blank and grey. They were not the same as the flesh-eaters; they were human, to an extent, and could follow orders. Their uniforms were black trousers with black tunics. Even their helmets were black.

Both were carrying rifles that looked different from the standard breech-loading rifle. Their backpacks were also black, leaving only their grey faces and hands-on show.

The two soldiers left after receiving instructions from the bald man. They both had horses and rode off toward the Uzhok Pass.

The remaining two robed riders linked up with the long limbs and bears. The bald man was riding a large donkey, which squealed as he kicked it to go faster. As it passed the long limbs, they hissed and twisted their heads at the beast.

One of the robed riders raised his staff, and they settled down. Thousands of flesh-eaters started to gather at the bridge and filter across. These priests had complete control over them, and they parted as the horses crossed the bridge. One large wolf followed them. Its job was to pick up the scent of the British and Austrian soldiers.

The remaining bears followed the riders across, and their long limbs pushed through the flesh-eaters to get to the front. It was a devilish sight—a mixture of creatures with one goal.

Once across, the long limbs set off to attack the convoy while the riders brought up the bears and flesh-eaters.

Major Richmond was happy with the speed at which they were riding but prayed that Captain Hayward and his men would make it across before the horde arrived.

The ten mounted riders hung back and acted as a safety net in case they were attacked from behind. Following Captain Egger's untimely death, Corporal Heinz was now in charge of them.

The group was happy when Von Bloch ordered them to stop. Everyone dismounted or hopped out of the wagons and carts. The wounded were eased out and laid on the grass for a well-earned rest.

He had stopped them by a stream outside of a small village. It looked to have around fifteen to twenty houses and a small church.

The scouts were sent ahead to check on the village. The ten mounted riders who were bringing up the rear had a quick change of guard. Von Bloch was fully aware of the implications of being attacked by a large group of flesh-eaters and did not want any unnecessary surprises.

The soldiers cleaned their rifles and helped set up the kitchen for the cook. Everyone was hungry and tired from the constant tension.

Private Brown and several others went to fetch water. Heidi joined him, and they took a moment to snuggle and talk to each other. The conversation turned to how she wanted him to meet her family in Vienna. He smiled. Part of him felt it was a little soon to meet the family; the other part thought, why not? The unfolding events made him unsure of life in the world and made him question some of the things he had learnt at school.

The long meadow grass swayed in a slight breeze, the trees were in full leaf, and the landscape was beautiful. They were told not to take too long as the general wanted to leave within the hour. Most people just wanted to eat and rest.

The scouts returned from the village and declared it empty. The cook rustled up a simple broth, and everyone ate quickly. Some of the soldiers mentioned the lack of wildlife. Birds and rabbits had been seen, but no farm animals. Some thought about being consumed by the flesh-eaters, although no one spoke out loud about the creatures—it was easier to ignore those thoughts. Most wanted to find the main army and hoped they would destroy this abomination.

Sergeant Green stepped forward to announce it was time to press on. There was a slight groan, but people understood the need to keep moving. The water barrels and wounded were loaded onto the wagons first.

The clouds started to gather overhead, and for the first time in a while, rain threatened. Major Richmond pinned another note to the tree. He wanted to keep Captain Hayward abreast of what was happening.

The convoy was soon rolling along again. The ten mounted soldiers hung back to bring up the rear, and scouts roamed ahead. The village was only a short distance away. Major Richmond had explained to his men that they should only stop for a short period of time to load up supplies and move on to Tokay.

The rain started to fall gently from the heavens. It trickled down faces, slipped off wagons and gathered in large puddles on the road.

Inside the village was one supply store. It had been raided but still had enough items for them to use. The food was mainly dried meat, flour, oats and anything pickled or in jars. There was the odd tin of biscuits and chocolate.

Major Richmond sent out search parties for wagons and carts. He wanted to get as many men as possible off the road, believing this would help speed up their movement.

Fortune was on their side as five wagons were found scattered around and then hauled in front of the general. He gave the order to load up and move out.

Meanwhile, Captain Hayward had seen the first note and was pressing hard towards Tokay. When they reached the village, they had to stop and rest and find water for the horses. Sergeant Butcher found the second note and was confident they could reach them by nightfall. They found some dried food and ate what they could.

Sergeant Butcher asked the soldier to take the horses to a paddock at the side of the village and let them graze. He then spoke to the captain about the plan for the evening. The sergeant felt they were a good day's march ahead of the horde. Captain Hayward pointed out that the long limbs were faster, more nimble, and surely on their tails. He also felt they stood more chance of survival if they regrouped with the main convoy.

After a short break, they set off. They had taken down the notices each time because every scrap of information was valuable. Captain Hayward took out his pocket watch: the time was three o'clock. He took another glance at the watch. It was a present from his wife, Rebecca. She had given it to him on his birthday the previous year, having noted how he admired it during his shopping trips to London. Then, on his special day, she surprised him with the watch. Looking at it brought memories of her and the children flooding back. It was the small things that sometimes hurt the most.

As dusk started to fall, they could see the convoy ahead. No sooner had they come into sight, ten riders surrounded them. Luckily, they soon saw who it was, and a hearty cheer went up. Smiles and pats on the back greeted them.

"How did you make it?" said Sergeant Green.

Captain Hayward shook his head and smiled.

"We got lucky."

They then rode on to meet the rest of the group. Von Bloch looked at the map with a lantern, working out a place to stay for the night. The general was confident they could rest for several hours and leave at dawn.

Major Richmond was delighted to see Charles and his men but was saddened to hear about Private Chamberlain's death.

A nearby village was checked and approved for the men to bring the wagons in. They were lined up on the road, ready for an evacuation should it arise. There was tension in the air due to the flesh-eaters on their tails, but they needed rest and sleep.

They planned to have guards all night and divide the hours among the Austrian and British soldiers.

This would only be a short stop, so supplies were sought first. Then, it was decided that the house on the edge of the village would be the first lookout for a possible attack. Captain Hayward and his men were given the night off sentry duty due to their heroic effort at the Uzhok Pass.

Charles found a relatively well-maintained house. The occupants had left in a hurry, but a photograph of the family was still hanging on the wall. He paused and looked at their faces. He couldn't help but wonder where they were now.

He looked at his pocket watch and pulled out a folded photograph of his family, brushing his thumb against the picture for a moment or two. He then slung his pack and blanket onto the bed and, using his coat for a pillow, laid his head down slowly. It did not take long for sleep to find him.

Chapter 9

Gunshots woke Captain Hayward. Quickly, he grabbed his Adams revolver and looked out of the window. He could see movement outside and horses rushing down the street. Loud shouts followed, and more gunshots.

He grabbed his tunic and dressed hurriedly. His eyes were slightly blurry, and his head was still fuzzy from sleep. He could hear banging at the door on the stairway, and without wasting any more time, he rushed downstairs. Half-expecting a flesh-eater to burst through, he raised the revolver directly in the line with the door.

"Sir, are you in there? We have a big problem."

On hearing Sergeant Butcher's voice, Captain Hayward un-cocked his revolver and holstered it, then rapidly undid the bolts securing the door. A concerned-looking Sergeant Butcher greeted him.

"Captain, we have been overrun by deserters and civilians."

The fresh air that wafted in was tainted with the smell of gunpowder.

They both took off down the street carrying their rifles, Sergeant Butcher leading the way. As they came to a corner, they found most of their group kneeling down with their hands over their heads. Von Bloch was being led to a wagon with Major Richmond.

Captain Hayward did a rough sweep of the group and reckoned they had nearly everyone.

"What shall we do?" Sergeant Butcher asked in a concerned manner.

Charles scratched his head. "I don't understand how this happened so quickly."

Both men stood still for a moment. Then, several rifles appeared behind them. They were Austrian soldiers, not Engineers.

They were asked in German to join the others. Sergeant Butcher looked to Charles for a signal that they should make a fight. He received a look which indicated no. The Austrians then asked them in broken English to move on and join the rest of the group.

They were led to the other officers. Captain Hayward asked Von Bloch and Major Richmond what had happened. He was informed of the betrayal: one of the young Austrian engineer soldiers on guard had been convinced that this Alpine Jaeger Corps unit was returning from a battle and that there was no need to wake the others.

He had allowed them to come through and settle their horses and wagons. The civilians followed behind, and soon, the whole village was surrounded. Von Bloch understood it was a case of betrayal. The young engineer had no need to worry, and why would he, with a fellow Austrian army unit? He should have reported it to his non-commissioned officer, but it was too late.

Whilst most of them slept, this marauding force took over the village. They rounded everyone up and took all the weapons. Luckily, no one was killed; there were just some minor injuries.

An officer came forward and introduced himself as Captain Sternberg. He was with the Alpine Jaeger Corps. Von Bloch could not withhold his anger and instantly demanded an explanation for the outrage. He declared that Captain Sternberg would face a court martial for his treason. His German was strong and direct; he wanted answers. In his mind, Austrians turning on Austrians was unthinkable.

"You must forgive me, General, but times have changed. We need your wagons and weapons."

The general looked shocked. He had not fully understood that this was an Austrian regiment holding them prisoner.

"We are Austrian Engineers returning from the Carpathian Mountains. Do you know what's coming after us?"

Sternberg paused.

"I fully understand what's coming, and that's why we must have your wagons and supplies. I would offer you to join us, but unfortunately, we are nearly four hundred strong, and there is no room for more."

Von Bloch walked closer to the Alpine commander.

"We have women and children and wounded men. Would you leave them to die here in this village?"

"Time is of the essence. I will grant you wagons for the families and wounded. We will also leave you some rifles, with the ammunition, on the other side of the village. I have no more time."

The commander turned to go but felt his tunic being grabbed.

"Why?"

"General, death is coming, and it will stop at nothing to consume us all. Austria is a proud country, but we must look after ourselves now."

Von Bloch shouted an order for the Alpine soldiers to stand down. His rasping German voice indeed had men lower their rifles. Some looked uncomfortable with this situation. For a moment, it seemed control would switch over to the general.

Bang.

The general fell forward, clutching his stomach. Captain Sternberg stood very still, his revolver out, pointing it at the general.

He then barked orders, and the soldiers and civilians started taking what they wanted. Major Richmond crouched down on one knee next to the old general. He called for an orderly to come and help and a staff doctor.

The major gave Captain Sternberg a fierce look, but it was greeted with impassivity.

"If anyone else stands in our way, we will kill them."

As they went about their business, scouts arrived at speed. They weren't Engineer scouts but Alpine Jaeger scouts.

News spread amongst the soldiers and civilians that the long limbs were closing in on the village. Panic set in, and Captain Hayward pleaded with Sternberg to let them go. He refused and said they would be allowed to go once their own convoy was on the road.

Thirty tense minutes followed. With the last wagon rolling out, Corporal Heinz helped organise the Austrian engineers and civilians, and Sergeant Butcher got the British Engineers ready. They had twenty-six rifles and several ammunition boxes with them. Sternberg had kept his promise and allowed four wagons for the wounded, women, and children.

General Von Bloch managed to speak to Corporal Heinz and Major Richmond. He wasn't sure how much longer he could go on. He then demanded to be left in a house to give everyone time. He could shoot from a window and hold the beasts back for as long as possible.

"Damn those creatures, turning Austrian against Austrian." Von Bloch groaned.

Blood was oozing out of his stomach, which he held with both hands.

"I'm an old soldier. Is there a better way to die?"

They reluctantly agreed to his wish. Some wounded soldiers wanted to be left with him. He commanded a lot of respect amongst the men. He refused to allow any able-bodied man to stay, stating that the others needed them more.

The goodbyes were swift. The general was left with five men and six rifles. They picked a house close to the road to station them in.

The mood was sombre as they left; the general had been a guiding light for them. He got two soldiers to hold him up. They then wrapped an Austrian flag to a pole outside the house.

The dawn sun started to creep across the village, highlighting the buildings' wooden panels and tiled roofs. It looked, for the most part, like a ghost town now—empty houses and broken lives.

The wagons set off at speed. They still had a map and a few supplies, but they would need to find food and water along the route. Tokay was still the next destination.

It would be a long walk, several days at most, for those on foot. Captain Hayward walked at the back with Sergeant Butcher. Corporal Heinz led from the front with the one remaining horse that was not being used to pull the wagons.

Charles looked back at General Von Bloch and the five wounded soldiers. They were all Austrians. He felt emotion flow through his body and knew this was the last time he would see the general and the men again.

The general saluted him. He stood still and returned the salute. They then moved into the house and awaited the onslaught.

The soldiers on foot picked up the pace, so they were jogging but not entirely running. The dark blue English helmets and red tunics came alive in the morning sun. However, their blue trousers and black boots were not as smart as usual, and even their white straps and packs were starting to show the wear and tear of this journey across Austria.

Captain Hayward was proud. He was proud that they were coming together to fight against this aggressor and were not resorting to the tactics used by the raiding party the night before. He prayed they never would.

Major Richmond, who had spoken to some of the Austrians, said one of them believed he knew a shortcut to Tokay. It could save them days, and a supply town was on the way.

The old general looked at his wounded men in the house as they tried their best to fortify their position. He stopped momentarily, thanking God for having such brave soldiers serving under him.

He then said that if any man wanted to leave, he would think nothing of it. Knowing he would die from his wounds, he accepted his fate, but he did not want any other man to follow suit on some folly that it was the right thing to do. He didn't know what was happening in the rest of the Austro-Hungarian Empire.

Each man shook their head when asked if they wanted to leave.

Groaning sounds crept along the road. The general had asked to be placed in the attic with a rifle and a pouch full of bullets. They followed his command. Three men were to be stationed downstairs in the living room and kitchen.

The house they chose was not huge, but it was sturdy. Two more Austrians were positioned upstairs. All the men had injuries, some worse than others, but they were willing to fight for their country in common.

The groans and snapping sounds grew closer and closer. Outside, the breeze picked up, and the leaves shook in the wind. There was also a stale smell—it smelt like death.

"Pick your targets! Today, they will find out what it is like to invade our country. No more running."

The general winced as he bellowed out his orders, and the effect on his men was galvanising. Each of them pushed their rifle slowly out of the window they had chosen. The house fell silent, and they waited.

Long limbs started to appear in the village, and some were sniffing at the houses. Their legs and arms could now be fully appreciated in the dawn sunlight. Their human-like heads, with giant teeth and dark eyes. They found a door open close to the Austrian house. One reared up on its hind legs and coughed – a deep, grizzly cough. Two more long-limbed beasts appeared behind it. They then followed the lead creature into the building, inadvertently closing the door behind them.

Ten to fifteen more long limbs were ambling along the road. Another house door smashed open as the soldiers' eyes followed the creatures. The long-limbed creatures came out; they were no longer looking around; their eyes were transfixed on one house.

General Von Bloch knew it was now time. He let the rifle sit into his shoulder and eased his face closer to the breech. His eyes rolled down the sights; he could see the lead creature coming forward.

Blood trickled out of the general's mouth. He turned his head and spat it out. Gritting his teeth, his mind raced with thoughts of his family, his grown-up children and his life in Vienna.

He whispered to himself: may God have mercy on our souls.

Slowly, he squeezed the trigger, and the roar of the rifle crackled through the air. Birds flew up, and animals scattered. The bullet was a killer. The creature was hit straight between the eyes, sending blood spurting from its skull and causing it to fall forward on its very next step.

With that shot, the stampede started. The long limbs coming along the road broke into a sprint towards the house. The remaining soldiers began to open fire on the two creatures directly in front of the house, killing one instantly and wounding the other.

The shots pounded out of the windows and echoed around the village. Several more long limbs fell under heavy fire. In the distance, the flesh-eaters started to pick up speed, sensing fresh meat nearby.

Three long limbs had managed to go unnoticed around the back of the house and were making a beeline for the back windows. One saw an opportunity to stick its head through a glass pane. That was the last thing it ever did as a bayonet pierced its flesh. The soldier twisted it hard but could not reposition himself in time as the other two came smashing through the back door and the now broken window.

They made quick work of attacking the wounded soldier, their giant claws and teeth ripping into his arms and legs. He let out a yell before being torn apart. The other two soldiers shut the kitchen door and made their way upstairs.

As the first soldier reached the top of the stairs, he heard a gurgling sound coming from behind him: his comrade was missing his head. Standing directly behind him was a long limb. The Austrian soldier raised his rifle and squeezed the trigger; nothing happened. He hadn't loaded his rifle.

Seconds later, he was food for the ever-increasing numbers downstairs. It was a quick death as they tucked into his body.

The two remaining soldiers shouted up to the attic that the house had fallen. They killed the next two long limbs that dared to climb the stairs. The general was feeling giddy and weak from the amount of blood he had lost. The attic hatch was shut, but the blood from his wound seeped through the ceiling of the room below.

The two soldiers fought gallantly, but the numbers slowly overpowered them. They tried to shoot each other as an act of mercy, but the creatures were already tearing at their wounded bodies.

The general watched as the flesh-eaters arrived, and the long limbs fought them over the food. The flesh-eaters were almost in a state of frenzy, waiting to eat. Suddenly, three dark priests rode up, separating the fighting creatures.

This was the moment General Von Bloch had been waiting for. He took aim and let off a round, shooting one of the riders through the throat. Underneath him, the long limbs were licking the ceiling and starting to look for a way up to the attic.

The priest slumped forward and rolled off his horse, his foot remaining in the stirrup as he fell awkwardly and making a snapping sound as he fell. He wriggled for a short moment before breathing a deep sigh.

The other two priests looked up at the attic. Their eyes were full of rage.

"Bring me that soldier alive!" screamed one of the priests.

The other priest then pushed past several long limbs that lowered their heads as he passed. The creatures on the second floor of the house had started to claw at the ceiling from which chunks of plaster were dropping off. The old general knew his time was coming to an end. His life was seeping out of him through the wound in his stomach. For a brief moment, he thought about ending it with the bayonet but then accepted he could not do that.

The other priest made two long limbs smash open the attic hatch. He directed one to stand on its hind legs and raise its head into the space. The loud gunshot was what he expected, and the creature fell back to the floor. Wasting no time, he hauled himself up through the attic hatch with his sword drawn and unholstered revolver at the ready.

The sight he met with was of the old general lying on his side, his rifle no longer in his hands and his eyes half open. The priest grabbed his arms and dragged him to the hatch entrance, instructing a long limb to take him to the other priest.

The general was unceremoniously dragged by the legs down the stairs and out into the street. His eyes were closed, and his breathing laboured. The priest got down from his horse as the general lay before him.

He wore a dark tunic and trousers beneath the robe. He knelt alongside the general, took off his cap, and rested it on the ground beside him.

"The priest you shot was my friend."

His German was fluent, and he had a scowl on his face as he said it.

The long-limbed creatures came in closer, the flesh-eaters edging in behind them.

"You put up a good fight. We could have done with a general like you. You probably want to know why. Well, let me tell you."

With that, the priest pressed his lips next to the general's ear and whispered their intentions.

The general's eyes opened. He did not have the strength to talk, even though he tried. With that, the priest raised his hand, commanding, "Let the flesh-eaters finish him." The long limbs begrudgingly moved aside as the flesh-eaters rushed in eagerly. They ravenously tucked into the existing stomach wound and then tore at any available flesh.

Their teeth ripped and bit into everything. With sharp nails and even sharper canines, nothing got in their way. Bones were crunched and fought over as more and more poured onto the general. His dying eyes stayed focused on the priest who had given the order; no screams, no calls for mercy. The coldness of these eyes made the priest move on from this final chapter in the general's life.

Feeding flesh-eaters was the last the priests heard as they rode off.

"I want that convoy. We must find them." "Should we request that the commander of the drones send reinforcements to capture this convoy?" questioned the junior priest.

"No, that would mean admitting defeat, something we shall never do. Get the long limbs to pick up the scent. Where are the bears? We may need them."

The subordinate priest turned and called out to the long limbs. Some were in the house, feeding on the dead soldiers; others were starting to fight with the flesh-eaters for the remains of the general.

"I believe I know where they're going. Send a drone and ask for the riders of the North to meet us."

Chapter 10

Captain Hayward kept everyone's spirits up as they jogged along. The soldiers were in good shape, and the speed was manageable, even with their backpacks and equipment on. Major Richmond spread the weapons out amongst the Austrians and British soldiers. Having only twenty rifles meant that their firepower would be minimal.

Sergeant Butcher checked on the women and children. They were coping well. No one wanted to be stuck in a cramped wagon, but the choices were simple: ride or walk.

The route Corporal Heinz knew would hopefully knock off several days' travel. Major Richmond had left this part of the journey to the Austrian corporal. They knew the distance between them and the flesh-eaters was slight at best. They did not know if these creatures needed to rest or could keep going at a constant pace. This troubled the major, not knowing any of the enemy's weaknesses worked against them. He missed having the direction and experience of the old general. The major was only slightly older than Charles and had not really fought in any considerable conflict. He had been educated at Eton and then at Oxford before doing his officer training at Sandhurst. He was engaged to marry a French duchess from Normandy. She was friends with Captain Hayward's wife and both currently resided in Paris.

As the day wore on, the sun started to heat up the weary travellers. Water played a key part in their journey, and regular breaks were needed to stop the soldiers from getting dehydrated. Food was also being rationed, as the raiders had taken nearly everything.

By late afternoon, Corporal Heinz pointed out where they were on the map. He was very pleased with their progress. They would shortly come to a bridge crossing a small valley further up in the hills.

Going this way would be tiring, but it offered them a chance to get to Tokay more quickly. He also had a cunning plan. There was a small stream that ran nearby. They needed to restock their water barrels and canisters, but there was another reason for going this way. By getting them all to walk in the stream for a mile, he believed the creatures, like dogs, would follow a scent and that this tactic would delay them. He also hoped they would follow the main road and not take the track through the hills. It was a risk as time was precious, but they had little choice.

When they reached the stream, they heard screams and calls behind them. Everyone looked at each other, their eyes telling the story. Fear gripped even the bravest soul. It had to be overcome, or they risked becoming paralysed to the spot.

Captain Hayward cleared his throat and led the first wagon into the water. They had to be careful not to get stuck on the rocks or in the sand. The other soldiers soon came to his aid and began to take the three wagons up the stream. It was wide enough and deep enough to hide the tracks, and fortune also shone on them, with the rocks and stones only being small.

The background noises did not fade, allowing them no time to rest on their laurels. They had to travel as far as they could to ensure there was no immediate trail to follow.

The water was cold but also refreshing. As they moved along, they filled barrels and canisters. Ten soldiers with rifles brought up the rear. Corporal Heinz held back on the horse.

He wanted to keep a visual on the woods and hills in the distance; if they were spotted, they would have to make a break for it.

After ten minutes, it was decided that they had to get back on the track. The stream had larger rocks than they first thought, making it hard to negotiate. With this, the wagons were eased out of the water and led to the side of the stream.

Soon, they were making good progress through the hills. Although they were wet, the afternoon sun was drying them at a reasonable speed. Most people were hungry, but there was no time to stop or eat.

The children clung to their parents. They were starting to look more anxious as the journey wore on. The soldiers who had children were promptly reminded of their own and how glad they were that they were not doing this trek now. They tried hard to make them feel at ease with the occasional smile, silly face or even a carved wooded toy.

The bridge was meant to be only a couple of hours away. The screams and cries were no longer within earshot, which gave them all hope that the plan had worked – for now.

The following two hours were hard going. The hills were unforgiving, and the men marching with heavy packs and little in their stomachs felt it more.

The convoy moved onwards at a steady pace. The mood amongst the soldiers and civilians had changed slightly as the imminent danger had subsided. Tiredness, though, was having an effect. The nervous tension had taken its toll on everyone— it was energy-sapping. The sight of the old bridge brought relief to most people's faces. The ravine it crossed was not particularly deep, but it would stop or delay a pursuing army, even if that army were not a conventional one.

Major Richmond did not have any dynamite, but he agreed with his captain that they should try their best to destroy what they could of it. The tools they had were limited, though. Each wagon had an axe and spade, and the soldiers could also use their bayonets to help lever up the wooden planks. Captain Hayward was wary of the effort needed to destroy the bridge and was willing to start the process once people had crossed it.

As they crossed, he felt that perhaps the job would be made easier than he had thought, with the planks creaking and rising in places. This bridge had seen better days.

The first swing of the axe split the wood with ease. They could not take down the whole bridge, but creating a hole in the middle would do for now. Captain Hayward led the way, chopping and breaking up wood as he moved backwards from the middle. Several other soldiers joined him, spreading out along the bridge and carrying on working backwards. As the hole appeared in front of them, they pushed the shattered planks into it and watched as they fell effortlessly down to the ground below.

It did not take long before a large chunk of the bridge was ripped up. They made sure it was not a distance a horse or animal could jump. The creatures would find it hard to gauge as this was something new to them. They didn't want to waste any more time and decided what they had done would have to do. Hopefully, it would buy them some time.

Food was on the agenda as they trudged along. Major Richmond knew they must eat to refuel their energy; the problem was the lack of food and time to eat it. Corporal Heinz said the track would take them through a hill village and that there might be some supplies there.

They travelled along the trail for several miles, briefly stopping to drink water. Two hours passed, and it was decided that they would eat what they had. The cook and others helped prepare dinner for them all. Scouts were sent out on horseback to check the forests.

The scouts returned with no news and tucked into the poultry dinner that had been prepared.

After an hour, it was time to move on again. It was evening now, and the village was coming into sight. Corporal Heinz rode off to check the village and hopefully bring back good news.

Private Brown found Heidi, who had been walking by the wagons to stretch her legs. Her smile made him feel a little more alive. They chatted for a short while as they sat on the track. Her hair did not glow in the same way it had at the fort, and her skin was also pale and undernourished. Heidi was a good reflection of the group. The journey was taking its toll on everyone. It was a challenging trek, and the added stress of something chasing them made it even worse.

Private Clegg came over and sat with them. He smiled at them both and remarked, 'Two lovebirds'.

"So, when's the big wedding?"

Heidi blushed, but even that did not lighten up her face entirely. She just held John's hand.

"I hope we all get through this. I would love John to see Vienna."

Private Clegg nodded. For him, it was a moment of normality in a very abnormal situation. After a moment, he got up and walked to the front of the convoy.

Corporal Heinz returned, shaking his head. After speaking to an Austrian soldier, he approached the captain and major.

"Those long-limbed creatures are in the village. I don't understand how they made it there before us. We had the upper hand."

Both men looked down. It was a bitter blow. It could be the end if they were to be cut off and surrounded. Twenty rifles in the open would find it impossible to hold off such a large force. The thought of being eaten alive scared everyone.

"Corporal, is there anywhere we can go? Is there another route to Tokay?"

"Yes, Captain, the caverns."

As the word caverns came out of the corporal's mouth, both officers looked at each other. Darkness was a friend to some and an enemy to others.

"How far away are they?"

The corporal scratched his head and then rubbed his beard.

"It's around an hour to the mouth of the caverns."

News rapidly spread around the group that they were heading towards the caverns instead of going to the village to get supplies.

It was a testing moment. Some of the Austrian soldiers and civilians looked anxious about this route. They started to huddle and discuss it in small groups. Major Richmond had some command of the German language and could tell that they wanted to try the village anyway. They believed it was better to fight than to starve in darkness.

It was hard to argue with hunger and tiredness. He spoke to Corporal Heinz, explaining that they could make their own choices here and now. The food would be divided, and the rifles would be shared again.

Corporal Heinz explained to the major that he would lead them through the caverns and did not intend to leave the group. He rode up to a tall man who was the blacksmith in the fort. He seemed to be discussing about leading a breakaway group.

The corporal and the blacksmith had a frank discussion. Their voices were raised, but never to the point of losing control.

The blacksmith was a large man, physically strong and very determined. He got his point across about what they wanted to do, and it was time to take that chance.

They could not discuss it forever—time was precious. Gathering some bits and pieces together, the blacksmith then called out that those who wanted to follow him into the village were welcome. He did not take long to amass half of the remaining Austrian soldiers and civilians.

They asked for half of the rifles as promised and a wagon for the women and children who were also coming with them. The major walked over and shook his hand, speaking briefly in broken German before returning to the others.

It would take them around an hour to reach the village, almost the same as it would take the others to reach the caverns. The remaining Austrians hugged and kissed their compatriots before waving them off.

They didn't waste any time setting off themselves. It had not taken long to share out the supplies as they were almost gone anyway. Only the water was well stocked. They had also been given more tools to use as weapons.

Corporal Heinz hoped they could overcome the long limbs and take what they needed. It would give him great pleasure to meet them in Tokay.

The rifle fire in the distance indicated that the fight for the village had begun. They hoped and prayed that their fellow group members would overcome the enemy.

The opening to the cavern slowly came into sight.

They had very little oil for the lamps, and darkness was not their friend. Corporal Heinz believed they would have to spend the night in the cavern. It would not be ideal, but it would give them a chance to rest and then progress to the other side the next day.

Reluctantly, they all crept into the opening. Its jagged rock face and awkward shape did not reassure everyone. For the most part, it was reasonably dry inside, and the opening was large enough for them to take the wagons in. Captain Hayward instructed some tired and hungry soldiers to cut down bushes to cover their tracks.

They toyed with the idea of pressing on through the caverns, but it would have been asking too much of the soldiers. Due to what had been hunting them, the pace had been set quite fast. After a brief discussion, Sergeant Butcher agreed to take the first watch, followed by Corporal Smith and Major Richmond. Ten armed guards would accompany each watch.

It was decided that should something kick off in the night, they would retreat into the cavern and continue to make their way through. The wagons, however, could not be brought deeper into the caves. Their best chance was to take the horses they had, half the frame of a wagon and two wheels and then build something on the other side. The idea was that they could fashion a makeshift cart for the children who could not maintain the pace they would need to escape the horde.

Corporal Smith asked if they could light some fires for warmth. Sergeant Butcher agreed it would be nice to have something warm in the caves but wanted to check that the fires could not be seen from the outside. This essentially meant they had to go in further and around a vast jagged rock to ensure that no light would be visible.

They then started to build a fire while Captain Hayward went outside the mouth of the cave to check if he could see anything. Fortunately, he was able to report back to Sergeant Butcher that it was safe and that no light was giving away their position. Wood was needed for the fires, and small gathering parties were set up to collect what they could. Half of each wagon was dismantled. The supplies would have to be taken in the soldiers' backpacks.

Corporal Heinz believed that travelling would take only a day and a half once they were through the caverns.

The night sky was clear, and the air was fresh. The gunshots had stopped; no one wanted to guess whether that was a good or bad thing. Everyone was working well as a team. Firewood was mounting up, and all they wanted now was a hearty meal. The cook was busy at work, trying to make something out of nothing. A couple of the civilians asked for permission to go hunting for rabbits.

Major Richmond agreed and sent the soldiers who also had experience hunting small game. They had a few farmers' sons with them, which helped set up a hunting party.

The rest of the group set about concealing the entrance and preparing for the evening. They could not cover it totally but could do enough to make it hard to see from a distance.

The beds for the evening would be basic. The caves were quite dry, but they always had a certain dampness and coldness to them. Corporal Heinz hurriedly formed a small cave party. He wanted to check the route they would set out on in the morning. He had mentioned by chance that he had once been there as a boy and worked through the caves with his father.

His father worked for the government and travelled around the country, visiting major towns and cities. On a trip to Tokay, they took a detour and visited the caverns. They spent a day and night in the caves with a guide, working their way through.

That had been a long time ago, but he knew some corners were marked out. This information could be crucial as they went along.

The lanterns were lit briefly as they needed to see what they were doing while preparing for the evening. After two hours, the hunting party returned. They had been successful. The sight of bundles of rabbits and wildfowl caused the noise level to rise within the cave opening. Food had been on most people's minds for a while. Now they were going to have meat.

The head cook had several people cooking at once while he prepped the vegetables. Many of the hunters already knew what to do, so they prepared some of the animals themselves and started roasting them.

Captain Hayward was wary of the smell of cooking meat, but he was intoxicated by the thought of eating warm flesh. When they started serving the meat, an orderly queue formed. It did well to maintain its shape and discipline. The women and children were allowed to the front first, and the men lined up behind. Major Richmond and the other officers went last. They wanted to make a point of showing that everyone was working as a unit and no one should receive special treatment because of rank.

Once the meat was handed out, it was quickly stripped to the bone. Jaws snapped at flesh, and tongues licked the bones. It was a most enjoyable meal and went down well.

The feast was an important morale booster. The satisfaction on everyone's faces was enough to convince Major Richmond that a hunting party had been a risk worth taking. The lanterns were blown out, and the fires stoked. It was not going to take long for sleep to overcome them.

Those on guard duty had been promised some time on the wagon to compensate for the lack of sleep.

Major Richmond spent a moment chatting to Captain Hayward.

"Do you think we will make it, Charles?"

Charles Hayward looked at the major.

"We're in a very sticky situation, outnumbered and running out of food. What we do have is a 'never say die' attitude."

They both smiled at each other. It was an impossible question to answer, but it was a comforting one for the man in charge.

"Get some sleep, Major. I'll wake you later."

The night air still carried a chill. Private John Brown was on watch near the entrance to the caverns. His eyes were heavy, but his instincts were still switched on.

He walked closer to the branches and bushes that covered the entrance. His eyes scanned to and from, studying the hills and woods in the distance.

A bat shot by the opening, making John step back. He saw a deer foraging. It all looked peaceful and calm, so, rolling his rifle over his shoulder, he sat down on a large rock.

His thoughts were of Heidi, her soft lips, long flowing blonde hair, and tight bosom. These thoughts helped him to get past the tiredness. He got up and decided to find Private William to discuss his growing love for her.

First, though, he wanted another look at the deer grazing because it made him feel there was still hope in the world. His eyes slowly worked their way up from the stony ground to the broken branches. He let out a sigh of relief as the deer was still there.

Then, a long limb sprang out in a flash and took down the deer. It didn't have time to let out a scream. Private Brown stood motionless; even though the attack was five hundred metres away, it was a reminder that they were close and out there.

When his adrenaline settled down, he spoke to Captain Hayward, who then informed the rest of the guards. The drill was still the same: no one was to be woken yet. While the long limbs were out hunting, everyone still needed to rest. If they started to make a beeline for the caverns, then it would be the emergency drill.

The night shift passed without incident. There was movement outside, the odd shriek, call and growl, but nothing more.

Chapter11

As the morning passed, they sat around, eating and drinking. The plan was to get to the nearest village on the other side of the caves and restock. The night's rest and food had given most people a spring in their step. The British and Austrian Engineers started to prepare for the trek through the caves. Oil was poured into the lanterns, and the rifles were cleaned and checked for battle readiness.

The officers gathered for a quick debrief. The message was simple: find supplies once through the cave or face starvation. With all the troubles evolving around the creatures, the basics still needed to be addressed: daily food, water, and sleep. The raider party had slowed them down, losing their supplies and mobility, which seriously hampered things. The small group of civilians and Austrian soldiers that were left lessened their fighting power, but it always came back to the basic needs.

Captain Hayward looked into the darkness of the cave. Corporal Heinz had informed him that there were openings in the cave ceiling on the way through, allowing natural daylight to creep in occasionally. He had recommended to the major that they set off in a couple of hours.

He watched a small lad playing with some stones. He had built a wall and was now taking shots at it. This was the first time in a while that the children could relax and be themselves.

Corporal Heinz took several soldiers with lanterns. He wanted to start on the route through the caverns. He would leave a lantern and mark the stone next to it at specific points. They were planning on leaving altogether, but he wanted to have a feel for the caves again. He knew there would be markings already there, but they would take time to find.

The idea of getting lost could not be allowed to soak into his subconscious. He wanted to focus on getting through and onto Tokay. There had to be a village en route, and maybe this onslaught had not touched it.

Private Brown took time to relieve himself in the bushes they had used to cover the main entrance. The night shift had been woken. They had a quick bite to eat and were now preparing to take over.

He stood there looking out at the same spot as the night before. He pressed his face closer to the leafy foliage. Suddenly, a face appeared in front of a branch, its eyes looking back at him. Then it moved forward, pushing through the thicket they had made. John fell back as he tried to move. He did not have a rifle, only his bayonet. The flesh-eater fell forward on top of him. It started to snap and claw at his body. He was in a good position to hold it back but could not lift it off. The rotting flesh had a putrid stench, almost dripping off the creature's face. It growled and snarled at him. Despite being half-rotten, its strength was a concern.

He tried to call out, but the creature had a hand on his throat, and as he thrashed around, he noticed another flesh-eater coming through the now partly broken entrance. It went straight for him like a bee to honey. The branch that had given way when the creature first came forward was now lying on top of his body, but it was also wedged under a rock. This was stopping John from rolling the flesh-eater. To make matters worse, the other creature was now bending down, trying to bite his legs.

He turned to see more and more of them shuffling up to the entrance. Private John Brown fought long and hard, but he faced the truth inside his head: time was not on his side. As the second creature grabbed his legs and a third staggered through the hole, he almost stopped fighting.

Then, a tremendous pressure was released from on top of him. A flesh-eater's head landed next to his shoulder. The second creature on his legs was smacked hard with a spade.

"Get up, John. There's too many to stay lying down."

John got up gingerly and was helped to his feet. The voice was Heidi's. She had come looking for him and saw the attack unfold. She wasted no time in stopping his attackers.

"Thank you so much, you've saved my—"

"You can thank me later."

She grabbed his hand and led him towards the others. Captain Hayward told the men not to fire as that could bring more. They would have to kill them with rifle butts or spades. If the numbers got too many, then they would follow Corporal Heinz through the caverns.

The hand-to-hand battle began in earnest. The first twenty were handled swiftly. This was one of the few times they outnumbered them, which gave them an advantage. At first, the situation was coming under control, but the creatures continued to stream through steadily. Unfortunately, several horses were startled by this attack, causing them to bolt out of the mouth of the cavern. This left them with one horse, which was brought under control and led into the darkness.

Major Richmond ordered them to fall back. He picked a moment when there was a lull between the creatures reaching the entrance and entering the cave. Nothing was known about how they communicated with each other or how they would track them in the darkness.

As more and more flesh-eaters reached the entrance, the blockade collapsed. Captain Hayward made sure the last man passed him and went into the tunnel. The caverns were now the only means of escape.

Corporal Heinz's work in laying out the lanterns saved time. The women, children and civilian men had gone ahead with the Austrian soldiers. The British Engineers started picking up the laid-out lanterns as they brought up the rear. At some point, they would catch up with the main group.

The deeper they travelled into the caves, the colder they became. The ground was damp and rough, making walking difficult. Shuffling and scratching filled the caverns. The predators were following.

The soldiers' red tunics and blue helmets had lost their spark. Sergeant Butcher made a comment to a young private about his uniform, which the soldier took seriously until the lantern was placed nearer to the sergeant's face, and he saw the wry smile.

Private Brown was with Heidi. She had saved his life, and he wanted to thank her. It was hard with so many other soldiers around, and he felt a little embarrassed.

"Heidi."

She looked at him.

"Dankeschön."

She smiled and kissed him on the cheek.

Moving through the caves at speed was not easy. The odd slip here and there was a dangerous game. Cries could be heard echoing around the tunnels each time someone fell onto a stone or rock. The whole group was amassed in a large chamber. Corporal Heinz held up a lantern – gathered around him were women and children. The Austrian soldiers were happy to see their British counterparts.

"Good to see you, Major."

"The same goes for you, Corporal. I'm afraid they're on our tails. No long limbs as far as we know, just flesh-eaters."

The conversation was brief; it was all about following the corporal now. The soldiers carrying the two wheels and frame were burly men. Other soldiers were carrying water barrels and the remaining supplies.

The cook wanted to stop and rest, but he knew there was no point in asking. They set off rapidly down a tunnel which had been marked. The groans that crept out of the darkness had menace. Some sounded throaty, others asthmatic.

It was a timely reminder to every person there: if you slow down, they will get you. The worrying thing was that they seemed to be getting closer even if the group kept up a steady pace.

Charles was concerned that they could end up coming face to face with flesh-eaters from the front of the tunnel and be trapped by the horde from behind. With so few rifles, it was a sombre thought to digest.

Major Richmond asked Corporal Heinz whether they could keep up this fast-paced walk, even jogging at times, without burning out. The soldiers were carrying the children to help share the load.

"We must get to the middle of the caves before they do."

This troubled the major as he thought they were already on the main route through.

"Why would we need to beat them there when they're behind us?"

"All roads lead to paradise, Major. There are other routes."

It was not exactly what he wanted to hear, but it was too late to start a protest.

The pace was kept up. The odd opening at the top of the caves let in light, which was welcomed but also sharp and painful on the eyes due to the prolonged spells of darkness. In some places, the caverns opened up to reveal larger chambers with ceilings hundreds of metres high.

The cavern's rock formations were peculiar, formed by water and ice over thousands of years. The stalactites hanging from the cave ceiling were long and cone-like. This was why Heinz's father had taken him on a tour all those years ago.

The corporal said he could only remember part of it, but he did recall his father saying something regarding minerals and other scientific things about the caves. For a short while, this was enough to take their minds off what had been happening and marvel at Mother Nature's creation. It was truly awe-inspiring.

"I believe if we can get to the main tunnel at the centre, we can rest there, and then it's one passage out after that," said the Corporal

Brief respites typically occurred in the larger chambers, where water was hurriedly consumed and the odd dry biscuit was handed out to the women and children. The children had done remarkably well. The constant echoes and grunts made sure no one slacked off. By the time they reached the centre, though, exhaustion was creeping in. It had been a hard slog, but without Corporal Heinz, it would have been nearly impossible. His knowledge of the marked cave routes gave them the edge.

They all collapsed as they reached the location. The chamber was large enough to hold them all. The passage lay directly before them, but no one was ready to use it. The soldiers with rifles were sent to three entrance points into the chamber.

They could rest there but were told to shoot anything that came through. Some lanterns were put down each entrance tunnel to give them fair warning of anything coming.

An hour passed, and fortunately, there were no signs of flesh-eaters. Everyone was thankful for the rest, but water was the only thing on the menu.

Captain Hayward asked Corporal Heinz if he thought it would be okay for people to sleep. It was only midday, but the journey had been frantic. The darkness also helped people lose track of time, and hunger made them weary. It was decided that they would rest as long as they could.

Captain Hayward checked his pocket watch by a lantern and then put his backpack and rug on a stone. It was damp, and the air wasn't fresh to breathe, but it was a good enough place to close his eyes. Major Richmond arranged for the tunnel entrance guards to change after an hour.

Sergeant Butcher fell asleep leaning against a rock.

Silence fell over the cave.

Chapter 12

A roar woke everyone up. It was startling to emerge from a deep sleep and be fully alert. No time was wasted gathering the group and setting off down the main passage out of the cavern.

The guards by the entrances to the other tunnels fell back quickly. The noise was coming at them fast, but they could not determine which tunnel it was.

The major stood with the captain and several armed soldiers, looking for what might come through. The lanterns had been blown out for fear of attracting flesh-eaters but were later re-lit.

The ground shook a little with the noise of the oncoming beast. The major ordered most of the men to leave, saying he would stay back with four armed soldiers. Captain Hayward wanted to stay but was ordered to retreat with the others.

The silence that followed the roar was unnerving. The major and the four men watched each tunnel. The lanterns flickered – still nothing. Major Richmond felt his heart as it pounded. The darkness was now more of an enemy than a friend.

Suddenly, movement came from the right-hand tunnel. The lantern shattered as a green flash went past it and into the chamber. The four men and the major were holding firm at the main exit tunnel. He did not want them to leave that position.

The thing that was now with them moved around at speed. They could hear its hard rasping huffs. The sound of grinding teeth and hissing was also prevalent.

"Sir, shall we move out and find the beast?"

The major put his hand on the soldier's shoulder, then put his finger to his own lips to indicate the need to be quiet.

The light in the chamber was dimmed because the right-hand tunnel had lost its lantern. It did not matter; the creature started to emerge from the darkness in front of them. Its head looked like a lizard's, but the difference was the loose fur covering it. The body was also lizard-shaped, again covered in loose fur.

It came forward, nostrils flared, and its shoulders revealed thick muscles as it moved. The monster was a giant. Its claws were a foot long, and its teeth protruded from its mouth.

Major Richmond stood firm. "Take aim, men," the recent order of shoot for the head was now mandatory. The beast stopped around ten to fifteen metres in front of them, its eyes following them all.

"Fire!"

The bullets shot into the beast, piercing its skin around the head and shoulders. It reared up and then charged. The shots were accurate, but stopping this creature would take a lot.

One Engineer was fumbling around with his bullet, trying to re-load it into the breach, when his eyes caught sight of teeth bearing down on his head. In one quick swoop, the beast ripped it off. It brushed the other soldiers aside, and its tail knocked the major into the wall. He was not carrying a rifle but an axe, which was flung into the darkness. Blood was now pouring out from the neck of the Engineer's corpse. The lizard creature swallowed the head in one quick flick and turned to attack the other soldiers.

They gathered their composure and started to bayonet its legs. The skin was almost like armour, and it easily took everything they could throw at it.

The men frantically jabbed and gored the beast but to little avail. It swung around an enormous claw and shredded a soldier from shoulder to abdomen. He screamed out in pain. Then, it turned in a small circle to lash out at the other two. The major came around to hear the thunder of rifle fire and see a flash of light. One of the remaining soldiers fired at close range into the beast's head. This seemed to have an effect on the creature as it burst out of the main chamber and disappeared down one of the tunnels.

Major Richmond was helped to his feet whilst the other soldier tended to the wounded man. The lacerations were deep, and his blood loss was considerable. He grabbed his friend and gingerly took out a folded cloth. Inside was a picture of his family: a wife and two small children. On the back was a short-written note.

Love from family – Catherine, Amber, George.

Major Richmond came forward and gently took the picture. He then leaned forward and listened to the dying man's request. The major took hold of him as his final heartbeat ceased. He then leaned him down and closed his eyes. They speedily searched the other soldier's body for any personal items.

A roar went up again. The monster was not done. It was injured but not finished.

"We must lure it out; it must be killed."

Major Richmond was adamant.

"How do you plan to kill it, sir?" A young soldier asked.

There was a pause.

"Get between the two rocks over there. We have to get it close. Then I'll strike with the axe from above." Major Richmond did this whilst retrieving the axe from the ground.

The two soldiers looked at each other. Their officer's idea did not convince them, but they had little choice. Rather than choosing who would lure the creature through the rocks, they decided they would both do it.

The rumblings around the chamber seemed to indicate that the creature was agitated. With no time to waste, they positioned themselves in front of the rocks. The men were then told to holler and shout. It did the job. The beast started to emerge out of the darkness, the centre tunnel highlighting its colossal frame. Its tongue rolled out of its mouth, licking at the blood streaming from its head.

The creature looked less nimble than before, but it still carried an enormous threat. It stopped before the soldiers, and they knelt to entice it closer. Then it charged. The major was on top of one of the rocks with the axe. He prayed he would not be knocked off when the lizard creature burst out at the men.

The beast powered into the gap between the rocks, maybe without the same vigour as earlier, but still with enough energy to take it almost all the way through. The key factor was that it got stuck for a second. That was its downfall. The moment that happened, the major struck, bringing the axe down with the full force of a woodsman splitting dead wood. It was a killer blow, straight onto its head and into its brain.

The wail was short, and the death instant.

They took a short while to take in what had just happened. The axe was buried deep in the lizard's skull, stuck fast. The major and the men cautiously got to their feet.

Whilst the action had taken place, the flesh-eaters had been drawn in by the smell of flesh and blood. They were now massing around the three men. Major Richmond was concerned. The two soldiers loaded their rifles but were told not to fire. The flesh-eaters were being drawn straight to the dead soldiers. It would give them a moment of opportunity.

As the creatures started to feed, the soldiers moved past them. One of the rifles had been snapped in half, and the other lay strewn on the floor. The major reached down to pick it up, and several flesh-eaters turned their heads as he did so. There was a moment when he stared at these sorry creatures. Their eyes were as dark as night, with flesh hanging off their bones. Human in looks, but animal in instincts. They stared back. He thought about telling the others to run but kept his cool. Fortunately, they were distracted as more turned up to feed.

The three of them moved carefully down the exit tunnel—they did not want to take any chances. After a hundred metres or more, they started to jog into the darkness. Their idea was to keep close to the soldier with the lantern.

It took them thirty minutes to catch the main group. The major explained that he had lost two men, but it did not lighten the mood.

Corporal Heinz continued leading the group. He thought reaching the other side would take another couple of hours.

Everyone felt tired, and the lack of food slowed the group down. The men carrying the wheels for the cart and frame were failing. The children had walked some of the way, but most of the time, they were carried. Luckily, the water levels were still reasonable.

They pressed on through the darkness.

Chapter 13

"Shall we send the drones after them through the caverns?" a young priest enquired.

The officer he was asking stroked his chin.

"They have been dealing with the flesh-eaters well. Maybe the Lizard Dragon caught up with them and finished them off."

The senior priest rode forward. He wanted to hear the discussion of the junior order.

"We shall send no more of our force after them. Tokay is the next target. The high priest wants it burnt to the ground."

The other two looked at him.

"Shall we take prisoners?"

"Spare no one."

He then turned and spoke to a drone commander. His eyes were dark black, and his yellow teeth showed when he smiled.

"I want the riders of the North to reach Tokay. They will help lead the attack. Your main force will join the flesh-eaters and long-limbs."

"Yes, my lord. Shall we send a request for more Lizard Dragons?"

The priest considered this option.

"The high priest is amassing an army. We shall let him be. The Dragons will be needed elsewhere."

The drone commander bowed his head and made his way to a soldier holding the reins of a horse. He then mounted the horse and rode off to join his men.

Massive cannons were being pulled by horses as big as elephants. The army marched to the beat of drums. Flesh-eaters were being whipped into line and led by dark priests along with the long limbs who had been herded together.

The drones had a large cavalry regiment, which helped protect the main force.

At the rear of the column were wagons and carts. The carts had pipes packed together and covered, whilst the wagons carried supplies.

Chapter 14

Captain Hayward could see light at the end of the tunnel. Its warmth hit them hard. After the dark, damp caves, this was a pure treat. They had to rest briefly and cover their eyes whilst adjusting to the brightness.

Everyone congratulated Corporal Heinz. He had led them through the caverns, and they were now within touching distance of Tokay.

A detachment of men was put outside the entrance to the cavern. The major said it would only be a matter of time before the flesh-eaters worked their way through the tunnel. He also briefed the officers about the lizard creature that had attacked them. He feared that if several of them were to turn up, and with the limited firepower they now had, it would make it a very hard fight.

A hunting group was organised again and quickly dispersed into the surrounding woods. A group was organised to gather water whilst the others were allowed to rest. Guards were posted around, most of them armed with spades or axes.

Captain Hayward shared a private moment with the major. He hadn't had time to think about what was happening and wanted to pick his brains about the insanity of it all. They both sat on a rock and looked over the valley.

"Could this be the end of the world?" Captain Hayward said this, wiping his brow.

The major took off his helmet and stroked his beard, which was a common sight on most of the soldiers' faces. Although they did have shaving kits in their packs, it had been the least of their worries.

The same applied to their uniforms: the famous red tunics and blue trousers were stained and dirty. The blue spiked helmets were far from blue now; a slightly tanned version had taken over.

"On the surface, the world has lost its order and code of conduct. Until we meet other officials, we won't know the truth. The way the Alpine soldiers robbed us suggests there is more to this than meets the eye."

Charles nodded.

"It looks like the creatures are being controlled. They are not randomly massing; they're being led. We need to know why and for what purpose."

Both men agreed it was not good to talk too much about this in front of the soldiers. They would already be having those conversations with their comrades, and morale needed to be kept up. Everyone was hungry and tired and wanted to be away from all of this madness.

As the hours passed, small fires were lit in preparation for the hunting group's return. Chalres still had his binoculars and used them to scan the horizon. He was first to see the hunting group return, shortly joined by the water collectors.

The hunting group had done well again; rabbits, berries, and wild roots had been gathered. It would not be a feast for a king, but it would be a feast nonetheless.

The cooked food was rapidly devoured, and the bones were buried. No risks were taken that could jeopardise their position or draw the enemy in faster.

They had lost another rifle in the caverns, leaving them with nine. The only other weapons now were spades, axes, and pieces of wood.

While most rested after the food, some of the engineers set about building the carts. They had brought enough material and wheels for two carts. These were envisaged to transport the children and what little supplies they had left. Some of the men were still carrying wounds from the battle at the fort, but these had not been too serious.

Once the carts were finished, everyone gathered and reviewed the route. Corporal Heinz was going to be the lead scout. He had maps of the local area and was confident in the quickest route to Tokay. If they had to take a detour due to being attacked or having their path blocked, he would find a way. There was a path nearby that led to the main road. This was the chosen route to the city.

The carts were loaded with children and supplies. The pace was less frantic than before, as there had been no sightings of flesh-eaters or anything else that could cause alarm.

The civilians had coped very well with the trek so far. The children had fared even better, and although they didn't have a choice, the complaints had been minimal. They had wondered what had happened to the other group that had left them before entering the caverns. Most speculated that the flesh-eaters or long limbs had got to them, and this was enough to spur them on to Tokay. It was far from home, but home would be wherever there was peace.

The Austrian Engineers were made up mainly of soldiers from Vienna, though some were more local and had Hungarian ancestry. They were concerned that their country was under attack and that their own soldiers had turned against them. They questioned whether a civil war was developing, but there was an unspoken question about the evil behind the swarm of death. The officers did not need to allay their own fears – it was obvious to them that this was no ordinary invasion.

Every farm close to the road was searched for supplies. There was some joy, with blankets and dried biscuits added to the collection. The cook had found vegetable patches and had organised a group to pick them. The farms looked abandoned but not ransacked. The major concurred that this had been an organised withdrawal, raising hopes that there was still a functioning government.

The weather was turning grey and overcast. Tiny droplets of rain were falling periodically.

The column moved at a steady speed, the carts being pulled by men as they only had one horse. Corporal Heinz was using this horse to scout ahead. It was a dangerous role: their safety relied on him keeping them from being spotted. They had thought about going through the woods or fields, but the tiredness affecting everyone was too much, so it had to be the easiest route for now.

The rain started to fall a little harder. It was refreshing; most people had not washed since they had been near the stream, and it felt good to have water falling on them. The leaves sucked in the cool water, seeming to come alive as Mother Nature quenched their thirst.

Two hours passed. The road had been in good condition, which helped their progress. In the distance was a viewpoint looking over the next valley. The corporal had already ridden off to investigate. He came back with a smile on his face. Tokay was now in sight.

The group gathered speed, the thought of warm food and a good night's sleep driving most souls towards their destination. The corporal had borrowed the binoculars to see if the city had fallen or not.

They had wondered why there were no other refugees on the road. No one could let the thought of the city being destroyed enter their minds. It was all about hope now. Nothing less would do.

Once over the hill, the city came into view. It was a beautiful sight: smoke was rising from the houses, but it did not look like uncontrolled fires; this was coming from the chimneys. The closer they got, the more they could see people scurrying around. It was not as crowded as they had thought it might be, but there were at least people.

They could see a makeshift defensive wall around the city. On top of this wall were a handful of soldiers. Cannons were pointed at them, so Major Richmond stopped the column and asked if Corporal Heinz could get permission for them to enter. The alpine soldiers came to mind; no one could be trusted too easily after that.

They waited a mile outside the defences. It was a well-earned rest, although most were very eager to get going and enter the city itself.

Corporal Heinz returned, looking relaxed. This helped encourage the mood.

"They were very surprised to see anyone coming from Unghvar. We can rest and eat. There are many spare houses in the city. Most of the population has moved on to Pressburg or Vienna."

He went on to explain that they were evacuating everyone. The fighting that took place at Unghvar had been brutal, and most of the Austro–Hungarian army had been destroyed.

There was talk of an army heading their way. Many people in the city had not seen the flesh-eaters or long limbs. They had only heard rumours of creatures not of this world taking over their beloved country.

They passed through the gates to Tokay. Captain Hayward smiled at the major, showing his relief.

The children started singing nursery rhymes in German, and the Royal Engineers responded with some traditional British songs. Even the sun's rays began to shoot through the clouds.

The further they went into the city, the more deserted it looked. Regular Austrian soldiers were moving supplies around, but most of the civilians had gone.

A soldier rode up to them on a horse. He looked stern and high-ranking.

"Guten Morgen, gentlemen. My name is General Haas. You British are a long way from home, ja?"

"Good morning to you, sir. I'm Major Richmond and at my side is Captain Hayward. We are the 37th Regiment of the Queen's Royal Engineers."

He spoke about the past few months and how they had been working with the Austrian Engineers in the Carpathian Mountains until the attack happened. Soon afterwards, more Austrian soldiers arrived with wagons and carts. They then helped load the civilians in. Nurses were stationed in each wagon and tended to sores and wounds. General Haas said they would discuss more after the group had rested. He appreciated that they all looked exhausted. He was saddened to hear of the loss of General Von Bloch, as he had been a friend and had fought alongside him before.

The sergeant called out for the British soldiers to come into line. This was a slight shock as there had been no marching in order since the fort. They were tired and hungry, but they followed orders and lined up. He then got them to about turn and started marching them behind the last wagon as they followed it deeper into the city.

General Haas had horses brought for the major and the captain. Corporal Heinz was still with them. The general apologised that he might not understand all the English being spoken, so it was better to have the corporal ready to translate.

The wagons and carts pulled into a courtyard. More soldiers were there to help unload people, and military doctors were on standby.

The civilians were led to houses that had been left empty, which were now ideal for refugees. Before they left, they took time to thank the Royal Engineers. Captain Hayward thanked the Austrian Engineers, particularly Corporal Heinz.

Sergeant Butcher and the other soldiers did the same as their captain. They had formed a close bond with their fellow Engineers, and seeing them go in another direction almost felt wrong. They had died for each other over the past several weeks, and it was hard to wonder whether they would meet again.

Major Richmond stood with the general and saluted them all as they passed. He intended to visit the Austrians later in the evening to wish them well.

The officers had their own quarters, with an orderly to bring them drinks or anything they should require. Captain Hayward took his time and prepared a warm bath. He let himself sink into it and let out a huge sigh as he immersed his body under the water. They had been given soap, and it was pure bliss to use it. The feeling of being clean was something Charles appreciated. He took time to shave and dress and then rang a bell to ask for a cup of tea.

They were due to meet General Hass for supper, but he still had an hour to kill, so he decided to write to his wife and children. The orderly was not gone long and returned with a hot cup of tea. Charles sat himself next to the window and pulled in a small round table to write on. He looked outside to see the odd soldier and civilian wandering about.

The main unit had gone to the barracks. Most of the regular Austrian army had been detached to Vienna, leaving hundreds of free beds vacant for them. The soldiers were grateful to be able to wash and change. The Austrians had supplied some general clothes to wear while their uniforms were being washed and repaired.

The Engineers were allowed time off from full duties. Most went to sleep or wander around the city. Supper was set for 7 p.m. All of them had been told not to leave the city limits.

Major Richmond washed and changed and then went to speak with General Haas. His headquarters were in the old city hall. He had moved it to be nearer the front of the city, where they thought an attack would most likely come from. The major passed several guards along the way. He was then directed up some stairs to the room. The door was slightly ajar, and inside, he found the general. He was smoking a cigar and looking over maps.

"Major Richmond, would you like some coffee?"

"Yes, thank you, general."

The general led the major to a luxurious armchair. He lowered himself into the chair, and the general brought over some coffee.

"They had a better suite over here. That's worth moving for, huh?"

The major looked around the room at the mini library and grand paintings. It was all very impressive. The view from the window allowed one to see over the city walls and out onto the valley ahead.

"What happened whilst we were in the mountains?" asked the Major.

"Major Richmond—"

Before General Hass could say anything more, the major interrupted.

"Please, call me Harry."

"Harry, the city will be totally evacuated over the next few days. The Austro–Hungarian Empire is coming to an end. This is what happens to Empires; they come, and they go. There is a new challenger on the scene. Europe had better be ready."

There was a pause as the general sucked in a large amount of smoke from his cigar. His eyes gave away his thoughts, and the look of bewilderment on his face was condemning.

"There is still hope, General. Your old friend Von Bloch gave his life for us to reach here, as did many others. I'm sure there will be an emergency War Council in Europe to discuss this latest attack."

The general looked him straight in the eye.

"Europe will only unite if they are all under threat. No one knows where this force is coming from and why they want the Austro–Hungarian Empire." He almost sat back in his chair, trying to reassure himself about his last comment.

The major stepped forward.

"Politics are not my game, but you're right about self-preservation. Many would not flinch should the British Empire fall. Empires have been built on war and domination. Colonial rule can not last forever. We will do our best to help Austria whilst we are here. I will make sure I put your case to the high council in Paris."

Both men took their drinks and looked out of the window. They then discussed the evacuation of the city, how wagons and carts would transport the civilians, and how steam trains would move soldiers.

He suggested they could travel with the Austrian Engineers to Vienna. Once they arrived, they could take a train to Munich and then to Paris.

The train would have cannons on it and even the newly purchased Gatling guns. The general said this weaponry would change modern warfare as they knew it.

They both sat chatting for a while. Corporal Heinz arrived and was escorted in. He was asked to help with some of the translation, although the major thought General Haas understood English very well.

The general started laying out his evacuation plans and explaining how he wanted the city cleared within the next week. Some civilians were staying behind. They wanted to fight for their land or houses. He had urged them not to undertake such a task as it could mean certain death, but their determination had been strong, and he understood that people would be patriotic. The major explained the rogue regiment and how they killed General Von Bloch, something that General Haas wanted to address. He wished he had a detachment to go after them and bring them to justice. Treason would be punishable by death.

His anger soon returned to the job at hand and the need to load up the trains and wagons over the following week. He was not sure how long the city had before it would come under attack. They could put up a small-scale show of strength, but if a large enough force arrived, they would soon seize on the weakness of the defenders.

After some frank discussions, the general recommended that the men get some rest. "Tomorrow, we will start the retreat."

Corporal Heinz looked a little down upon leaving the general's office. Hearing about the downfall of your country was never going to be easy for him—he loved his homeland. He was also concerned about the welfare of his family. They lived on the borders of Prussia, and he hoped that the evacuation would take them somewhere safe along with the other civilians leaving the conflict areas.

He wondered whether he could resist not travelling to his family town to find them if news came of it being under siege. He was aware it would be a court-martial offence but did not know how he would react. No one would be left at the front if every soldier abandoned the fight. He told himself it would come down to how the war was being fought and that the chances of total defeat would affect his decision.

Just before they went their separate ways, Major Richmond spoke to the corporal and assured him that Europe would rally against this force of evil. He tried to install some hope, but it was hard to be totally convincing. He had witnessed something out of this world. A new type of enemy not only wanted to beat you but also wanted to consume your soul.

They saluted each other and returned to their quarters. Major Richmond looked at his family pictures before blowing out the candle in his room.

Chapter 15

The sun was warm early in the morning, lifting people's spirits as they set about their duties.

The British and Austrian Engineers were allowed to rest longer that morning. Private Brown was concerned about not seeing Heidi again, but she asked permission to go to Vienna with the soldiers. She was also undertaking basic nurse training, as they needed more help with the sick and wounded.

The other civilians were moving out by wagon and cart. It had been hard on them as they had had only one day's rest in a proper bed. The train of thought was that it would be better to leave now at a slow pace and not risk being attacked or chased along the route.

The supplies were packed into several wagons, and there was plenty of space for everyone. They had a small escort to take them to their next destination. The general wondered whether his country would surrender rather than risk a total collapse of society. Speaking to Major Richmond and Corporal Heinz had painted a dark picture of their new foe. Not much was known about the long-term plans for the invading force.

Heidi waited outside the barracks for an hour to catch Private Brown on his way to wash. Normal military practice was being observed back in the city. John took a moment, though, to break off and take Heidi behind a supply shed,

"John, I've missed you badly. It's hard not having you lie next to me at night."

"Heidi, I feel the same. We've had some luck, and you can transfer to Vienna with us. How is the training going?"

Heidi smiled and explained that it hadn't really started yet. She looked forward to it and wanted to help people wherever possible.

Heidi had a very caring side, and John liked that. He didn't want to speak about what would happen after Vienna. His detachment was surely going to be posted back to England or France.

He hoped that Europe would rise up against this force, but he knew that, as his father once said about their town's local mayor and the red tape surrounding getting things done, "Things were never easy in politics."

John and Heidi spent five minutes kissing and holding each other. Sergeant Butcher arrived on the scene and reminded the private that he was still in the army and would have to let the nurse return to her unit. He said this with a sympathetic face, however. Even the sergeant was missing his family.

Corporal Smith arrived at the captain's quarters. He knocked on the door and brought in fresh coffee. Charles took a moment to have a sip of the warm drink and then grabbed his helmet and parade stick. He thanked the corporal for bringing him coffee and said he would see him outside.

Captain Hayward joined Major Richmond on the parade square. The soldiers had not lined up for a while. It wasn't about checking uniforms but was about informing them of their current evacuation plans.

The men looked fresher. The day of rest had done them the world of good, and the cooked meals had helped. The Austrians had supplied them with rifles and extra clothing. The soldiers were once more wearing their smart red tunics and blue trousers.

As they stayed lined up, the corporals and the sergeant issued a roll call. Then, they were split into small groups to gather supplies from the munitions store and replenish their backpacks.

Private Brown and Private Clegg were assigned to guard the wall. The Austrians had requested some relief for their own soldiers as they also needed to prepare to leave.

The parade did not last long, as time was of the essence. The men were called to attention. Charles saluted the Major and gave permission for the soldiers to stand at ease and then fall out.

Private Brown and Clegg went with the group to the wall. They were surprised to see only a handful of soldiers guarding it. The Austrians that stayed with them only had limited English. There were lots of hand signals going about and laughter as they tried to understand each other. Private Clegg showed the Austrians his interpretation of the flesh-eaters and long limbs. They tried to keep a straight face, but it was hard seeing a soldier doing a crab walk and then shuffling towards them with his mouth open. He was applauded for his efforts and given some homemade ale as a reward for his performance.

The wall gave them an excellent viewpoint over large swathes of grassland where cattle were still grazing. The soldiers guessed they could not take all the livestock with them, so letting them feed away as usual made sense.

Several towers along the defences gave an even higher advantage point to check over the surrounding countryside. John went with William to have a look.

The wall turned out to be more relaxing than they had initially thought. Corporal Smith liaised with the sergeant every hour, leaving them some time to stand down. They knew how quickly things could turn nasty, so they kept an eye out for the horde.

The rest of the group set about loading the trains in the northwest of the city. The armoured carriages were loaded with extra sandbags. They had five armoured carriages for each train, three carrying cannons and two carrying Gatling guns.

The soldiers were boosted by seeing the heavy weaponry on each train. The British Engineers knew what was out there and appreciated having as much firepower as possible to face potential threats.

The day passed by with General Haas overseeing many of the operations around the station. The country might slowly be consumed by an invading force, but efficiency remained firm. The civilians would be leaving the following morning. The convoy was in place and ready to roll out.

With the sun going down, the work parties returned to the barracks. A hot meal and a good night's rest were on most people's agenda. The next morning, the Austrian soldiers gathered to see off the remaining civilians.

No stone was left unturned. This was a thoroughly thought-out plan. By the early afternoon, the wagons rolled out with the last civilians. Heidi was with the nurses' unit now, and anyone else who was left was mainly either an Austrian military officer or a British Engineer. There was the odd civilian group who wanted to stay and fight.

Scouts had been sent out to check the outer perimeter of the city and any local farms for enemy movement. No sightings around the wall had been reported. The general was not taking any chances and believed this was only a ploy to lower their guard.

That evening, over supper, he announced that the wall night duty would be trebled. He knew this meant some long shifts for the soldiers, but it also meant they would have a more substantial chance of survival should the city come under assault.

The British Engineers had the first shift after supper. The whole unit was out there. Major Richmond wanted to show his Austrian counterparts that they were willing to help in any way, especially after their support.

The British force was not that strong, but it was rested and alert. Captain Hayward had around forty men to patrol one half of the city wall, with Major Richmond covering the other half with a similar force.

The soldiers were in their regular British military uniforms. The blue spiked helmets were now more respectable than before, and the buttons and buckles were polished. This had not been an order from the major; the soldiers had done it of their own accord.

A small contingent of mounted soldiers patrolled the city. General Hass focused on the walls facing the open farmland and beyond, but he was wise enough to be prepared for an assault from anywhere. The barracks and living quarters were near the station. Should they need to pull out quickly, this option was kept alive.

The general arrived in the afternoon and explained that the leaving date had been pushed back one more day. He gave the reason as logistics, but others pointed to the rumour of his cousin returning with a cavalry detachment. This could mean bringing in extra carriages for the trains to take the horses.

The general had not publicly suggested as much, but he had been a bit ambiguous about the delay.

By late afternoon, the Austrians had arrived to swap the shift. The British were glad to stand down. It hadn't been the most challenging shift, but it had been a vigilant one.

Captain Hayward spoke privately to Major Richmond about being in the city another night. They were respectful to their hosts but had due care for the soldiers under their command.

The British filed back to the barracks. Normality was starting to creep back into their lives. Routines were good for the soldiers. They wanted to be directed and kept busy. That said, none of them wanted to face the enemy in a hurry.

Major Richmond went to find General Hass. He wanted to emphasise that the enemy was a mobile force that could attack with lightning speed, leaving them open in this situation. He found the general by the old station, mounted, and looked at the trains waiting to leave the next day. All of them were full of supplies and heavily armoured. The sun was slowly disappearing behind the skies. Its last shadows shot out from around the station house and down onto the well-trodden soil.

"General, I would like a quick word, if I may."

The general looked around and dismounted. He nodded to a nearby soldier, who came over and took the reins.

"I have heard the rumours as well, Major. You think I'm mad for waiting another day. Believe me, this has not been an easy decision. I've got my cousin's interests at the back of my mind, but the truth is we needed this extra day. I've sent scouts along the track to the 'deep gorge'. This area of the train line could leave us vulnerable to an attack."

The major nodded. Rumours were always out there, and careless whispering cost lives.

"Sorry for questioning your decision, sir. It has been a mad few weeks, and the men are wary of most things now."

The general agreed and said they would board the trains at first light and after breakfast. The major returned to his quarters feeling a little more assured about their current situation. He needed to ensure the general was not losing direction on where they should be heading.

Settling into his bed, the major gazed at the ceiling. A candle burnt to the side of him on a well-furnished dressing table. He wondered if the Austrian family that had once lived in this house were refugees now moving towards Vienna. It was not a happy thought to sleep on, so he tried to think of warm bread and a hunk of cheese. Fresh coffee also came into his mind. Soon, he was asleep.

The morning light broke, and breakfast was served to everyone. The Austrians laid on a fabulous spread of meats and cheeses. The soldiers were told to fill their boots as the train was not due to stop until late afternoon.

Sergeant Butcher called out to the British Engineers to line up. They did so with full military aplomb.

"Right, you horrible lot; let's show the Austrians how to march to the station in style."

This was said in good jest, not wanting to offend the Austrian military and the great hospitality that had been bestowed on them. They started to march to the station. It was only a five-minute trek, so the men did not see it as a hardship. It was a good reminder of who they were and what they stood for.

As the soldiers got underway, a rider burst into the courtyard. He rode straight to an Austrian colonel. Colonel Kiesl was a tall, broad man with blonde hair. He was working his way up the military ladder and was hungry for success. His eyes almost lit up with what he was hearing.

He then turned and went to the general, who was watching the British march out of the courtyard. The outer city walls had only a small force as most were now returning to board the train. The early morning news had been quiet. This had all changed. The horizon was now a dust cloud for miles around; the flesh eaters were on their way. The small detachment on the wall did not have horses or wagons with which to escape. They were worried but standing firm. The cannons were loaded, and the rifles readied. Some of the Austrians rushed up the turrets.

The obvious problem was the lack of men. The wall could not be adequately defended. They were just too few.

In the courtyard, the order was given to double their speed boarding the train. The general had asked for volunteers to take horses to the wall to evacuate the soldiers there. Colonel Kiesl had put himself forward. He wanted to face the enemy head-on, and this was his chance.

Being a God-fearing man, he said a quick prayer before riding out with a group of mounted soldiers with extra horses.

The general ushered Captain Hayward and the major to the station. As they were arriving, cannon fire started to echo around the city. The soldiers gave each other knowing looks. The enemy was at the gates.

What they did not expect were shells starting to land within the city. They were under bombardment. The general was concerned by the long-range artillery. The Austrian army had no weaponry that could fire that distance.

As he pondered this, a shell exploded twenty metres away, destroying a house and sending debris shooting into the air. Many soldiers took cover, but the general stayed on his horse. He was covered in dust and pieces of grit and fine dirt. A small cut above his left eye emitted blood. It was not a deep cut, but deep enough that a small trickle of blood slowly crept down his left cheek and dropped onto his tunic. He refused help and wiped the blood away with a glove.

A corporal stood up and called for a military doctor to come and assist. They came over straight away. The general turned his horse and started barking out orders. The major admired his courage under fire and his determination to get the soldiers and medical staff on the trains.

The shells continued to land around the city. They had not accurately targeted the station, so this gave them time to load the carriages. Supplies and everything else were ready. Steam engines had their fires stoked, and water was topped up.

The British Engineers rapidly boarded one of the trains. The general was acutely aware that if the enemy could get in front of them, they would destroy the track, leaving them vulnerable.

Time was of the essence.

The dust had settled down in the distance, but a mass of movement of figures filtered across the plains before them as far as the eye could see.

The soldiers stood in awe at the sight unravelling in front of them. The cannon fire was not directed at the wall; the enemy fired over their heads and into the city. The shells had incredible power and destructive capabilities.

Houses were being blown to smithereens around them. The noise was ear-splitting, inflicting a sharp ringing sound in the ears of those close to the blasts.

The Austrian Sergeant on the wall was taken aback and watched this army unleash volley after volley. Their cannons could not even reach the enemy's first line as their range was that of a typical field cannon. The gunners were accurate enough but were no match for this type of power.

The cannons ceased firing.

The sergeant told his men on the wall to brace themselves. Then came loud thunderclaps, followed by shells smashing into the outer walls. The defences were taking a battering, with large chunks of rubble being flung up into the air. They were targeting specific areas along the main wall. This bombardment lasted several minutes. One part now looked decimated. This left some soldiers shaking their heads, but luckily, no one had been hurt. It was an unmanned section.

The following noise they heard was a collective mass of horns, which then fell into a roar. It was hard to make out. It was a mixture of creatures and shouts rolled into one.

A mass of figures came at them at a furious pace. The soldiers were told to hold their fire until the enemy came into range. This all unfolded as Colonel Kiesl arrived with more horses. He sent a soldier up to the walls to tell the men to leave with them immediately. The timing was awkward. The mass of creatures and humans was now in firing range. The cannons on the walls opened fire.

The mounted soldiers struggled to hold onto the extra horses as the volume around them intensified. They could also detect something else coming, making them very jumpy.

Colonel Kiesl did not want to wait around. He hopped down off his horse and made his way up some stone steps.

He witnessed the first Austrian volley rip into the approaching soldiers dressed in black. The effect on their tightly packed ranks was devastating; arms and limbs were torn from their bodies.

Charles's eyes fell upon what was coming with them: giant bears with two heads, lizard-type monsters and a mass of walking humans with rotten flesh.

He could see that men were leading them in long black robes. He deduced they looked like Priests, but what Priests, he thought, would control such an army of darkness?

The fight was in full flow as the cannons roared and the small detachment of men shot from the wall parapets. The soldiers lacked the firepower to stop the enemy from approaching the broken outer defences. They started to spill into the city with great purpose and vigour.

The drone soldiers arrived at the manned part of the city defence. Their faces were taut and gaunt. Their eyes carried rage, fuelling a frenzied desire to reach the soldiers holding the line. Colonel Kiesl launched himself straight into action as he noticed a ladder arrive next to where he was standing.

The first enemy soldier did not last long as he hurriedly ascended the ladder and tried to get on top of the wall. He placed his hand on a merlon and began to heave himself up. The colonel was quick to react and drew his sabre before unleashing a deadly blow upon the drone. The soldier's head rolled clean off and dropped down amongst his comrades. Bullets started to whizz through the air as the soldiers below opened fire on the Austrians.

"This is not the time to die here, men. Fall back to the horses."

Colonel Kiesl's voice was strong and clear. The noise around the wall was muffled, but most began to fall back. The flesh-eaters were streaming into the city via the broken battlements. Hand-to-hand fighting erupted everywhere as the Austrians started falling back down the steps. Those who were not able to retreat died fighting where they stood. They all understood that no prisoners were being taken.

The men formed a line and kept firing as the others tried to get the wounded onto the horses and away from the oncoming enemy. Gunpowder had been lit around the cannon ammunition, adding to the haste with which they needed to retreat.

As Colonel Kiesl mounted his horse, some of the Austrian soldiers were still firing from their saddles. The shock on their faces when a giant lizard creature with scaly thick skin appeared from around a house was compelling. They had not seen what was happening on the other side; this was their first sight of the new enemy. It lurched forward, bullets cutting into its skin but having little effect.

Two soldiers who were holding horses were directly in its line of sight. The creature tilted its head as it moved forward and bit into the leg of the nearest soldier. The man let out a scream as he was thrown into the air and then promptly slammed to the ground. The creature was interested in the horse for a moment, and the poor, injured soldier tried to move away from the beast with his leg practically hanging off.

The giant lizard was being hit with bullets and decided to grab the dying horse and leave for cover. The other men then ran forward to help their wounded comrade. It was of little use; he had passed out, and his blood loss was uncontrollable.

The priest's men were now flowing over the battlements and down the steps from the walls. To the side of a long road, the colonel could see a shifting army of flesh-eaters coming their way. On the other side were several two-headed bears bounding towards them.

It was time for composure under tremendous stress. Colonel Kiesl got as many men mounted as possible. Some just grabbed already mounted soldiers. Bullets were still whizzing through the air towards the Austrian men. A horse was stuck in the chest by a bullet. It fell to the ground, writhing in pain. A couple of soldiers were also struck as they came under heavy fire.

The creatures and the enemy were closing in.

"We must fall back to the train station." The colonel bellowed out this order.

The group began to fall back, some running alongside the horses. The men's shock and fear as they saw the flesh-eaters and two-headed bears were evident. They had heard the stories from the Austrian Engineers, but seeing was believing.

The colonel led the men down a narrow street. The main group was told to push on to the station. The priest soldiers and creatures were compressed into a small area, which opened the opportunity to fire volleys into their tightly compacted ranks.

There were around thirty Austrian soldiers. They dismounted and formed three rows.

"First rank, take aim…Fire!"

"Second rank, take aim…Fire!"

This continued through each rank, crushing the approaching force. They were not organised in their advance, and the creatures were hindering their progress. The bears were caught further back and crushing whatever was in their path to get to the front.

The dead bodies started to mount up, almost forming a wall. A couple of bears started to get through to the frontline but came under intense fire to the head. They fell amongst the other enemy dead.

This was the moment to retreat, and the colonel acted. Some horses had escaped, but all the men were helped to ride onto the station. Those who had not made it from the wall or were stuck in nearby buildings were either hunted down and shot by the drone soldiers or eaten.

The trains started to roll out of the station.

Two tracks ran parallel to each other. Both of them led to Vienna. Four trains started to pick up motion. The fourth train was going slower to allow time for the Austrians coming from the wall. The British Engineers were camped in the second train.

Shells began to rain down on the old station. Debris was flung up from the railway ticket office and shot over the fourth train as it pulled away. Some of the glass shattered in the end carriages, but most had sandbags to cover the windows and help lessen the impact.

Fires had broken out in the city as the shells brought mass destruction to the tightly packed houses, factories and shops.

The railway sheds were still full of food and other supplies that they could not bring with them. The general had not given the order to slash and burn as they retreated, and the information from the high command was minimal.

As Colonel Kiesl arrived at the station, he could see the fourth train pulling away. They had made it just in time.

While several soldiers rode on to meet the train, he kept a small number back to shoot from the saddle. Their covering fire would hopefully be enough to allow time for the others to get onto the moving train.

The shells were still falling around them, and thick plumes of smoke drifted across the tracks. The enemy was not yet upon the station. Colonel Kiesl waited to see them, but nothing came. The fourth train was starting to move out of sight.

He was satisfied the others had boarded the train and now wanted his remaining men to join them.

They galloped at full speed. The shells were still coming down around them, but luck was on their side, and no one was blown from their horse. Once close enough, they calmly took it in turns to board the train and let the horses gallop off. They had wanted to take as many with them as possible, but keeping all of the livestock on the train meant having more carriages, something that could not be spared.

The shelling suddenly stopped. This left smoke rising from the damaged buildings and fires burning across the city.

The steam engines puffed along as they picked up speed. An eerie sound filled the cobbled passages, and the roads carried another noise, something that reminded the men of distant thunder. The soldiers operating the Gatling guns and cannons could pick up on this noise wave, which was approaching fast.

General Haas was in one of the leading trains. He wanted the trains to move quicker as he feared they were still vulnerable to shelling. The noise made him turn his head as he made his way to the engine room. The sound was strong enough to carry into the carriages. It made the British Engineers come to the windows and try to peer out as best they could.

Their eyes fell upon a sea rolling in. It was thousands upon thousands of flesh-eaters. They were not running but moving at a quickened pace. Their collective groaning was what was making the noise. It was a humbling sight. The sheer numbers were hard to comprehend. General Haas was worried. He now thought of what lay ahead. They had not faced a vast force like this before. They were like African soldier ants consuming everything in their path.

He thought about how the British had come across the Jaeger regiment on the run and how they had turned on their own countrymen and General Von Bloch. Austria was in grave trouble. He wanted to reach the capital as quickly as possible.

The four trains began to pick up a good head of steam. The flesh-eaters were sweeping over the station and onto the railway tracks. They were coming from almost everywhere. The roads were covered with this horde. Fortunately, they could not keep up with the trains, which brought a sigh of relief from everyone. The tough veterans did not let this show in front of the others, but even they knew the battle for Austria was now on.

The corporals with the cannon crews and Gatling guns had been ordered to save ammunition and not fire on this walking army of death. They preferred to save what they had and use it when necessary.

As the trains left the inner city and moved through the industrial side, all became quiet. The occupying force had not yet reached that part. It all looked surreal as they passed empty factories and dormant warehouses. It was like a ghost town waiting to be filled. There were supplies left stacked up, but nothing could be done now to destroy them. They were the enemy's prize assets.

Captain Hayward walked amongst his men and reassured them they would shortly be returning to England.

A tunnel was soon approaching, which signalled the end of the city. The trains shot into the darkness at a brisk speed. There was a brief moment as candles were lit, that illuminated people's faces. It was haunting to see the same expression. Their minds wandered, thinking about what life had in store for them now. The British Engineers thought about home, but the more experienced thought about derailment in the tunnel. That thought stayed in the back of their minds and was not allowed to fester. With the sea of flesh-eaters staggering after them, it would mean a grisly death.

Smoke bounced in from the tunnel walls and filled the compartments. The windows were promptly shut. General Haas made his way to the officers' carriage. He had designated the middle carriage of the second train as his HQ. Once he arrived in the office, he swept a table clear of documents and grabbed a map of the train route to Vienna. He had studied it before, but his mind wanted to go over every possible scenario.

The light swept in as soon as each train burst out of the tunnel. Relief was evident on many faces. The four trains were in close proximity to each other. The men and women on them began to relax and let their guard down. For many, it was a good time to sleep or play cards. There were different shifts for the cannons and Gatling gun crews. The men operating them needed a rest and a change of scenery.

Captain Hayward pressed his head against the window, thinking of his wife and children. In these moments of calm, his family came to the forefront of his thoughts. He started to close his eyes and eventually fell into a gentle sleep.

Chapter 16

"My lord, the trains are carrying the last survivors from the city and the British soldiers from the fort."

The high priest rode forward.

"Everything is going to plan."

The Junior Priest who spoke lowered his head.

"My lord, I do not fully understand."

"That is why I am in charge, and you are listening to my orders. Bring me the commander of the drones."

The junior priest kept his head lowered as he backed away.

Five minutes later, the drone commander arrived. He was not as pale as his soldiers and had a slight nervous twitch. He was a chubby man with grey hair and rough stubble.

"Your Highness, I hear you want to speak with me."

The high priest turned and looked at him.

"The war is being won. I need you to have the riders of the North track and destroy this fleeing army. These British soldiers initially amused me, but now they are growing tiresome."

The drone commander nodded in agreement with everything that was being said. He was scared of the high priest. It wasn't helped by the fact that his ruler had leprosy.

It was in the early stages, but his skin was starting to be affected, and he was binding his fingers with cloth.

"I do not expect you to fail. If you do, then you know what will happen."

The man began to shake. He couldn't help himself. Rather than hanging around, he bowed his head and left as quickly as he'd come.

A small group of priests re-joined their commander. They sat on their horses, watching the drones and flesh-eaters destroy the city. The larger creatures had been reined in and were being led to any captured livestock for feeding.

Prisoners were being led away. These had been captured from the wall. They all looked concerned about what would happen to them. The flesh-eaters were being held back by drones and the occasional priest on horseback. The city had fallen into the enemy's hands. Tokay was no longer part of the Austro–Hungarian Empire.

The trains passed through villages and over hills. The engines were well stocked and did not need to stop for water or more fuel. The scenery was breathtaking, but most of the Austrian contingent paused to reflect on the ramifications of this hostile takeover.

Private Brown went outside to an armoured carriage. Cold air whistled past. The cannon crew had gone inside to eat, and a new watch was taking over. He wanted to see if the train next to him was okay because this was the train carrying the nurses. Heidi was in there looking after the injured or sick men. He thought about her and prayed she would be safe as they travelled to Vienna.

Fields passed in a flash as the train sped along. Along the way, there were herds of cattle and sheep wandering aimlessly, eating grass and looking carefree. This gave them hope that the horde had not reached them yet.

The trains continued into the night and early morning. Most soldiers and nurses slept the best they could. In some cases, the carriages had been converted and did not offer the same sort of comfort they would have wished for when travelling a long distance. These thoughts, though, were kept to themselves. The alternative was walking to Vienna, which was less appealing considering what was out there.

The general wanted to put a reasonable distance between themselves and Tokay. They decided to stop and rest the engines at the next town. It would be good to restock the water for the steam engines.

Captain Hayward spent an hour walking around the train talking to the men. The soldiers liked his personal touch. They found the major a bit more regal, whereas the captain had a softer military approach. The Engineers asked how they planned to get back to England. They did not want to forsake the Austrians with whom they had formed a strong kinship, but they also wanted to know the route home.

Charles said they would have a fair old journey ahead. It would involve more travelling by rail and possibly road. The men liked the fact that there was a plan in place.

A town was coming into sight. The crews with the cannons and Gatling guns looked for any sign it had already fallen. There were two main risks: an ambush in the town when they stopped or a railway track pulled up, causing a high-speed derailment. Both had their nightmare scenarios attached, but really, there was not much they could do but carry on and see.

The general did have one trick up his sleeve: He brought the trains to a halt a mile or so outside the town and then requested a small detachment of mounted cavalry to investigate.

The men mounted their horses and set off in earnest. They did not want to stop the trains for too long as it would take a while to get the steam up and running.

General Haas hopped off the train and went to speak to the major. He liked to be involved with strategy and planning. He firmly believed battles were lost through bad communications.

The other soldiers and nurses came out onto the armoured carriages for some fresh air. They all looked to the horizon for movement. The atmosphere was relaxed, but nonetheless, people were on guard. The Gatling crew slowly rolled the gun from side to side. This was a new weapon of warfare. The Austrian army had not tested it before.

The horses could be seen riding back at speed. It was hard to see from a distance if they were spooked or generally making good speed back. The general was alerted to their return as he spoke with the major. They both immediately left the train and walked towards the front of the steam engines.

The scouts arrived, looking relaxed and calm. The horses' nostrils flared from the galloping, and it took a moment for their riders to steady them.

The scout spoke to the general in German. His accent was quite thick, so the major did not pick up everything being said. He was instructed to fire up the engines and move the trains into the town.

The scouts stayed mounted and almost escorted them in. This allowed them to take a wider berth and give them views further afield.

The general turned to the major.

"We can let everyone take one hour to stretch their legs and get some fresh air. The train crews will replenish what we have used."

The engines were primed and stoked, and the steam pressure built up, and they were off. The town was empty, but there was no sign of fighting, raising hopes of a civilised retreat.

Once the engines pulled into the station, the different groups set about their tasks. Some were allowed just to stretch their legs, but most wanted to muck in and help out where possible. The town was beautiful as it was coming into bloom. Captain Hayward looked at the empty houses and streets. No children were playing, no hustle of carts or voices talking the day away. He paused to reflect on how a war had disrupted a community and country.

His mind promptly turned back to the duties at hand. He sent Sergeant Butcher to gather some cushions and anything that could make sleeping more bearable. The Sergeant gathered around ten men. He wanted to get this done in one fell swoop.

The hour passed, and it was time to set off again. The trains were fully loaded, and the sleeping quarters improved.

The bugle was sounded, which gave the order for people to return.

John managed to have a quick conversation with Heidi. Every time she was close, his heart jumped. Her soft lips, long blonde hair and piercing blue eyes made his legs feel wobbly. When she touched his skin, his heart would miss a beat. They both walked back to the trains.

"John. Please take care."

She smiled at him. Her English had a German twang to it, which he found endearing.

"We will get through this, Heidi."

A tear rolled down her cheek. He put his rifle over his shoulder and moved in closer. With the side of his hand, he brushed it away. She then leaned forward and kissed him. By then, they did not realise they had become the backdrop to hundreds of soldiers and nurses. The whistles went up, and they banged on the windows and sides of the train. It was all good-natured, and even the commanders took relief in a moment of natural human behaviour.

They looked at each other briefly and smiled before turning around and getting on their corresponding trains.

Once everyone was boarded, the trains started to roll out. The town slowly became a dot on the horizon as the railway line rose and fell through hills and valleys.

Lightning flashed in the distance, and thunder broke the silent backdrop. There was an old wives' tale about how far away the storm was by counting the time between a lightning flash and thunder. The younger soldiers tried this, beginning to count after the flash and before the thunder followed. Each number represented one mile from where the storm was. No one was sure how accurate it was, but it helped pass the time.

Captain Hayward sat in his quarters looking out of the window. He had blown out the candles and moved the sandbags blocking the glass. He knew this was not meant to be done due to the risk of attack, but he felt the need to look at the storm and think about other things.

A heavy rain shower swept in, pounding the carriages. It was hard on the soldiers outside handling the guns.

The general passed an order to get the men in whilst the storm raged, reasoning that if visibility were poor for them, it would be for the enemy. All the commanders on each train carried out this order as common sense prevailed.

The rain had a soothing effect on most. As it began to fall more gently, the sound became less intrusive and more calming, sending many to sleep.

The sergeant took a moment to observe the sleeping soldiers. He then took out a cigar and went out to an armoured carriage. He lit it and looked out at the darkness. There was an area which was covered from the rain, so he stood there to smoke. One Austrian soldier joined him and lit up a cigarette. He spoke German to the sergeant. The sergeant had learnt a little German but not enough to understand everything. He spoke back with some broken sentences. There was an awkward silence for a while, and then the Austrian reached into his trouser pocket. He pulled out a cigarette case and slowly opened it.

Inside was a picture of a woman and three children. The Austrian looked up and smiled. In broken English, he managed the word "family". The sergeant reached into his tunic pocket and pulled out a thin metal container. Inside was a photograph. He showed it to the soldier and said it was his wife and four children. The Austrian looked at the picture and counted the children in it.

He then laughed and raised his fingers to show four. He then spoke German and pointed to his three. He finished his cigarette and threw the stub down on the ground. He then shook the sergeant's hand and returned inside.

The sergeant did not want to finish the cigar, so he puffed on it one last time, letting the smoke sit in his mouth for a while before slowly releasing it. He then returned and found a suitable place to bed down for the evening.

The night journey would take them to Pressburg. They hoped this city would be well-defended as it was close to Vienna. The general planned to gather an army there and then report to Vienna before going to help defend the Austro–Hungarian Empire from her attackers.

Morning broke, and the train was flying along at a good pace. The train crew had swapped several times in the night due to the hard work involved in shovelling the coal into the furnace to keep the steam engines going.

They estimated they would arrive in Pressburg at lunchtime. Both sets of soldiers were very relaxed. Some were still sleeping; others played cards. Many of them had gone outside to wash amongst the cannons and Gatling guns. The officers had warned that they must be quick due to the nature of the situation and the fact that it would soon become full daylight. The captains had been asked to keep all the men and women on full alert.

For breakfast, there was porridge, which was very well received by the group. The cooks on the train worked very hard to please so many with little space to work in.

Pressburg started to creep into sight.

The thought of getting out of the carriages appealed to most. The journey was going fine—better than walking—but the lack of space was challenging. The soldiers cleaned their rifles and got themselves ready. Some of them expected to join land units that might be waiting in Pressburg.

The general pored over the maps. He was already working out a counter-strike option. His mindset was now on war.

The Austrian captains had come to his temporary HQ and left after he had debriefed them. The general continued to stand, posturing over a desk, holding a large cup of warm coffee in one hand and a magnifying glass in the other.

The silhouettes of the buildings were now in sight, with a tall church steeple proudly sticking out and industrial factories scattered across the outskirts of the town. The surrounding fields were starting to come to life with crops, and livestock was grazing freely. There were no visible signs of humans, but the farms still looked as though they had been well-kept until recently.

The passengers studied the buildings they passed for movement of any type. They were happy to see the animals feeding, birds flying around, and other general normalities. The only thing missing was the people.

The general did not concern himself with this. The civilians would have been evacuated long ago, and this would become a military region. He wanted to strike back as fast as he could.

The train continued towards Pressburg. They did not even send out scouts because they were confident about what was awaiting them. A busy, excited vibe spread through all four trains. Soldiers started to gather outside the armoured cars.

The nurses came out of the second train. They waved at them, which raised the excitement level. Some of the British Engineers were eyeing up the Austrian girls. Private John Brown made sure he pointed out his girl and warned everyone off. This, of course, brought a lot of teasing and bragging about how some of them would win her off him. It was all good-natured.

The train line passed into the central part of the city. As it inched further and further in, the expressions on faces changed. Piles of clothes were stacked along the train track.

Shoes and boots followed. Then their eyes fell upon another pile. Teddy bears were gathered in a large mound by a tree.

There was not a single soul around. The general had come out after noticing that the noise around the four trains had died down. He figured that something was wrong and wanted to find out what. He stood alongside his countrymen. His eyes fell upon the sight that stopped the train.

There were small mountains everywhere they looked. The whiteness glistened in the sunlight. The trains slowly came to a halt even though they were still a good mile away from the central station. The general got down from the train, followed by many of the soldiers. It was a moment without much thought; most of them were unarmed and vulnerable to an attack, but they were drawn to the sight in front of them.

Some of the nurses joined the soldiers as they walked over to the piles. Flies hovered around in their thousands. The closer they got, the more the air almost turned black as they shot up and buzzed around everyone.

One nurse realised what she was witnessing and started to cry. These mounds of white were bones. The flesh had been stripped off them entirely, and all that was left were parts of the skeletons. Skulls, spines, legs and arms filled the piles. No one knew how many had perished to make them, but some guessed it to be in the thousands.

The cold, hard facts were dawning on them. There were no people in the city; they had already been eaten.

More soldiers were starting to arrive, and more tears were flowing. The atmosphere was one of anger and shock. Many had not seen too much of the enemy that was invading their country.

They had only heard from the others that these things were sent from the Devil himself and only wanted to feed on human flesh. Others pointed out that they had also seen soldiers dressed in black, looking almost human but much greyer and more lifeless.

The major joined the general. They both agreed it was not the time or place to bury the bones as it could take weeks to do so. He instructed the captains and sergeants to get the men and women back on the trains. They wondered why the track had not been destroyed. The one theory that sprung to mind was that the enemy had been using it themselves to speed up the invasion. It was the most logical one; otherwise, they would have been stopped by now.

The trains took a short while to get going, but it did not take long for them to arrive at Pressburg station. Scouts were sent from the bones to scour the city on horseback. There could be no room for error. An ambush was the last thing the general wanted.

He returned to his quarters looking broken. His idea of raising an army in Pressburg and setting off after the enemy was now fading fast. He did not know what to think and wanted to press on to Vienna. They had to stop and refuel with coal and water. There would also hopefully be time to eat and stretch their legs. No one wanted to hang around, but there was little choice.

The scouts returned and reported that they had seen nothing untoward in the city.

Captain Hayward spoke to the major. He wanted to know his thoughts on whether they should travel to Vienna.

"The situation has taken a turn for the worse, my old friend."

Both of them stood there looking at the empty streets.

"Should we disembark here and make our way on foot into Prussia?"

The major turned and looked at him.

"I've let that thought cross my mind. The problem I have is that we are around one hundred men strong. With the Austrians, we are a regiment of nearly a thousand men. We need to know more about what is out there. Vienna could hold the key."

Captain Hayward nodded. He agreed with his Commander, but his thoughts lay with escaping Austria.

While the trains were attended to, the passengers took the time to stretch their legs. Guards were stationed around them in a five-kilometre perimeter. The Bugler would sound the call to arms if there were any signs of movement. Several units of mounted soldiers patrolled further out into the city.

The general took a while to come out from his quarters. He looked visibly shaken by what he had seen and what it entailed for them. He got down from the train and was lost in his own thoughts.

His officers were busy gathering information from each other and discussing ideas. Their confidence was still high. Colonel Kiesl approached the general and looked more in tune with the situation. He had faced this enemy and was fully aware of what they could do en masse. The towel was not thrown in yet, though, and he would fight to the death for his beloved country.

Colonel Kiesl took a moment to discuss their route with the young officers around him. Some were in their early twenties and were wet behind their ears, but most wanted to meet the enemy as soon as possible. Images of glory flashed through their minds – it would be their chance to boast about heroics on the battlefield and even tell tales to their families. The older officers calmed them down and explained that warfare was never straightforward. The new breed of foe was something else. They only knew what they had experienced. The British Engineers had advised about headshots on the flesh-eaters and other unworldly things.

The drone soldiers were new to everyone. An army of human-looking people, but with a slight edge, they all looked sick. Not in the same way as the flesh-eaters, but nonetheless, still different to a normal healthy human.

The priests had been seen, but little more than that was known about them.

Captain Hayward and Major Richmond joined them at the table.

The British Engineers did not know the topography as well as their hosts. They studied the maps with keen eyes. They were closing in on Vienna. General Haas composed himself and began to point out the route the train would take. They would shortly be entering a large farming area mixed in with grassland plains.

He felt confident that the Austro–Hungarian army was waiting there to gather as many forces as possible before counter-striking. His bravado was returning. His voice grew stronger and more confident. His eyes rolled at the thought of fighting the enemy with a decent army. He spoke in German to the gathered officers and then in English to the British officers.

"Gentlemen, we shall travel for several more hours before reaching Vienna. Then, our British counterparts can start on their long trek home. This war is in its early stages; we will turn it on its head and destroy those who challenge us."

The officers clapped at his rousing words.

The discussions lasted about half an hour. The young and old officers were at loggerheads over which approach would be best to tackle the enemy.

They knew that they were great in number; some even suggested they were Russians. One young officer said they were probably just sick patients from the prison camps whom they painted red and sent into battle. Colonel Kiesl was there smoking a cigar and leaned in on the conversation.

"There is worse than ill patients from the prison camps. Have you not seen the bones, gentlemen? They are not here to conquer; this is total domination. There are other things, half-people, half-creatures with long, stretched limbs. They have a common desire: to feed on flesh."

Some of the young men looked in horror, while others rolled their eyes as if to confirm it was mere stories to bring their youthful exuberance into line. Kiesl was not in the mood to discuss what was out there. He had seen it with a small group of soldiers. He knew the British had been experiencing it for well over a month. Colonel Kiesl strongly believed the young officers would also get their chance to meet it very soon.

They had stayed longer than an hour. The call went up for everyone to return to the trains. The scouts loaded their horses back onto the railway wagons. The steam was built up as the coal fires were stoked. Then, slowly, the four trains started to move. The drivers were congratulated on their fine work getting the soldiers to Pressburg. It was predicted they would reach Vienna by nightfall.

Pressburg crept out of sight the same way it had come in. Some of the soldiers watched it disappear into the distance. Their thoughts remained around the bones and the driving force behind such destruction.

The trains were travelling at full speed, and their passengers relaxed and reflected amongst themselves. Vienna was now only hours away.

Corporal Heinz passed Captain Hayward. The captain tapped him on the shoulder. He had not spoken to the corporal for a while. With the increased numbers on the four trains, faces blended into the crowd.

They spoke about the situation and the corporal's growing fear for his family and country. Then, a bugle call rang out, breaking their conversation. The calmness in all the trains was shattered, worried eyes searching for comfort in others. Both men took a second and nodded in expectation of what was there. They then joined the rush to gather rifles and ammunition.

Bags were hastily arranged in front of the windows. Firing holes were made on both sides. Major Richmond met Charles as they went outside to one of the armoured cars. At first, neither man could see what the call to arms had been for. Charles took out his binoculars.

He surveyed the hills and surrounding grasslands. Then dust clouds came into sight. Out of the dust appeared horses with riders. These were no ordinary horses; they were twice the size of a shire horse, and their riders looked twice as big as ordinary humans.

They were massing on one side. The horses were quick, as fast as the trains when galloping. General Haas studied their movement and worried about whether they had destroyed train tracks further ahead. Either way, he had to give an order: try to increase speed or slow down in case of derailment. He chose to slow down the trains. They were close enough to the other trains for notes to be thrown across by rope. Soon, all the trains were going at a steady speed and not at full pelt.

Then, the attack started. The riders came in from the right, attacking the two trains on the outer tracks. Whilst they approached at speed, a large group of riders attacked from the rear. The cannons were loaded, and the Gatling guns steadied. The British and Austrians got ready with their rifles.

The major was the highest-ranking officer on that side. The men looked for his order to fire. The enemy slowly came into range. They had war paint smeared across their faces. Several priests could be seen riding amongst them.

"Fire!"

The noise wave that rolled around the trains was intense. The cannons recoiled as they let off their first volley. The shells landed with deadly accuracy, blowing men and horses to smithereens. The Gatling guns started to open up – this was the first time the British had seen them in full operation. The rattling humming sound was mesmerising, and the effect was overwhelming for the enemy. Scores of men and horses fell like dominos. They may have been twice the size of normal humans, but the deadly effect of the machine guns was laid bare for all to see.

It cut through them like a warm knife through butter. They did not need headshots to kill them, although they took many hits before falling. The soldiers opened fire with their rifles, killing even more of these giants.

The wave of riders was being hit hard, and it began to fall back. They had not even fired one shot. The Gatling guns needed to be reloaded. One had overheated during the battle and was left to cool down. The young officers around them appreciated the new weapons. It only took one soldier to turn the crank and fire, but they still had a team to help reload and were prepared in case he was killed and someone else needed to take his place.

General Haas was receiving messages from the other trains. The armoured cars at the back of the trains had also seen off the rear attack. The general opened his map. He realised they would soon be able to see Vienna, although it was still a good distance away. The track veered towards a passage through a small hill.

He instantly grabbed some paper and began to write a note. The soldiers were reloading. They were not excited about the casualties they had inflicted on the enemy.

The general rushed out of his quarters and towards an open area of the train. He then threw his note across on a weighted rope as the train entered the passageway between the hills. The general had foreseen what the riders might do.

The note landed on the opposite carriage at the same time as bombs were being thrown from above. Explosions started to shake the ground around them. Glass shattered as the devices landed near the tracks. A bomb fell and landed on one of the back armoured cars, destroying the Gatling gun and killing three men.

The bombs kept falling, but fortunately, nothing landed directly on the steam engines or within the packed carriages. The hillside passageway was ending, but now fires had broken out around the trains.

Captain Hayward rushed around, helping the men put out the fires and prepare for another attack. The casualties were few, but those injured needed medical attention, which the orderlies set about providing. An army doctor was on each train, which helped the situation.

The trains burst into the open land, sending steam and smoke shooting behind them as they sped along. The trail left the rear carriages almost in a cloud.

Orders were thrown across from General Haas's train to tell everyone to prepare for another attack. He expected them to come from both sides.

The ground had levelled out now. On either side of the railway line was a small woodland consisting of silver birch trees, which had been coppiced back.

Captain Hayward checked on the soldiers. The British Engineers had no significant injuries to report. Some men had been wounded by flying debris, but nothing serious. There was constant movement, and weapons were reloaded and readied for action.

A bullet smashed through a window and into a soldier's neck next to the captain. The man fell back due to the impact and held his neck, blood pouring out of the wound. Charles grabbed some cloth that was near to him and tried to stem the flow of blood. The man tried to speak, but his throat was too severely damaged. The call went out for the orderly and doctor. One arrived within seconds and started to help.

Bullets smacked into the carriages from the surrounding woodlands. The riders appeared again at speed. The general was right about them attacking from both sides.

All four trains went under attack at the same time. The Gatling guns opened fire, and the cannons began to unleash pandemonium amongst the riders' ranks.

The sandbags stood up well to the intense fire and prevented the bullets from penetrating the crowded spaces. The soldier who had been hit in the neck died whilst the doctor worked on him. Charles shook his head and closed the man's eyes. He grabbed his rifle and moved to the middle armoured car to assist the Austrians.

More riders came from the rear. They used the smoke as a screen to get close to the back of the trains. One rear train was on fire, where the bomb had destroyed the armoured car and Gatling gun. The smoke from that was blowing across and causing visibility problems for the other rear Gatling gun.

They opened fire when they saw the riders coming out of the smoke. This instantly had a huge impact, sending giant men and horses crashing to the ground. While concentrating hard on the riders, they failed to notice two riders boarding from the side.

These men were carrying new weapons of war. One of them opened fire with a hand mortar rifle. The grenade fell between the Gatling gun and its crew. They did not see it until it was too late. The explosion killed them and several others in the blast. It also destroyed the last rear remaining Gatling gun, which now left the back of the train exposed.

The two riders started to smash their way into the back carriage next to the smouldering armoured end car. These giant men were a good match for a small army, let alone the soldiers who were now facing them.

While the soldiers were firing out of the windows, the two Northern riders started to attack them. They were armed with revolvers and swords. An Austrian soldier noticed something out of the corner of his eye and turned to see what it was. As he did so, he felt a sharp pain in his stomach. He then fell to the floor.

This alerted the other men in the carriage as they tried to fight the riders back. One soldier shot at the two intruders, missing by inches. They came forward, cutting and firing as they went. The Austrians were being cut to pieces; arms were being hacked off, and deep lacerations sliced across their torsos as these man-mountains moved forward.

A young soldier held his ground. He was out of ammunition but fought hard with his bayonet attached to his rifle. Colonel Kiesl arrived to witness the carnage that was unfolding. To make matters worse, fresh riders were appearing outside. Two were proving hard to kill. What would ten or more be like?

Colonel Kiesl was more experienced than the soldiers in there but was taken aback by the sheer size of these foes and the power they wielded. But he was a soldier, and his job was to fight anything that got in his way.

The young soldier was trying his best to hold them back. He was jabbing and using his rifle butt to lash out when he could. Luck was on his side as he rammed his bayonet into the leg of one of the attackers. The giant let out a roar, and his fellow attacker brought his sword down on the rifle, cutting it in two. He then raised it again, but a gunshot filled the room. The bullet looked as if it had missed its target, and the young soldier braced himself for the strike. The giant then looked down at his chest and fell to his knees.

Colonel Kiesl did not waste any more time and slammed his sword into the neck of the wounded man. He then began to fight with the other rider, who still had half the rifle sticking out of his leg.

He was a big old brute with long dark hair and a scraggy beard. His eyes were bloodshot red, and his mouth revealed dark yellow teeth. A pungent odour filled the room as he moved about. He was not like a flesh eater or a long limb, but something was not right about his demeanour.

Colonel Kiesl was thrown into a pile of sandbags. He gingerly got up and saw five soldiers arriving on the scene. They had already aimed at the giant, who turned and grimaced, baring his teeth at them before a volley of bullets ripped into his chest and head. He then collapsed in a heap onto the floor.

Heavy steps could be heard coming along the roof. They were now boarding the back of the train and moving along the carriages. Windows were being broken as they fought to gain access. Charles knelt by the side of one of the dead men. He picked up his hand-mortar rifle. He had heard of this type of weapon before, but not this version. He did not have much time to study it more.

Outside, the battle was raging. Despite their losses, the riders continued attacking. They had already boarded one of the back trains and were now trying their chances on the other rear one.

Communication was proving a problem, as always in battle. The two front trains were being kept occupied by riders attacking them. Soldiers were shooting at the riders the best they could inside the carriages. The orderlies were bringing fresh cartridges. They also assisted any wounded soldiers they came across. The reserve ammunition was being spread out throughout the train to minimise the risk of explosions.

The smell of gun- and cannon fire filled each compartment. The nurses were kept busy helping out where they could. Some had taken up rifles and were firing out of the windows.

Both rear trains had Northern riders on them now. Captain Hayward took five British Engineers and climbed on the roof of their train—bullets whizzed by as the riders shot from their horses at them. The captain took out his rifle and opened fire back. He was using an Austrian Kropatschek rifle. It had a different feel to the more familiar Martini-Henry rifle. He knew they all had to adapt since losing most of these rifles in the raid by the Alpine Jaegers.

One of his five men was hit in the leg, which made him stumble and roll off the train. Unfortunately, they could do nothing for him as he hit the ground hard. The riders showed no mercy and speared the fallen soldier as they rode behind the train. Charles shouted at his men to keep low. He aimed and breathed in, slowly squeezing the trigger.

Boom.

The shot was accurate, and it crashed into a rider coming forward on the rear train's roof. It was a neck wound, causing the man to fall to his knees. The other riders did not wait to check on the man. They kept on coming forward and pushed him aside. He fell in between the rear trains.

Hand-to-hand fighting was raging throughout the end carriages. Corporal Heinz was with the remaining Austrian Engineers. They were stationed with the British and doing very well with their kill ratio. Fortunately, there were many hunters amongst both groups.

Flames licked up from various parts of the train, with smoke bellowing out from broken windows and cracks in the roof. It was making it difficult to put up a decent defence. On the rear left-hand- train, one armoured carriage crew had been wiped out. The riders were trying to turn the cannon on the other compartments. Luckily, this was proving difficult for them. A Gatling gun was left abandoned due to a lack of ammunition. Engineers were still piling bags on the sides of an open carriage and using it as a firing post. Both forward trains' roofs had soldiers on them, trying to help their fellow countrymen.

Colonel Kiesl was organising a retreating party from his train. He realised the best option was to get to the forward trains. The general was considering the same thing. It might be time to destroy the two rear steam engines.

The decision to have the horses in the forward carriages was now proving to be a masterstroke.

The Northern riders were causing panic as they pushed forward. Their sheer size and brute force were hard to contain. Soldiers had been ordered to help get nurses off the rear left-hand-side train. Their steam engines were now touching the armoured carriages in front of them, allowing them to move from a rear train to a forward train.

All this was happening whilst under heavy fire. John was watching from a distance, concerned that Heidi was on the wrong side. The sergeant reassured him she would be fine and told him to concentrate on shooting at the enemy.

John waited until Sergeant Butcher had gone down the carriages to check on the other men. His close friend William was kneeling down and reloading while pressed against several sandbags.

"John, go now and get on the other train and find her," William said while reloading.

"What about my post? The sergeant will surely see that I'm missing." John was unsure about leaving his position.

"You'll be okay; I'll cover for you. Go get her and bring her back. Then come back here." He looked at William. Actions like that could mean a court-martial, and in extreme cases, that could mean a death sentence by firing squad.

William made it sound like the only possible option. John was a young soldier, and his heart ruled his head. He loaded his rifle, put it across his back and made his way to an open carriage. The wind was blustery as the trains moved at speed. Bullets whizzed through the air, and suddenly, the idea became more dangerous. There was a ladder leading to the roof. Letting himself think only of Heidi, he climbed up slowly. Keeping low, he moved along the train. Captain Hayward and several soldiers could be seen in the distance. They were involved in a furious fire-fight.

A smokescreen was made from various compartments that had been hit in battle and were now quietly smouldering away. The smoke travelled away from the train as it shot forward, intermittently covering John. He used it to his advantage and lay there for a short while, plucking up the courage to jump from his train to the next.

The smoke faded momentarily, and John looked up at a deep blue sky. It was very appealing. The clouds were scarce, and it was a calming sight amid the action. He raised himself to his feet and then took a leap of faith.

He landed just short but grabbed onto a rail and pulled himself up.

An Austrian soldier was coming up a ladder to investigate the sudden thud on the roof when he saw it was a British Engineer. He wiped his forehead in a sign of relief, and John smiled. The Austrian then disappeared back below, and John carried on his way.

The nurses were no longer being transported from the rear steam engine. John had to climb down and wade through a packed end carriage. His eyes scanned for Heidi, but he could not see her anywhere. A friend of hers came into view, and he promptly made a beeline in that direction.

The girl's name was not known to him, but she seemed to notice his red tunic and blue spiked helmet making its way through the other uniforms. A bullet ripped into the crowded carriage, and Private John Brown fell backwards. He looked down to see blood covering his hands. He waited for the pain to kick in, but nothing happened. A doctor and nurse came across and assisted him on the floor.

The bullet had hit an Austrian soldier who had been in front of him, causing the man to stumble back onto John and splattering him with blood. He offered to help the wounded soldier, but the doctor said they could manage.

Heidi's friend came over to John and explained she thought Heidi was with a group stranded in the middle carriages, as the riders had taken either side. A young officer saw Private Brown making his way to the rear armoured car and followed him out onto it. The Gatling gun crew was busy trying to find spare ammunition and preparing grenades.

The odd soldier was still coming across, and the steam engine crew looked anxious as more soldiers left their train. John did not look back as he stepped across from one side to the other. The steam crew talked to him in German, pointing to the rear and shaking their heads.

Soldiers were guarding them, but they were all getting jumpy.

John nodded that he understood. He knew it would be dangerous to return there, but he had made up his mind. He would now rather die than not attempt to find Heidi, even if she had been killed. He had to know.

The guards helped him onto the roof of the steam engine. He did not wait around. He moved from carriage to carriage. Gunshots were ringing out below, but he carried on, making his way to the middle. The fire was spreading from the back of the train.

A hand grabbed his leg. His instinct was to lash out with his rifle, but that was over his shoulder. He bent down to remove the hand and saw it was an Austrian. It was the young officer from the other train.

His English was quite good, and he apologised for startling him. He explained that his cousin had not returned, and he wanted to know whether he was dead or alive.

The men lay on the roof next to each other. There was no real plan. It was more of a case of going down a set of ladders and trying to help those trapped inside.

The door leading into the compartment had been destroyed. Once down the ladders, they lowered their rifles and fixed bayonets.

"Good luck, Englishman."

"The same to you, my Austrian friend."

John led the way as he moved inside. It was hard to see, and the air was stale. Bodies were strewn over seats and scattered across the floor.

John pointed to his eyes and then to the considerable figure crouching down in front of them. This rider was the biggest they had seen. He reeked. It was a soiled smell of a man who had not washed in a long time. His clothes were a mixture of animal skins sewn together. He had an axe strapped across his back and a large knife. He was also carrying a rifle and revolver.

Both men stood still. To their horror, four more riders came into view further down the carriage. Size was starting to matter.

The young officer smiled and pulled out a grenade. He suggested they take cover behind some spare sandbags. They could hear gunshots and deduced that the survivors were holed up in the middle compartment. The young officer lit the fuse and threw it past the large rider and nearer to the four other attackers further down in the carriage. The explosion was powerful in a confined space and killed the four riders instantly.

John's ears were ringing when he picked himself up. The young officer was a little groggy as well. The large rider was lying face down, making murmuring sounds. The Austrian picked up his rifle and slammed the bayonet into the man's head. The body flinched as he did so. He then drew it out and repeated the action. Blood now flowed from the wound.

John thought it was brutal, but if the giant rider were not killed, he would pose a considerable risk to their lives. With no time to waste, they moved towards the middle compartments. They could see it had been barricaded up as they went further down the corridors. This was the only reason the riders had not broken through yet.

John and the young officer did not want to get shot by their own side. The Austrian called out in German that they were there to help. Silence followed, and then a German voice asked them to step forward. Both men prayed that this was their own soldier; otherwise, they would be vulnerable to being shot without knowing a thing about it.

As the door started to be smashed open, neither of them raised their weapons, as such an action could bring danger to this situation. The atmosphere relaxed when the first Austrian soldier came through. Several nurses followed him, Heidi not one of them. John's heart sank. The soldier spoke with the young officer as John entered where they had been holding up. In the far end, he could see Austrians firing through another barricade. The giant riders were attacking that side in earnest.

John wanted to know what had happened to her. Time was against them, but he went into a small room to the side of the compartment that was being used as a safe point for the nurses. He looked around for anything that could have belonged to Heidi. Then, as he came out, he heard his voice being called. Heidi had been further down helping a wounded man. She came forward, wrapped herself around him, and gave him a massive kiss on the lips.

John looked at her and smiled.

"I'm very proud of you, Heidi."

She smiled and stroked his cheek.

"You have saved us. I don't have words for your bravery."

John pointed out that he was not alone. The young officer bowed his head and moved past them to inform the others that the retreat was now on. John helped to gather the wounded and move them towards the train next to them. The nurses helped carry the men and waited whilst soldiers were fetched to help carry them across.

John made sure Heidi got to the adjacent train. She looked at him with doting eyes.

"John, stay safe."

He ushered her to join the others and then returned to the young officer fighting to hold back the riders.

"Did you find your cousin?"

He nodded.

"Thank you. We need to move; they're going to come through the roof."

John could hear clumping and banging from above. He gathered some ammunition from the floor and took up a firing position. The remaining Austrian soldiers began to leave the barricade and make their way back slowly. Some looked at the front, while others scoured the ceiling.

Swords and axes started to rip through the piled-up wood and sandbags. The grunts and shouts were enough to put every man on tenterhooks. The ceiling began to split and come apart as they tried to break through. Small splinters and sections of lacquered roof fell on top of the retreating men.

They did not waste any bullets as they pulled back. The idea was that it was better for the riders to break through the roof rather than follow the retreating men to the end of the train.

The young officer lit a fire in one of the supply rooms. It did not take long to flare up. Bullets were still ripping through the windows and into the panelling around them. The steam engine crews had already left the rear trains and were now running unmanned. The soldiers had attached thick chains to the back of the armoured cars and connected them to the steam engines behind them. This was a short fix to allow the others to cross should the engines start to slow down.

The fire was spreading well. They left explosives in a couple of compartments. It would only be a matter of time before the fire hit the dynamite and blew that part of the train to pieces.

The opposite train was being evacuated at the same time. The riders were advancing in both rear trains. They had not managed to get a grip on the forward ones and were relying on jumping across to the other two.

Captain Hayward was crouching with his men and taking potshots at the giant riders as they came forward. The heat and flames were delaying their advance in some way, but so was the accuracy of the British Engineers. The headshots were taking their toll. With the wolves, flesh-eaters and other ghoulish creatures they had faced recently, it had helped to focus their shooting.

Captain Hayward was the last man down from the opposing train roof. That train was burning sporadically throughout. He ordered his men to leave and join the other train. He got down and steadied himself. The ground was becoming less flat now, affecting the Northern riders' battle plan. They could no longer ride by the side of the trains.

As he turned to leave the armoured car and catch up with the others, a grunting sound could be heard behind him. He reached for his revolver and turned around rapidly. A rider was standing in front of him with a hand-mortar rifle. He looked at the captain and smiled, showing some enormous teeth that were as yellow as the sand of Arabia. The gun was pointing at him. Charles did not know how long he had before the rider would pull the trigger. He lowered his revolver to buy thinking time, which made the giant laugh.

Something whistled past his right ear and made a cracking "thud" as it hit its target. The rider had blood spouting from his forehead.

He then fell forward and crashed onto the floor.

Charles wasted no time leaving the train. He did not see who had fired the shot but reckoned it had come from the other side.

Northern riders were now firing at them from both rear steam engines. The large chains had been released on both sides. The Austrians and British were cramped in both forward trains. The armoured cars at the back had their Gatling guns directed at the steam engines behind them.

Rather than wasting bullets, the soldiers were left to maintain a level of covering fire. The decision was to hold them off for as long as it took for the two rear trains to be separated.

The general stayed with the men. He had his helmet on and revolver drawn. He wanted to get at the enemy but knew their size and power well. Grenades were being thrown over, but it was hard to get them to land on the trains behind as they kept on rolling off. The British were mixed in with the other Austrians on the left-hand forward train. The Northern riders could no longer keep up; their animals had tired as the terrain became uneven.

The riders burst to get on both end carriages, but the Austrians and British had established a good line of defence. Sandbags were stacked high, and the men waited for the enemy's surge. When it came, the volley fire was fantastic. It was a small victory for the defenders. The riders were being struck left, right, and centre.

Those who remained on the rear trains had to try to disable the two forward ones if their reinforcements were to have any chance of helping them out.

The Riders of the North attack was strong, but they could not withstand the sustained casualties and slowly began to fall back. Even their large size was not enough to overpower their enemy in this instance.

The gaps between the trains were now widening. It would not be possible to jump between the two now. There was a sigh of relief as the rear trains slowly disappeared from sight.

The loss of the rear trains was significant to space but not to food supplies. They still had the horses and plenty of ammunition. The general remarked to his officers that he believed the Austro–Hungarian armies would be massing around the capital city.

The wounded were treated and helped to water. It was a good time to have a breather.

Major Richmond found Captain Hayward and shook his hand.

"I'm glad that out of all the officers I had with me, you were one of them."

Charles smiled and thanked him.

They then joined other British Engineers on the roof of a carriage. The air was now clear and fresh. No bullets whizzed by, just calmness around them. They took the time to survey the hills and forests for movement. The land could not possibly sustain a horse attack. Even if the horses were extra fast, they needed flat ground to maintain their top speed.

They used their binoculars to follow the smoke from the two rear trains. A screeching, twisted metal sound followed. The noise of the steam engines and carriages blowing up behind them was powerful. It sent tremors along the railway tracks. The soldiers and nurses on the armoured carriages stood and watched the smoke rise in the distance. They were glad to see the riders had broken off their attack. Many had not seen action before; this was their first baptism of fire. A silence fell across the compartments. Records of the dead were taken. The casualties had not been too high, but this was war, and bullets were claiming their victims.

The wounded were moved to the infirmary compartments. They had doctors and nurses waiting to care for them.

Notes were thrown across from General Haas's train to Major Richmond's, reporting on injuries and casualties. Likewise, news was carried out from the major's side. It was essential to see what supplies were left and what the state of the morale was. Two of the machine guns were now jammed, and frantic work was being carried out to repair them.

In his last note, the general wrote that Vienna would soon be in sight. He fully expected to be greeted by a checkpoint along the railway line, so he ordered the trains to ease off a little. They continued to update each other for a while.

The trains climbed a short hill and made their way up a narrow pass. Von Bloch had said that once over this hill, they would "feast their eyes on beautiful Vienna." Vienna would be used as a staging point to turn the tide of this war.

What their eyes fell upon, however, was destruction on a grand scale. The city was a good twenty to thirty miles away, but fires were burning brightly. The houses and farms in the surrounding area were also burning. The tide of war had changed, as the general said, but it had turned against them.

The general's legs gave way, and he would have collapsed had it not been for Colonel Kiesl. The horror on everyone's faces summed up the Austro–Hungarian plight. This all-consuming enemy was now overrunning their capital.

The trains slowly came to a grinding halt. Scouts were sent from the front and rear to check the surrounding woods. Some Austrians started to climb down from the carriages, almost falling to the side of the tracks.

Soldiers lay down their rifles on the ground and sat on the grass next to the tracks or even on the railway lines. The air was one of abandonment. All hope had drained out of them.

The British Engineers tried to appease their Austrian counterparts. They pointed out, in the little German they knew, that their armies may be massing elsewhere.

The truth was summed up by the look in Captain Hayward's eyes as he left his compartment. He walked down the steps from an armoured carriage and made his way over to the general's train. There, sitting nearby, was the general. He had found himself an old fallen tree and was using it as his bench. Charles was unsure of his age – he initially thought around the early fifties – but as the afternoon sun fell upon his face, he looked older. The life had drained out of his skin; he no longer had character in his expression.

His shirt was untucked, and his hair ruffled as if he had repeatedly reviewed a plan by rubbing his head.

He went and sat next to the general. They did not say anything at first; they just sat there thinking.

"My country is finished." the General sighed.

Captain Charles Hayward looked him in the eye.

"General, I do fear the worst for your country. This force is larger than we could have ever imagined. The fighting that has taken place here was not the same army that attacked us."

"I planned to raise an army and return to destroy this evil. They have no right to be here. If this is judgement day, I want to go down fighting."

He buried his face in his hands.

"You should come with us to England, or at least Prussia or France."

The general shrugged his shoulders. His look was blank and unresponsive.

"Charles, can you come here, please?" Major Richmond called out.

He stood on top of one of the steam engines, his binoculars out, and looked into the distance.

Charles arrived at the engine and proceeded to climb up carefully.

"Is everything all right, Harry?"

"Not really, old boy. The smoke in the distance has died down a little, but what concerns me is the dust cloud movement. It reminds me of when we were near Unghvar."

Charles took out his binoculars. His eyes hurriedly surveyed the landscape for movement. When they fell on the cloud, his heart dropped.

"My God, I do believe they're coming."

Chapter 17

"Your Highness, Vienna has nearly fallen."

A tall, dark-haired man came forward on his horse. He had a scar across his throat.

"I am happy with our progress so far," gloated Nazar.

He scratched his beard and licked his lips.

"I want all their souls, all of them."

Half his face scowled at that thought. His eyes rolled from side to side.

"Tonight, the Austro–Hungarian Empire is no more. They have a new king. His name, Nazar, will be whispered from their lips."

A short bald man joined the High Priest. He was a Priest but lacked the rank to control the whole army. A collection of younger priests on horseback watched a spectacle unfold from a small hill. They laughed and pointed together. Down from the hill was a makeshift arena. It was crudely put together but was doing the job for now.

Inside was a large creature—a cross between a bear and a Siberian tiger. This animal was big, with razor-sharp claws and teeth that could snap through bone. It was causing a commotion while having to fight five Austrian men who had been put in the arena with it.

These men had been given sticks to use as weapons, but they were no match for this beast. Judging what sort of danger they represented, it looked at them for a moment or two, and then it attacked. The animal lashed out at two men, knocking them over before biting and clawing their bodies. Their screams carried across the valley.

One man ran to climb out of the arena but was pushed back down by some drone soldiers. By that time, the creature had killed the remaining men, leaving this lone man to face certain death.

While this scene was unfolding, Nazar had ridden over to the makeshift arena. He had dismounted and climbed the wooden stockade, watching the drama unfold. As the beast began to come in for the kill, a shout from Nazar was enough to bring the creature back. Five drone soldiers bearing long poles with spikes went in. The animal soon backed down.

The priests spoke about this new breed and called them razor-tooths. They then watched their high priest enter the arena and go over to the man, who was on his knees crying. He asked the man to stand up and then led him out of the arena.

"Has he spared the man's life?" one Priest whispered to his nearest companion.

The man was still shaking from the experience. The high priest said nothing except to draw his sword and then bring it down hard on the man's left leg, cutting it clean off from the kneecap.

"You should have fought like a man, not run like a child."

The man writhed around in agony as blood poured from his wound.

"Feed him to the flesh-eaters."

He was dragged off, leaving his lower leg on the floor. Nazar cleaned his sword and got back on his horse.

The young priests were silent. None of them wanted to catch his eye as he rode off.

Chapter 18

Decisions were being made on where to go. The trains were being unloaded, and supplies were transferred to carts. They would be short of wagons, so it would be a case of finding what they could along the way.

A route had now been discussed and agreed upon, although not all parties would stay together. General Haas would hunt around the other side of Vienna to find any units that could still be mobilised to fight. Some of the nurses would go with them. Corporal Heinz and Colonel Kiesl had been ordered to retreat with the British into Prussia. They thought about using the River Danube from Vienna to Passan. Then, they would go through the mountains to Ratisbon and then onto Stuttgart. This was just a basic plan, but it gave them hope.

The Austrians that were coming with the British believed their families would have fled to Prussia. The constant threat of war with Prussia in recent times was a cause for concern, but the truth was, there was nowhere else to run. The thought of losing their families amongst the refugees was enough to inspire them to quicken their step and move faster.

Colonel Kiesl had reached an agreement with the major regarding leadership and rank. Although the British numbers were larger than the Austrians in the new group, it made sense for the major to lead them. Should this change, the colonel would take command.

Scouts were sent ahead to check the route in both directions. Several guards were posted on top of the trains to keep an eye on the encroaching enemy. The general gave everyone an hour to get ready. It was a case of moving out as soon as possible.

The dust cloud was gaining pace. Captain Hayward stood with Colonel Kiesl and discussed the enemy and their tactics. The Austrian was awestruck by how they were swooping across his country and wiping out anything that got in their way.

He felt that having creatures that had not been fought against before gave them an overpowering advantage on the battlefield.

The flesh-eaters did not seem to tire, nor did the long-limbed beasts. The drone soldiers could march until they dropped dead. Then, there were the giant riders and bears with two heads. It just went on.

With the dust cloud coming more and more into focus, it was time to say their goodbyes. The general thanked everyone for helping them get this far and wished them all Godspeed to their next destination. He shook the hands of his officers and men.

He stopped when he got to Captain Hayward and Major Richmond.

"I owe you a lot, my friends. Thank you for helping us Austrians. May you get home without losing any more lives."

The pain of his country being swallowed up was written all over his body. A horse was brought over to where he stood, and he mounted it. Riding to the front of his group, he moved them on.

The horses were split amongst both parties. Most were being used to pull carts, but some were for scouts. This left the rest on foot. The British and Austrian Engineers planned to go around the south of Vienna and see what boats could be found to help their journey.

Both groups set off at a reasonable pace. A Gatling gun and one cannon had been taken by each party. The rest of the weaponry on the train had been destroyed. Nothing was being left for the enemy.

Captain Hayward spoke to Corporal Heinz about leading the scouting party. He would be in charge of five men, all Austrian. Their use of German in Prussia could save time and lives.

The nurses within the British group included Heidi. She was concerned for her family and hoped and prayed they would follow the rest of the refugees into Europe. Their group numbered over two hundred people, roughly the same size as the group that had left the fort several weeks ago.

The major was on foot, with the captain in the middle of the convoy. Sergeant Butcher was with a squad of men covering the rear. Colonel Kiesl was at the front with twenty or so Austrian soldiers.

The plan was to get to the villages along the Danube. They knew they would have to take a chance to see if there were any boats there.

The noise of banging drums filled the air behind them. It was a good motivator to keep moving. The convoy was being steered south of Vienna. They were taking a chance as Vienna had recently fallen. The scouts had not been into the city, but the fires and smoke could be seen from miles around. General Haas was also heading south, but they were moving towards Graiz. He hoped there would be forces there and they could unite with family members as well. He had not given up hope on the Austro–Hungarian Empire.

The timing was imperative; they did not want to be outside in the open after dark. Judging by the enormous dust cloud, the force that had destroyed Vienna was considerable. That would mean the enemy would have lots of scouting parties around its main force, which could cause the British and Austrians a lot of trouble if they were found.

The track they were using bore the marks of a retreat. Broken carts and clothes were scattered along its sides.

However, no one could see any signs of fighting or dead bodies. This hopefully meant the villages were intact, but would there be any boats left? This was an overwhelming question going through Captain Hayward's mind.

The pace was starting to slow. They could amble along for a short while but never stop. The fact that there were two groups would benefit both parties as this would split the would-be hunters.

Corporal Heinz was returning to update Colonel Kiesl on the situation. They had mounted their group's Gatling gun on a cart, stationed in the middle of the convoy. Should there be a surprise attack, they would have some firepower to hold back a considerable force. The major commented on how he wished they had had that at the Uzhok Pass.

The nurses with them were fit young women. Most had grown up on farms and were used to hard work. They helped carry supplies and could use weapons if need be. The extra rifles were kept near the Gatling gun. Colonel Kiesl had commandeered an enemy weapon. It was something he had heard was in development in Europe, but now he had his own. He had several grenades for it and was eager to try it out but was in two minds, as that would mean they were under attack.

The hours passed, and the day was drawing in. Judging whether they should press on or find somewhere safe to spend the night was important. The scouts returned and made that decision. There was a small empty monastery ahead. It was not ransacked, and there was even some food – some unused vegetables – left in there.

They were close to the Danube but not close enough to walk through the night. At that moment, the dark belonged to the creatures.

The group arrived at the monastery and quickly got everyone in the courtyard and shut the gates. They backed up the Gatling gun to face out of the gates should they be attacked in the night. The monastery was not heavily fortified, but it did have a large stone wall around it and one tower by the main entrance. There were several buildings inside, all very modest and in keeping with a monk's lifestyle. The stables were clean and ready for use, and there was a good supply of fresh hay.

After feeding and watering the animals, the cook began his endless task of preparing food for this large party of hungry people. He had a small team of helpers, and he was happy to work from a reasonable-sized kitchen.

The guards were posted in the tower and told to stay low. They did not want to attract unwanted visitors to this site. Their experience taught them that the long limbs and anything else that was quick on its feet would be first on the scene.

A few beds scattered around the monastery were given to the wounded or nurses first. The soldiers were just happy to sleep under a roof in dry conditions. It was less crowded than the train and more spacious. The nights had been mostly dry, but the chance of rain was higher at that time of year.

The vegetables were peeled, and a broth was prepared. As usual, the food was appreciated, setting the mood for people to relax and unwind. They found that being around buildings brought some normality back to the proceedings. In a way, they could switch off from what was happening outside.

Captain Hayward and Major Richmond could not switch off. Colonel Kiesl joined them to review the route and decide what action to take in the morning.

The soldiers had been asked to keep the noise levels down. They did not want an evening attack of any sort. The decision was made to set off early and scour the villages along the river for boats.

Private John Brown took a moment to break off from his duties to speak to Heidi. She had been helping some wounded men with food and water. Their eyes lit up upon meeting each other. They embraced and hugged. Then they kissed for a moment or two. John liked the way her soft lips felt pressed against his.

"Your uniform is kind of appealing," John said quietly.

She looked at him with a smile on her face.

"You look kind of appealing yourself, soldier boy," whispered Heidi.

They both giggled, then kissed again. It was not the time or place to find somewhere to have an intimate moment, so they had to make do with that brief encounter.

"Heidi, don't stray too far away from me. Whatever is happening to this world, I want you close to me."

She smiled and nodded her head as she walked back to her quarters. John returned to check the ammunition and the status of the carts.

Dawn broke with a sudden downpour. It was hard to get going with the rain falling, and most people wanted to stay in the warmth until it stopped. They felt safe and secure from what was out there. The major understood this but realised that should they be found, they would be swarmed within minutes, and then there could only be one outcome. They had to move on.

A disused wagon with a canvas canopy had been found. It was perfect for the wounded to go in and would free up more space. The cook took what extra fresh food he could. The carts were loaded, and the group set off for the river.

The track was waterlogged in some places as the rain continued to fall. The horses pulled the carts and wagon along through thick, sticky mud and kept the convoy moving.

There was no sign of the enemy, but this did not relax anyone. When the enemy followed them from behind, it at least gave away their location. Now, they could be anywhere. The scouts were sent out in all directions, and each soldier was told to be extra vigilant.

Hours passed before they came across a small village. It was close to the river but did not have any boats. They hurriedly searched it and left, as nothing of use was found. Their maps pointed to a fair-sized town a couple of miles further down the Danube. Setting off at speed, the group covered the ground quickly. The town was within reach, but the scouts were first sent to check it over.

They came back, reporting that a small group of drone cavalrymen were stationed there. It also had a large steamboat moored. This was seen as a moment of sheer luck. They had to get on that boat at all costs. The scouts estimated the drone group to be around thirty-strong. Some were guarding the ship; others were sitting around drinking coffee. Their full unit strength was unknown, so it would have to be a lightning attack. As far as they knew, they outnumbered them.

A battle plan was drawn up in the soil. Colonel Kiesl would lead around ten mounted soldiers to the east of the town and cause a small diversion. Then Captain Hayward would take eighty British soldiers to attack the village from the front. Reinforcements would come down to the major, should they need them.

Private Brown was told to help guard the nurses and wounded men. The operation was to happen immediately, as they did not want the enemy to spot them coming. Rifles were readied, and bayonets fixed.

Captain Hayward got the men to advance slowly as the mounted soldiers rode past at speed. The soldiers looked at each other as they advanced through a field leading up to the small town. The grass blew in the wind, and the leaves shook as a soft breeze carried the men towards their destination.

The soldiers were formed into two groups of forty. They slowly closed in on the outskirts of the town, and the layout of streets and buildings was unknown. Sergeant Butcher would take forty men through the main streets while Charles led the other forty to the boat. The boat could not leave under any circumstances. The drone cavalry might not be part of a more significant force in the area, but it still meant the enemy was this far south in Austria and represented a massive threat.

The soldiers who had been drinking and sitting outside the townhouse were now loading a wagon with supplies. Their Commander was sleeping outside the town hall. The British entered the village as quietly as they could. Two drone guards were dispatched with bayonets as they casually strolled around. The element of surprise and lack of concern from the enemy played into the British's hands.

Captain Hayward had his revolver drawn and moved with his men towards the dock. The thought of getting to the boat was racing through his mind. He wondered how long it would be before the first gunshot would get the boat moving off down the river.

Major Richmond followed his men through his binoculars. Their red tunics and blue spiked helmets helped him locate them as they advanced.

The first shot fired was at a drone cavalryman who came out of a building carrying water. He looked shocked to see the soldiers coming through the town and started to sound the alarm when a bullet pierced his lungs, sending him flying backwards. He wriggled around in agony, arching his back and flailing his legs.

No soldier should enjoy watching another soldier die. The soldier who shot him went over and finished him off with a bayonet through the heart. This all happened quickly but still allowed the other drones to rush to their rifles. Gunfire now broke out around the town. For once, the British had the upper hand and were well-placed to exploit it.

Captain Hayward started to run with his men to the boat. A couple of drone soldiers were frantically trying to release the ropes that were anchoring it. The British Engineers began shooting at them as they moved forward. One man was hit and fell back. The other raised his hands. The captain rushed past him and onto the gangway. His revolver was drawn, and his men followed him. A couple had hung back to collect the surrendered drone soldiers and wait for more orders.

The house which had the drone Commander in it was surrounded. The fighting was fierce. The British used the other buildings for cover and broke into the houses which were situated around the drone soldiers' stronghold. Bullets shot past as men tried to get closer to the building. An Engineer fell, holding his face. He died almost immediately.

Colonel Kiesl arrived with the mounted cavalry. They had swept through the town to ensure there were no more hidden men. They then joined in the fighting. Sergeant Butcher was crouching behind a wall, rising up as soon as he thought it was safe to shoot. Shards of masonry pinged off the bricks as the bullets impacted into them. Glass windows were broken to shoot out of.

The colonel spoke to the sergeant and suggested they rush the house from the side as it was only being covered by a small window at the top. This would give them a chance to get closer to the building and throw in a couple of grenades. Colonel Kiesl asked for two soldiers to help. The Austrian Commander then led them on a daunting run to the base of the house. The drone soldiers tried to shoot at them from the solitary window but found it hard to get a good aim. Once the men reached the side of the house, they pressed their bodies up close and tight to the wall. Then, the colonel took two grenades and lit them. He smiled at the two soldiers with him and then rushed around the corner. He threw both grenades into the building and then peeled away and ran back to the two British soldiers.

The explosions shook the house. Colonel Kiesl seized the moment and rushed back around and into the building, where he found several drone soldiers looking shocked and dazed from the explosion. He had his revolver drawn and shot three of them as they went to aim. His British counterparts followed him in. The gunfire in the house was intense, as they were practically on top of each other.

Colonel Kiesl used this to his advantage, shooting an oncoming drone soldier in the chest as he burst into the living room door. Two more could be seen darting from the room to the bottom of the stairs. They glanced up to fire their rifles at the commander and his men. Bullets punctured the walls behind them. One of the British Engineers tipped over the kitchen table and then used it as a shield. As this unfolded, several more soldiers started coming in through the ground-floor windows to join the three men in the kitchen. Colonel Kiesl told the unit to direct their fire at the bottom of the stairs. They loaded cartridges into their rifles and shot at a reasonable rate. One drone soldier fell forward with multiple hits. His comrade was now crawling up the stairs. The British Engineers cautiously approached them.

The colonel got them to stand back and launched a grenade upstairs. After the explosion, they rushed up the steps.

They were greeted with five dead bodies and four wounded men. The drone commander was holding his stomach. His eyes looked weak, and blood was trickling out of his mouth. The soldiers tried to help the wounded men. They spoke in a language which was close to Russian. Colonel Kiesl was unsure of it and tried to speak German first and then English to them. There was no reply.

He knelt next to the commander and asked if he needed a drink of water. The man looked up and nodded. The wound was deep, and the blood from it was now seeping through the floor.

"I can speak some English," mumbled the drone commander.

Colonel Kiesl leaned in to hear the man better.

"You will all perish. This is not a war to win."

The colonel took off his hat and put it next to the pool of blood.

"You may have the upper hand at the moment, but wars are messy things. Maybe the devil is backing you, but rest assured, many will fight you to the bitter end."

The dying man looked up.

"This is the end."

He let out a huge breath and then passed away.

"We need to lock the prisoners in the barn. We can leave them with medical supplies. They will be found soon enough as the fighting will bring more here now," said Colonel Kiesl.

Captain Hayward cautiously searched the ship. They had encountered little resistance since they had come on board. The drone soldiers had been relaxing and playing cards when they were startled by the inrushing British. They were then frogmarched out of the boat onto dry land and taken to the others to be locked in the barn.

Major Richmond did not waste any time in moving the rest of the group towards the town. He wanted to be in the boat before the gunfire brought the attention of other units in the area.

Colonel Kiesl came out of the house and received a salute from the men. They were impressed by his bravery and his fighting skills. Some of the Engineers had not seen this type of action: this was up close and personal. Real soldiers were made from these situations. The colonel did not bask in his bravery but instead ordered two pairs of Austrian mounted scouts to check on the outskirts of the village. He knew time was of the essence.

The enemy's horses were taken with them to load onto the boat. It was a steam ferry of good size. The supplies were swiftly loaded on board, and the wounded were taken to the spare cabins. There was an air of excitement and nervousness around the town. Lady Luck was on their side; several Austrians had worked on boats before and had reasonable knowledge of the engine room. Two of the railway crew who had survived the Northern Riders' attack were with the group. They expressed their wish to help get the boat fired up and ready for use. Their knowledge of steam power was an asset.

Major Richmond congratulated the colonel, captain and sergeant for a sterling attack. They had taken the town with only minor injuries. The speed and surprise of the attack had prevailed.

The officers went to visit the prisoners.

A small detachment of men guarded them. Inside the barn, the group of drone soldiers gathered, speaking some sort of Russian dialect. All of these men looked ill. They were still human in appearance, but all carried some sort of ailment.

The major asked the prisoners if anyone would come forward and speak to him. He knew it was a long shot, but any information could be valuable. An older drone soldier approached him and said a few words. His English was not bad. He muttered something about medicine. He tried to explain that the wounded would need some extra medicine, or they would "change".

The major did not understand.

Whilst they were there, one of the wounded drone soldiers passed away. Then, after a pause, the dead man started to twitch. The sergeant thought it could just be something to do with his body, like a chicken that moves even after its head has been cut off.

The dead drone soldier then sat up, his eyes wide open and teeth bared. It was now obvious: dead drone soldiers became flesh-eaters. This army had a double use.

A cry was heard from outside. The major ordered the flesh-eater to be shot immediately. The other drone soldiers had backed away from the now mobile flesh-eater. Captain Hayward took out his revolver, shot it through the head, and then followed the major outside.

Several soldiers were rushing towards the house from where they had fought for control over the village. They burst in to find two flesh-eaters fighting with a British Engineer. He had been bitten on the arm and leg. The major took out his revolver and shot both creatures. The order was given to double-check that each dead drone soldier was either shot in the head or decapitated.

The injured man was helped to steady himself. The bites were deep, and he needed medical assistance from the army doctor.

The remaining drone soldiers looked on at the major. It was the first time he had seen sadness in their faces. They were not right; something was affecting them, and death only brought them back to life. After a short while, they sat back down. The major deduced that some were more affected than others. There was a difference in intelligence between them. Some were more aggressive than others. He wanted to learn more, but it was not the time to find out.

They shut the barn doors and doubled the guards. Everyone was doing things in haste. Steam was being built up in the boat's engine room. Soldiers had been sent down there to help shovel coal. Supplies were being found in the town. They had been lucky; due to the evacuation of the area, some stores and buildings had been left totally full. They took what they could.

Corporal Heinz arrived, bringing news of movement in the woods to the east of the town. He was not a hundred per cent certain if it was the enemy but decided he needed to alert the group.

Upon hearing of this, Major Richmond ordered the boat to be boarded. Most of the supplies and items were now loaded. The last horse was taken aboard, and the gangway was deserted. The engine room was hot and stuffy, with coal dust filling the air. The men down there were working very hard to get the steamboat moving. The train crew was a great help, and the Austrians who had worked on steamboats before were indispensable.

The boat left the harbour at a steady speed. One of the Austrian doctors was in charge of steering this vessel. He had captained a boat before, although he admitted he was not totally up to speed with a large steamboat.

He explained that his father had been in the Navy and wanted his son to follow. His father was Prussian, and this had been a problem since hostilities grew between Prussia and the Austro–Hungarian Empire.

As the town began to get smaller on the horizon, they saw long limbs coming to the water's edge. There were around a hundred or more in number, so the group was immensely relieved to have gotten out when they did. The long limbs stood up on their hind legs and sniffed the air. Then, some gravelly-throated bellows followed. It was a deep and vibrating sound that carried for a reasonable distance and was most likely alerting anything in the area to their find.

A British Engineer drew his rifle and wrapped his strap around his arm. He took a steady aim and was about to squeeze the trigger when a stern voice recommended him not to do so. It was the sergeant. He pointed out that the gunshot might bring in more and that every bullet needed to be saved for now. The soldier nodded and lowered his weapon.

The boat was of a good size, allowing much more space than previously enjoyed in the trains. The nurses were hard at work looking after the wounded and making up beds where possible. The Austrian and British set about mounting a Gatling gun to the rear of the ship and a small field cannon to the front. They had taken grain bags to use as cover around the windows and heavy weapons.

The long limbs followed the boat for a while but lost interest after an hour or so. Captain Hayward watched as they broke off and disappeared into the woods. He was not sure how much they were aware of people being on the boat or whether they were just following the scent in the air.

He took out his binoculars and watched the shoreline for a short while. Given this enemy's mobility, it was hard to relax.

Private John Brown arrived behind Captain Hayward.

"Sir, I hope that's the end of it now."

Captain Hayward scratched his head and turned to face Private Brown.

"So do I, John, so do I."

He turned back to watching the shoreline again. He was confident that they were moving in the right direction and that once they were in Prussia, they would surely see life return to normal. The only nagging thoughts were about this new breed of enemy, the creatures they had under their control, and the motive behind this sudden war.

They travelled down the Danube at a good, honest speed. The boat was holding her own, and the makeshift crew below handled her demands well.

The water broke off the bow gently and serenely. As summer approached, the broad-leaved trees were coming into their full glory. Corporal Heinz spoke to Captain Hayward about the history of the river and its importance to the Austro–Hungarian Empire. He talked about its trade routes and how the Romans utilised them. The river also had flooding problems, meaning major cities were built further up the river.

As he spoke about this, Charles could see a twinkle of sadness in his eye. He loved his history and that of his country.

"This does not mean your country will never be in Austrian hands again. You may have lost the battle, but there is still a war to be fought," stated Captain Hayward.

Corporal Heinz rubbed his forehead.

"You're right, but have you ever encountered a force like this? We don't know anything about them. It seems they have some plague that makes them want to eat flesh, but something drives them, an unholy force of nature."

Both men stood there in silence. Talking about their situation was not always helpful; it highlighted the uncertainty. Charles missed his wife and children and yearned for them more now than ever. In his role as leader, the men needed guidance under fire and, even with this long and tiring retreat.

Moments of relaxation were followed by tension. It was hard to fully unwind as most of the soldiers and nurses thought about what lay ahead. The Austrians had lost their country, and the British wanted to return to theirs. They thought about the men who had died in their regiment during this long journey.

The day eased into the evening. Major Richmond was conscious about travelling down a river at night and decided to moor the boat close to the bank. He ensured this was done before nightfall so they had reasonable visibility to carry out the task confidently. The usual routine of picking guards for the night shift was handed out and was followed by a hearty meal. The cook was good at knocking up different food, even using the same ingredients. The general consensus about his cooking was that some days were better than others. He would argue that he had to work with what he had, and if they didn't like it, they could go without.

The evening was a quiet one. The anchor was pulled up at first light, and the boat set on its way. They had some good maps aboard to help keep them from grounding her. The ship's captain was very pleased with that.

The morning passed quietly as they made their way along the Danube. There were no sightings of the enemy. The weather was fine, and spirits were high.

The terrain was varied. Hills and farmlands were abundant and mixed in with woods and forests. They spotted deer and other wildlife going about their business. It truly was refreshing for everyone.

Captain Hayward had slept on the floor in one of the storerooms. He felt it was only right that someone else got a chance to enjoy a decent night's sleep in a proper bed.

A soldier brought him a cup of coffee, and he sat back on a deck chair to enjoy the view. They were making good progress.

Chapter 19

By late afternoon, Melk Benedictine Abbey came into sight. It was truly spectacular. The abbey itself was on a hill, set back a little from the river with an inlet flowing by it. The walls of the abbey were huge, and its architecture was exquisite.

Colonel Kiesl said it was of great spiritual importance to the Austrians. Leopold II had given the castle to the monks in 1089. It survived the Napoleonic Wars and was, unfortunately, now under threat again.

The group wanted to go inside the monastery. It was a strange moment. Many soldiers and nurses on the boat believed in God and felt drawn to this abbey as if it could save their souls. Some did not believe in anything, but the sight of this overpowering landmark urged them to do the same.

Major Richmond had a decision to make. They had not seen any life or movement as they passed into Melk. There were neither Austrians nor enemy soldiers. He spoke with the other officers, and they agreed they should get closer to see.

The major had a large group of people under his command. The estuary was narrow and would be a great risk should they be attacked. He pondered for a moment and then agreed to sail the ship to the entrance of the estuary and moor her there.

Several soldiers and nurses agreed to stay behind with the wounded and guard the ship. The rest of the British Engineers and Austrians disembarked. They travelled light. Most soldiers only took their rifles and a pouch full of bullets.

Corporal Heinz was wary of the silence and yet drawn to the abbey's presence. They made their way through woodlands and found an old track that took them close to the water's edge. The abbey was slowly coming closer and closer. They stopped short of its walls as houses came into view. It was the start of the town. Captain Hayward and Kiesl took two groups of twelve men and did a quick scout of the surrounding area. When it was deemed safe, the group continued.

The town was empty but did not carry any signs of war. The odd cat roamed the streets, and it felt like an early Sunday morning.

They were in awe of the abbey's size. It was genuinely overpowering. The group moved through the side of the town at a constant speed. They felt like mice going about their business as swiftly and quietly as possible.

The road they were on weaved through the narrow streets and then took a sharp left. They cautiously made their way to the entrance. The soldiers had fanned out to be ready for anything. There were no signs of fighting, just cold, stone silence.

The wooden doors to the abbey were shut. Two of the Austrian soldiers approached them quietly. Then, with their rifle butts, they banged on the wood three times. Everyone took a few steps back and waited. All eyes were on the doors. Some felt they were holding their breath as time stood still for a moment.

Then, it began to creep into life. The giant frames creaked and slowly opened to reveal a collection of monks standing there with a large crucifix. They came forward and spoke German to the men in front of them. The soldiers then turned to the other anxious faces and beckoned everyone in.

The grandeur of the place contrasted with the monks' lives. Theirs were simple and committed to God's worship. The group was taken into the courtyard and met by a Father who was left in charge.

"I take it you're the relief force, then."

He may have been a monk, but he had a sense of humour.

Major Richmond came forward and, in his broken German, asked if he understood English. The man smiled and nodded his head.

"Dear Father, we have travelled from the Carpathian Mountains on a horrendous journey. The Austro–Hungarian Empire has been consumed by evil."

The major was almost stuck for words as a sense of this whole occasion sunk in. They had witnessed things that they believed not to be possible or had ever expected to experience.

"My son, the Austro–Hungarian Empire has crumbled. We know only a little of what is happening out there. We have had the odd person seek refuge with us over the past few weeks, but most depict a story of total annihilation. The townsfolk and army left a week or so ago. We were offered a chance to come with them, but we are committed to the abbey, regardless of what happens."

He then said they would not have much time. Reports had come in of priests and giant men on horses riding towards Melk. With that, he took them into one of the buildings. The paintings on the ceiling were powerful and daunting. Major Richmond asked if he could go and pray in the church, which pleased the Father.

"Do so now, and we shall give you some food to take on your way."

A monk then led them to the church, which was just as spectacular inside as it was outside. They all gathered in the aisles, and the monk blessed them and led them through some prayers in German.

It was a special place to think and believe in other worlds and lives. The sermon was not too long. The Father returned and beckoned them to follow him—they had carts waiting in the courtyard. There was a good collection of vegetables and even some warm soup. The Major was very grateful for this kind gesture. He asked once again if they would think about coming with them.

These invaders would not spare anyone; they were not here to take prisoners. The Father shook his head.

"The abbey has stood for a long time, with or without us. We shall face our destiny together."

As he said this, a younger monk came racing across the courtyard carrying a telescope. He spoke to the Father and pointed in the direction of the river. The Father spoke to him quietly and then returned to talk to the major.

"I have one favour to ask. A young lad has recently joined us. His family have been killed in this conflict. His name is Benedict. I would be very grateful if he could accompany you on your boat."

The major nodded his head.

With a flash, the young lad was brought forward. He was around eighteen and not as young as the major had thought he would be.

"He knows the Danube well, as his father used to be a merchant on this river. He can help guide you to Ulm if that is where you're going?"

The major thanked the Father for having the foresight to help them on the river. Small gunfire could be heard in the distance, sending a wave of panic throughout the group. The boat was not well manned now, and they needed to return.

The Father said he could help them one more time, which drew a puzzled look from the major and Captain Hayward. He then led them into a building and down some long, winding steps.

"Follow these until you see an iron cross. You will be then next to the Danube."

Everyone thanked him as they passed. Food was manhandled off the carts as there was no time to take them to the boat. The cook looked at the soup and dipped one finger in it to get a quick taste. He smiled and nodded with satisfaction, then shook his head with regret as they had to leave it behind. Lanterns were lit as they made their way into the dark tunnel.

Benedict led the way.

Time stood still as they made their way through the dark. It was murky down there, with water knee-deep in places. The odd rat could be seen watching them from their tunnels, probably hoping for some kind of food trail to be left. Just as people started to wonder about the tunnels' destination, Benedict called out in German about the Iron Cross. They had reached the Danube.

The tunnel did not open directly onto the river itself. It was set a good thirty metres back and emerged from a slight bank. Colonel Kiesl went out first. He had a rifle strapped to his back and his revolver drawn. Two more British soldiers followed him out. There was an anxious wait in the tunnel whilst they checked that the coast was clear. Eventually, a call came out for everyone to exit the tunnel as fast as they could. Gunfire could be heard closer now, which put everyone on edge.

They clambered out of the tunnel. The soldiers gathered on each side, kneeling, at the ready with their rifles. Major Richmond spoke to everyone.

"We have little time to get to the boat. We must move quickly and keep together."

Corporal Heinz led the group, cutting past five broad Austrian pines and through a large thicket. They then broke into a fast jog. The nurses found it hard as their dresses were more extended and less forgiving. An Austrian Sister had taken note of this as they ran. She had a plan for them, which would involve shorter dresses. It would be considered unladylike, but they had no choice.

They moved through an open field, and the boat came into view. As they ran, whooshing sounds fizzled through the air. Shots were being fired at them from across the river. The muzzle flashes were all they could make out. Bits of dirt were flung up sporadically as bullets hit the ground. One soldier got hit in the arm and was knocked over. He was picked up and helped along.

They entered another wooded area, which gave them more cover. The boat was now only a short distance away. The soldiers on the boat could see them coming and tried to lay down, covering fire to help them.

The group got in as close as they could. Then, the soldiers helped the nurses wade into the water and towards the boat. After that, they carried their rifles over their heads and moved towards the anchored ship. Ropes were thrown down to help them climb in. The nurses were sent up first, but they found it difficult in their clothes. They certainly impressed the men around them with their sterling show of determination and willpower to get up there.

It took around fifteen minutes to get everyone on board. The gunfire was now increasing from the other side. Loud bangs and thuds could be heard as the shots hit and ricocheted off the metal sides of the boat.

The major went to the wheelhouse and ordered their immediate departure. The engine room had been kept busy while they were away. Steam pressure was not allowed to drop too much, which gave them the advantage of leaving rapidly.

Captain Hayward joined the cannon crew as they directed the weapon at the opposing bank. Drone soldiers could be seen arriving and taking aim at them. The Gatling gun was also primed.

Some soldiers took off their wet red tunics and joined the others, taking cover behind sandbags and anything protective on the ship. Charles saw an excellent opportunity to open fire as a clutch of drone soldiers came closer to the water's edge. The cannon was loaded, and the sights were adjusted to take in their position. With a flick of his hand, it kicked into action, and a thunderous pounder shot left the side of the boat and almost instantly smashed into the other side of the riverbank. Lumps of dirt and flesh were scattered into the air.

He then shouted the order for everyone on that side to fire. The Gatling gun opened up on the bank, cutting across trees and bushes like a scythe threw hay. Foliage filled the air in a thin mist. Mixed in with that concoction were pieces of flesh and blood.

The steamboat rolled into action, pulling away and picking up speed as it went. Waves broke off her bow and rebounded onto the banks. The drone soldiers tried to follow her, but the thick alder trees along the river's edge hindered their movement.

The order was still circulated around for most soldiers and nurses to stay below deck as sniper fire could still be a problem.

This order was only relaxed after an hour or so of travelling. The spotters were stationed around the boat, looking for cannons and other things that could endanger the boat's welfare.

Captain Hayward went to check on the wounded. They had only sustained one significant injury, and that was the man who had been shot in the arm as they ran back to the boat. He was being worked on and was fortunate to have several doctors looking after him with a good number of nurses to provide valuable assistance.

Colonel Kiesl arrived on the scene and checked on the man. He was concerned for the welfare of all the soldiers now fighting together. Something was troubling him, and he made clear to Captain Hayward that he wanted to speak to him about it in private.

They then left the makeshift hospital and entered a small cabin on the middle deck.

"I believe we have a small problem, Charles," said Colonel Kiesl,

He then led him to the room where a man had been bitten by the flesh-eaters in the village. The man was lying there looking very sick; his wounds had been festering. A nurse arrived and explained that they had kept everything clean, but these bites almost looked like they carried poison. They thanked the nurse and then left to speak on the top deck.

Standing and looking over the rolling hills, Colonel Kiesl spoke his mind.

"I believe we need to keep an eye on the private who was bitten. I think there is more to this illness than we know."

Charles stood and thought for a moment. He remembered the dead drone soldier coming back to life and thought about the implications of that. Once they came back to life, they were fuelled by hunger.

"This is a worrying turn of events, Colonel. We could be on the verge of something terrible here."

Both stood quietly for a moment or two. Captain Hayward took out two cigars from his army pouch.

"I've been saving these for when I thought things had worked out well. Now, I'm not certain of the future. We need to make sure that what we think will happen actually happens."

Colonel Kiesl took the cigar and thanked him. He struck a match and puffed on the cigar until it got going. Captain Hayward then did the same. They were lost in thought for a while. Smoke wafted around them, and Captain Hayward leaned forward onto the outer railing.

"We have to stay near the man tonight. This could have massive implications for Europe; if the flesh eaters are carrying a virus, it could be worse than the bubonic plague."

Kiesl agreed and suggested that they take turns waiting outside the dying soldier's cabin. Captain Hayward instantly agreed.

They smoked for a good half an hour before returning to active duties around the boat. There were animals in the fields as they travelled along. Farmhouses still had smoke coming from their chimneys. It looked as if war had not arrived in these parts yet. The odd person was seen scurrying along, but they were not stopping to look at the steamboat; they were just going about their business at a fast pace.

On the surface, things looked normal, but most suspected that something was coming from the East and spreading fast. They knew that those who were left could either flee or wait to see what cards fate dealt them.

Corporal Heinz stood next to Sergeant Butcher.

"They don't know what's coming."

The sergeant looked up.

"None of us knows what's really coming."

Both men followed the silhouettes of people as they disappeared into the distance.

Charles was happy with the boat's travelling speed. The young Benedict was a huge help, as he knew the ferrying routes well and where best to steer the boat in the river.

Linz was the next port of call. The mountains rose up in the distance and profoundly affected the landscape. Their beauty was matched by their danger. Many armies had perished crossing mountainous terrain. In recent times, when Napoleon had failed in his conquest of Russia, the elements played a huge part.

Captain Hayward thought about this as he sat in a cabin across from the sick British soldier. He had spoken to the major about the situation and what they thought was unfolding. Now, it was just a waiting game. Colonel Kiesl would see out the shift from 2 a.m. Captain Hayward spoke to the nurse and said he would lock the wounded man's door and keep the key himself. She was unsure of this and spoke to a doctor who came over and asked why such actions were needed.

He was reluctant to reveal his suspicions but quietly spoke about what they believed could happen.

The doctor's face dropped. He was horrified by this concept and yet fascinated by its medical implications. He asked if he could help the wounded man in any way. Charles suggested morphine and agreed.

When they entered the cabin, the soldier could hardly open his eyes. The room had a dark, unforgiving odour. His wounds now stank of pus and were almost rotting; the infection was like none other the doctor or Charles had ever seen. The man whispered something, and the captain bent down and got closer to hear what he was saying.

The words were hard to decipher, but family and love were amongst them. Captain Hayward put a hand on his shoulder and helped administer the morphine. The soldier then fell unconscious. His breathing became rapid and then shallow. They left him in peace and shut the door behind them.

"Do you have to lock it? How can we hear if he needs our help?" the doctor asked anxiously." I understand this is difficult, but it's for everyone's safety. The nurse can check on him every thirty minutes but must fetch me if anything changes."

It was agreed, and the doctor left Charles to return to his cabin. Every half hour, a nurse would appear and check on the man. On the third visit, he had passed away. The door was locked, and the nurse was instructed to tell the doctor. Captain Hayward checked his pocket watch; the time was midnight.

His mind thought of the witching hour, and he let his head rest back on the cabin bunk for a second or two.

A thudding sound and a slight groan awoke him. It was enough to bring him out of his slumber. He checked his watch. The time was twelve thirty-three.

He rubbed his eyes and buttoned up his tunic, which must have come undone while he slept. He then took out his revolver. The groaning was getting louder, and the sound of gnashing teeth was more intense. The noise stopped when he left his cabin and walked over to the other side of the boat.

Charles stood still; his heart rate sped up. The light was not great—some oil lanterns provided the only backdrop. He brought himself closer to the door and listened. Still, nothing. Could it mean they had been wrong with their first theory?

An aggressive smack on the wooden cabin door broke through his thoughts.

He cocked his revolver and went to the door. A figure appeared to his side, making him instinctively turn around and point the gun in that direction. He was taken by surprise and almost pulled the trigger. It was Colonel Kiesl.

"Easy, my friend. You could ruin my night shift."

Charles half smiled and simultaneously let out a deep sigh.

"It's happened, I'm afraid."

They both then turned to the door as it shook. Colonel Kiesl drew out his revolver as well.

"We have to take care of this now."

Charles agreed.

"On the count of three, you open the door, and I'll shoot it in the head."

Charles looked down.

"His name is Richard Smith."

Colonel Kiesl nodded.

"Yes, I'm sorry. Richard Smith. He would not want to be in this way, Captain. Should I ever get bitten, please end my life, too."

A simple nod said it all.

"One. Two. Three…"

The door was unlocked, and out staggered a flesh-eater. Richard Smith did not look human anymore. He looked like a sick creature and had an evil desire in his eyes. They did not wait around as he staggered towards Captain Hayward. Colonel Kiesl shot Richard Smith once in the head, killing him directly.

Charles re-holstered his gun and bent down over the dead soldier. They had taken Richard's personal belongings and would return them to his family. The official line was that he died in combat.

"Charles, strange that only headshots kill them," commented Colonel Kiesl.

Three guards appeared after hearing the gunshot. The captain and the colonel explained they would debrief everyone in the morning. They ordered the body to be thrown overboard and the room locked. They were not sure if the room could carry the bacteria or not.

That night, they moored outside Linz. Charles had his best night's sleep in a long time. He did not think about the consequences of what a single bite from a flesh-eater could do. His mind was free to dream of his family.

The next day, after breakfast, they moved through Linz. It had some distinct buildings close to the river. The group looked on from the boat. More people were making their way out of the town. A small group of soldiers was helping direct refugees.

They were manoeuvring a cannon so that it faced the boat, but Corporal Heinz positioned himself at the highest point on the vessel and waved an Austro–Hungarian flag. There was still a moment when they were unsure whether to fire, but Colonel Kiesl instructed some nurses and the remaining Austrian troops to go on top deck. He wanted to show the other soldiers that they were not the enemy.

The boat gently rocked closer so they could call out and ask what was happening. A young officer appeared from a building and instructed the men to leave the cannon and continue helping the refugees. He then shouted back to the soldiers on the boat that the enemy was at the gates, and there was little time. He told them not to moor, or they could be captured.

As he described what was happening, shells started to fall on the town. Plumes of thick masonry smoke filled the cobbled streets, and flashes of explosions lit up around them. He saluted them as they passed on. The major considered taking on more passengers but was concerned about how many he could accommodate. As the bombardment intensified, refugees disappeared in all directions. There was no sign of drone soldiers or flesh-eaters, but the order was given for the Bugler to give the "call to arms" blast.

The British and Austrian soldiers took their positions as the boat continued down the Danube. Gunfire could be heard on both sides of the river.

Linz started to fade into the distance. The men and women looked at the flames coming from the town. It was a sad sight. For many weeks, there had been no people; now they saw so many running with fear in their eyes.

The river was winding this way and that past the fields and forests. The sounds of fighting had died down a little since leaving Linz. Colonel Kiesl spoke to the Austrian soldiers on board the boat who felt they should be fighting the enemy rather than sailing to safety. It was a challenging question to justify. He felt the same. He had dark thoughts in his mind and was unwilling to share them with the men just yet.

He explained that the population of Austria would now be on the move, and more than likely, that meant going into Prussia and the surrounding countries. Everyone wanted to fight these aggressors, but it was better to pick a time and a place to fight this war. That meant making some hard decisions.

The officers were summoned to the wheelhouse before lunch. The major had been looking at maps with Corporal Heinz and going over the river route with Benedict. The speed of the enemy advance meant they had to think on their feet. Towns and cities were falling rapidly, and whilst the boat was moving at a good speed, the risk of being flanked on both sides by enemy cannons was disturbingly real.

In all fairness, little was known of the remaining Austrian forces. The route they were considering would take them into Prussia. Basic needs like supplies and wagons would be essential. The soldiers could march at a reasonable speed, but they needed to be quicker than that. They had horses on board, which would help with the movement, but they needed to find wagons and, ideally, more animals.

Ammunition was being counted along with Gatling gun rounds and cannon balls. The grenade situation was dire.

An order had gone out for bayonets to be sharpened and all weapons checked and prepared. "No stone shall be left unturned," was the message sent out.

Maps were being traced so each officer could navigate the local area in case of separation from the leading group. This would not give an end destination as such but more of an idea of where to go if that situation occurred. As this was being done, rain started to fall effortlessly. It began as only light drops but soon became a torrential downpour.

Major Richmond asked Benedict if it was better to moor for a short while and let the storm pass. Benedict shook his head, said this was nothing new to him, and helped the captain plot their next course.

The rain eased, and the skies cleared to reveal a wonderful rainbow. It was a pleasing act of nature that caught everyone's imagination for a moment or two.

The light broke through the trees and reflected off the water. The calm was blissful while it lasted. Spring was giving way to summer.

The next few days were spent cautiously working their way down the river. They stopped and sent mounted scouts out where Benedict had told them of the narrowness of the waterway. This added time to their journey but also secured their safety.

Passan was known as the City of Three Rivers, with the Inn flowing in from the south and the Ilz from the north. They would journey through this and continue along the Danube.

The next obstacle was negotiating access into Prussia. The relationship between the two countries was frosty, to say the least. They hoped the war unfolding on their borders would help ease their access.

The British flag was holstered up the mast. It was hoped it would prevent unnecessary attacks as they approached Prussia. The days passed by with ease. They stopped and moored every evening but never let their guard down.

Major Richmond spoke to Colonel Kiesl. He wanted to make sure all the Austrians were aware of their actions and that no one could be too sure of the reception they would receive.

"I must implore that you explain to all your men that we are entering a country that could take any unfamiliar action as hostile," said Major Richmond.

Colonel Kiesl nodded.

"The Austro–Hungarian Empire has recently had its differences with Prussia, but we must put that aside. We are struggling as a nation, and I hope they will not take advantage of this!"

The major listened, waiting for reassurance that they would remain calm as they approached the border.

"We will take your command as we enter their country," reassured Colonel Kiesl.

This was enough to satisfy the major. He shook the colonel's hand and went off to his quarters. He wanted to compile his thoughts. He had kept a journal of their whole ordeal since the fort, and now it seemed even more prevalent that he did so as evidence would be needed to understand what was happening.

The following day, the boat edged into Prussia. There were no checkpoints or guards anywhere, which was very odd considering the recent feelings between these countries.

The boat cruised along at a gentle speed. The striking image came when they passed through a small village to find it empty. It was a familiar sight to them. There didn't seem to be any signs of a struggle or fighting.

Captain Hayward looked on, concerned. He then went to find the major and knocked on his quarter's door.

"Excuse me, sir, have you seen that there is no border control or civilians in the village we have just passed?"

The major looked up. He had his reading glasses on and slowly took them off.

"Yes, it is not a good thing."

He pointed to a fresh coffee pot sitting on a coaster. Charles helped himself.

Holding his coffee, he spoke to the major.

"They must have started to attack Prussia. Surely, they wouldn't be so foolish. The Prussians have a huge army and some of the most modern weapons around."

The major took a sip of his coffee.

"Yes, they do, but as you and the colonel found out the other night with Private Smith, they have weapons of a different magnitude. The plague from those flesh-eaters could do even more damage than we know."

Captain Hayward sighed.

"You're right, Harry. This could be the start of something very, very terrible indeed."

Both men stared into the corners of the room, lost in their own thoughts.

"We must keep up morale amongst the soldiers and nurses. We have several doctors on board – perhaps we should have kept Private Smith's body to see if they could have gained any valuable information on the sickness."

They spoke briefly before Charles returned to the upper deck. He took three deep breaths and calmed himself before meeting the rest of the men.

The scenery along the river was breathtaking, with hills rising and falling in the distance and meadows coming into bloom. It made a mockery of this dangerous situation that was now developing. Captain Hayward was a soldier, but he loved nature and was an Engineer at heart. He had no strong urges to fight a massive battle or command a whole regiment. He was pondering going into civil engineering and working for the government.

The death and destruction had brought him down to earth on warfare and the harrowing side of its nature. He wanted to spend more time with his family and watch his children grow up. Seeing the human bones piled up and knowing a lot of them were not adult ones sent an intense chill through his body.

Charles had grown up in a relatively comfortable Victorian family. His father had worked with the railways, and his mother stayed at home and looked after the children. They did have a nanny who was involved in his and his brother's upbringing. His brother Michael had not joined the army and was working in America. He had told Charles: "This country is going places". They were close growing up, and still wrote at least three to four times a year. Michael tried to come home and visit family and friends at least once a year. He was wealthy enough to do that.

Their father was not overjoyed when Charles joined the army. He was more of a mathematician and wanted his boys to go into commence rather than the forces. The Empire was very powerful and allowed young men to see the world and earn money. The dangers were out there; with any fighting force, death was just a neighbour.

He convinced his elder son that the Royal Engineers would offer him a chance to use his skills more than normal soldiering. He wanted something for his son after the army. Charles' father had some contracts through the railways in India and had encouraged Charles to study to become an officer at Sandhurst.

He had done well and took to the Engineers like a duck to water. The moment his life changed was when he met Rebecca. She was a young lady who was the daughter of an army general.

There was a summer ball for the officers who had qualified. Charles had gone there with his friends in full uniform, feeling very proud of his achievements. The place was full of nobles and important people swanning around. His father had instructed him that this was the time to make acquaintances and help get his career off to a flying start.

It started well when he met the MP for Surrey. He was a round, pompous man who liked to talk up a storm about how he would change the country and give the people more power. He said he wanted the Empire to take back America and had many other unreasonable ideas. The two of them did not hit it off, so Charles took a bottle of wine and went to sit outside in the gardens.

He found a quiet spot and looked up at the evening stars. The night sky was awe-inspiring. The wine flowed from the bottle too quickly, and he soon got up to fetch another when he heard a commotion from behind a hedge near him. As he walked along, he saw a young lady arguing with a navy officer. Charles did not know them and tried to keep moving, but she called out to him. The last thing on his mind was getting involved in someone else's argument.

"Are you a Royal Engineer?" questioned the woman.

Charles was amazed she knew his uniform.

"Umm, yes. Can I help you?"

The navy officer with her looked like he was going to explode with anger. Charles did not know what to say.

"Bloody hell, Rebecca, I did not sleep with the maid or Camilla. They're just army rumours. And you, sir, might as well move on."

Charles didn't like his attitude, but this was not his battle to fight.

"I am moving on as you have broken the silence I came out here to enjoy."

The man sneered at him, and the lady smiled politely. He walked for several minutes and found a large oak tree, then dropped himself at the base of the trunk. He could see the arguing couple in the distance. The view was good but with less sound. Charles thought about his past relationships: some had come and gone in a moment; others lasted for a while and then petered out. He was a bachelor at that moment and happy to enjoy life a little before being posted abroad.

He watched the couple break off and go their separate ways. The navy man went back into the ballroom, and the lady started to walk in his general direction. This was not something he wanted, but he found himself stuck to the spot. He hoped if he stayed still, she would just walk past him. It was fairly dark in the garden, with only lanterns scattered around on various bushes.

Charles thought about closing his eyes and pretending to be asleep. He tried it for a moment or two but could not help forcing himself to open them to gauge where she was. He was pleasantly surprised when he did and found she was no longer in front of him.

"You're not drunk, are you?"

He nearly jumped out of his skin.

"You scared the life out of me."

She laughed.

"Some soldier you'd make!"

Charles felt himself going red.

"I'm not drunk; I was out here to gather my thoughts."

She leaned closer to him.

"You look drunk but very handsome."

Charles looked confused.

"Umm, thank you. I should really introduce myself. Er, Charles Hayward."

He only really took in her beauty once she came close. His heart did a quick cartwheel. She was very attractive and had sharp, piercing eyes.

"Please to meet you, Charles. My name's Rebecca Lundin. My grandfather was Swedish, wouldn't you know."

They looked at each other and smiled. There was a comfortable silence.

"Your father is the general here, isn't he?"

"Yes, he is. Does that bother you?"

She said this with a smile.

"Talking to the general's daughter is not a crime as far as I know. Upsetting her might be. I guess that was your chaperone for the evening?"

She nodded.

"I'll speak to Father; he'll be dead by morning."

She said it with a deadpan face that unnerved Charles a little.

"Don't worry, I'm not like that. We have seen each other for a short while, but he does not share the same passion for life as me."

She took Charles's hand and led him off towards the lake. Charles was starting to sober up – fast. First of all, he did not want to upset her. She was the general's daughter, after all. He was taken by her charm and beauty but was cautious, nonetheless.

They walked for five minutes, maintaining small talk, and then arrived at the lake. It was a fair distance from the ball, but music could still be heard in the background, adding to the ambience.

Charles looked around. As he did so, Rebecca started undressing.

"May I ask what you're doing?"

He was puzzled and a little shocked. She turned to him, totally naked, and waded into the water.

"Well, I'm enjoying the evening. It's been a lovely summer's day, and I need to cool off. Join me?

She beckoned him forward. Charles was taken aback by her approach and stood still for a moment or two. He then thought it was all too crazy and turned around.

A splash from Rebecca soaked his back. It was a warm summer evening, and the water was refreshing.

"You must have seen a lady naked before, Charles."

She said this laughingly, not in a condescending way, more flirtatious than that.

"Right, I'm coming in!"

He then awkwardly started taking off his clothes. The alcohol had had more effect on his judgement than he realised. He stumbled several times and wondered how safe it was to enter the water. As he took off his long johns, he looked around to see if Rebecca was looking. She was nowhere to be seen. Blind panic set in. Being naked and at the scene of a missing dead general's daughter would be unexplainable. He wasted no further time and threw himself into the water.

He dived several times, but there was nothing. His heart was pounding, his mind out of control. He started to swim for shore to raise the alarm and get more help when a rush of water in front of him brought up Rebecca. She breathed hard for a second or two and regained her composure. "I've broken my personal record, I do believe."

"What are you playing at? I've been diving for your body. You're bloody mad. This is not at all good manners. I was worried sick."

She leaned forward, pressing her naked body against his.

"I'm sorry."

She brought her mouth to his and kissed him. Her lips were soft, and her touch was special. Charles was captivated by her. They carried on kissing. She splashed him with water, and he did the same back.

When they returned to the ball, there were several glances at their wet hair and slightly dishevelled look. Her former companion for the evening had since left with another woman.

Charles went and fetched Rebecca a glass of wine, and they sat for a while, soaking up the atmosphere. Then, when she had finished her drink, she placed the glass on the nearest table and took Charles by hand.

She led him to the centre of the ballroom as couples started to dance to the next piece of music. Charles just stood there. The music filled the room. Couples swirled at great speed around them, but his eyes were transfixed by his female companion. Then they started to dance. She started them off, and Charles led from there on. He was not the greatest dancer – his mother had proclaimed he had two left feet – but he had not given up and was taught to a respectable standard.

Rebecca leaned in and pressed her head against his shoulder. Her soft, sweet smell filled his senses and made him look around at the room. It was happening so fast, but time stood still as his heart fell for the woman in his arms. Her eyes met his. He felt sheer energy flow from her into him.

His dream started to fade.

"Rebecca, Rebecca…"

"Captain, you've been dreaming. We're coming towards Passan," said a young Private.

He snapped out of his half-sleep and saw a soldier standing before him. He had a half-open map and pointed to their position.

"Thank you, Private. Let me gather my thoughts, and then I'll go to the wheelhouse to meet the other officers."

The soldier saluted him and returned to inform the others.

Captain Hayward looked out over the beautiful countryside and thought once more about his wife and children. He had enjoyed reminiscing about her and now wanted to see them even more. He was aware that letting it overtake his thoughts could be dangerous. There was still a lot of land between himself and Paris.

With no further thought, he took the map to the wheelhouse. There, waiting, were the major, Colonel Kiesl, and several other officers.

The major laid down the map of Passan.

"The Prussians could be massing their armies around this town with preparations to defend their borders. We don't know what reception they'll give us."

Colonel Kiesl scratched his stubble.

"I have spoken to my men about lying low until we understand their intentions more."

The officers continued to discuss the route and the best place to disembark. The boat was currently giving them the fastest route away from the enemy.

That night, a feast was prepared. Everyone enjoyed what the cook had served up. He had quite a few kitchen helpers scheduled in a tight rota. With so many on board, there was plenty to do in the kitchen, and a lot of the time was spent washing up afterwards.

Wine was available. It was not generally allowed during times of heightened danger, but with Passan within reach the next day, this rule was relaxed a little. Bottles were passed around for several men and women to share.

The nurses were kept apart from soldiers in the evenings. The officers had warned the men that they would be dealt with severely if they started sleeping around. Many perceived this as harsh, but the simple fact was that discipline had to be maintained in any army. If they allowed that to fall, then mutinies and disorder could follow.

The nurses had flirted with the soldiers during the daytime but kept a keen eye on the rules during the evenings. Sergeant Butcher and two Austrian sergeants were ordered to keep an overview of this. There was one exception, and that was Private Brown. He had gone to the major and declared his love for Heidi. She had done the same to Colonel Kiesl, and they agreed that they would be allowed more time together. The evening sleeping ban still stood, though. They knew that if the two of them flaunted the rules, others would feel aggrieved if they could not do the same.

During the evening, guards were posted outside on the upper and lower decks. Windows were covered up to make sure minimal light escaped. Nothing was taken for granted. Distant rumbling sounded like fighting, but the sentries pointed to a storm over the mountains. Watching the lightning from his room, Major Richmond wrote in his diary. He hoped they would not be blown out of the water tomorrow before even getting a chance to speak to the Prussians. He thought, too, about the lack of border control entering Prussia and the enemy's ability to move at lightning speed.

After writing his thoughts, he poured himself a glass of water and put his weary head on his bunk pillow. He said a prayer and calmly fell asleep.

The morning started well with a fresh breeze and a sunny outlook. The storm had cleared the skies and eased the pressure that was building.

Passan was coming into sight. There was no smoke bellowing into the skies, no gunfire, or warning signs of such, but they were still cautious. Their fear of this being a trap and limited escape routes stuck with them.

The major asked for most of the soldiers to be on the lower decks so as not to give off too threatening an appearance. He also requested the Austrians to stay below due to the current feelings between the Austro–Hungarian Empire and the Prussian Empire.

The British Engineers raised the Union Jack and ensured the soldiers would not be carrying their rifles. The Bugler would be ready on the lower decks should a call to arms be needed. Then, the soldiers would be prepared to man the cannon and Gatling gun. The rifles were lined up in a row on the middle deck. Ammunition boxes were opened in case they needed to reload quickly.

The first farms on the city's outskirts started to come into sight. They were deserted. Livestock was still wandering around, oblivious to what was happening in the nearby country.

The cook gazed at the chickens roaming around and imagined catching a few for a roast chicken with herbs and onions. His stomach started to rumble with delight at the thought of such a feast. He looked around to see if anyone else was contemplating such an idea. He was met with Colonel Kiesl's look of refusal and then asked politely to go down below.

The ship kept on moving towards its destination. As they crept along, the soldiers on the top deck looked on with horror as large groups of long limbs moved towards Passan.

The boat was not making enough noise for them to be interested in it, so Benedict kept them as close to the middle of the river as possible.

There was sporadic gunfire as they approached the inner city. Captain Hayward spoke to the major about whether they were witnessing an assault and whether they should get as much firepower up on the top deck as possible. The major pointed out that this was probably just a skirmish, as there was no heavy artillery in use or a mass army advance.

The soldiers on the top deck crouched down. Their weapons were kept on the middle deck, and they felt vulnerable to any attack.

"Harry, we have to get more men up here and arm the others," insisted Captain Hayward.

The major thought for a moment or two and then nodded with approval. Sergeant Butcher then got the men moving, and Corporal Heinz did the same with the Austrian soldiers.

As the boat moved stealthily along, swathes of drone soldiers could now be seen moving in large groups. The city was coming under a sustained attack. The full force might not have arrived yet, but these shock troops were attacking purposefully. The officers used their binoculars to scour the horizon for movement and cannons. There were no flesh-eaters in sight – yet.

The further down the river they went, the more anxious they became. The gunfire was getting heavier. Street-to-street fighting had broken out. The central part of the city effectively had the Danube running through it. The weapons were now readied. They watched for movement. It was now that the major feared a heavy assault would leave them sitting ducks. A giant razor-tooth was seen moving through the lanes. He was followed by several drone soldiers carrying what looked like handheld mortars. Captain Hayward recognised them from the one he had taken from the Northern riders.

They were at a safe distance from this marauding group but still watched them intensely. As they moved along, gunshots came closer and closer. Then, the boat came under fire. The soldiers took cover and looked around for where it was coming from. It was soon located in an area to the south side of the city. Drone soldiers had seen this large target and started to shoot at it. As the bullets snapped into the boat, there was a feeling of resilience in her. It was their guardian angel at this moment in time, taking them through the dark and delivering them into the light.

They did not return fire; it would have been a waste of bullets. The boat slowly pulled out of their range and pushed further along the river. Then, Corporal Heinz spotted a group of Prussian soldiers with their distinctive helmets, light blue jackets, and darker blue trousers. There were around ten of them running at speed. Moving rapidly behind them was a group of long limbs.

The soldiers took turns firing and moving as they retreated. The long limbs outnumbered the Prussians three to one. It was only a matter of time before they were on top of them. They had a chance to take cover in a house, but they probably realised that that would leave them trapped.

The corporal shot to his feet and asked if they should set out a rowing boat to collect the men. The major looked at Charles and then gave the nod. He grabbed a mixture of British and Austrian soldiers and was then lowered down to the water. They rowed at speed towards the Prussians.

The Prussians had not seen them and kept falling back. They took notice when the boat's cannon fired a shot at the advancing long limbs. The shell was accurate and landed between three long limbs, sending flesh, bone, and dirt flying up into the air and onto the houses around them.

The Prussians looked at the steamboat and the rowing boat coming their way. They did not waste time and got close to the water to be rescued.

Corporal Heinz was the first to greet them in German. They were a little taken aback and surprised by having an Austrian soldier rescue them.

A Prussian officer came forward and introduced himself as Jurgen Müller. Introductions were short as they clambered into the boat. The long limbs were coming from all angles. The cannon could not be fired with the soldiers at such close proximity, but the steamboat could offer covering fire from the soldiers on the top deck.

The long limbs climbed into the water after their victims, waded in deep, and even tried to swim after them. Some of the Prussians in the boat fired at their bobbing heads. The creatures' eyes focused only on their prey, but the rowing boat pulled away at a decent speed, giving them less and less chance of catching the group.

Soon, the remaining British soldiers threw rope ladders down from the side of the steamboat for the men to climb onto. The rowing boat was attached and hoisted up. Smoke rose from all quarters of the city, and thunderous bangs could be heard.

"Why are you here?" the Prussian captain asked pointedly.

"We are fleeing this invasion. The Austro–Hungarian Empire has fallen," said the Royal Engineer.

The Prussian looked at the men to gauge the truth in this statement. Major Richmond and Captain Hayward came over and were swiftly joined by Colonel Kiesl.

The major introduced himself and got a salute back.

"I'm the commanding officer here. We have come with the Austrian Engineers from a fort in the Carpathian Mountains. A war is happening all around us, and we must keep moving."

The Prussian captain swept his hair to the side. "I am Captain Müller." He stopped for a second before continuing.

"There have been reports of large movements of refugees coming from the Austro–Hungarian Empire. We sent an expeditionary force out two weeks ago, but they have not returned. I have been in charge of a small detachment covering the northern part of the city."

He went on to say that the other detachments were spread out. Their remit had been to wait for reinforcements from Ulm, but these forces never came. Then, small waves of drone soldiers started coming at them, testing their numbers.

"Then came the long limbs." Captain Müller's face showed his disbelief about what he was talking about. "Are we fighting the Devil?"

He continued to explain that this was all that was left of his detachment. His men looked battle-worn and a little shabby. They had beards and dirty uniforms. He explained that they would do what they could to help.

He suggested they raise the Prussian flag in case cannon batteries further up the river got a little jittery and opened fire on anything unfamiliar to them.

The steamboat moved rapidly away from the pursuing long limbs. The order was given to cease fire and save bullets, as the creatures were not going to reach the boat.

A Prussian soldier came forward and brought out a flag. An Austrian soldier received it; he was a little reluctant to place it on the boat's flagpole but realised they had no choice.

The officers spoke for a while about what they had been through. They were slowly moving out of the city's outskirts and further along the Danube. More soldiers had been seen moving around in the distance, but Captain Müller told them they should go to Straubing and see Brigadier Von Schwen. There was a castle in the mountains, and maybe he would be planning Prussia's defence strategy for this invasion from there.

Captain Müller spoke quite highly of this brigadier. He was well-educated and had a good command of the English language. Captain Hayward felt a little ashamed at the way others knew at least something of his language, while he only knew snippets of theirs. His French was improving, though, and regular visits to Paris helped.

The officers entered the boat's wheelhouse while the Prussian soldiers patrolled outside on the upper deck. It was suggested that they take this first river section after Passan until it was felt safe enough to swap groups. The weather was much warmer now, and it was recommended that the British Engineers take off their tunics when on the top deck. This would reveal their blue shirts and be less threatening to any forces camped along the river waiting for a target.

As the officers discussed recent events, they agreed to discuss them in further detail when they reached Straubing.

The Royal Engineers took this moment to rest and unwind from the tensions of passing through Passan. Their thoughts were mostly of their families back in England and their friends serving in the other units around the world.

Private Brown was allowed time to visit Heidi. She was assisting a wounded man when John met her. He watched her careful touch as she dressed a wound and how painstakingly observant she was of the soldier's welfare.

When she was finished, she spoke to the man for a short while and then took John off down a corridor into a storage room.

"Heidi, we must be careful. The rules have been laid down very strictly."

She smiled and kissed him.

"We're not going to make love here, John, but it does give me some time to talk to you alone."

She hugged him and kissed him again. The feeling of her body against his made John a little giddy. He wanted to tear her uniform off, but it was not the time or place. Rules were rules; this time, if he were caught, he would be in a whole world of trouble.

"I want to ask you something. It's quite a big thing, but just something I have to get out of my system."

John looked into Heidi's blue eyes. Her pupils were large and intense.

"You know you can ask me anything."

"Well, we're kind of courting now. I want to be with you, John. I will come to England with you if that is what you want."

There was a pause.

"I need to find my family, and I pray they're safe. Hopefully, they are in Prussia now with the other Austrians."

John nodded. "We can find them. There must be a large camp with many refugees in it. Maybe they can come to England."

He did not know what the setup would be for refugees in England or elsewhere. He had not really experienced anything like this before. The scale of destruction was massive. He tried not to let himself think too much about what lay ahead. They were not out of the thick of it yet and there could be more difficult moments further down the line. The couple hugged and kissed a little more before slowly returning to their duties.

The boat was cruising along at a steady speed now. The soldiers who had been working in the engine room were doing a sterling job. Captain Hayward and Major Richmond took time to go down there to thank them.

Captain Hayward was looking over maps and roads to the castle in Straubing. Corporal Heinz had a keen eye for a route and pointed to various possible shortcuts. Captain Müller spoke in German to Corporal Heinz. His voice had a sharp tone, and his words were followed by an index finger that traced over the map.

"Do not fret over the route to the castle. I know the route well," reassured Captain Müller.

"With all due respect, Captain, we like to check out all angles in case the route you have in mind has been compromised."

Captain Müller's face showed a look of half-acceptance, half-annoyance.

The evening came and allowed the Prussians to swap shifts. They were tired from the persistent fighting and were glad to rest. The cook had prepared a small meal, and the men gladly tucked into it.

The evening light was fading, but they kept on going as long as they could. The soldiers listened to the distant gunfire and cannons rumbling. The smell of war filled everyone's nostrils. The soldiers who were not veterans were coming to terms with fighting on this scale.

Days passed as they took their time heading towards Straubing. The new Prussian soldiers seemed to fit in well. At first, there was an air of hostility toward the Austrians, but it passed as stories were told about the new common enemy.

Major Richmond pulled Captain Hayward to one side.

"Will you go with the Prussian captain to the castle? I would like there to be a mixture of British, Austrians and Prussians at the meeting."

"Very well, sir. Corporal Heinz can help translate the more difficult German."

They both stood looking at each other for a moment.

"I know you're thinking the same as me. This is getting bigger by the day. We may play a key part in how it all unfolds. I would come to the meeting, but I know you are a better rider than me, and we cannot be stationary for too long."

Captain Hayward paused for a moment.

"Harry, they are moving at incredible speed. Do you think they have grand plans for Prussia, or is this just a warning for them not to get involved?"

Harry looked up.

"I'm not one hundred per cent sure to tell you the truth."

They stopped just outside Straubing. They had not encountered too many Prussians on the way. The villages and towns were deserted, reflecting the same pattern they had witnessed in Austria.

The boat was anchored, and a small group of men was selected for the four-day trip into the mountains. The horses had been in good health and had been allowed to exercise when the boat could moor.

Captains Hayward and Müller led the way. There were ten men: four Prussians, four Austrians, and two British Engineers.

Sergeant Butcher was selected to ride with the captains. He had good horseman skills, which would be useful if there was any trouble.

By the next morning, the horses were prepared for the journey. The major explained to them all that they could only wait four days at the maximum. With the enemy's rapid movement, they had no other choice.

The journey was expected to take around a day and a half. It did not give them much time to spend with the brigadier. The sun started peering through the clouds as they descended a farm track. Captain Müller was at the front with Captain Hayward. One of the Prussians was sent ahead with them to scout with Corporal Heinz.

They rode along at a steady speed, and the river soon disappeared behind them, giving way to a thick blanket of trees. The pines stood tall and firm. Sunlight poured down onto their needles but was prevented in places from penetrating below.

Wildlife was more abundant in Prussia than in the Austro–Hungarian Empire. With the onset of summer, nature was in full bloom. The meadows had an array of flowers and insects feeding on them. The colours were magnificent and gave a false air of calm.

Deserted cottages came and went. The odd farm had animals still wandering around in the fields, feeding away without a care in the world. The Prussian scout knew the route towards the castle and took them there as fast as he could. Captain Hayward had maps and a translated description of what had been happening over the past few months.

The idea was to pass on as much information as possible. They did not know how much Prussia knew of its aggressor. Captain Müller said the defence of South Prussia fell in Brigadier Von Schwen's hands. He was a prudent man. "He likes to assess the situation before jumping in."

Captain Hayward wanted to know what sort of army Prussia had at her disposal, but it was not something he thought he would get a response about. There had been a massing of forces since the relationship with the Austro–Hungarian Empire became strained. The main issue was the size of the enemy force, but this was not known. The virus that the flesh-eaters carried was a concern that was being kept close to the officer's chests for now. They wanted to understand more before causing a panic.

The plan was to inform the brigadier of what could possibly happen. They needed to know that the drone soldiers were dangerous, dead or alive. This was a substantial physiological weapon.

As they rode higher, the mountains' presence unleashed an overpowering feeling. They were spectacular, and their size and aura created a wonderful backdrop.

As they rode higher, the mountains' presence unleashed an awe-inspiring feeling. They were spectacular, and their size and aura created a wonderful backdrop.

Captain Hayward wanted to visit Lower Bavaria when this was over. He reached inside his tunic and pulled out a small photograph. The image of his family helped relax him, and their smiling faces lit up his heart and kept them close to his thoughts.

The group carried on through lunch and into late afternoon. There were no signs of the enemy or civilians. As they rode further and higher along the tracks, the pine forests became more extensive and the mountains more dominant.

Captain Müller stopped at a viewpoint and surveyed the landscape for movement. He could see dust clouds in the distant valley and small fires burning. He could not work out whether they were friends or foes. He reported this to the group and said they should be very wary when camping that night.

He was fascinated with the war waged against his country. Prussia was a strong nation; in his eyes, this was a formidable mistake by the would-be conquerors.

As night fell, they set up camp within a condensed thicket and started a small fire. They dug a hole in the ground and used stones piled up at the sides to help keep the light to a minimum.

Their food consisted of dried meat and freshly caught rabbits. The weather was relatively mild, although the mountain breeze was cooler than the air by the river. The food was greatly appreciated, and the horses were brushed down and tethered.

Captain Müller sat down with the men and started to eat. Three of the soldiers had been selected for the first watch. It would be a rotated role, with Captain Hayward and Sergeant Butcher volunteering for the night shift.

Captain Müller took a large bite of warm, cooked meat and licked his lips.

"You've had some fortune with the steamboat, would you not say?"

Corporal Heinz answered.

"Sometimes you need a little good fortune."

Captain Müller had not spoken much since being rescued and looked contemptuous as he spoke with Corporal Heinz.

"I guess, as an Austrian, it was easy to take something that was not yours."

The corporal looked slightly annoyed with this comment and was about to answer when Sergeant Butcher tried some basic German. It was something along the lines of, "The weather is good this time of year." He had not understood the tension in the German that was being spoken. Captain Hayward was picking up more and more of the language but still followed facial expressions better.

The Prussians and the Austrians looked at each other. The sergeant inevitably broke the tension, and he was answered with a simple "Ja."

The group carried on eating. The food was much appreciated, and soon, bowls were being readied for second portions. The clouds had come in while they sat and ate.

There was some light conversation before the group settled down to get some rest. The guards wandered around, trying hard to concentrate on the darkness and what was in it.

Captain Hayward felt the rain falling down. The gentle drops made a soft noise on his thick blanket. The group had moved a little to shelter under the larger trees, offering more rain protection. When the shift change came, he felt a little groggy. The soldiers were glad to climb under their blankets and get some well-earned rest. The first couple of hours passed without notice. Then, something caught the captain's eye. The horses were a little uneasy, enough for him to signal that to Sergeant Butcher.

Both men told the other guard, who was ordered to get closer to the sleeping men. Then, Sergeant Butcher followed his captain off in the darkness. At first, there was nothing; it was just a soft breeze with light rain. Their senses sharpened as twigs snapped to the side of them.

Moonlight broke intermittently through clouds, illuminating the darker woods. Their eyes adjusted slightly to the dark, and they were convinced they had seen something moving.

Charles lowered his hand down towards his bayonet. He then indicated to the sergeant to do the same. They both drew their bayonets and moved deeper into the wood. The sounds were stronger the closer they went in.

There, in the darkness, were three flesh-eaters feeding on a freshly killed deer. The guts and intestines were being ripped out and devoured with fearful speed. They were unaware of the two men creeping up on them, as the feast was the prize asset.

"Captain, how can they be here so soon?"

"I'm not sure, Sergeant, but we must do this as quietly as possible."

With the bayonets drawn, each man chose a target. It would then be a case of dash and kill. The third flesh-eater would be left for both of them to take.

The creatures did not hear the men dart forward and set on them like lions catching their prey on the Serengeti. The quick thrust and twist to the heads of the first two gave them the upper hand. The third took a while to react, content to eat at first. Then, eyes focusing on fresh meat, it moved out of its slumber. The plan was simple: let it come after one man whilst the other stabbed it from behind. This went exactly to plan. The creature focused on Sergeant Butcher and was unaware of Charles coming from behind it to stab it in the head.

Once the attack was over, they sat down, hearts pumping. They were disturbed that the flesh-eaters were already this far into Prussia. How quickly was this enemy force moving, and what was the level of the infection from the flesh-eaters?

They did not dwell there too long and silently returned to the group. The other guard was alert and looking a little edgy. The horses had calmed down and were now resting. The soldiers spoke to each other briefly and decided it was fine not to wake the group. There had been no more signs of creatures moving about; even if there were more, everyone still needed to rest.

The flesh-eaters were not particularly fast, but they did not seem to tire. The only real way to kill them was to destroy their brains.

The sergeant and Charles spoke briefly about what was causing them to come back to life. They could not understand why it had never been seen before and why they were not attacking the Priests. The drone soldiers were half infected, which made them less attractive to the flesh-eaters.

As they took leave of their shift and returned to their sleeping place, their thoughts lingered on being bitten or eaten whilst asleep—the new change of guard. They had been warned about the flesh-eaters and told to be prepared for more.

The rain had stopped in the night. The sun was out early, and the weather was already looking good. Breakfast was rustled up and devoured instantly.

They set off early and were making good progress by lunch. The castle was set amongst a sharp backdrop: steep banks of the mountain and rugged terrain surrounded this fearsome place. The walls were high, and the turrets were tall and thin. It was not the largest castle in the world, but it had a dominant feel to it.

The Prussians now led from the front of the group. A flag was flying from the keep, and movement on the battlements gave hope that it was still occupied. Captain Müller said it would be best for him to ride ahead with two of his men. He pointed out that if it was a trap, there was no point in all of them dying. His English was harsh and sharp like his German, but he had a fair point.

The other men dismounted. They did not draw out their rifles as this was not the time to raise suspicion. They hoped Brigadier Von Schwen was still residing in the fort; otherwise, this would have been a wasted journey.

One hour passed before Captain Müller returned with five more Prussians. They promptly told the others to follow them towards the castle. As they rode at speed, the actual size of the castle started to come into view. It did not seem that big from a distance, but the closer you got, the higher and stronger the walls became.

The drawbridge came down, and the gates opened. Two cannons were positioned almost directly in front of the gate, surrounded by a ring of sandbags. The castle was not teaming with life. A couple of soldiers were moving ammunition boxes around, but overall, it was quiet.

An old-looking man in a smart uniform was waiting for them at the top of the stone staircase. Captain Müller went straight to the bottom of the steps and dismounted. He then saluted the man. This was Brigadier Von Schwen. The rest of the group dismounted and saluted the brigadier. The non-German speakers were told they would have all the information translated to them.

The brigadier's uniform was pristine, with polished boots and brass buckles. He may have been an older man, possibly in his mid to late sixties, but he still looked strong. His eyes were inquisitive, and he searched for information from his guests.

Captain Hayward came forward and saluted the brigadier again. He then shook his hand.

The brigadier welcomed him in broken English. Then, a young Prussian soldier came forward to help translate. They were all led up the steps and into the dining quarters.

"The brigadier wishes you to have something to eat before you help us with information on this war that is now being waged," said the translator,

In front of them was a long table with a feast fit for a king. Several large cauldrons of soup, fresh bread and cheese, fruit, and wine were also on the menu. The men tucked into this smorgasbord with relish.

The brigadier let them eat for thirty minutes before returning to the dining quarters. He then spoke to Captain Müller and Captain Hayward. He suggested they both should follow him. They walked across the large dining hall and down several corridors. They then followed him up a winding turret staircase. It seemed to go on forever, and each man had to work hard to keep up with the brigadier.

At the top of the stairs was a well-furnished room with a roaring fire and tables covered in charts and paper. The view from the windows was jaw-dropping. After a few minutes, the young interpreter joined them.

The brigadier sat the three men around the fire and fetched more wine.

He spoke to the interpreter, who then translated.

"The brigadier would like to know how you have ended up in Prussia and what you know about this invading force."

A chair was pulled closer to the three men. The brigadier sat down and looked at Captain Hayward. The captain then began to tell them the story. He paused now and again to allow the interpreter to catch up. The brigadier's face moved with shock and revulsion at some of the things he was being told.

This conversation went on for half an hour. When they stopped, Charles was offered more wine. The interpreter told him that his information could be vital in the war with this new enemy. Reports had reached the brigadier about flesh-eaters in the hills and mountains around the castle. Their appearance in Southern Prussia played heavily on his mind.

Captain Hayward was told they had reached the castle just in time as they intended to join the main army in Munich shortly. The discussions rambled on for another hour. They were shown maps and possible future defensive points. The brigadier felt Prussia had an army that would equally match this aggressor and glanced at an old picture on the wall of Prussian soldiers fighting an epic battle. It was like a statement, something to give him comfort. He was proud to be a soldier and would probably die being one.

The men pondered over more battle plans and were only stopped by a hard knock on the door. A staff sergeant came into the room and saluted the brigadier. They spoke briefly, and the brigadier nodded. Captain Hayward got the gist of it and realised it was probably time to start heading back to the boat.

They shook hands and, left the warm inner quarters of the brigadier's world and made their way back down the steps.

Soon, the horses were being mounted, and the men were preparing to leave. The brigadier came over and spoke to Captain Müller with the interpreter by his side.

"Good luck to your band of warriors, and maybe we will meet for the greater good on the battlefield in the future."

With that, Charles saluted him one last time and turned the horse to leave. The gate was opened, and they rode out at speed. It had occurred to them to stay overnight, but it meant risking missing the boat should they hit trouble along the route home.

The sun was slowly going down, so they agreed to ride for an hour or so and then make camp. Their full bellies had restored some drive, which helped them press on.

The graveyard shifts were swapped. Noises could be heard in the distance as the woods no longer carried the usual night sounds.

They awoke early and left for the boat. Time was on their side as they rode at speed.

They pressed on into the following evening and came across the boat, still moored. The guards had initially demanded a password, which was "Fatherland" in Prussian. They were granted access to the boat once it was established that they were friends, not foes. The horses would be loaded on board in the morning, meaning several men would have to camp outside to protect them. The idea was passed around to leave them tied up unguarded, but they were just too precious for that.

Chapter 20

The next morning, the boat was brought closer to shallower waters and moored near the bank, allowing the horses to be winched in. It was a slow process but a worthy one.

As the boat Captain gave the order to move, the upper decks started to fill with soldiers and nurses taking in the scenery. It was hard at times for them to understand there was a war on, surrounded as they were by such beauty.

Charles spoke with the major about their brief meeting with Brigadier Von Schwen. They hoped their talk had convinced him to warn other parts of Prussia about what was coming. Flesh-eaters in the mountains were also mentioned. The major was concerned to hear this, as the movement and spread of the enemy were faster than first feared. They were joined by Colonel Kiesl and Captain Müller, who added their thoughts to the discussion.

"Could they have infected people and already sent them from Austria to Prussia?"

It was a decent question from Colonel Kiesl, to which Captain Müller responded:

"Prussia would have known about such an outbreak before you arrived on the scene. You are clutching at straws. Just because the Austro–Hungarian Empire could not cope—"

The major stopped him mid-sentence. He could see both men getting angry with each other and did not want to turn the boat into a mini battlefield between the Prussians and Austrians.

"Gentlemen, this cannot turn into a competition of who can piss the furthest. We are facing an enemy that has an army of walking dead. Creatures that no man has ever seen before! The picture is a lot darker than you can imagine. We must focus our energy on constructive solutions."

There was a look of disdain from both men, but they agreed to stop fighting.

Benedict set the course for Ulm and believed they could do it in several days, depending on unforeseen stoppages. The brigadier had ordered the Prussians to stay on board and see them out of Prussia.

The warm, sunny weather and idyllic countryside fooled the mind about what was happening around them. It helped them relax but carried a worry for Captain Hayward that if they let their guard down, it could prove fatal.

The plan was to get close to Ulm and then make their way to Stuttgart, which would require more horses, wagons, and carts. Captain Müller believed he could find these requirements and was confident of getting the soldiers and nurses from Stuttgart into France.

In the evenings, the boat moored as usual, and the inhabitants took their supper and prepared for sleep. There had been the odd moment of tension from being cooped up in the boat for so long. Austrians and Prussians were finding it the hardest. They had ill feelings towards each other that needed to be buried. The British Engineers made the difference between fighting breaking out.

Forests gave way to pastures, giving them greater visibility. They were not going to march into Ulm. The fact was that nothing was known of the enemy's whereabouts, but Captain Hayward hoped they would be far enough away to disembark from the boat.

This wish was shattered in the afternoon. A detachment of Northern riders were seen riding down a nearby road. Captain Müller pointed out that this was the road to Ulm.

With this sighting, the soldiers were put on alert. They were not sure if they had been spotted or not. The steamboat was cranked up a notch or two, as speed was going to play a key part in their escape.

Two hours later, a strong odour started to fill the air. It was rotten and touched the very taste buds in everyone's mouths. Then groans and snapping sounds could be heard. Nothing was there to see, just empty fields until the river made its way around a sharp bend. What fell upon everyone's eyes was hard to take in. Scattered across miles and miles of fields were bodies: soldiers, women, children. They were not alone. Flesh-eaters, possibly tens of thousands, were feeding like wild dogs.

They were tearing off flesh and innards. These half-human, half-dead creatures fought over the remains of Arms and legs. This army of flesh-eaters was too busy eating to notice the boat quietly pass them by.

No one could take their eyes off what was happening. Everyone was in shock.

Rumours quickly circulated that the dead were the inhabitants of Ulm and that it had already fallen.

One thing was clear: they would have to sail on for another day before disembarking. Panic was starting to bubble under the surface; even the veteran soldiers were now worrying about what they were up against.

Major Richmond ordered a staff meeting in the wheelhouse.

"Gentlemen, you have all seen the fields of the dead. Make no bones about it; this war is spreading faster than we can control."

Captain Müller looked still to be in shock. Seeing so much destruction and knowing that the dead were Prussian women and children almost broke him. He trembled with anger.

The other officers could see his anguish, giving him space to collect his thoughts. The river forked and bent around giving them plenty of opportunities to land. Benedict was confident he could find a small village with a port for them to get close to the bank.

"Major, how long do you think we have until the enemy knows how to stop us on water?" Captain Müller spoke with a blank look on his face.

The young officer had a point. The major looked up and paused briefly.

"My dear man, we must disembark before nightfall. We need to locate wagons and carts as soon as possible. That will mean finding a farm that still has livestock."

The Prussian captain looked up.

"Nothing will be left now – we're doomed!"

"You're in shock, man. Get him a stiff drink, and let's get planning," snarled Major Richmond.

The major might have felt the same as Captain Müller, but he was responsible for safeguarding his men and the people on this ship. Captain Hayward brought over a strong whisky for the captain. He knocked it back in one swift action. His second-in-command seemed to control his thoughts and nerves.

"I'm sorry for that outburst. I have never seen this sort of thing before. Those creatures – humans – are monsters, and they are killing my people."

Captain Hayward put his hand on the captain's shoulder.

"We have a fight on our hands for sure. They are driving deep into Europe. We do not understand their mission or how they have managed to change into these creatures or infect humans with that disease. We must stay strong, and find answers."

Within three hours, a village came into sight. It looked deserted, and there was no sign of life anywhere. It had a small dock, but big enough to moor the steamboat. Two detachments of soldiers on the top deck covered the banks on both sides. Nothing was taken for granted.

Once the boat was docked, they sent out a scout party. The Gatling gun surveyed the buildings that were in close proximity to them.

Corporal Heinz was sent with ten Austrian soldiers to check the village house by house. The sun was rising, and the heat warmed the air around them. The village was serene and typical of the others they had encountered. There was no damage anywhere, just a feeling of quick departure. There was still food in most of the houses and enough items that could be collected and used.

The real find came a few hours after the boat had been disembarked. Corporal Heinz took a horse and went out to a large country house on the outskirts of the village. He found what they needed: several wagons and carts were stored in a barn. The owners must have left in a hurry and could not take them all.

He took his time to move around the house and its corresponding farm. Next, he found some chickens, which he thought would be useful. They were wandering around carefree. He was about to turn and gallop back to report his good fortune when he saw another barn. The door was half open, catching his eye as he moved past it.

He brought the horse to a halt and looked into the darkness. Then he rode over to a post, tied the horse and pulled out his revolver. He kissed his crucifix, which hung around his neck, and slowly approached the entrance. The warm sun licked at his arms and head. He slowly shuffled forward, his body tense and ready to react to any sort of movement.

His feet were turned slightly outwards, something his mother had always commented on to his father. He thought about that as he walked into the murkiness of the barn. His eyes adjusted pretty quickly, allowing him a picture of what was in there.

To his surprise, seven to eight horses stood perfectly still. He couldn't understand why they had not escaped to their freedom. The door had been left open on purpose, yet they had returned to the barn.

They started to stir and become agitated. Corporal Heinz backed off, but they continued to move about in a panicked fashion. The deep, gravelly growl was enough to send the corporal stumbling backwards. The noise was not coming from within the barn—it was coming from outside.

He slowly worked his way to the open door. The light hurt his eyes briefly before he could focus on where he had tied his horse. It was still there, but it was becoming increasingly agitated. Coming in from the left was a long limb. Its eyes were transfixed on its next meal, and it was crouching as though getting ready to strike.

He knew that his shot had to be good. The long limbs were no easy kill, and this one was hungry for food. He raised his revolver as it moved forward. Each step he took left a mark in the dirt beneath his feet. The horse started to rear up and struggle to break free from the post it was tied to.

The long limb had not seen Corporal Heinz. He had the upper hand. He squeezed the trigger. The first shot landed in the creature's right shoulder. It recoiled with pain as the bullet embedded into its muscle.

With that, it changed its course immediately. The corporal let off another round and then another. Both these bullets hit the chest area of the long limb. It kept coming. Its eyes and mouth looked ferocious. He had to keep his nerve. The next shot was good; it landed plump between the creature's eyes. With that, the long limb fell forward and crashed to the ground, blood spurting from its head.

Corporal Heinz stood there motionless, his heart still thumping. He took a moment to regain his composure and then closed the barn door, re-saddled and left for the main group. He thought about the discovery of the horses and wagons and how they would be crucial to a quick retreat. For a split second, he thought about what he would have done if there had been two or more. His reaction was to acquire a sword as soon as possible.

On his journey back, he met a small detachment of riders coming towards him. It was Captain Müller and three Prussians.

"Are you okay, Heinz?" expressed a concerned Captain Müller.

A little shocked at their concern, he informed them of his find and the location. He explained the long limb and his worry that the gunshot may bring more to the area. Captain Müller echoed his sentiments, recommending they return and get the group moving.

As the men returned to the village, Captain Müller enquired in more detail about the corporal. He wanted to know how long he had been in the Austrian army and what family he had. The conversation was a surprise; he had not expected the Prussians to care about the Austrian plight, but now, of course, they were being sucked into their own full-scale war. After witnessing the mass flesh-eating army, it was time to put their differences aside.

It was another hour before enough transport could be found to take the food and supplies away from the boat. They towed a cannon behind a cart and mounted a Gatling gun on a wagon, which was then put at the back of the convoy.

Major Richmond thanked the corporal for his good work and the great livestock find. The cook thought about the chickens and planned to take several with them—he wanted fresh eggs to cook with. The boat was left docked. The men who had served in her engine room clapped as they disembarked. Benedict was also praised for his navigating skills.

The nurses moved the wounded and sick, although most could walk freely, and only a handful needed assistance. They then joined the injured on the carts and wagons. A selected few decided to walk for now.

The soldiers followed behind the wagons. There was a small collection of mounted cavalry to respond rapidly if needed. Captain Hayward rode at the front with Corporal Heinz. The corporal took them to the country house and farm as quickly as possible. The main group waited on a nearby track and prepared to move on. Everything was about swiftness.

They arrived at the country house farm with ten men. The first sight that greeted them was rats feeding on the dead long limb. The effect of carrion feeding on infected creatures was unknown. They knew the bite from a flesh-eater could infect you, but the other creatures they had encountered did not seem to carry the same danger.

Two guards were posted outside as the men rushed around, fetching the carts and wagons. Chickens were collected and put in wooden cages found in another barn. The horses, which had been sheltering in the large barn, were still there. They were agitated but rounded up and harnessed to a cart or doubled up on a wagon.

Once this was done, they made a beeline to the main group. Some of the men wanted to search the house for more items, but they were warned that a horde of flesh-eaters could be on their way and that this was not the time or place to start a battle.

The group was glad to see the men returning with food and more transport. The extra horses were welcomed. This meant they could rest soldiers en route to their next destination. The summer sun made it thirsty work, and freshwater was needed for both humans and animals.

They drank what they had conservatively. Barrels had been filled with water and bottles for each soldier. The idea was to stay on the outer rim of the villages and towns where they could. Most farms had wells or even freshwater streams they could drink from.

Flowers and long grass became familiar sights. Cows and sheep grazing still existed, which gave a false picture of this whole war. The lack of people, however, was a key indicator that something was amiss.

"This is an adversary of great distinction," Captain Müller said whilst lost in his thoughts.

Captain Hayward looked over at him.

"They are not here just to conquer. I pray to God we can stop this disease that is spreading from Russia."

The day was long and arduous. They stopped where they could and rested if the weather allowed it. The boat had given them a safer environment, and sleeping in the evening was not quite the same as it was on the water.

They were not going into Ulm. Cities had proved to be dangerous unless you could confirm that allied forces definitely controlled them.

The next couple of days were spent travelling and resting. No enemy was sighted, just roaming livestock and wildlife. However, meat was put on the menu, which was greatly appreciated.

Stuttgart was their next destination. Spirits were high, and bellies were full. Songs broke out as they travelled along. The Prussians were talking about fighting with their countrymen as soon as they could. The Austrians knew what it was like to retreat from the enemy but had an inner desire to fight back. They wanted to find out where the refugees were heading. Brigadier Von Schwen had spoken about refugees escaping to other countries. Prussia was a neighbour and would be a natural route by which to leave the Austro–Hungarian Empire.

With night falling, it was time to set up camp. An old, disused farm was perfect. The barns offered some shelter, and there was a stone wall to use as a defence should they need it.

Chapter 21

Lightning struck a tree, and flames lit up the night sky. Groans and mumblings wafted in the night air. Light rain fell from the heavens against a backdrop of clouds clapping together. The mood was tense amongst the drone soldiers. The high priest had gathered his generals and given orders on his plans.

"The Prussians are putting up a strong fight. They could have bided more time if they had let the Austrians fight with them. Their hatred of each other is such a good element for us. I want more drone soldiers, more flesh-eaters, more Northern riders. This war has just started; heads must roll before I am seen as the supreme ruler."

"My lord, your queen has arrived with fresh wolves. She has brought more razor-tooths and bears."

The high priest's smile lit up his face. "Where is Lev? My brother was meant to have taken South Bavaria by now."

The smile disappeared as he watched a group of prisoners being marched past, their faces white and down-beaten. The high priest Nazar asked for a rifle, took aim and shot a man through the head. Fellow prisoners went to help him, and a second man was then shot in the shoulder. He lay there in agony, his hand raised. The other prisoners could only turn their heads, their faces carrying the anguish of the man's pain and the utter feeling of defeat.

He did not lie there for long as two drone guards came and dragged him away from the walking prisoners. The high priest nodded, and six flesh-eaters were led over to the man. His eyes focused on these half-human, half-monsters slowly staggering towards him. Their mouths were open, and groaning and whining sounds resounded out.

The screams could be heard all around the surrounding area as flesh was ripped from the living man's body. The feeding frenzy was a reminder to those who wanted to rise up and fight back against this champion of evil.

A drone general came forward.

"General Georgiy, my favourite general. Tell me, I hear that British Engineers have made their way through the Austro–Hungarian Empire and are now working their way through Prussia. Is this true?"

"Er, I have heard these rumours too, sire."

Nazar leaned forward and slowly drew his sword.

"What of Benedict?"

The general lowered his head.

"He escaped from the abbey. They were last reported going down the Danube."

"Mmmmm... How does the sickness feel, Georgiy? It must be nearly time for you to drink from the blessed water, is it not? Or join the others…"

His finger pointed to the walking army of flesh-eaters.

"Double your efforts. Bring me, Benedict, before they discover his true value in this war."

The rain started to fall more heavily, and lightning lit up the sky around them. The landscape was now covered in hundreds of thousands, if not millions, of marching figures.

Chapter 22

"Major, we must remember not to get too close to Stuttgart; the cities are dangerous now."

"Charles, we must get close enough to ensure we do not miss a chance to get help from a major force. We number barely over two hundred men and women. We are sitting ducks out here in the hills and mountains."

Captain Hayward nodded, but his body language, for once, did not agree with his superior officer. He felt that there had been too many sightings of the enemy in this area, and if anything, Stuttgart would be next on the list for them to take.

The convoy was moving at a steady pace. Soldiers had swapped with others from the wagons to rest their weary legs.

Captain Müller was speaking to Colonel Kiesl. Although they were from opposing nations, they still found it interesting to discuss tactics. The Austrians liked the rifles the Prussians had and wished that the Austro–Hungarian Empire had invested in more breech-loaders before they were invaded.

Both men remarked on this sudden outbreak of war and how interesting it was that no one saw such a large army being built up. Russia was thought to be behind it at first, but they commented on the lack of flags bearing their emblem. If Russia had fallen, why did news not reach the rest of Europe quicker?

They agreed that limited information had been passed around for several months since this invasion started. Captain Müller spoke honestly about Prussia.

"There has to be a new headquarters leading a counter-offence. Prussia is too big for us not to crush the enemy that dares take our land."

Colonel Kiesl gave a sympathetic nod.

"Very true, you have a wonderful army. One that Europe has been afraid of for some time. But Russia and Austria also had large armies, and we have seen nothing but destruction."

"Dear man, do you think Prussia has already fallen to these foes? Think again; we are too powerful for that. Yes, they may be heavily involved in the south of Prussia, but our generals will have a plan, and I intend to join the force that crushes them."

Colonel Kiesl said no more and chose to ride on, leaving the Prussian to think about what lay ahead.

The track became more expansive as they approached a few copses on either side of it. As they moved towards a rising hill, there was a slight gradient. It was hoped they would see the outer city limits of Stuttgart from there.

Everyone's main concern was food. It had been many hours since they last ate, and their stomachs were rumbling.

A scout rode ahead to see the lay of the land. Spontaneous songs broke out as news spread of a short rest with a good meal.

This happiness was short-lived. As they reached the brow of the hill, a gunshot rang out. The scout who was riding ahead fell from his horse. Multiple gunshots followed. A nurse was hit in the neck, spraying blood onto the track. She was quickly pulled around, and pressure was placed on her wound.

Two more soldiers collapsed with wounds to the torso and legs. The Bugler blew for the call to arms, and the men rushed to take cover. The nurses were helped down from the wagons and carts whilst under fire.

It was too early to determine where the main focus of the fire was coming from. The Gatling gun could not be used as the range and whereabouts of the shooters were still unknown. The cannon was released from behind the wagon and wheeled into place. Shells were brought close, preparing it for action.

"Get me a line on the enemy fire," ordered Captain Hayward.

He had dismounted and was frantically searching for the drone soldiers. Then, to the side of a small hut, he saw movement. It was maybe four or five men moving around. He could see more arriving from the side and some larger figures galloping towards them in the distance. His heart missed a beat as his initial reaction was: Northern riders. They were in better cover now as the men and women moved into the copse on either side of the track.

If it were a brigade of Northern riders, they would have a fight on their hands. He quickly located Major Richmond, who had Colonel Kiesl and Captain Müller in close attention.

"Should we try and double back and leave some men to cover our retreat?" questioned Captain Müller.

The major was scanning the horizon with his binoculars.

"That may well be a good idea," commented the major.

Captain Hayward arrived with an update. Bullets were hitting the trees and dirt track around them.

There was a terrific explosion as the hut was blown to pieces. The band of Northern riders, which was cutting across a field, came under fire, causing them to change direction. A charge of Prussian Lancers then met this. The officers and soldiers who had binoculars eagerly watched from the hill.

"By golly, we've actually found some friendly forces." The major was excited to see this unfold.

Captain Müller nodded.

"They're the... Lancers. Just in the nick of time."

The Northern riders struggled to deal with the attack. Although they were influential on horseback and foot, they could not match the Lancers.

The gunfire slowly relaxed as the enemy rapidly retreated and was forced back by the Prussian cavalry.

On top of the hill, the wounded were being treated. Soldiers had retrieved the injured scout and loaded him onto a wagon. The nurse with the neck wound was in a bad way. She had suffered massive blood loss and was fading fast. The others were being seen to by the army surgeon.

The captains scanned the hedgerows and fields for further movement. Coming up the track was a small group of mounted soldiers. Captain Müller quickly pointed out that these were not enemy soldiers and the order should be given not to fire. He got up and took a Prussian soldier with him as he moved cautiously along the track.

The Lancers were rapidly arriving to join them at the top of the hill. Major Richmond came forward and thanked them in his best German. Then, through a translator, he was informed that this was a brief window of opportunity and that they should move quickly to get past Stuttgart.

He even went on to say that refugees were pushing into France and that Prussia was retreating on all fronts. This news was not taken well by Captain Müller; the sheer idea of his country retreating was unthinkable.

In his eyes, they were formidable and mighty, and it would take a force of gigantic proportions to beat them. He saw the enemy as weak and inferior, to be outthought and outmanoeuvred.

He was left to his thoughts as the wounded were loaded onto the carts. The nurse passed away. She was a fond member of the tight Austrian medical group, and the strain and stress were starting to show. Tears began to flow as they wrapped her body in an oat sack. There was no time to bury her now; she would have to be transported and buried at a more convenient time.

The wagons started to roll, and soon they were passing the smoking hut and dead drone soldiers; close by were pockets of fallen Northern riders who had also been killed in the attack.

The Lancer escort could not stay that long, as they explained they had to move and rejoin their main unit. They thanked the Lancers for helping and told them they would be more than welcome to continue with their group. Major Richmond wanted numbers and firepower as they swept through Prussia.

The road they were now on was clear. The fighting could be heard to the east as they moved along. No one was singing anymore; the mood was bleak.

A small trail of blood dripped from the cart carrying the dead nurse. Private Brown looked on with a heavy heart as each droplet landed effortlessly on the track, lost amongst the traffic of hooves and marching boots.

They could smell the burning buildings as they made their way along the road. It was late in the afternoon, and scouts were sent ahead to find a place to rest for the evening. The dark clouds in the distance were black smoke rising from the burning city. Strasburg had been their intended destination, but they kept to the rule of not entering a major city unless they thought it was safe.

The Prussians in the convoy had made it clear they would join the next main regiment that came their way. They wanted to fight back now as they felt the group was nearing the Prussian–French border.

The mountains around Ulm were imperious in size and had taken a lot of energy out of the group as they made their way to Stuttgart. With Stuttgart now crossed off the list of cities under Allied command, it was all about the dash to the border. The news from the other Prussians that the country was collapsing was demoralising and disturbing.

The atmosphere improved a little, with the gunfire slowly dispersing in the mountains and hills. Tiredness crept into the men's legs. The sheer distance was sometimes overwhelming, even with the scheduled breaks and changing over of passengers on the wagons and carts. Captain Hayward had dismounted his horse and offered it to several weary men along the route. This gesture was carried out by all the officers. The major even did his share. This was taken well by the men, as they believed in those who led them.

With darkness approaching, they found a suitable place to rest and set up camp. Wagons were arranged in a circle, and the carts were used to fill in the gaps. Guards were set in groups because of the recent engagement with the enemy, which could mean more people were searching around in that area. They also took time to bury the fallen nurse, which was a poignant moment for this group. Many of them stood in silence and tried to understand what was happening around them. Colonel Kiesl said a few words in German before they dispersed to carry out their tasks.

Private John Brown met up with Heidi afterwards, and they spent time gathering wood for the fire pits, stopping occasionally to kiss and cuddle. Both of them expressed their sorrow at the nurse dying and how thin the line was between life and death. John did not want to think about the consequences should his new-found love be injured or even killed.

Chapter 23

Rain was falling, not hard, just consistently, making the road muddy and waterlogged. Trees soaked up water, and ferns gave off a sweet smell as the water touched their stems.

Standing to the side of the road was a small boy. He was sobbing uncontrollably. Even a snorting sound behind him failed to break his lonely stance.

A white horse pulled up alongside him. The boy's soft brown hair was wet as the rain mixed with tears rolled down his face. He was not scared when this towering figure blacked out the light around him. The sharp blue uniform with a white strap across the chest and white helmet stood out. The boy just pointed down the road to an overturned cart.

The lancer leaned down and collected the young lad in one quick swoop. He gripped him tight as they embraced each other. He then rode over to a red horse chestnut tree by the side of the road and placed the young boy on a fork in the trunk.

"Climb the tree, Jack."

"Yes, Father."

The lancer turned to face the overturned cart. His horse reared a little as its senses picked up danger, and his hand tightened on his lance. Slowly, he urged the horse on, the rain still falling slowly, giving rise to a damp smell. The cart had been violently hit and knocked over. The driver had been ripped in half, and all that was left were his legs, still caught up in the seat.

Then, the first image came into sight: a group of flesh-eaters were feeding over a small girl's body. Her legs were on show, and her white dress was now another colour. The strands of blonde hair that remained were scattered around the feeding group.

There was a razor-tooth sitting close to a tree. Its colossal frame pawed at several dead bodies, guarding its food with intense ferocity.

Further up a small bank was a large man dressed in black priest clothes. He was pressed on top of a badly injured woman. She was still trying to push him off, although her life was slipping away from her. The man was kissing her and raping her defenceless body.

None of them had seen the lancer. He stopped for a second, and a tear ran down his cheek. This was to be his last for now as rage started to engulf his body. He took out his knife and cut his arm. This renewed his concentration. With that, he lowered his lance and began a full charge at the razor-tooth. It was too busy eating to notice the lancer approaching it at full speed. When its eyes caught the glimmer of light reflecting off the metal spear, it was too late. With deadly precision, the lance was thrust into the animal, rupturing organs and piercing its heart. The beast gave out an almighty screech as it keeled to one side. Breathing heavily, it tried to roll over, but the wound was fatal. The lancer leaned forward as the creature drew its last breath, making sure the animal saw his eyes as he took his sword and cut the beast's throat.

This commotion had stirred the flesh-eaters. Two of them started moving from the girl and going over to the lancer. He withdrew his lance and sheathed his sword. Dismounting from his horse, which stood by the dead razor-tooth, he started walking towards them. The first flesh-eater quickened its step. It could not run but sensed fresh meat. The blow that came down on its head sent it tumbling to the ground. The lance was then jabbed through its skull.

The other flesh-eater kept on coming. The three behind him had also left the body and were moving slowly towards their foe. The lancer controlled his anger well and kept a cool head as he struck the lance into the left kneecap of the flesh-eater nearest to him.

He then brought the pole around and knocked it down. The creature tried to stand but was instantly knocked down with a kick to the head and was then decapitated with a rough cutting action from his knife.

The other three flesh-eaters were now in range. With his lance, he struck one in the head, bursting the spear through its face, then, quickly withdrawing it, he brought the pole around and knocked the legs of the other two away. Whilst they struggled to get up, he finished them off, bringing the lance up and down on both of them, paying meticulous attention to their heads.

He turned around to see that the priest had risen from the woman he was attacking – the Lancer's wife. He was a large, muscular man with a strap across his chest and a sword attached to his belt. He had a fresh scratch down the side of his face. His eyes fixed on the lancer; he began to clap and gesticulate as if he were enjoying the performance. The lancer stared motionlessly back.

The priest wiped his mouth and glanced over at the dying woman. His eyes then focused on the lancer again. It was then that a shred of fear crept over him. He would not just be fighting a soldier; he was now fighting the husband of the dying woman and the father of the dead child.

Sensing the moment, he drew his sword, picked up an axe from the ground and came at the lancer. He moved quickly for a man of his size and used the bank he was on to gain speed to plummet down on his victim. The lancer stood still and waited. Three hundred yards, two hundred yards, one hundred yards. The priest let out a war cry as he prepared to slash the soldier in front of him. To his amazement, the lancer lowered his lance. The priest was closing in and did not really know what to think. He wanted to make this a quick kill and return to his unit.

The lancer calculated the distance and let the pole hit the ground. He then swept his right hand to his side and drew his revolver. He was fast and took aim within a fraction of a second of the gun being drawn. His finger squeezed the trigger, and the round burst out of the chamber and nestled into the charging man's stomach.

The priest kept on running for a moment or two before falling to the ground. He dropped his axe and sword and clutched both hands to his stomach. The pain was spread across his face. The light around him went dark, and he looked up with desperation at his executioner.

The lancer took off his white gloves and tucked them into his belt. He then knelt down to maintain eye contact with the priest.

"You will pay for your sins here today."

The priest tried to shake his head.

"Show me mercy, I beg you."

No sooner had he let those words slip out than he received a kick in the stomach. Then he felt a sharp pain in his left, then right shin. The lancer ensured he could not walk again by piercing flesh and bone with his sword. He then grabbed the man by the hair and dragged him over to a large rock. His head was placed on the stone. The priest tried to move, but the pain stopped his body from shifting.

The lancer went over and picked up the priest's axe. He slammed the butt of the axe into the priest's head, not killing him but leaving him stunned. Whilst he took a moment to come round, the lancer used the axe in quick succession to take off both the man's arms.

He looked at the lancer. His eyes were full of desperation and pain. With one fell swoop, the lancer took his head off. He stood there for a moment or two afterwards, breathing heavily.

He then turned and ran over to his dying wife and held her in his arms. She was fatally wounded and struggled to talk. Tears ran down her cheeks as she looked into her husband's eyes.

"Look after the children; look after them, my love."

Her voice was weak as he pressed his face next to hers. He would never tell her that there was only Jack left. She took a deep breath in and passed away.

Shock hit him. He held his wife and cried, and for the next few minutes, he was lost as he gripped her body tightly. The pain was too much.

He had to refocus. He knew Jack was still waiting up a tree. He carefully laid down his wife and fetched his horse. He then went and retrieved his son and placed him by the cart. He told Jack not to look over at the creatures. Jack knew his sister was dead but did not know his mother had passed away as well.

The lancer found a small shovel in the cart and began digging a shallow grave. Holding back the screams within himself, he carried his daughter to the hole and gently placed her down. Then, he brought his wife and placed her alongside his daughter.

He called Jack over to him. The lad could hardly walk and fell to his knees on seeing his mother's face. The shock of losing his sister and mother was almost too much. The lancer wanted him to say his goodbyes the best he could before he buried them. The lad lay on the ground shaking as his father bent down and hugged him.

"Jack, we do not have much time, my beautiful boy."

He picked his son up and held him tight. Both of them began to cry, which helped to release pressure. Five minutes passed, and Jack whispered that he wanted to kiss his mother one last time. He knelt down beside her and kissed her on the forehead. He also kissed his sister's hand. He then went and stood by a tree and told his father to do what he had to do.

The lancer buried them and made a makeshift cross. He went over to Jack and hugged him again.

They collected the horse and saddled it up, then, with a slight kick to its side, started off down the road, leaving the carnage behind them.

Chapter 24

The morning broke, and Captain Hayward went to wash his face in a small stream. A kingfisher landed on a branch hanging over the cold running water. He watched this elegant bird, its bright plumage and sharp pose. Then, the bird darted off briefly, returning with a small fish.

Captain Hayward smiled, something he felt conscious of doing. He then got up and walked back through a small woodland to the rest of the group. They had been resting from the arduous journey and were quite settled where they were. The officers looked over the maps and picked at each other's route plans.

The major did not allow much more time to rest or discuss routes. It was time to push on and get moving. The wagons and carts rolled into action. The horses had proved invaluable and had probably meant the difference between life and death.

Scouts pushed ahead to be the convoy's eyes and ears. Mountainous terrain was proving hard work for all of them. The weather had been fine for an extended period of time but was now starting to become more wet and stormy. This made walking on the small tracks and roads harder. The waterlogged routes cut up easily, causing mud to stick to their feet, which meant changing their direction often to find a different, more accessible route.

Two days followed of hard rain and thundery weather. They were grateful for the lack of enemy sightings and the small mercy of having enough food and water in their bellies. Morale was low. Sores were starting to be a problem for most of the soldiers who marched alongside the wagons and carts.

The medical staff had ointments and various herbal remedies, which helped, but the primary need was for a sustained rest. They guessed they were three to four days away from Strasbourg, which was playing on the major's mind. He felt they were so close that a rest would be suicidal.

The decision was taken from them when a fever broke out amongst the British Engineers. It spread rapidly over the next day, and it meant they needed to find shelter from the conditions and get the main party healthy again.

The scouts had located many places along the route and informed the officers of such farms or stately homes. Villages, towns and anything more significant were considered too risky as enemy forces would target those places first. What had come up was a large manor house several miles from their current position. With sickness spreading amongst the soldiers, it was decided that this would be the best place to rest. It had a good farm wall enclosing the main house and some barns and other outbuildings where they could rest.

The major toyed with the idea of pressing ahead with the fit and able, leaving a detachment with the sick and wounded. He let the idea float through his brain, but when he suggested it to Captain Hayward, he was reminded they had come too far to split the group. Numbers had counted for a lot in this war so far.

As usual, a small reconnaissance party searched the building. Nothing could be found in the grounds or the manor house. This was ideal. It had enough rooms and space to sleep everyone. The horses could be rested and bedded in the stables. The major pushed for two days' rest at the most, but some thought this could be closer to a week.

The army surgeons and doctors expressed their gratitude to the scouts for finding a place to shelter them from the elements.

Securing the surrounding area was quickly mentioned. The appearance of the buildings lifted the current mood.

Sleeping rough had been fine when the weather was good, but it was more demanding on the non-military people during this rainy period. The soldiers were expected to tough it out, but this break was needed, with the fever spreading throughout the group.

The wagons were used to block gaps where the walls did not offer cover. A six-foot wall surrounded most of the house. The courtyard was also walled, but it had a large entrance that was no longer gated.

The manor house was quite lavish inside. The rooms were divided out, and the nurses were allocated to the top floor of the house. Some of the soldiers were moved to the barns and other outbuildings. The quartermaster went to work, dishing out the chores straight away. Clothes needed to be washed and weapons cleaned. The house was searched again, but only the cellar was left untouched. It was a large property with a Georgian feel about it. The décor was exquisite, and it must have been heart-wrenching for the owners to leave. Some plinths were empty, which suggested that statues could have been taken. The truth was that anyone who had been chased by the enemy and their army of darkness would soon realise the actual value of the possessions they undertook to save.

A small squad of British Engineers was assembled to check the cellar. They were given lanterns and candles to find their way around. The cook wanted to know if there was wine in the cellars as he was starting to prepare a feast for the group. He had a small team of helpers, mainly those who liked cooking and wanted to get out of other duties. They had not always run a central kitchen. More often than not, it was split into small groups, and they would then cater for themselves. The cook would oversee the food supply but liked to get everyone involved when he could.

The twelve men entered the cellar through a long, winding staircase in the main hall. They would have sent fewer men in normal circumstances, but twelve felt suitable for a dark place with so many interconnecting passageways.

The cellar was dry and smelled of dried fruits. It was quite a strong smell but not overpowering. They found several barrels of wine, which was a pleasant surprise. There were many other treasures down there, and it would take another day to search the whole area properly.

As the men left the small, cold room which housed the barrels, one of them thought they heard something. "It's a rat!" barked an older veteran. The noise was louder the second time, making all the men stop.

Each soldier started to feel the familiar anxiety creep over them. The passageways were narrow, and it was a maze underground. "Is anyone there?' The same veteran took control, raising his lantern as he tried to make out if he could see anything.

Something shuffled across an opening and moved back into the darkness.

"Look, lads, it's time to move out of here. There are plenty of supplies, but it's too risky. We will have to tell the captain and see what he thinks."

As the veteran finished his sentence, a voice called out.

"Help me. I'm scared, and I need help..."

The voice was English with a German accent. The men had their rifles pointing at every opening now. The slightest movement could have caused a hail of bullets to rain down on the unfortunate victim.

"Come out and show yourself. Make sure you do it slowly, though, as we don't want any accidents to happen," said the Veteran.

"All right."

A silhouette started to emerge to the right of where they were standing. Its frame was small, and its posture a little awkward.

"We'll put a lantern down and then expect you to walk next to the light," the Veteran said cautiously.

There was no verbal response, but the figure did move next to the light. Now, the soldiers could see the outline more clearly. It looked like a priest of some sort. His head was lowered to one side so they could not see his face.

"Come forward more so we can see your face," the Veteran was clear and to the point.

The figure did not move.

"Benedict, where is Benedict?" The voice was gravelly and had a slight rasp.

They noticed something strange about the figure's hands. It had extra-long fingers and sharp nails. It was breathing heavily and letting out hissing sounds.

"Benedict? The boy from the abbey?

"Yesss."

The veteran raised his rifle.

"You'll never get the boy. Arthur, take Thatcher and tell the others they're after Benedict."

The veteran pushed the men behind him.

The figure raised its head. It looked human, but when it smiled, its teeth were long and jagged. Its eyes were dark and wide, its nostrils flared, and its tongue came out to an unnatural length.

"We'll see about that." It licked its lips and smiled in an eerily overconfident way.

"Time to meet with God." The veteran raised his rifle and squeezed the trigger, hitting the figure in the stomach and forcing it back. This unleashed hell.

Flesh-eaters started to appear from the passageway, coming at the group from all angles. The veteran told them to pick their shots and use their bayonets where they could. "Keep a close formation as we fall back."

A soldier let out a cry as teeth sank into his arm. He spun the flesh-eater around and head-butted it in the face. Falling into the dark was a mistake as they fell on him like piranhas scenting blood. His shouts and cries were quickly muffled as he was devoured.

Arthur and Thatcher broke off from the main group and pushed their way towards what they hoped was the exit. Puzzled by the number of different routes, they moved as fast as they could, with Arthur holding his arm out with the lantern hanging from it. It only gave them a short view in front of them, but after a few wrong turns, they managed to find a staircase. Without thinking twice about where it would lead, they rushed up it, and both of them were surprised to come out in the courtyard.

The scenes that greeted them were ones of chaos, as the whole place was fighting a battle for survival.

In the cellars, the fighting was intense. The lanterns were being knocked over, and the lack of light made fighting in the dark nearly impossible.

The veteran still had three soldiers with him. His sheer size and strength were keeping them alive. They had made their way to a staircase leading to the hallway. Gunshots could still be heard in the chambers below, and they tried in vain to call out to the missing men.

A voice came out of the darkness. It carried the same rasp in its tone and an air of menace.

"Where's the boy?"

The priest moved past a lantern. He was on all fours and moved more like an animal than a human.

One soldier charged the priest with his rifle and bayonet attached. The bayonet went into the priest's body. His eyes changed colour just before it bit into its victim. His body then began to shake violently, almost as if he were having a fit. The soldier stood back in astonishment and wondered what was happening.

The priest then stopped moving. "Is it dead?" came a call from behind him.

"I think so," said a private nearest to the body.

Then it started to move again. The flesh around the stomach and chest began to bubble. An extra piece of flesh started to rise from the bubbling skin. This flesh then changed shape to form two arms. They were longer and thinner than the priest's other two, but the claws on the hands were just as sharp.

"Kill it!"

The young soldier stabbed at the developing limbs and tried to make an impact on the whole body.

As he jabbed and worked the bayonet, a flesh-eater emerged from the darkness and sank his teeth into the soldier's shoulder. He yelped in pain and fell back. The priest had now got to his feet, mouth open and teeth on full show.

This thing let out a snarl and attacked the injured soldier on the floor, knocking the flesh-eater to the side. It was like a ferocious lion, biting and tearing with consummate ease. The poor soldier did not stand a chance as he tried in vain to fight off his attacker.

His fellow comrades began shooting the creatures back but to little effect. The darkness was making it hard to make a decent shot. The flesh-eaters were also pushing them further and further away, so they had to retreat up the staircase.

Outside in the bright sunlight, the fight was in full swing. Thatcher and Arthur were shooting and reloading as they moved. They were taken aback by the sheer number of flesh-eaters and the fact that they had arrived from nowhere so quickly.

"We must find the major or Captain Hayward," Arthur shouted.

Thatcher nodded and slammed another bullet in the breech, pulling the lever to cock the rifle, then pushing it back and taking aim. Boom! A flesh-eater fell to the ground. It was a clean headshot. The British Engineers would not go down without a fight.

Both soldiers fought their way through the courtyard, helping other soldiers as they went. Some men had formed small lines and were laying down volley fire to increase firepower by sheer numbers.

The Gatling gun crew had been pushed back, which meant the heavy weapon was out of use. Thatcher looked in its direction.

"We can do it."

"No, we have to relay the message first."

Both men stood still for a moment. Fighting was happening all around them. Even though they had seen many flesh-eaters before, the shock always crept in. Some looked like recent victims; others were more decayed. They all shared one common goal: living flesh. They hungered for it, and it drove them to wander the land in search of it.

"It's too risky. If we fail to relay this message and die, it could have massive consequences on the war."

Thatcher nodded. He realised they had to find the major or captain and pass on the information. With that, they started to fight their way through the sprawling mass of bodies, using their bayonets and rifle butts to clear a path to the house. As they moved along, several soldiers joined them to swell their numbers. The shouts and cries of Prussians and Austrians could be heard around the manor house. The British were spread out, "Doing the Empire proud," as Sergeant Butcher declared.

The two men made it inside the house with some help from the other soldiers. Major Richmond was located via a corporal who directed the privates up the stairs. The gunfire was sporadic, and ammunition was distributed accordingly.

They both went up the stairs to find the major, but he had moved, and the soldiers shooting out of the window did not know where he had gone.

Captain Hayward was fighting alongside several soldiers and nurses at the rear of the house. The ammunition was not close to hand, so it developed into hand-to-hand combat. The flesh-eaters were more dangerous as a group, so being surrounded by them decreased your chances dramatically.

The men had discussed this scenario many times during their long, arduous march to safety. If the worst happened, they would use their last bit of energy to break through the ranks and get back to a fixed object. Of course, this was not always possible.

"We need to get more bullets," Captain Hayward cried out.

The captain was covered in sweat and blood. The carnage was everywhere, and at that moment in time, they were not able to stem the flow of flesh-eaters. The sudden surprise attack had raised questions, and the volume of the enemy this far down was considerably worrying.

Major Richmond was in the house but was now on the lower floor. He had secured the building the best he could, but there was also the small matter of the cellar. Drone soldiers had been spotted around the building and in the cellar. They assisted in the attack by opening doors, gates, and anything the flesh-eaters could not negotiate. They had not engaged directly in combat, which the officers believed indicated there were not many of them. The main body of attack was from the flesh-eaters.

The major had managed to get some sharpshooters on top of the manor house. They were having a devastating effect on the oncoming enemy. The Allied casualties had been kept to a minimum by close ranks and covering each other's backs.

The Prussians were doing a sterling job at guarding the barns. They had carried several cases of ammunition and were laying down heavy fire. They were the first to see light at the end of the tunnel. The shuffling army was starting to lose numbers. This sudden mass attack did not have reinforcements and offered them a chance to gain the upper hand.

A Prussian soldier was sent to climb the outer manor wall and get word that the remaining flesh-eaters were the last on the horizon.

This soldier was nimble as he pushed and barged his way through the beasts to the wall. His fellow soldiers helped pick off some of the creatures that started to track him. Once on the wall, he made his way to the courtyard. He could see that the fighting was still intense and that the lack of ammunition made it more difficult.

He shouted in German about the enemy's numbers starting to wane. This was not picked up at first. Then, an Austrian acknowledged the information and helped spread the news. This was translated for the British soldiers who had formed a line and were advancing, bayoneting everything they could. It was a formidable line led by Captain Hayward. He was taking full control, and this war was now bringing out the soldier in him.

"You've heard the news, men. Keep driving forward. We can win this battle," was the captain's battle cry.

The men rallied around his orders, with rifles and bayonets becoming devastating weapons. Major Richmond was now in complete control in the house and was sending more men into the cellar. The priest had come out into the courtyard and had grown in height and mass. He was snarling and spitting. His extra arms made him look more threatening, and his movement was erratic. The soldiers tried to get a clean shot on his head, but he darted from one side to the other. Coming out of the cellar with him were six drone soldiers carrying grenades and rifles.

They threw the grenades at any groups of European soldiers grouped together. As the men took cover, they began opening fire. The initial explosions killed four men and injured three more.

Ammunition was brought forward to the Gatling gun. This was then loaded by the returning crew and swung into action. The deadly force of the weapon was instant, cutting through the walking flesh-eaters trying to come into the courtyard.

The Gatling gun cut them to pieces, ripping through bodies with ease. They then spun it around to face inside the courtyard, but the mixture of British soldiers and flesh-eaters meant that the risk of using it was too high.

Arthur and Thatcher reached Major Richmond just as a call went out from the courtyard that the priest was heading to the house.

"Sir, they're after Benedict."

Major Richmond looked puzzled.

"The boy from the abbey?"

Thatcher came further forward.

"We don't know why, but the priest is coming, and they want him."

They did not waste any more time; the major led the men to Benedict. He was apparently loading rifles for the soldiers on the roof.

The Austrian sharpshooters had moved on to the barns and were now finishing off the remaining flesh-eaters in the surrounding area. The priest lashed out at Captain Hayward as he moved towards the house. The drone soldiers fired at the British as they moved along with their master.

The sharpshooters on the roof trained their fire on them. One drone soldier got it in the shoulder and went down instantly. Two were killed with clean shots to the head, showering shreds of hair and skull onto the muddy courtyard.

The volley fire now raining down on the drone soldiers was having a subduing effect on their morale. The priest snarled at the stragglers as he approached the building.

The remaining three drone soldiers tried to rush the door but were also cut down. A barrage of bullets was hitting the priest, but they were having little impact. Even headshots were not enough to kill this beast.

Instead of trying to get into the house, the priest changed tactics and began to climb it. Its extra arms and claws gave it more agility. The soldiers watched in shock as it scaled the building. Captain Hayward did not waste time. He sent soldiers to collect more ammunition, and those who had some rounds left followed him into the house. The major grabbed Benedict and asked him what he knew about these invaders, but the lad shrugged his shoulders. The major pondered this. Maybe they had got it wrong, and he knew nothing. Still, the creature was climbing the house, and it would be upon them.

The priest did not climb all the way up. It swung its body through a large window, smashing the glass and the wooden frame around it. The order was given to kill it at all costs, but the knowledge of how to do so was still unknown.

The house was a good size, and it took nearly a minute for them to arrive at the right room. A suitable number of guards were left with Benedict, and the rest followed the major. Coming up the stairs was Charles. They stood outside the room they thought was holding the priest. There was a silent lull, followed by a ripping, banging noise.

No one could figure out what was happening, but it sounded like a builder's workshop. The men were ordered to be prepared to burst in. Soldiers gathered on either side of the door and waited for the order.

"Keep your wits about you, men. This one's different," said Captain Hayward.

They went on the count of three. The door flung open to reveal a hole in the ceiling, and a leg disappeared through it in the darkness.

"It's going to the roof. We must get up there."

Captain Hayward led the way. He withdrew his revolver and pressed on up the stairs with a detachment of men behind him. The fighting around the house had now stopped, and the area was slowly secured. This only left the priest.

Thatcher and Arthur stood by Benedict with bayonets raised. Austrians flanked them on either side.

The priest burst through the ceiling, teeth snapping and deep growls coming from within. Its legs and body had become more extended, not in the same way as the long limbs, but it was still an awkward sight. Once out of the gap, it came under heavy fire from the sharpshooters on the roof. The fear in their eyes was evident as the bullets were swallowed into its body. Blood gushed out, but there was no stopping its advance. Its eyes were transfixed on Benedict, and that's what drove it on.

Charles arrived on the roof, immediately removed his sword, and charged the beast. His men followed as the priest rose up onto his hind legs, and standing at least ten feet tall, he let out a deep belly roar. His tongue licked out of his mouth like a lizard's. The men flung themselves into his legs, and as they did so, two of them were brushed aside by the power of his arms. The claws cut through their tunics and straps with ease. Captain Hayward managed to get close to the creature's chest.

He slammed the sword down into the ribcage. This opened up a deep cut. The eyes of the beast turned on the captain, and within a quick flash, he was picked up and hurled to a corner of the ceiling. The impact was bone-crunching.

As it moved closer to Benedict, two Austrian soldiers jabbed at the priest to try and keep it back, but again, in a quick lunge, the beast bit one soldier's head clean off and put his arm through the other man.

It now focused on Benedict.

Thatcher and Arthur fumbled to insert bullets into their rifle breeches. The creature's sheer size and lack of apparent ways to kill it troubled them.

They looked at each other as if to accept their fate. Neither man would run. They would stand their ground.

He went onto all fours and dealt with the other soldiers trying to hold him back – lashing out, sending them flying and wounding indiscriminately. Major Richmond arrived with three grenades.

"Back it to the edge, and I'll go over with it," the major called out.

He kept the grenades out of sight and lit the fuses on them. The priest turned, and half smiled. He had lost most of his human features, and his robes were torn and ripped from his expanding size, but you could still work out the grimaced smile. Captain Hayward took his chance, charged the beast once more, and attempted to push it to the edge. His body hurt from being thrown violently before, but he pressed on. His shoulder hit the priest hard, and he jabbed the bayonet into its side. The priest grabbed Captain Hayward and stood back on his hind legs. It pushed him to the corner of the house. The priest opened its ever-expanding mouth, exposing colossal teeth.

Charles thought of his wife and children and closed his eyes. The priest's breath swept across the captain's face, and he prayed for a quick death. The wound on the priest's chest had not fully closed as the others had done. Then, a whoosh of air passed Charles, and a slight thud followed. He slowly opened his eyes. The priest's grip had lessened, and its legs started to collapse. Both of them fell hard to the floor. The beast's tongue rolled out of its mouth; it sighed once and then lay motionless.

The shot had come from a fair distance away and not from the top of the roof. Charles was grateful but had to watch in hope as the major threw the grenades off the back of the manor house. He tried to get them away from soldiers that were down there. The thunderous noise that followed shook the building, but fortune shone on them, and it claimed no allied victims.

Soon, the army medics and nurses were on the scene, helping where they could. The major turned to the captain and gave him a grateful look. The body of the priest lay there. The remaining soldiers picked themselves up and prodded it with their bayonets. The order was given to take it down to the courtyard and burn it.

"Charles, old boy, that was a bloody close thing."

The major said this with a massive grin on his face. He was slightly trembling from having three live grenades in his hands moments earlier. Captain Hayward got up onto a brick chimney stack. It had a slight edge, which he lent against.

"I do believe that shot saved my life."

Major Richmond had a wry smile.

"You'll have to buy a bottle of champagne for that sniper unless the bullet was for you?"

The major helped Captain Hayward to his feet. The captain grimaced as he stood up.

"Get Doc Brown to check you over."

The captain nodded.

"Why was that priest after Benedict? This was a calculated attack. They must have had men down here before we arrived. How could they get so many flesh-eaters here?" stated Charles.

The major sat next to the captain.

"You're right, Charles. Maybe, just maybe, they have already sent this plague into Europe. We've been in the mountains for a whole winter. We never heard back from the garrison. They could have been planning this for years."

Both men sighed and put their hands over their faces. Corporal Heinz arrived on the roof. "Major, the area is secure!" He was pleased to announce this and gave them a brief update on the wounded and dead. The corporal lowered his head and announced that five men had been bitten. This now left them feeling empty. Decisions would have to be made on the men's welfare.

"Dear lord, this is getting worse by the minute," said Major Richmond.

The major was downcast on this latest news. The corporal continued to debrief Charles on the situation. Army doctor Brown arrived at the top of the building. He was a little out of breath but happy to see the men alive. The corporal left the doctor with the officers and went to check on the Austrian numbers.

Colonel Kiesl arrived next with news that a British Engineer had come out of nowhere and claimed to be from their regiment. "We nearly shot him. Fortunately, one of your men recognised him," After that brief update, a soldier emerged from the door leading onto the roof. It was Private Alex Chamberlin.

Captain Hayward wanted to get up, but the doctor stopped him. The major needed this small boost of hope and leapt up to shake Chamberlin's hand.

"My God, man, how? Just how?"

The major smiled when he said this. As the officer in charge, he had kept his emotions in place, but he couldn't help letting go a little, with a man he thought had left his stewardship now returning.

Alex smiled and reached forward to shake his hand.

"It's been a long journey, and I have much to tell you."

Charles stopped the doctor, dressing his wounds. "It was you, wasn't it? You have a fantastic shot on you, Private."

Private Chamberlin smiled.

"I had to gauge the wind first as I didn't want to hit you, sir."

He went on to explain his escape from the dead forest, and the story of the three long limbs was breathtaking. His horse had been the difference between life and death, and the ability to leave an area at speed was paramount. Alex told them of his observations and the fact he had seen civilians being marched towards Austria, possibly Russia. He spoke for around ten minutes about everything he had seen and the perilous nights and lack of sleep. "I haven't seen the enemy for a while apart from this attack today." He was confident they had some time before the priests arrived with more extensive reinforcements.

Fresh orders were given to secure the outer walls and dispose of the dead and flesh-eaters bodies. They had a dilemma with the noise this battle had generated.

The common thought was that it would bring in more enemy forces, even if Private Chamberlin thought otherwise. The other dilemma was the fever—half the soldiers were now complaining of having it. They needed to rest and see this out. The journey ahead was a long one.

The major offered to stay with a small group of soldiers and the sick, whilst Captain Hayward would push on with the nurses and the rest of the group. This thought process was stopped in its tracks. "I'm sick, Harry."

"Dear friend, not a bite."

He had sheer panic in his eyes.

"No, it's the fever. I've felt it since this morning. I can stay, and you go, Harry."

"I can't leave you all now!"

The major ordered them to stay as long as possible. Spotters were posted on the roof, and the men left to join the others in the courtyard. The officers and men greeted Private Chamberlin and were overjoyed to find out he had survived. It was a good morale-boosting moment, and the officers knew it. There had been little to cheer about, but seeing a man come back from the dead was a sign of hope.

The men who had been bitten were taken to a servant's quarters. They knew what this meant, and it was now only a matter of time. This was taking its toll on Charles and the major. They did not want to execute their own men, even though they knew they would change at some point. The decision instead was to offer them the choice: they could end it themselves or be cared for until the sickness killed them. Then, they would be humanely dealt with.

The officers could think of no other way. It was not an easy process, as it could be any of them soon.

"Damn this war and these wretched creatures. They poison our men, and even a hollow victory like today pales into insignificance when it keeps taking more."

The major hung his head and excused himself to go and talk to the wounded. The operation around the manor house was in full swing. The nurses were having to help out due to the number of soldiers now falling ill. Sandbags were being filled to help plug the gaps, and the cellar was searched extensively for any remaining flesh-eaters. Several were found and dealt with swiftly. They also found three more entrances, which were sealed.

The dead allied soldiers were buried outside the manor grounds. It was a hard slog for the remaining soldiers as not enough hands were available to dig or move the bodies. The flesh-eaters were being burnt with their leader. The dead drone soldiers were being stabbed in the head to make sure they would not be coming back.

The major visited the men who had been bitten. They were in good spirits despite the death sentence that had been handed down to them. He was moved deeply by the notes and messages handed to him to pass on to their families. He could not bring himself to offer them the option of taking their own lives, but this actually became their own request.

The virus was spreading rapidly. It seemed to affect different people at different speeds. The men all felt woozy and light headed. The bite wounds became infected even if they had been cleaned. The change in skin colour around the wound was disconcerting for each victim and helped pass the final judgement on what they should all do.

Each man had a drink of whisky from the manor house. A good year was found, and the bottle was passed around. Then, five revolvers were brought into the room they were in.

The men decided to take their own lives in that room. They had many visitors to wish them farewell before they did so. Their fellow soldiers were distraught that it had come to this and begged the doctors to find a cure or cut out the infection. Sadly, there was no cure; it was an infection that had already taken over the body. The Austrians and Prussians came in and paid their respects. The mood was sombre around the camp.

The gunshots sent shivers down everyone's spines, and the realisation hit them of how life and death were in the balance every day.

The rest of the day was spent clearing the battle debris and preparing for the night and what it might bring.

That evening passed well, and so did the next. In fact, a week quickly shot by before a scout came back with news of a dust cloud across the valley that went on forever. It was now time to move.

They had prepared, so there was no major panic. The fever had swept through the group and passed without taking anyone. The odd Prussian soldier had passed the manor house in search of food and shelter. They gratefully joined the group and bolstered the numbers, which had been slightly depleted since the attack.

An hour later, they were on the road leading away from the house. It was a place that would hold mixed emotions. It had helped them survive the fever, but the attack had claimed many lives. The question over Benedict remained. Rumours were circling the group that he might be working for the enemy, but the Austrians quickly dismissed these. They said the priests had killed his father, and the monks took him in for a reason.

Benedict held his head in his hands and started to cry. He did not understand why they would come after him, but the major and the captain tried to reassure him.

His eyes then lit up.

"I'm sure my father went to Russia on a trading visit many years ago and returned with a small chest. I asked him what was in it, and he said an old map of a castle in Siberia and things."

"Well done, Benedict." Captain Hayward patted him on the back.

"Do you know where that chest is now?"

Benedict looked uncertain. "I think my father hid it in the cellar of our house."

The major and the captain told him that was a good start and that he should tell them if he could remember more.

Both officers then left him to get some rest.

"We have to find out more about why they want him, Charles."

"Maybe the castle in Siberia is where these priests originate from. There has to be a link," suggested Charles.

Harry nodded his head in agreement and recommended they should investigate this further.

The major was riding up front with the captain. The wagons were in tight columns, and the last wagon had a mounted machine gun. Scouts flanked them on either side.

Captain Hayward looked concerned. "Do you think the priests have infiltrated across Europe?"

"We have no idea how far they have spread and what their objectives are. Major cities have been falling and their armies are being swept aside with ease. They have the numbers, Harry, and creatures like none we've ever seen before."

The men discussed the broad implications of where this whole thing could be going and the role the British Empire must play in stopping it. When it first started, they thought it was a case of Russia trying to flex its muscles, but now it turned out that Russia had capitulated months ago and was overrun with this new force.

They rode all day and stopped for a short rest before it got dark. There had been no sign of the enemy, but that meant nothing now. They no longer trusted their vision; the enemy could already be in front of them.

A small wooded area was found for the camp that night. They were only a few miles from Strasbourg. It was meant to be a joyous occasion but was dampened by the realisation that the vast dust cloud was sweeping through Europe. The question on everyone's minds was: Would it stop in Prussia?

There was talk that the dust cloud could be the refugees fleeing Munich. This was not allowed to sink in, as the idea was to keep moving. They did not enter Strasbourg. The cannon fire put an end to that.

The major thought about the week they had spent in the manor house and how much time they had lost, but for now, they had not seen much movement, enemy or allied. The Prussians were a little reluctant to leave their own soil. The recent Franco–Prussian war would not be easily forgotten in France.

The days passed as they moved down through hills and mountains. Food and water were being kept under close control. The wounded men were starting to show promising signs of recovery.

Colonel Kiesl and Captain Müller discussed Haut-Koenigsbourg castle. They thought it would be a good place to go and decided to speak to the major about it. He was reluctant to go off course but knew they needed to restock and rest a night in secure premises. There was always the worry that they would be in serious trouble if this area were already taken, but that was the risk they would have to take.

Heidi was walking along with Private Brown, who was at the back of the convoy. They both cherished that moment.

"I don't know how much more of this I can take, John."

John squeezed her hand tight.

"We'll make it. We must believe that!"

Her face lit up a little.

"Make it where John? Europe is falling. The generals might talk about how they can stop this enemy, but we've seen what things they can do. I am only a nurse, but these things are demons. I—"

She began to cry. John stopped them walking and stood there holding her in his arms. "We must believe. I know you're concerned for your family and country, but we must believe."

She kissed him, and he wiped away her tears. They continued to walk and hold each other. The weather had improved over the past week, and when the sun broke through the clouds, its warm rays lifted everyone's spirits.

It was a hard slog up and down tracks and roads, but the castle was in sight. The scouts checked the area and reported empty farms and villages, which sadly had become the norm.

The usual tactics were applied, and a small detachment of British soldiers and Prussians, accompanied by Captain Hayward and Captain Müller, was sent ahead.

Haut-Koenigsbourg castle was an overpowering fortification. It sat high on a mountain top, overlooking the valley, with imperious qualities. Caution was always taken with any fort, town, or village.

This time, the soldiers were greeted by a weary-looking Prussian division. They were happy to see so many soldiers, but their faces were despairing. Many were exhausted and worn out, some had injuries, and some looked sick. These people caught Charles's eye. The notion that they had been bitten was now playing on his mind.

Captain Müller spoke German to the guards who greeted them. They were an Alpine Jaeger corps division retreating from Munich. Several generals were camped in the castle, and General Schmitt was the one to greet them. He was a middle-aged man of stocky build with a hard-looking face.

He first greeted them in German and then welcomed the British officer. "We do not often have the pleasure of having members of the Empire in our country. I hope you are not behind this invasion?" He said this with a half-smile. He was not sure who to trust, and that was obvious.

"We number nearly one thousand men in this castle. We're preparing a counter-strike against the enemy." General Schmitt said confidently.

He led the men to their command headquarters. A roaring fire had raised the temperature in the room, and strong words were being exchanged between the different officers there. Captain Hayward looked at the men and a large model map of Prussia. They used small model soldiers to mark out the Prussian armies and the enemy forces. The Prussian men were blue, and the enemy were black. What interested Charles was the number of enemy soldiers believed to be in Prussia. It covered the map from nearly top to bottom.

The visiting officers were brought water and fresh bread. General Schmitt decided to speak to Captain Müller and began questioning him for any information he may have. Hayward could not keep up with all the German being spoken. The questioning was forceful and almost inquisitive about why Müller was with the British and not fighting the war with his fellow countrymen.

They all waited with bated breath for his answer. Captain Müller knew he had to be courteous in the presence of generals. He explained that he was ordered to accompany the British and Austrian soldiers to France. Brigadier Von Schwen had passed this down. The moment he mentioned Austrians, the mood turned darker. They started shouting at the Prussian captain and wanted to know what the Austrians were doing in their country and under the assistance of Prussian soldiers.

Captain Müller soaked it all up.

"If I may be so bold, I was given orders and have been following them out."

The snigger that followed around the room was enough to put Captain Hayward's back up. He could grasp what they were getting at, but everything seemed a little out of order.

"Gentlemen. I have travelled from the Carpathian Mountains through Austria and most of Prussia. The whole of Europe is under threat from this army. We must work together. I have so much respect for your captain here—"

He was stopped halfway through his sentence by General Schmitt, who took control.

"How many are you?"

"We're nearly two hundred, General. This includes some army medical staff and nurses."

The room went silent.

"Nurses, you say? We could do with some support for our sick men."

Charles looked at the general.

"Have you come across the flesh-eaters?

The general looked at him with steely eyes. "The demons who are already dead?"

"Yes, they're the ones. They're everywhere, we think…"

Again, Charles was stopped in his tracks. This time, the general raised his hand, palm and fingers open, in a halting motion.

"We know about the creatures with the long limbs and the giant riders. Let me get to the point. They are camped not too far from this castle, and we intend to hit them at night. Having an extra hundred men or more makes this more viable. Hell, we can have the nurses care for the wounded and mount a defence from here."

Captain Hayward wanted to be strategic. This was not the time or place to disagree.

He had not had a chance to tell them about the side effects of being bitten and what happened to the victim. The tension in the room was at a fever pitch. Sweat was dripping from their foreheads as the fire crackled away. General Schmitt walked over to the window ledge and glared out of it.

"Captain Müller will go back and fetch the others. You can wait with us."

He did not trust the British captain to return; now, they were trapped in his web.

Captain Müller looked on anxiously as he left the room. Charles hoped he would tell the others to leave and not return for him. This idea was quickly quashed as the general ordered a small detachment to return with him.

Captain Hayward turned and looked around the room. He then went and sat in an empty chair. The other officers and generals began talking again amongst themselves. The room was too hot and needed a window opened to allow some fresh air in. In his best German, the captain suggested this and got a young officer to open the window. The cool breeze wafted into the room, easing the intense heat.

Charles let his mind wander as the background noise became almost a humming sound. This half-sleep was broken by shouting and then gunfire. A corporal came in looking distressed. General Schmitt approached Charles and explained that some of the men who had been bitten had changed.

Suddenly, the call to arms bugle sounded. Long limbs had been spotted in droves coming up the west bank of the castle, followed by riders from the north.

Charles felt that this was the time to speak.

"I must return to my men. They're in danger out there."

General Schmitt looked at him long and hard.

"The armies of Europe are meeting at Reims in France. Go with God's speed and tell them as much as you know."

The sudden attack changed the atmosphere, and the hard stance towards Charles leaving evaporated.

"I'm sorry for the previous demands. We're under a lot of stress, and numbers matter in this war with the Devil," said General Schmitt apologetically.

He extended his hand. This time, it was to shake Charles's hand, not stop him.

"I understand, General. It is about us all fighting together now. They have one goal, and that's becoming obvious."

With this said, he left the room. A young officer led him to the courtyard. His horse was being held but was getting a little jumpy as flesh-eaters emerged from the barracks. The Prussian soldiers were dealing with them as there were not as many as in the manor house attack.

Charles took to his saddle, looked around the castle, and left as the gates were closing. He rode fast as he heard barks and growls, which he had now become familiar with. The long limbs had reached the gates.

Captain Hayward was glad to see some British soldiers on the lookout. They smiled and welcomed him back. As news of the invading party broke, the makeshift camp was being hurriedly packed up.

The detachment from the castle was offered the chance to return but was warned by Charles that the gates were now shut and that the long-limbs and Northern riders had arrived. This left the twenty men with one real choice: to join the new group and move into France.

Captain Müller was on hand to ease them into this multinational force.

The convoy set off at speed. The scouts returned with reports of long limbs coming through the woods in large packs. A small road took them away from the castle and out of the forest. The last wagon had the Gatling gun mounted on it, and its crew kept a keen eye out for movement.

There was a contingency plan to have a small detachment of mounted riders ready to fall to the back should the convoy need protection. The rumblings in the distance kept the tension level high.

The extra Prussians gave them twenty more horses and some local knowledge of the area. Their next destination was Luneville.

After an hour or two, the major gathered his officers. The speed of their movement had left the enemy far behind them. The pace slowed down, giving him time to talk to his commanders before entering France.

"Gentlemen, we have been told by Captain Hayward that the armies of Europe are amassing at Reims. This is our future destination."

There was some small talk amongst the men. The Prussians and Austrians wondered whether their armies would gather there as their own countries fell into enemy hands. The answer was still the same: "This will be where we can face these priests and their armies of flesh-eaters."

Crossing the border offered little insight into the Allied situation. The road was empty, and the buildings around the border were deserted.

A pungent smell and a fine dust in the wind carried in the air from the East. There was a distant noise that occasionally wafted on the airwaves. It sounded like thunder, but there were no clouds to carry the menace of a storm.

One soldier thought it was drums. His fellow soldiers laughed at him, but Corporal Heinz, who was riding past, agreed. They knew that a vast army was coming their way; how many was another question.

Luneville was deserted. The convoy took time to rest and restock where they could. There was not a great share of extra food, but the odd farm animal roaming freely was rounded up and slaughtered. The cook set to work with some helpers preparing the food, and guards were posted around the village. The major spoke to Colonel Kiesl about the French retreat and the refugees' plight. Both agreed it would not be long before they caught up with the allied forces and civilian population.

Chapter 25

"Nazar, we have news of your cousin."

The high priest looked up from the chair he was sitting on.

"Pray tell me, messenger."

"He has been found dead in a forest on the border of France. They found a lance at the place of this death. It seems he attacked a small group of women and children to pleasure himself."

Nazar looked at the soil beneath his boots. His anger was boiling over. He brushed his long black coat to one side, revealing a dagger and a small pouch. He beckoned over one of his generals.

"Get me a thousand humans – now."

The priest nodded and scuttled off.

"My darling, we will get through your pain. I've brought the wolves," said the High Priestess.

"Oksana, this is not the time to appease me."

He brushed the high priestess aside and then walked over to watch his armies passing. There were thousands upon thousands. The ground moved with marching feet. As far as the eye could see, various creatures and drones moved towards France.

"I told him not to leave the main group unless he had good reason. Pleasuring oneself is not one."

He was interrupted by a drone soldier.

"Sire, the civilians are lined up."

"Then bring out the Gatling guns."

Nazar turned to his Priestess and told her to come to his side.

"The only message I can send them is this." He pointed to the drone commander and nodded.

The prisoners were malnourished and scared. Their eyes focused on the guns. They huddled together as the drone soldiers began to fire. The bullets were unforgiving, and the devastation was quick. Their bodies were left slumped on the floor, some twitching and some groaning. Nazar then smirked and pointed to the long limbs.

"Let them feed."

He sent an order to all his commanders to gather and join him on the ridge overlooking his troops. It was time to plan the battle with the European forces.

"We will meet them head-on at Reims. It is time to destroy this European army. Make no bones. I want rivers of blood to flow through the heart of Europe."

His commanders gathered in closer. One drone general was a little slow to move; before he could adjust his step, he felt a blade to his throat. He looked up to see Nazar's eyes locked on to his.

"It is all about speed and movement." Nazar slowly drew the blade away, cutting a thin line across the man's neck. The others looked on with wide eyes and cautious tongues.

"Do not fail me, my brethren. We have waited a lifetime to get here and must be ready to fight to the death."

He summoned maps and reviewed every building, village, and hill in the area. Forests and woods were marked, and fortifications were singled out.

He then turned and led the men to the marching horde of flesh-eaters. They were being kept in line by drone soldiers on horseback with whips.

"We have the numbers to crush any army that stands in our way. They are not ready for this."

A young priest dared to speak.

"My lord, they still have Benedict?"

Nazar's eyes rolled over to the young priest. He briefly showed his razor-sharp teeth and a tongue longer than a normal human's.

"They may have Benedict, but using his information is another thing. We will deal with the Benedict problem in due time. I have despatched friends to bring me my prize."

The generals around him smiled. Several female priests arrived on horseback. They were in charge of the Northern riders and were armed with bows and arrows. Each one dismounted and joined the group. Nazar spoke about what part they would play in the battle.

Giant cannons rolled past, and then regiment upon regiment of drone soldiers dressed in black with carbine rifles, some with long barrels and some with short barrels. This pleased Nazar; rifles that could hold up to seven bullets would play a huge part in his war.

He mounted his horse and rode to the top of the mound. The drone soldiers cheered him as he reared up on his horse. "Now we ride with the Devil to victory!" shouted Nazar.

Chapter 26

The rain fell hard as the convoy moved towards Nancy. Major Richmond had taken advice not to enter the city but to go around it. They were well-supplied and moving at a decent speed. The weather was not dampening spirits too much, either.

The grey clouds made everything look lifeless. The drums could still be heard, like distant thunder. They never stopped, just a constant humming.

The approach to Nancy was difficult. Piles of clothes and possessions lined the route. A teddy bear caught Captain Hayward's eye. It was crumbled into a heap and tucked half under a small case. He dismounted and knelt beside it. Without thinking, he placed the teddy in his pouch and mounted his horse.

Hours passed before they encountered something they had not seen for a long time. Refugees were walking everywhere in front of them. The camp that now confronted the convoy stretched on for a mile or so. They stopped moving forward. Captain Hayward rode up to the Major with Captain Müller and Colonel Kiesl.

"How should we pass them?" Captain Hayward asked.

The men sat on their horses, looking at this sprawling mass. The major took out his binoculars.

"There must be governmental forces in charge here. The French authorities would not leave this camp unmanned."

The others agreed. Captain Müller offered to take ten men and ride into the camp.

The major agreed to let him go but warned him to be careful and ready to escape should the situation get out of control. Captain Müller thanked the officers around him and set off with the ten men.

The French authorities were few and far between, and the crowd rose to their feet and gathered around the soldiers entering the camp. Captain Müller spoke good French and tried to calm the civilians around him. He had picked several other soldiers who understood French. The crowd wanted food and medicine, and many looked malnourished. At first, there were just ten to twenty people, but soon it became hundreds, then maybe a thousand. They pulled at the horses, trying to find food. The men felt the situation was getting out of control and began to turn around. A gunshot rang out, and the crowd settled down. Captain Müller had withdrawn a revolver and now had it in the air. The civilians around them parted a little as they rode out.

They returned and told the others of the problem that lay ahead. No official had come forward, and none of them could see how they could make their way through this large camp. The decision was taken to go around it.

As they started to turn back, a small group of riders left the camp to the east of them. Twenty men or more carrying French flags were heading their way. The order was given to stand ready.

Approaching at speed, the riders waved a white flag to indicate that they meant no harm. They were met with a wall of mounted riders, stopping them from getting to the main group. Captain Hayward rode out in front of them, speaking reasonable French. The delegation was made up of police and former government clerks. They had old rifles and looked a little shabby.

"Where have you come from?" said a government clerk.

Charles explained their plight whilst studying the men and women before him. He had grown more cautious of everything around him since the Austrian Alpine soldiers had raided them over a month ago.

They agreed to help them pass through the camp and would put them under the category of "victims of flesh-eaters". Stories had broken about being bitten and how victims would turn into one of them. This had brought panic at first, with all those suspected of being bitten being abandoned or segregated from the main group.

"We have few soldiers or police here. There are tens of thousands of people, and our daily task is to find food and water for them. We have different diseases breaking out daily. Sanitary problems and hygiene are worrying issues," the clerk said with a solemn face.

Charles listened sympathetically.

"Your camp needs to move. The humming sound that carries on the wind is drums. They beat to the sound of death. There is an army coming that will consume everything in its path. This is why we will join the armies of Europe in Reims. It could be our last chance."

The shock and disappointment of hearing about the enemy movement seemed to deflate the French contingent more.

"There is no way we can leave quickly. We have women and children and old people who cannot walk fast. There are several nationalities here. How will we do it?"

Charles looked around the site.

"We have limited supplies and little firepower. If we did stay and fight, two hundred or more soldiers would not stop what is coming! Two hundred thousand would not stop what is coming."

Again, the greeting party looked despondent.

"We are mainly Engineers. We can perhaps destroy the local bridges and delay their advance where we can," Captain Hayward explained sympathetically.

Their eyes lit up for the first time.

"There have been rumours of refugees making their way to Great Britain. Maybe we can start the evacuation and head for the coast," the clerk had hope again in his eyes.

They spoke amongst themselves briefly.

"I cannot promise there will be a straight passage to Great Britain, but you will stand more of a chance than staying here." Charles was as honest as he could be.

The discussions did not take much longer, as they agreed they would start the evacuation. Captain Hayward explained he would ask Major Richmond for permission to help them. He rode back to the main group and explained what was on the cards. Major Richmond was not sure about the plan. Captain Hayward had pitched it straight and simple. The main group was to continue to Reims, and a handful of soldiers would help destroy local bridges and make things difficult for the enemy to advance.

They would set up a base on the other side of the camp, allowing them to move out more rapidly if necessary.

As this was being discussed, the French group returned to the camp with an escort carrying blue flags, which must have meant some rite of passage. Thus, the hungry refugees stopped surrounding the convoy en masse when they passed through.

"Charles, you must not take any unnecessary risks. Europe will need your expertise at Reims. But I fully understand your desire to help these civilians. You're a bloody good soldier and an honourable man," said Major Richmond encouragingly.

Charles looked at his friend and felt the concern in his voice. The distant drumming was growing louder by the hour. Nobody knew how long they had, but a scouting party would surely be on the prowl.

The convoy fell in behind the escort and followed them through the camp. The wagons' covers were kept shut. This was to help give the illusion of sick or wounded men. Many of the crowd came out to see this group pass. Some wanted to come forward and investigate, but the blue flags made them wary. The soldiers in the convoy were told to be ready but not give off an aggressive stance. The sheer number of refugees meant that once inside, things could turn nasty in the blink of an eye.

It took nearly half an hour to go through camp. They looked on at many weary, worried faces. The children looked unfed and lifeless in many ways. This was a sorry sight, and it made Captain Hayward sure of his decision to stay and help. The group set up a HQ a mile outside of the main camp. This would be the Engineers' base after the rest had gone. Major Richmond would move the rest out at first light the next day.

No one slept very well that night. The drumming noise was playing on everyone's mind, and the thought of scavengers coming into the camp whilst they slept was more than a little unnerving.

The morning came around with a burst of sunlight. It was a pleasant feeling. No one had come over from the main camp, indicating the blue flags were doing the trick. The men who chose to stay behind to help Captain Hayward were volunteers. He could have handpicked his men but felt it fairer to ask for help.

The soldiers and nurses cooked and polished off a hearty breakfast. The moment of realisation came when the rest were getting ready to leave. The men who had chosen to stay started shaking hands with their fellow comrades. Captain Hayward shook hands with Major Richmond.

"Don't do anything silly now, Charles."

He smiled back at him.

"We're meeting you in Reims, Harry. Don't you worry!"

Captain Hayward then wished 'God's speed' to the other officers and men. It was a longer farewell than normal, maybe because the situation was grave and there was a chance they might not come back.

Corporal Heinz had asked to stay with the captain along with Sergeant Butcher. Charles felt that the detachment needed a scout, and Corporal Heinz had proven himself to be among the best.

Soon, the wheels were rolling, and the carts were drifting out of sight. For the twenty men left, the base camp would still be in the same place. It was on the right side of the main camp, should they need to escape at speed.

The refugees stayed put at first, but they began to move out after a day. They started leaving in dribs and drabs but soon became thousands.

Their sheer numbers meant the soldiers had to move around them. The base camp was far enough away from the exodus that it was not under immediate threat of looting. This did not stop Charles from posting two guards there whenever the main group was away.

The first thing they did was to meet with some French officials and plan out the nearest bridges to the camp. Dynamite was needed, but it was in short supply. The refugees were not ex-soldiers and had few weapons apart from tools and wooden clubs. The gunpowder was brought to the Engineers on the second day. The drumming was distinctive now and bore a greater purpose. There had been reports of long-limbs and drone soldiers in the nearby woods scouting out the area for enemy strongholds. This meant Charles pressed his small force into action.

That afternoon, they went to work on several bridges. The explosives were a little crude but did the trick on the wooden supports. The problem arose when they discovered that the main bridge into Luneville was made of stone. This was going to take a little more time to deal with.

They began blasting the wooden middle planks and then worked on digging a ditch on the far side leading onto the bridge. The same was done on their side. It was time-consuming, and the noise of the drums became ever closer. The camp was starting to empty quickly, leaving vast areas with empty tents and belongings that were no longer deemed worthwhile.

The bridge was nearly ready, but it would take a little more time. Captain Hayward decided to stay the night by the bridge. It was an edgy evening, with the now familiar sounds of long limbs lurking in the nearby woods. The river was deep enough to stop them from closing in, but this did not mean they would not try to cross the bridge.

At sunrise, the men awoke and began working effortlessly on making it difficult for the bridge to become operational. Later in the afternoon, they saw the arrival of enemy scouts. At first, it was three to four priests. They did not open fire; they just gathered together and watched them.

Captain Hayward told the men to concentrate on doing their jobs and only worry should they come under fire. That moment came when several Northern riders arrived. They started opening fire on the Engineers straight away.

Captain Hayward did not want to get into a fire-fight and got the soldiers to remount and leave the area as fast as possible. The bridge was damaged enough to possibly give them a half-day head start. The ride back to the refugee camp was at a fast pace. Once inside, they found the main headquarters, and Captain Hayward reported that the enemy was within touching distance. The evacuation had gone very well; nearly everyone had taken on board the gravity of the situation and had packed up, leaving for the coast. There was a group of elderly people who had decided they were ready to meet their maker. They had been warned that the enemy would spare no one.

Sergeant Butcher asked what their next plan would be. He scratched his head. The truth was they were twenty men, and their firepower would not stop a large scouting party, let alone a reconnaissance force. It was a case of packing up and leaving to join the armies of Europe. The camp was almost deserted within the hour. They then set off towards Nancy. The work on the bridges would bide them time but nothing more.

The journey was going well. The men were not restricted and could flow more easily without the hindrance of tracks and roads.

The night sky lit up with flashes – not thunder, but cannon flashes. Artillery firing in the evening was rare. Having no target meant indiscriminate shelling.

The soldiers guessed it was the enemy firing at some fixed French positions. The camp officials had said there were some lines of defence even if the main force was now heading towards Reims.

That evening, they sat around a small campfire dug into the ground and stones stacked around it. The meal was a broth made of various vegetables and dried meat. Sitting alongside Captain Hayward was Sergeant Butcher. The men spoke quietly about the conflict and their longing for home. They were aware that Corporal Heinz no longer had a home as such and tried not to dwell on this subject. Breaking the silence and self-reflection time, Sergeant Butcher started to sing a Cornish folk song.

"With a good sword and a trusty shield
A faithful heart and true
King James's men shall understand
What Cornish men can do
And have they fixed the where and when?
And shall Trelawny die?
Here's twenty thousand Cornish men
Will know the reason why."

He was a proud Cornishman and loved the county he was from. He spoke highly of the stunning views, small country lanes, and hard-working farmers. His special praise was reserved for the pubs. His wish list included a good steak pie and a fine ale to wash it down. His reminiscing refreshed the atmosphere and made the evening enjoyable, which was long overdue.

The next morning, Corporal Heinz led the way. He was a keen scout and followed the earth's natural paths wherever possible.

He was excellent at picking out tracks and identifying what sort of animal or man had made them. His skills and ability to read maps and find the best route available to them were also prevalent. Captain Hayward had thanked him on many occasions, saying that he was the reason they had got this far alive.

He had confided with the men that he was adopted. His step-parents had been relatively old and had passed away many years ago. This meant he was ready to go anywhere now with the British Engineers. He would, of course, join his own regiment if it still survived.

The men passed by huge forests and thanked the Lord they had not had to enter them so far. The creatures that now stalked this land were adept at striking in deep, thick, wooded areas, and it could be a foolish decision not to heed their gut feelings about these places.

The next stop on their route was Bar-le-Duc. This small crossroads town was ideal for taking stock and resting.

Corporal Heinz was the first to arrive. He checked for enemy soldiers and creatures. The town was a little rugged; it had seen many refugees and soldiers pass through it, which reduced the chances of finding food and supplies.

They did not stay in the town itself, as it was easier to find an empty farmhouse and rest there. The extra incentive was that they could barricade the doors and lower windows. The horses were locked in a barn, and several soldiers slept high in the barn rafters.

Morning came with a call to arms. A rider had been spotted coming towards the farm. He was not dressed in black, and the men thought he was a cavalry cuirassier. He had a steel helmet and steel breastplate.

A fire had been lit in the farm kitchen and was hurriedly stamped out. Soldiers raced to the house's second floor and prepared to cut this cavalryman down should they need to.

The rider did not seem to be stopping at the farm and carried on past them. Corporal Heinz was dispatched to bring him back. Taking good care not to startle the man as it could have dire consequences, he caught up with him and persuaded him to turn around and come back.

They arrived at the farmhouse and saw Captain Hayward waiting to greet them. The French cavalryman did not dismount, coming across as anxious.

"Where have you come from, my friend?" Captain Hayward calmly asked.

The man did not answer at first.

"I have come from Nancy. It is finished. The whole regiment is gone. They came at night; the woods and forests are teeming with the walking dead."

Charles just nodded.

"Are you going to join the main army at Reims?"

The man just looked at him.

"Why?"

Captain Hayward was taken aback.

"We have to amass our forces there and drive them back."

The horse reared, and the French soldier looked at all of them.

"This is not a battle that we can win. Save yourselves and run."

He then kicked his horse with his spurs and made haste off down the track, disappearing into the distance. His words stayed with the men as they packed up and left the village.

Sergeant Butcher was still thinking about it as he rode next to Charles.

"This is going to be one hell of a battle. They have a force like no other, gathered on earth, with creatures never recorded before."

Charles shook his head.

"Whilst man walks the planet, we will fight them to the bitter end. The Empire was built on courage and strength. We will need that now."

The wind picked up as they rode. The clouds darkened a little, and rain threatened to fall from the heavens. Fortune eventually shone through, and the clouds slowly dispersed. The veteran was not the best rider and sometimes found it hard going. He was a burly man who had worked on the docks before the army. Rumour was he was once a bare-knuckle fighter on the streets of London. His size and stance made this believable, although he did not come across as an aggressive man.

It was a good time to reflect as they rode along. The sweeping French countryside was breathtaking at times, with its quaint farmhouses and picturesque villages. Food amongst the men was getting low. They needed to take some time and scout out a village for what they could find. The issue was the number of refugees that had been passing through. This meant that most villages had already been ransacked.

Rationing food had become the norm. People had started skipping lunch and just drinking water to quench their hunger. With any war, the fundamental things of life still played their parts. Food and water were key requirements, and without them, you would join the dead.

They rode solidly until evening and then, exhausted, collapsed in an old barn. The next day, they got an early start, and by lunchtime, they arrived at Epernay. The town was empty, but fires were still burning in some of the houses.

Captain Hayward received a report from Corporal Heinz. He was concerned by the freshness of the situation. Although no enemy soldiers were to be seen in the current vicinity, his nerves were still on edge.

The major find came when Sergeant Butcher declared he had come across some fresh bread and cheese. The soldiers' eyes lit up; finding such luxury items was a fantastic treat.

It wasn't long before a couple of bottles of wine were added to this feast. The men tied the horses and came in to sit at a large table. The building must have been a town hall, and it was in good order. The occupants had left but had not taken things with them. The food was devoured with appreciation; every morsel was enjoyed and cherished.

Charles let his eyes sweep around the room at the men eating. They had served him well, but he worried about what lay ahead. As they sat there, one of his men took a hunk of bread and a slice of cheese and left to keep guard upstairs.

"Horses!"

The sudden shout broke the slumber and sent the men dashing around for their weapons, each of them loading bullets into the chambers. The house was quickly surrounded.

Charles had told them to hold fire. They were close to Reims, and this could be a friendly force. While he worried about getting to their horses, a French voice called out for them to show themselves. The order was given to stand down, and Charles was first out of the door. He left his weapons behind and came out with his hands raised.

The French soldiers were part of a scouting group and promptly lowered their rifles. The officer in charge spoke to Charles. He smiled, which was a good start.

"We need every single soldier we can muster. There is a dark cloud coming from the East that covers most of Europe as we speak. We have more refugees than we know what to do with," the French officer worriedly said.

Charles ushered his men out.

"We'll do the best we can. We've heard the armies of Europe are meeting in Reims to counter the enemy's advance."

"This is true. It has been a while since a large British force has landed in Europe. They number over a hundred and fifty thousand," the French officer looked happy to pass on this news.

Charles was surprised at this number. Although there were many British forces around the world, it was astonishing to him that an army this size could be mustered.

"How many does Europe have to combat this invading force?"

The French soldier looked a little smug.

"Over a million."

Charles was shocked but a little relieved. It had been a long time since he had encountered what could be a turning point. The officer said they had armies from Sweden, Spain, France, Italy, Prussia, Austria and Great Britain.

"I can inform you more as we ride to Reims. The enemy scouts have been seen in this area. I will take you to the British army."

The men gathered what food they could take and joined the French scouts. A familiar sound started to ring through the air, and the incessant drumming began again. They were close, very close.

They rode for half a day through a vast forest south of Reims. As they drew closer to the town, they encountered small pockets of European forces preparing defences. The mood amongst the riders was almost euphoric. Seeing so many soldiers gave me a sweet tingling of anticipation. Maybe, just maybe, they could turn the tide here at Reims.

As they slowly emerged from the forest, they came upon a magnificent sight: a walled defence that seemed to go up into the skies. Small silhouettes, highlighted by the sun's rays, could be seen walking along the ramparts. Cannon barrels extended out from the wall's edges.

The men looked on in awe at how impressive and extensive this defence system was. It stretched for miles in either direction. The French soldiers kept on riding past the wall. They were not heading into the city but towards the east side, where the main forces were gathering. A French officer rode next to Captain Hayward.

"I'm taking you to your units. We have kept the armies of Europe in their respective countries. We have so many men it makes sense to fall under the command of their own officers."

Charles nodded.

"I've never seen so many forces altogether. How long have they been gathering here?"

"Since news broke of Russia falling, we have been monitoring the situation. You can understand that it takes time to get different cultures to agree. Prussia and Austria were the hardest, but as their nations fell to the enemy, they came around."

Charles considered everything as they rode along a road towards the British camp. The French officer stopped them and said he could send a rider with Corporal Heinz to the Austrian camp, but before he could finish, Corporal Heinz rode in front of them.

"I've have decided to stay with the captain and his men. This is a war against the whole of Europe, and I have fought alongside him for six months now. That is if you would like me to stay, Captain."

A smile broke across the captain's face.

"It would be an honour to have one of the best scouts I have ever seen ride with us. We need to fight this war as one to stand a chance."

The men rode on, passing huge, long pits filled with water and spikes. There were fields of stakes rammed into the ground. The wall was a good mile or so from this first line of defence. The idea was to meet the enemy head-on on the city's east side. They had prepared other armies further down in the south of the forest and around the north of the city, but it was hoped they would come at them from the front. This was a gamble, but one they had to take.

The camps for the European armies were on the other side of the wall. They were like small towns; new roads had been built, and small supply stores were placed strategically along the route. Ammunition was a talking point, as different armies used different rifles. There was insufficient time to convert all the European forces to one stand-alone rifle. Politics had played their part, and each country had its preferred option.

Cannons were being mounted on swivel iron turntables. Sandbags and barricades were placed around them. There were Gatling guns all along this frontline – close to a thousand or more – which was a breathtaking sight. Confidence grew the further they rode along the defences.

Eventually, they reached the British defences. Work was being carried out frantically, and the distant drums kept everyone on their toes.

"This is as far as I can go; I must return to my units. Good luck in the battle, and may God have mercy on our souls." With that, the French soldier turned and left.

It was a lot to take in. The men sat on their horses for a moment or two. Sergeant Butcher saw the Royal Engineers' flag and got them to head over to the main unit. They passed many units along the way. The Black Watch, Duke of Wellingtons, Highlanders, King's Royal Rifle Corps, 44th Regiment of Foot, it went on and on.

Several King's Dragoon Guards cavalry officers promptly greeted them and asked where they should be heading. Captain Hayward asked to be taken to the Royal Engineer Corps regiment.

They picked up speed as they galloped along.

"We're not sure of how long we have, old boy, so speed is of the essence," urged the Dragoon.

The officer also informed them that the British top brass, including Field Marshal Prince George, Duke of Cambridge, was present. "This is our real chance for glory."

Captain Hayward wanted to know how long the British Empire had known about this uprising in the East and what lengths were being taken to evacuate the refugees from France and Europe.

"There were rumours months ago that a war was raging in the Austro–Hungarian Empire. It only started to escalate when Prussia asked for help. Ships are taking people across the British channel, but Great Britain is buckling under the sheer numbers."

Captain Hayward could now see the flag and the Engineers at work. "One last thing. How many soldiers of this European force have seen the enemy yet, or better still, fought them?"

The dragoon looked at him. "Maybe half. I've heard rumours of giant dragons and men the size of mountains. This cannot be true."

Charles smiled.

"They are probably tall tales at best, but take heed. A darkness is coming, and it's a lot more dangerous than people believe. Good luck, sir."

They saluted each other, and Charles took his men to join the other Engineers. Major Richmond appeared from a tent and looked delighted to see them all alive.

"My God, we have been lucky. The news we received was of general despair and loss. Not many have been coming from the East now, and yet my eyes treat me to a wonderful sight."

Major Richmond was a little emotionally overcome and took a moment to compose himself. "Come, feed. You must be hungry. I'll bring you up to speed as fast as I can."

The soldiers dismounted, and orderlies came and took the horses. The Engineers were still at work, building defences and laying mines in the fields. The major instructed Sergeant Butcher to take the men and rest for an hour or two. Some tents were outside the defensive wall to cope with rain showers and other elements. The army supplies were of the utmost importance and needed to be kept in a pristine condition where possible.

Captain Hayward asked about the Austrians and Prussians who had been with them. Major Richmond explained that they had joined their own national armies. He felt a little sorry he hadn't been able to see them before this battle.

Once the other soldiers had left, Charles and Major took time to look over the maps. Lieutenant Colonel Wilbury appeared from outside the tent. He was well-known to the captain and major, and both considered him a good leader and tactician.

"Gentlemen, the hour is almost upon us. I have heard all about your bravery, and both of you will get a mention further up the ladder. Believe me, when this mess is finally over, it will do your promotions the world of good."

Captain Hayward had only been back ten minutes, and already, he was being bombarded with questions from the colonel: "What sort of firepower did the enemy have? Did they have Engineers? How good were they?" He felt obliged to answer them all but added his own questions.

"I have never seen a British army this big, " added to the fact that most of the European nations also have their armies here. I do honestly believe we will need every one of them."

The colonel gave him a stern look.

"Come, come, Captain. We are discussing a military operation dealing with over a million men here. What army in the world could stop a force like that? We shall push on from here and drive them back to Russia."

The colonel was almost boasting about how the British had the centre stage in this fight. "We have Gatling guns along this whole front and heavy artillery ready to smash the living daylights out of them."

He then described the role of the Engineers, how the defences had been strengthened with the expertise of "our regiment," and how sandbags and stakes would help slow the enemy and cover the troops.

"Have some supper before joining up with your men," suggested the Lieutenant Colonel.

The colonel then turned and left to meet some of the other senior officers. Captain Hayward smiled at the major. "It's bloody good to see you."

After eating some warm food, Charles was ready to help out. The major informed him he would be in charge of the same detachment from the fort. This was the best news Charles had heard in a while. The thought of not being with them during the conflict now felt wrong. The major admitted he wanted to be there with them as they did the hard graft but said he had been ordered to check on all the Engineers serving in the field.

Corporal Heinz had been given special dispensation to continue serving under Captain Hayward. Sergeant Butcher was glad they were being kept together, as the whole episode had created a firm bond.

Private Chamberlin was loading a wagon with Private Brown.

"Cheer up, mate. She's only behind the wall."

Private Brown half-smiled.

"Thanks, Alex, but you know what's coming. Yes, this is the biggest British force I've ever seen, and I've seen how many other foreign armies are here! How can we lose? But you've seen those things; this isn't about men versus men. We're up against something far more sinister."

Alex's smile faded.

"Look, if things start to go wrong, go find her and flee to Britain. I hope and pray we win, but war is war: someone will lose."

Private Clegg and the veteran joined the two men. They continued to load the wagon with stakes and then set off to the front line. The dust cloud in the distance had started to settle, telling them what they already knew: they were here.

Captain Hayward had his horse brought to him. Before joining his men, he rode to the top of one of the man-made mounds. It was a fantastic vantage point. He could see all the different armies preparing for battle. The Swedish army was to their immediate right, followed by a French division, and the Italians were next to them. In the forests to the south were Prussians and another French division. To the immediate left of the British forces was a Spanish army, followed by the Austro–Hungarian army. Covering the north was a French and a British cavalry brigade.

The stakes covered miles of fields, and small mounds were being built in front of each army. On these mounds, Gatling guns were placed with sandbags around them. The height was sufficient to avoid killing any men below. The idea was to have as many rows of soldiers behind sandbags below the Gatling guns as possible. Heavy artillery was placed further back. There were long-range and short-range mortars and artillery at a lower level to support the soldiers on the front line.

Captain Hayward left the mound and joined his men in the field. It was good seeing them, and the response he received indicated that they were happy to see him. Charles Hayward was not a man to sit and dictate work; he got stuck in. The mines being laid were an acceptable distance from the stakes. Ditches were being dug and filled with barrels of oil and explosives. Most of the hard work had been done, and the soldiers in the fields were putting in the finishing touches.

It was interesting watching their engineering counterparts work next to them; so many nationalities came together for the common good of Europe. The scouts had been stationed in small villages outside the city. Nothing had been reported yet, but the air was one of anticipation and nerves.

The hours were swallowed up with planting mines and creating sandbags. The Engineers were not alone; whole regiments used the soil from the freshly dug ditches to fill the bags. By late afternoon, Charles felt like the entire day was catching up with him. His men looked like they had hit the same wall.

Sergeant Butcher reported that the mines and other stakes were finished. The British were slightly ahead of the other countries, but only by a whisker. Several men were finishing off a dugout that would be used to ignite the mines. The men in it would then have to run as fast as they could through the fields of stakes, over the ditches and back behind the rows of sandbags before the mortars and Gatling guns opened up.

As the light faded and the men talked about food, a small group of riders came across the fields. Snipers took aim. It was of utmost importance that the riders were carrying their countries' flags; otherwise, they would have been shot. It turned out to be French and British scouts. The news was filtering in that the enemy had been spotted.

A minor skirmish had broken out in Nogent-l'Abbesse, a village less than three miles away. The enemy scouting party was huge and rapidly overran any resistance in the village. Directly in front of Nogent-l'Abbesse was a small forest. This gave the enemy the cover they needed to launch an attack. However, it was also hoped it would slow them down when they began their assault on Reims.

The different field marshals ordered all armies to "call to arms." They hoped this would prevent a night battle.

Major Richmond thanked his men as they gathered for supper. Different units were pushing onto the front lines, but for now, the Engineers were allowed time to rest and eat.

"You've all done well, men. This is a defining moment in a conflict that threatens the whole of Europe." All the Engineers could not hear his speech as there were so many, but he made sure he got his officers to pass on the information.

The generals fretted over their flanks. Precautions had been made to cover them with units in the south and north, backed up by large cavalry regiments. Still, not knowing about the enemy's tactics troubled many.

Field Marshal Prince George hoped for one more evening before the battle commenced. Communication was paramount to the European army's success, and ammunition was not far behind that. Tactics had been discussed, as many were still linked back to the Napoleonic years. With weaponry changing and firepower increasing, question marks were raised over the soldiers fighting in lines. The problem was that the eve of battle was neither the time nor the place to undertake a major reform.

Soldiers filled the forward positions quietly and together. The artillery crews checked the cannons and prepped the Gatling guns. Fireworks were loaded into mortars to use should they need some sort of night guide in the eventuality of an evening attack.

The Engineers were allowed to move back to the camp behind the wall. If an attack materialised, they would join the front-line soldiers. Their primary role had been to assist behind the scenes, building bridges and carrying out engineering tasks, but this war had brought them much more to the forefront of warfare.

Charles Hayward spoke to his friend Harry about the pending battle. He wanted to have clear instructions in case he did not return from the battlefield. The men took each other's notes and tucked them away inside their tunics.

Cooking for this vast army was a mission in itself. The camps had small farms working away to provide fresh meat for the different nations. Captain Hayward wondered if the enemy could hold out for a month or two. How long would this force be able to cope? The sheer attrition involved was monumental.

The soldiers from the fort in the Carpathian Mountains gathered together. They were all under Charles's command, and it was a good time to enjoy their food and rest. Nervous tension was still hanging over them all. The wait for the first gunshot or cannon rumble defined the mood.

A few small fires were lit, and folk songs broke out sporadically. Music was an acceptable way to relax, bringing the men closer together. There were some good singers amongst the group, and it was a harmonious event when they joined together in chorus.

Soon, the food was served, and the mood turned to rest. Charles became lost in his thoughts and looked at his family picture.

Chapter 27

Outside Nogent-l'Abbesse, other preparations were being made.

"My lord, they have built a large defensive system stretching around Reims. What should we do?"

Nazar sighed.

"Have you seen my army? What man-made wall will stop us?"

He pointed to a sea of drone soldiers, flesh-eaters, long-limbs, wolves, bears and heavy artillery.

"Oksana is taking the battle to them in the north of Reims. She will drive the enemy into confusion, and in the South, General Georgiy will squeeze them through the forests."

The general kept his head lowered and waited to be spoken to again.

"We will attack tomorrow. I want to see them suffer with my own eyes. Prepare my forces, and victory shall be ours."

He turned his horse and made his way towards his tent.

"Remember, I don't want them all killed. I have a need for some of them alive."

Chapter 28

It was early August, and the sun felt warm even at seven thirty in the morning. The officers noted this and sent out orders for water to be prepared and sent to all men at the front. The logistical side of any army was massive; with so many men, excellent preparation had to be taken by the orderlies and supply service.

The soldiers on the front line ate some breakfast as fast as they could. The Bugler could sound the alarm at any moment, and it was hard to tell when they would get another chance to eat.

Many of the men were enlisted only a short while ago, and their pre-battle nerves showed through. Some were throwing up, and others were drinking a little alcohol discreetly to calm themselves. This was all done under the keen eye of the officers. There's no point in having drunk soldiers in a battle situation.

A flock of blackbirds sprung up from the forest directly in front of the British forces. They did not resettle in the forest but flew over the soldiers as if leaving whilst they still could.

Silence followed. Tea was drunk, and food was consumed. Then, a whizzing sound burst through the air above, followed by an explosion as a shell slammed into a patch of fields. The shell was off-target but left a huge crater.

The Bugler called for the soldiers to stand. All the home nations complied. The men leaned against the sandbags, waiting for their first sight of the enemy. The Gatling gun crews primed their killing machines and scanned the horizon. Nothing came.

The morning passed, and the heat grew stronger and stronger. The orderlies administered water as often as possible.

The occasional soldier passed out and was swiftly replaced. The sick were taken to the camp to be assessed. Any soldier could face a court martial if he was caught faking it.

Captain Hayward rode to the front with a small detachment of Engineers. The major, along with several other senior officers, was pondering over a map on the back of a cart. Translators were on hand to feed information back to the command centre, where the field marshals were congregated.

Lunchtime came and went. There were no more shells or movement. An order was given to send out a small reconnaissance squad to gain an idea of what was happening on the enemy front. Rumours circulated that they had thought twice about attacking such a large modern army and turned and made haste with their tails between their legs.

A rider came charging past with news from the North. In his dispatch: "An army like no other has descended on us, fighting bravely. Not sure how long we can hold out without reinforcements."

A hurried meeting was called, and the order was given to send the reserves to the North.

Within thirty minutes, over half the Allied reserves were marching to the North to add to the divisions there. No sooner had the soldiers left than despatch riders noticed a gigantic army pushing through the forests south of Reims, led by a female priest.

The field marshals had feared they would try to flank them, but not from both sides and with such force. The worrying truth was starting to come to fruition. Captain Hayward arrived at the front and greeted Major Richmond. Whilst he dismounted, shells began to crash into the defence all along the front line. They took cover behind some sandbags and watched in horror as men and horses were torn to pieces in the explosions.

The damage to the defences was considerable, and the bombardment did not let up. The troops had some field artillery in the form of eighteen-pounder cannons, but there was nothing to fire at.

The bombardment lasted around ten minutes. When the smoke dust settled, there was a sea of destruction. Men were seen walking around without arms or crawling without legs. Casualties had been high, even with the added protection of the sandbags. The army medics with orderlies arrived promptly on the scene, taking away the injured men as well as they could.

Captain Hayward took out his binoculars and scanned the forests for movement. At first, he could see nothing but oak leaves gently swaying in the summer breeze, but then came the familiar drumming sound. The noise grew louder as figures started to emerge from the forest. Charles could see a mass of flesh-eaters, their lines only broken by drone soldiers on horseback, seemingly guiding them to their target.

It took a few minutes for the senior officers at the front to react. This was mainly due to the fact that many had not seen the flesh-eaters before, staggering along, mouths half open, and flesh hanging off their decomposing bodies. The officers were still watching through their binoculars when Major Richmond jumped on his horse and rode to the nearest field artillery with the eighteen-pounders. He was short with the officer in charge of that particular unit: "Open bloody fire on them!"

"I'm afraid, sir, that we must get an order from the field marshals to open fire."

Major Richmond shook his head.

"For the love of God, fire, man, before they are upon us."

The field battery officer was caught in two minds and pondered over what to do. Fortunately, the Swedish field cannons were the first to open fire, triggering a massive, thunderous barrage of shells flying into the oncoming enemy ranks.

The mortars also started to open fire, followed by the heavy artillery further back. The shells caused carnage unseen before, on this scale, to the advancing ranks. Limbs, heads and torsos were blown to pieces, and yet still the enemy advanced.

The noise along the front line was deafening, with all the nations firing their cannons. Cannon smog drifted over the soldier ranks and briefly blurred their vision. The enemy kept advancing, their casualties increasing by the minute, but this did not stop their momentum.

Fresh shells were constantly brought to the frontline. The field marshals were anxious about the fighting in the South. The forests would act as a defensive shield as the soldiers fought hard to control the enemy's advance. Only a small reserve force was left, but the decision was made to let them leave to reinforce the South.

The front-line British soldiers could now see the oncoming flesh-eaters and drone soldiers. The heat and dust left every man's mouth parched, but water was difficult to come by during battle. Orderlies were heavily involved with taking out wounded men and bringing fresh munitions.

The Gatling gun crews prepared to unleash hell upon this army of darkness, but they had to wait until they came into range. Soldiers prepared themselves behind the sandbags, and officers braced themselves for battle. The field artillery was now firing at close range at the oncoming force.

Captain Hayward was with Major Richmond. The major commanded a small engineering force and was involved with helping with any logistical needs around the British army. The captain's main force was helping with the defences at the wall.

Sergeant Butcher and Corporal Heinz were alongside him. They watched the battle unfold from a command mount that had been heavily fortified. As the enemy came into range, the first Gatling guns opened up. The rattling sound was just as piercing as the cannons. It was the absolute destruction of flesh and bone. It started to cut through the enemy's ranks with ease. Thousands died. Even the soldiers at the front were surprised at the sheer power of all the machines and their destructive combined force.

They were not allowed to dwell on this as the order was given to open fire. This coincided with the Gatling guns reloading or overheating. The soldiers with their breech-loading rifles were equally deadly. The repeated volley fire was spellbinding and started to push the enemy back. The shells continued to land amongst the retreating enemy, killing yet more in their thousands. The drone commanders wasted no time in redirecting their forces, and rumblings of sheer joy, as their enemy retreated, could be felt in the air.

The senior officers did not celebrate this first taste of victory. The scores of foes killed were ghastly and had not been seen in this number on a modern battlefield, but the nations that had previously fought the beast already expected more. They had seen the effect of what this new predator could do and how it had swallowed up most of Europe in less than six months.

"Charles, there is news that an army has been seen marching towards Paris. They have overrun the North," Major Richmond appeared concerned.

Captain Hayward looked out across the battlefield. In his eyes, it reflected the carnage of war and the sheer destruction of lives.

"Our families are there, Harry."

They both stood looking at the smouldering fields. The orderlies worked very hard to remove the wounded and resupply the front line. The Engineers were also involved in this process. Captain Hayward gathered his men and helped with this requirement.

The field marshals were behind the defensive wall, constantly having dispatches brought to them. The scene was chaotic as commanders worked relentlessly to get each other's views across about battle plans. This was stopped momentarily as explosions hit the south side of the wall.

The order was given to pull the Prussian and Italian units inside the camp and defend that side of the wall. It had to be a speedy manoeuvre, as the long limbs were breaking through from the forest and attacking soldiers as they retreated. Shells were also falling amongst the retreating armies, causing confusion and heavy casualties.

The jaws and powerful limbs of these creatures were difficult to fight against. Their numbers meant they were isolating small pockets of soldiers who instinctively tried to help their comrades. The disorder did not help, and the sight of drone soldiers advancing with flesh-eaters created an overwhelming need to retreat and to get inside the camp.

Brigadier Von Schwen was in charge of the Prussian force and fought alongside his men all the way back.

The Swedish army started to wheel its forces around to close the gap between the wall and the south side. British General Watt offered to help plug the gap with the Black Watch. The regiment was well respected on the battlefield and known for its fighting prowess, and the Swedes were very grateful to have them alongside them.

As this unfolded, the north wall came under attack. This meant the Austrians and French had to enter the camp and defend that side of the wall.

The British and French regiments that had been fighting in the North were now dispersed and scattered around, fighting hard not to be totally annihilated. The countries now left on the front line were Spain, Britain, and Sweden.

Northern riders were attacking the wall to the north with flesh-eaters, long-limbs and drone soldiers accompanying them. The Spanish forces had moved swiftly to plug the gap but had left holes. Their generals were trying in vain to fill them, but faced with such numbers and artillery fire, it was proving difficult.

Major Richmond helped at the British front line. The mines and bombs that had been set early were now being readied. They had been saved in the first attack; now was the time to use them. Captain Hayward was on his hands and knees, making his way to the dugout they had made in the fields to set the bombs off. He was with Corporal Heinz and two other soldiers.

The sound of warfare filled the air. The sun beamed down, making it hot, sweaty work. The soil was hot to the touch, crumbling a little in Captain Hayward's hand after each movement. They all slid into the dugout, hurriedly checked the fuses, and readied the detonators.

Their focus was changed when the drumming sound started again. The men looked up to see a mass of moving figures. The enemy was sweeping forward. The secret was setting the explosives off and returning to the British line as quickly as possible. Sitting there watching a sea of flesh-eaters coming towards them tested every man's nerve and inner soul.

The urge was to get up and run, knowing that all the creatures wanted to do was feed on their flesh and bones.

Captain Hayward tried to stay focused on the job in hand. He could not help but think about Paris and the army on its way to take it. His wife and children played on his mind. It was only a bullet hitting a wooden stake next to them that made him come round. The worrying point came when they realised the bullet had been fired from their own lines.

"Private Jones, go back and bloody well tell them we're in this hole to set the charges. Give them hell."

Jones almost looked relieved to get out of there. The sound of moving bodies and groaning got louder and louder. The creatures' teeth snapped back and forth, and, in a strange moment, Captain Hayward swore one of them seemed to catch his eye and shuffle faster. It was about holding your nerve, waiting as long as possible and setting off the fireworks.

They started to get within a reasonable range. Still, Charles waited.

Sweat dripped off Corporal Heinz's nose; his eyes told of the fear and loathing this wait was causing. Each staggered step towards them was a lifetime in anticipation of what would unfold. The men's focus turned to the fuse.

"Soon, men, they're nearly upon us."

As he said this, the oncoming mass of bodies parted. A sea of long limbs was charging through the ranks, directed by drone soldiers on horseback. Razor-tooths and double-headed bears supported this attack.

Charles lit the fuse, and the men started to run. The noise of the beasts and enemy force closing behind them helped keep their speed up.

By the time the explosion hit, they had made it to the first line of sandbags. The earth jumped with the size of the blast, knocking them to the ground. Captain Hayward came around with a high-pitched whistling hum in his ears. The rattle of the Gatling guns rapidly replaced this.

Sergeant Butcher helped him up and the other soldier with them, feeling relieved to have made it just past the killing range. Carnage greeted their eyes as they looked back. The crater left in the centre field was huge, but it had been rapidly swamped with flesh-eaters falling into it and then slowly crawling out the other side. The Gatling guns were now doing the same damage as before; the only problem was that there were not so many armies raining down bullets on the oncoming force.

They did not hang around and were helped over several more lines of sandbags with soldiers waiting patiently behind them, bayonets already fixed. The field cannons started to open up, but the enemy kept on coming.

The small group re-joined the major on the mount. They were in time to see the Gatling gun crews retreating as the machines overheated or simply ran out of ammunition. The enemy's sheer numbers were weighted to their advantage. Thousands were dying, but an endless stream of dead replenished them.

The heavier creatures were used to batter the sandbags and were herded towards the cannons. One cannon crew let fly with a volley, ripping a two-headed bear in half and cutting down hordes of onrushing long limbs. The army around them saw the rapid fire of these crews. They would never leave their post and would keep the cannons firing until the bitter end.

The front-line soldiers were laying down a repetitive volley fire. It was again having an overpowering effect on the enemy lines, but the larger creatures absorbed the impact on the smaller bodies behind them. This was enough to get the flesh-eaters to the first barricade. It then became a battle to hold them back.

Bayonets were used to good effect. The soldiers had been told that only headshots or bayonets to the head would kill the flesh-eaters. Being faced with creatures wanting to rip your intestines out and eat them was something different for these soldiers and became so real when anyone fell victim to this unforgiving opponent.

Watching from the mount gave Charles and the major a clear indication of how the battle was unfolding. The Swedish and Spanish armies were being hit hard, and the enemy was trying to break through at the sides.

News broke of fighting within Reims. The drone soldiers were launching an assault on the city. This meant they were pushing up behind them.

Captain Hayward spoke to the major about plans for a retreat and how it might be time to fall back to make sure they were not totally surrounded. He agreed with his old friend, but the order had to come from the field marshals.

The fighting was intense on the front line. All the Gatling guns were now out of action and some of the field cannons were also lost. The King's Royal Rifle Corps and 44th Regiment of Foot were now involved in heavy hand-to-hand fighting. Orderlies tried to hand out extra ammunition where possible and even joined the fighting when needed.

Long limbs smashed into the lines, hissing and biting as a group, using their large frames to gain an advantage.

Razor-tooths being ridden by drone soldiers had the upper hand in the hills north of the battle. The Spanish forces were torn apart and on the verge of collapse.

Captain Hayward's men were behind the main camp wall, helping with supplies and reinforcing the wall when needed. The major was with his Engineer regiment and got them to form a circle around the mount. Captain Hayward could see the dark priests on horseback fighting alongside their men and creatures. It was the first time he had seen so many of them.

No order came through about retreating, and the battle raged for another hour before the sheer number of flesh-eaters started breaking the lines. Regiments were forced into forming squares or circles in a last-ditch stand. They soon realised no quarter would be given.

Shells started to rain from the sky, killing men indiscriminately. They did not care that they were also killing their own forces. Large explosions saw men and horses blown to pieces, arms and legs ripped off and multiple injuries occurring all over the battlefield.

A wave of staggering flesh-eaters buffered the Royal Engineers. Their first volley fire killed hundreds. The trouble was that thousands were coming in behind them. Drone cavalry charged at the fragmented units. Captain Hayward looked at his dear old friend.

"Harry, give the order. There's still time."

His eyes signalled his response. He leaned over and gave Charles an envelope. There was a horrible moment of realisation. Both men stood there motionless for a second or two. A single tear rolled down Captain Hayward's cheek. He then saluted the major and hugged him.

Corporal Heinz shook the major's hand.

With no time to spare, Charles left with Sergeant Butcher and Corporal Heinz.

"Why are they not retreating?" questioned Corporal Heinz.

A little hoarse in his voice, a soft answer came out from Captain Hayward.

"Too proud and too stubborn. Without an order from the high command, he will stand his ground until the end."

Corporal Heinz helped hold the horses as they mounted. They broke out of the circle, knocking over flesh-eaters who were coming from all angles. Captain Hayward looked back at his dear old friend. A single nod was his last contact.

They galloped at speed to the entrance of the main camp. Fighting was spread out over a large area around them. Some Spanish and British forces tried to regain some sort of line, but the enemy was using the larger creatures to break this and was now bringing in the drone cavalry to help pick off smaller groups.

The flesh-eaters were tearing into soldiers. Screams and cries of fallen men being devoured alive filled the battlefield.

The Grenadier Guards holding the gate were trying their best to keep the advancing hordes out.

They were also trying not to lay down friendly fire on their own soldiers, which was difficult in the melee that was occurring around them.

A brigadier came forward on his horse. Several dragoons escorted him.

"Captain, bring your men through."

The men squeezed their way through the tight ranks into the camp. The brigadier was a friend of Major Richmond and had been advised that Charles would be returning to his men.

Inside the walls, the defence was coming under heavy fire. It was starting to crumble around them. Captain Hayward quickly got to his detachment. They were busy reinforcing a wall and helping out the orderlies where possible. Shells were coming into the camp and taking their toll on units gathered close together. Army surgeons were doing their best they could to stem the loss of blood from severed limbs and flesh-eater victims.

A razor-tooth had broken over a breach in the wall but was swiftly dealt with by a roaming unit of 9th Lancers. They charged it together, and even though several were thrown from their horses, they managed to inflict enough wounds on the beast to bring it down and plunge lances into its head.

Private Brown was helping Private Clegg with several sandbags. His mind was on Heidi, who was helping the sick and wounded not too far away.

"If you're thinking of deserting, pick your moment, John."

John gave him a quizzical look.

"I'll judge the situation if it comes to that. I love her."

The two soldiers looked at each other and smiled. Amongst the fighting and raging battle, there was a moment of normality. It was promptly broken, though, as a shell landed near them.

Charles asked Sergeant Butcher to check on the troops. Morale was fairly high amongst the men, as they all worked in close proximity to each other, their rifles stacked nearby.

Captain Hayward was lost momentarily, thinking about his friend Harry Richmond.

He wanted to ride out of the camp and collect him from the mount, but the fighting had become overwhelming in all directions. The camp walls were starting to buckle under the pounding they were receiving. There were several Gatling guns being manoeuvred into spaces where the wall was being overrun.

The field marshals discussed the next battle move, but their resources were now stretched. The front line was fractured, and the European armies split into hundreds of splintered groups. The enemy was throwing everything at them. The fields around Reims were a sea of flesh-eaters. The drone soldiers were now being used to focus the fighting on areas deemed of strategic all-importance.

Major Richmond gathered what he could of his regiment and formed a circle on top of the mount. He could see the high priest orchestrating the battle and realised a fair few were fighting alongside this fearsome army. His men were running low on ammunition. Some Black Watch Highlanders soon joined them under the excellent stewardship of General Watt. The General had fought bravely and hard against unrelenting odds and had seen his regiment decimated, leaving just a small handful. Some Swedish soldiers had come to the mount and joined in this last stand.

Karl Lundin, a sergeant in the Swedish foot patrol, went up to the Major and explained they had seen the Swedish army destroyed, and now the last of his nation's men were fighting in small pockets around the front entrance. General Watt joined them, sword in one hand and revolver in the other. He was covered in blood and had the look of a wild animal about him. He was known as the fighting general, and his men loved him for that. The mount was soon surrounded by flesh-eaters and drones fighting to kill everything in their path.

Long-limbs were pushing to the front, biting and slashing at what they could. The British and Swedish forces were almost entirely out of ammunition. It was hand-to-hand on the mount.

Thick, oily smoke drifted across the battlefield. Major Richmond and his small band of Royal Engineers retreated further up the mount, stumbling over fallen soldiers and discarded weaponry. General Watt joined him with a handful of Black Watch Highlanders.

Long limbs were breaking through the lines, allowing flesh-eaters to surge in. With limited ammunition and dwindling ranks the fight was reaching its climax at the front. As the flesh-eaters surged amongst them, Major Richmond was knocked to the ground, dropping his revolver in the process. Two staggering flesh-eaters homed in on him. One was a woman in her later years, her grey hair matted with blood and her skin rotting around her cheeks. The other was a young lad, possibly a teenager, before becoming infected. His mouth was missing lips, and his teeth were broken in places. He seemed to move faster than the older lady and soon grappled with the major's legs.

The first bite took out a large chunk of calf muscle. The major let out a roar as the pain hit his senses hard. The creature went to take another bite but was kicked back by the major's flailing legs. By this time, the older lady was trying to bite his arms. He was fighting hard, and with the whole mount engulfed by flesh-eaters, there was no chance of escape. She managed to tear a strip of skin from his forearm. The major tried to push her back and reach for his revolver. Suddenly, a sword swung down and decapitated her in one clean swoop. The teenager came back for more but was ruthlessly shot in the head.

Standing over the major's wounded body was General Watt. "It's nearly our time, laddie!"

This was said with a stone-cold face. General Watt helped him up, and they stood with three other men at the top. The remaining soldiers were being taken down and feasted on. The sheer volume of flesh-eaters dulled their screams and shouts. A Highland soldier loaded his last bullet.

The major quickly drew out his photograph of his family and looked at his wife and children one last time.

Then, the general looked at the men; the creatures were coming at them from all angles.

"If you don't mind, gentlemen, I'd like to die the Highland way."

They looked at him and nodded.

Then, leading from the front, General Watt let out a roar which could be heard all around and charged down the mount with the major and the other three soldiers. They were able to cut, kick and slash several flesh-eaters before being swallowed into the masses.

The order was never given for them to retreat.

Captain Hayward told his men to gather their weapons and form a group. He wondered if they would share the same fate as his good friend Major Richmond.

"Corporal Heinz, get me news from the field marshals," ordered Captain Hayward.

Corporal Heinz left quickly to find a horse and ride to the HQ within the camp. The British lines were slowly retreating from the front. The uniforms were mixed as different European soldiers fought side by side. Such was the sight all around the main walls.

The cannons and Gatling guns could not easily be used on the advancing enemy, as the front lines were heavily populated with Allied soldiers.

Captain Hayward could see this all unfolding and spoke with Sergeant Butcher about getting ready to pull the men out of the camp. Rumours had surfaced about the city being surrounded. Corporal Heinz returned swiftly, looking perplexed.

"The headquarters have been overrun." Captain Hayward turned immediately to the Sergeant and gave him an order. "Sergeant, move the men out now. We must fall back through the outskirts of the city and get to Paris."

The men had their packs and supplies nearby. The preparation had been good. This was a difficult decision to make, but units were starting to fall back and run. The officers were lost in a sea of confusion. The noise of gunfire, shouts, and roars filled the battlefield. Smoke and dust helped create confusion for the ensuing force, which was relentless in its pursuit of flesh and bone.

Orderlies and medical staff were trying to help the wounded into carts and wagons. The buildings that had been used for hospitals and supply dumps were chaotically emptied. While the Royal Engineers were retreating, Colonel Kiesl arrived on horseback with a small group of men. He had seen the Royal Engineers' flag carried away from the front. The European forces were now in full flight, and pockets of outstanding bravery erupted as they pulled back. This gave various units time to regroup and fight a semi-organised retreat.

Private Brown appeared next to Captain Hayward as they fell back.

"Sir, may I?"

"Be quick, man. This city will fall very shortly."

John left to find Heidi. Private Clegg joined him in his search.

"Attach bayonets," signalled Captain Hayward.

Captain Hayward split the group into two hundred-man-strong detachments. Colonel Kiesl took one detachment and Captain Hayward the other. It was not the time to worry about an Austrian captain leading a British force. The men knew him and trusted his judgement, and so did Captain Hayward.

Behind them came a sea of hungry flesh-eaters, stumbling, crawling and hell-bent on eating anything that got in their way.

The two groups moved rapidly through the south of the city. Fighting had broken out earlier, with Gatling guns firing from supply buildings. Shells were falling hard on the buildings around them; masonry bits fell from the skies.

The cohesion of the European force was now gone. The sick and wounded were being moved out of the city, but inevitably, most were left to fend for themselves as the city was swallowed up.

Captain Hayward's men came under small arms fire from several drone soldiers who had occupied a large apartment block. They had broken the windows and were firing on anyone retreating near them. Two of the Engineers were killed in this exchange of fire. This was not a time to be pinned down, as long limbs had joined in the city's occupation. Streets were filling with these incessant creatures, like a broken dam allowing water out of its containment.

Luck was on their side as two massive shells landed on the apartment block. The explosion blew out glass and debris across a vast area. Some of the men were injured, but there was no real time to assess how badly. Colonel Kiesl, whose detachment was in close proximity to the captain's, quickly grabbed the chance to move. If the men inside had survived the hit, they would return to their posts.

They pushed on past the smouldering building. Privates Brown and Clegg had found Heidi; John kept her close. She was not the only one; with the help of three doctors, John had helped rescue ten more nurses. It had been hard – the wounded could not be taken with them, and some of the medical staff decided to stay behind with the soldiers. Sadly, it would mean certain death.

Private Clegg looked into the building as they passed. His eyes feasted on a drone soldier's body. It looked severely mutilated from the explosion. To his horror, he saw it twitch and move. He knew the drone soldiers were always one step away from turning, as they had witnessed in the village before. Still, this whole scenario added desperation to his mindset as he felt they could not compete with an army that, once killed, came back even stronger.

John saw his friend flagging and told him to knuckle down and keep moving. The dust was making most of them cough, and it was also hard to keep everyone together. Some of the streets were narrow, and they did not have a great understanding of where they were going. Corporal Heinz was the leading light, and he directed them as well as he could out of the city.

A clearing coming up ahead offered a chance to leave the city. However, this moment was quickly lost as six long limbs with fifteen or more wolves circled the area. No priests were guiding them, but for some strange reason, they stayed put as if told to wait and guard.

Captain Hayward had no choice. He asked Colonel Kiesl to ready his men for a charge.

"Alexander, get on the roof of the nearest house. I'll send two men with you. Work your magic with that rifle, son," ordered Captain Hayward.

"As God is my witness, I shall give you time."

Alexander left without another word.

The two detachments lined up behind a large building. The enemy was closing in through the city, shouting and intimidating them as they approached their position. It was now or never.

Captain Hayward looked up at the roof and saw Alexander and the other men move into position. With that, he raised his hand, and the men charged, bayonets reflecting the afternoon's dying sun.

A long limb looked up and growled as the advancing soldiers ran towards them. The wolves, larger than normal, looked imposing as they reacted and charged at the soldiers.

The first bullet from Alexander's rifle was filled with anger. It struck its target straight between the eyes. The long limb fell to the ground in a heap and was rapidly surpassed by the others. They came all at once, clambering towards the British and Austrian soldiers. Captain Hayward gave the signal to Colonel Kiesl. He bellowed out his orders simultaneously as the sergeants and both detachments lined up into two rows. As this unfolded, another long limb came crashing down, followed by a wolf. Alexander was taking no prisoners.

"First rank, take aim…Fire!"

"Second rank, take aim...Fire!"

The shooting was accurate and deadly. Long limbs collapsed onto wolves, and the once menacing pack of animals rushing them looked weakened. The volley fire was effective and backed up by excellent marksmanship. The order was given to advance and fire. The creatures had been dealt with effectively, and for once, the firepower had been enough to kill the advancing foe. The remaining long limbs and wolves were in two minds whether to attack or run. They stalled momentarily without a drone soldier or priest to push them on.

Alexander seized this opportunity to kill them. Bullet after bullet was loaded into his rifle, and each time he squeezed the trigger, a creature fell silent.

The soldiers moved into the open, and Captain Hayward waved so that the men could leave the rooftop. They waited a couple of minutes for Alexander and the other soldiers to arrive and then set off across the fields. Smoke was rising from the city rooftops, and gunfire was breaking out over the southern area.

The men's heavy backpacks slightly restricted their speed. The weather had been warm, and the ground was at least dry.

"Halt."

Sergeant Butcher stopped the soldiers and nurses in their tracks. On the horizon, some fifty-odd Northern riders gathered on a small embankment. The men's gut feeling was that this was a desperate situation—caught out in the open with no real heavy firepower.

Captain Hayward sighed but did not let the others see his obvious disappointment. He questioned himself why he had not sent Corporal Heinz out to check the surrounding area, but he knew the answer was simple: the enemy was everywhere, and this would be a fight-and-run chase from now on in.

There was no point in running, so he ordered the Engineers and Austrian soldiers to form four lines. The nurses and army medics were the only ones allowed to move towards a copse.

The riders fanned out and prepared for a full-on charge. Emerging from the outskirts of the city was the dreaded sight of flesh-eaters. They must have picked up the scent of fresh meat and moved on it.

Private Brown looked over his shoulder at Heidi disappearing into the distance. She had kissed him on the cheek and told him to come with her. She had said they could just run and never come back. But the truth was darker: their chances of survival depended on numbers, and alone, it would be ten times harder. Her red eyes stayed in his mind as he loaded a bullet into the breach. He looked over to his dear friend William.

"Bloody mess all of this, eh?"

William nodded.

"Don't worry, you'll see her again," William reassured John.

"Face up, lads, here they come!" shouted the Sergeant.

The noise of the giant horses shook the ground. The Northern riders then let out a shriek, their swords and axes catching the last of the daylight.

"Wait until you see the whites of their eyes," Sergeant Butcher focused on the men.

The yards fell away at speed.

Hands grew sweaty, and hearts sped up in anticipation of the impact. The men aimed and prepared to fire. At that moment, a bugle sounded. A thunderous roar filled every person's ears.

The 16th Lancers had appeared from the right flank, tearing down the hill at speed, their blue uniforms outlined with white straps and white helmets. It was a beautiful sight; they possibly outnumbered the Northern riders three to one. Their impact on the charging enemy was dramatic. They were ill-prepared for the attack from the side, and the Lancers wreaked havoc as they swept through their prey.

Some Northern riders tried to re-adjust to this surprise attack, but the damage was already being done. Their fellow soldiers were being mowed down and slaughtered without mercy.

The officer in charge cut a dashing figure. His approach was daring and brash. The enemy soon broke off from the attack and fled to the city. The order was given not to pursue them as flesh-eaters were emerging from different parts of Reims.

Captain Hayward seized the moment and got his men moving out of the open. The officer came over to the captain and introduced himself as the commanding officer of what was left of the 16th Lancers. He explained they were escorting the wounded out of the city and heading for the coast. France was falling, and Great Britain was now the only escape route.

Although he seemed normal, his eyes were dead. He carried a deep burden and was now happy to fight for the cause of Europe. He told Charles that his son was with a small convoy that they were going to join.

Most of the flesh-eaters drifted back into the city as they picked up different smells and noises. Some wandered after the soldiers, but their speed was enough to gain a good distance quickly. After ten minutes, they had reached a thicket, amongst which was a small collection of wagons and carts. The commandeering officer went over and hugged his son. Their bond was strong, and the relief in the boy's eyes at seeing his father return was heart-warming. John was also close to tears when he realised the Austrian nurses and army medics were also there. Heidi came forward and kissed him on the lips. She did not care about military rules at that moment; it was all about her love for John.

They promptly set off for the coast. Captain Hayward and some of the other men were given horses from fallen Lancers. The captain had one thought in mind: Paris.

His wife and children were there, and now a sea of darkness would descend on the city without an army of noticeable size to defend it. The thought made him feel a little dizzy. He had a duty to his men, but his heart told him to ride for his family. The sergeant could see him fighting an internal war of conscience as they rode along.

"Sir, I'll ride with you now," said the Sergeant.

Charles looked up, a little puzzled, until he realised his trusty sergeant had figured out his thought process. Corporal Heinz came up to enquire about what was going on. He was asked if he would ride to Paris with them. His scouting skills would save time and keep them out of danger.

Captain Hayward approached Colonel Kiesl and asked if he would take command of his men while he was away. The men knew the colonel and respected his leadership skills. He was very understanding about Charles needing to ensure his family's safety; leaving your regiment was not standard procedure and would typically result in a court-martial. However, as things stood, the whole of Europe was in chaos. The enemy was swallowing up towns and cities with ease.

The commanding officer of the 16th Lancers came forward. His demeanour was robust and decisive.

"I've heard you're planning on leaving us, Captain."

"Yes, it's my—"

"I understand a lot of the officers have family in Paris. You should leave now whilst you still can. Stay off the roads and beware of razor-tooths. They will be in the forward hunting parties."

The Lancer officer explained they would be heading for the port of Cherbourg. The ships and boats were leaving, and there was a chance they would get on a vessel back to Britain.

The men shook hands, and Charles noticed a trinket hanging from the lancer's neck. The officer touched the trinket before wishing him Godspeed.

Charles wasted no more time and left the convoy in transit. The soldiers wondered where their leader was going, but it was not the time or place to question it. Colonel Kiesl would inform the men when they next stopped for a rest.

Captain Hayward felt guilty as he left his detachment but also felt they were in capable hands.

The route to Paris was not easy. They moved from thicket to copse and tried to use small woodland areas where possible. Soldiers' movements were also something they could not avoid. Many men and women were still fleeing the oncoming mass of flesh-eaters. The roads were packed, and disorder was evident at each step. Panic had set in, and orders were not being translated down to units.

The French army in charge of Paris was already fighting a losing battle. The wolves and Northern riders had arrived with the high priestess, causing a stir with a relentless assault on the city. Reinforcements were being sent from Nazar, and she already boasted half the city.

The men rode well into the evening but agreed it was too difficult and dangerous to navigate through the countryside. Charles had a strong urge to press on, but he knew his heart was now ruling his head. They had already seen several razor-tooths feeding on animal and human carcasses. The sheer speed of the enemy advance and their raiding parties caused complete dismay within the retreating forces.

That night, no one slept. The sounds crept through the woods and hung in the trees, causing the wildlife to retreat deeper and deeper into the forests. Darkness was coming across the land.

Captain Hayward was up early with the dawn chorus, preparing the horses. A crow cawing woke the other two men. Everyone had grown to dislike these birds as they fed on the dead. Soon, the three of them were riding again. It took several days before they began to get closer to Paris. It was nearly lunchtime when Paris came into view. The north of the city was on fire, and sporadic shells were landing heavily on that side. The captain's heart sped up. He felt a sickness come over him as he panicked about his wife and children. Their faces and voices filled his mind and ears. His thigh muscles released his grip on the saddle, and he began to slide a little. The sergeant's hand came across and steadied him.

"Gentlemen, this is as far as you have to go. Save yourselves," suggested Captain Hayward.

Both the sergeant and the corporal shook their heads.

"We will follow you in."

"I cannot allow that. If you must wait, then stay here. Give me two hours; if I do not return, ride to Cherbourg and save your souls."

The sergeant looked up.

"Godspeed, Charles."

He shook both men's hands and spurred the horse on into Paris.

Chapter 29

As Captain Hayward rode closer to the city, his eyes fell upon the devastation. Small cottages were burning, and bodies lay strewn outside on roads and in gardens. This enemy was a killing machine. It knew no mercy and was consuming everything.

Someone was sheltering inside a house, looking out with haunted eyes. Charles looked up helplessly, full of sorrow about their plight. It was the end for that poor soul, and he knew he could do nothing to help. The people left in the city were trying to evacuate but were being caught before they could escape.

His horse stirred, and he patted her side while whispering to calm her. The thick smell of burning flesh filled the small streets and penetrated the very clothes covering his body. His thoughts lingered on about his family. He prayed they had retreated to his cousin's house on the south side of the city, as this was where he was heading.

A scream burst out from a large town apartment. Then several small calls and yelps and then stony silence. Charles's hand hovered over his revolver.

He rode on for another five minutes before coming to the house. He dismounted and ran to the door, knocking hard for a minute. No one answered. He tied the horse to a fence post and ventured around the back. The door was locked, but he forcefully threw himself at it, repeating the action until it began to split. He then kicked the door with a desperate, frenzied motion.

It eventually gave way, and he burst inside. He cried out to anyone who was there. He called Rebecca's name and Arthur and Emily, but no reply came. His heart sank, and his eyes fell upon a picture of all of them at a ball in Paris the year before. Thoughts of his beautiful wife and darling children caused a tear to roll down his left cheek.

He closed his eyes and revisited the moment captured in the photograph. Rebecca looked so radiant that evening. Her face was enchanting, and he pinched himself – he had to be the luckiest man in the world. When they embraced, her soft perfume filled his senses, and her skin was like silk as he pressed his face next to hers. They danced and kept eye contact as he spun her around. Once the orchestra stopped playing, she leaned forward and kissed him on the lips. In high society, this was not considered good manners. This is why he loved her – for her spontaneity and rebellious side. They both looked over at young Arthur and cute little Emily as they sat with his cousin, laughing and joking.

Rebecca pressed her lips to his ear. "Charles, never forget this moment."

He pulled her close and looked into her eyes. "I love you."

Outside, a shattering window brought Charles out of his daydream. He looked at the picture once more. He then checked upstairs and in the cellar to make one hundred per cent sure they were not there. He touched his fingers to his revolver. Then, something caught his eye on the mantelpiece. It was a note with his name on it. He recognised his wife's writing.

Dear Charles,

I pray to God you're alive. It feels like a lifetime since I last kissed your soft lips. The world has gone mad. There is talk of people who are dead walking the land, and nowhere is safe anymore. The children miss you; it's hard not knowing where you are. I know you will read this, and we will see you again. We have gone with Catherine to the church on the south side of the city. Church Sainte-Anne de la Butte-aux-Cailles. It's in the area of Maison-Blanche. We have all been there several times with your cousin.

My dearest husband, take care.
We love you so much.

Rebecca, Arthur, Emily xxx

It was the kick he needed. He wiped his eyes and burst out of the house. He came across a flesh-eater moving towards his horse. The animal was doing well not to get too spooked, but it was tied to a post and could not escape if it wanted to.

Captain Hayward withdrew his revolver but was aware that noise attracted their attention. He had the element of surprise, so as it closed in on the horse, he moved forward and kicked it to the ground. He then withdrew his sword and plunged it into the creature's head. He wasted no time mounting the horse and riding towards the church.

The journey was littered with despair. People were running from building to building. Some were thieves, taking plunder where they could, not genuinely comprehending the situation and the consequences of their decisions. Others had left it too late and were confused about where to go.

Charles could not help. He had to reach the church, even if that meant passing flesh-eaters feeding on corpses. His gut instinct was to attack them, but he had to be wise and keep moving. Every narrow street had to be avoided – the risk was too significant. His heart was pounding as he reflected on his family.

Smoke drifted out of apartment blocks. A French soldier came out of a doorway and looked at the captain. He did not speak or express emotion; his eyes followed the captain's until he was out of sight. Captain Hayward had to take a detour as a collection of priests and Northern riders passed him two junctions in ahead. He thought one of them looked like a female priest, but he could not be sure.

This thought was taken away from him as he was knocked from his horse. His body hit the ground hard, and it took him a couple of seconds to regain his composure. As he did so, a large wolf pounced on him. Its teeth ripped into his helmet and swung him around like a rag doll. He tried in vain to reach his revolver, only for it to slip from his holster and be kicked away by his trailing left foot.

With a paw on each shoulder, the wolf lowered its giant head and opened its mouth. The teeth were sharp, and its breath was foul. Saliva dripped onto the captain's face and ran down his chin. Thud. The creature fell on top of him, its weight pinning him to the ground. He had no idea who had shot the beast, but he was grateful as he fought hard to roll it off.

His horse had not strayed far, and Charles was able to remount and continue. The city was now probably the most dangerous place in France. The enemy had overrun its streets, and the creatures spearheading this war were taking their victims in a ruthless fashion.

Charles approached the road towards the church with anxiety and excitement. As he got closer, he saw a small group gathered around. From a distance, they looked like women and children. He spurred his horse on and quickened his pace. To his dismay, the road had been barricaded with high iron gates. These gates had been wrapped with broken glass and nails. He scoured the sides of the walls. There were no entrance points or windows to climb. He thought about standing on his horse and trying to climb over, but these gates had been made with one purpose: to keep people out. He would need explosives to clear his way through.

He could see across to the other roads leading to the open square where the church was situated, and they had been blocked in the same way.

There was only one clear route to the far left of the church, which was not blocked. Negotiating his way back to another crossing could take ten minutes or more. His eyes fell upon the most glorious sight: Emily. Her hair had been made into a French plait, and she was holding her teddy bear.

"Rebecca! Emily! Arthur!"

He shouted as loud as he could.

All three of them came forward and saw Charles standing on the other side of the blockade.

"Daddy!"

They ran towards him at full speed. Emily dropped her teddy, but seeing her father was more important, so she kept running. Rebecca and Charles had tears in their eyes.

"My sweet wife and children. Thank God you're alive."

Tears flowed from all of them, and Rebecca could not hide her excitement. "Charles, I knew we would see you again; I just knew it."

He put his arm through the iron railings, and his family snuggled into it. He was able to kiss his wife through the gap, avoiding the glass and nails. The children then wanted a kiss as well.

"We don't have much time. I need to get you out of Paris."

Their euphoria was broken by the sound of a horn being blown, and then a shout burst through the open air.

"They're here!" screamed a woman by the church.

The flesh-eaters were coming along the unblockaded road. A couple of French soldiers tried in vain to halt them, but they were quickly overrun and set upon in a frenzied feeding attack.

The fear in the children's eyes turned Charles's stomach. "I must get you over." He started to climb the iron gates, but it had also been oiled, making it virtually impossible. Blood streamed from his hands.

"Daddy, they're coming."

Panic had now fully set in. He searched everywhere around him. In his mind, there had to be a way.

"Rebecca, get yourself and the children inside the church."

She looked at him with a sorrowful face.

"We've tried, but all the doors are locked."

Arthur came forward.

"I don't want to die, Daddy."

Charles fell to his knees. He couldn't stop himself; he cried uncontrollably. Reaching through the iron gates, he pulled his family in close. They held each other for a moment.

"I love you, Charles, and I always will."

"Rebecca, I love...I love all of you."

Their tearful faces looked upon their father's, and they smiled.

"Go, Charles. You must not witness this."

"I cannot, and I will not leave." With that, he reached for his revolver and placed it to his head.

"We shall all go together."

The flesh-eaters were closing in. Their groans and grunting sounds became more evident the closer they came. The people outside the church were desperately banging on its doors.

His eyes scanned his wife and children for the last time. He had decided that at the moment the creatures struck, he would pull the trigger.

Through the noise and sheer haze in his mind, he heard a voice. "Madam, Madam!"

He opened his eyes and saw an old woman standing halfway out of a cellar door. The remaining people were funnelling down into the cellar. She called over for Rebecca and the children to come.

"Rebecca, go now. I'll cover you and the children."

They let go of their father just as the flesh-eaters closed in. Charles turned the revolver on the first creature nearest to his family, took aim and squeezed the trigger. The body fell to the ground from a clean headshot. Another came into his sight, and again, he dispatched it with aplomb.

Rebecca had Emily and Arthur in each hand. She darted towards the woman who was waiting patiently at the cellar entrance. This was very brave, as flesh-eaters were closing in. He squeezed the trigger two more times, killing two more creatures in the process. Emily was handed to the woman first and passed down into the cellar. Then, as Arthur was picked up, a flesh-eater stumbled from an unsighted part of the church.

The angle was not good for Charles to risk taking a shot with his wife and son there. The flesh-eater grabbed Arthur's leg and lowered its face to bite.

Rebecca lashed out with a kick and pushed the creature back. She passed Arthur to the woman and then returned to give the flesh-eater a good punch in the face. This stopped it for only a moment, but it was enough for Charles to take aim and shoot the beast in the head.

Rebecca looked over quickly and blew a kiss before disappearing into the cellar. The doors were promptly shut after her.

Charles fell to his knees. He was shaking and not entirely in control. The flesh-eaters tried in vain to reach him through the iron gates, their arms stretching through, not feeling the glass cutting their rotting flesh.

The next voice he heard made him spin around with his revolver drawn.

"Sir, are you okay?"

It was Corporal Heinz.

"What are you doing here? Where's the sergeant?"

"He's coming. We could not leave you in Paris alone. We've come too far."

Corporal Heinz could see Charles was an emotional wreck, but he held back on asking any questions. He did not know his family had escaped into the church cellar. Instead, he advised him to leave with him and regroup with the sergeant.

"I must find another way to the church. They're in there, underground," said Charles anxiously.

Sergeant Butcher was waiting at a nearby junction. He had his rifle drawn and was reloading it as the other men approached. "Quickly, Northern riders are in this vicinity," explained the Sergeant. The corporal led the way. He believed he knew another route to the church. Unfortunately, that route was blocked, making them turn around and head for a bridge over a small stream.

When they arrived in that area, they were greeted by a constant flow of priests and drone cavalry. The high priestess could be seen leading her troops. The wolves were circling, and flesh-eaters were filling the streets.

"We can't go this way, Captain," the Sergeant said softly.

The captain was agitated. He was not thinking clearly.

"I've got to get to them. They're my family."

The other two men agreed but knew not how to help. Corporal Heinz then remembered that many of the churches had underground passages. It was possible they even entered the catacombs. He went on to add that these were the old stone mines under Paris.

Charles sat on his horse, pondering what to do. His soul wanted to charge into the street and ride to the church, but he realised his family might no longer be there and could very well be heading underground and out of Paris. It was an impossible situation; he did not know what to do. The noise of gunfire broke out close by. The enemy was closing in fast.

"I will ride with you to Caen. From there, you can go on to Cherbourg," Said Captain Hayward.

His intentions were clear. Once he left his men at Caen, he would try and wait in France as long as he could and scour the various ports for his family.

The men turned their horses and broke out of Paris at speed. The last of the city was being surrounded. Small pockets of soldiers were fighting a losing battle against overwhelming odds.

Chapter 30

The journey to Caen was long and arduous. They camped twice in small thickets and woodlands along the route. Bridges had been destroyed, adding time and costing them extra energy to navigate. They stayed away from all the villages and towns—nothing could be trusted now.

Bodies littered the route. Some were wounded soldiers who had perished on the retreat; others were sick or malnourished civilians. It was a mixture of old and young – they could not look at any children lying by the road. Each man kept his sorrow to himself and grieved in silence.

When they finally reached the outskirts of Caen, a small group of marines emerged from a dilapidated farmhouse. Lieutenant Hazewater was in charge and quick to point out chaos along the whole coast. Ships were coming backwards and forwards, trying to rescue as many as possible. He admitted that soldiers were getting first priority, and civilians had to wait.

"My wife and children are amongst those civilians, Lieutenant."

He looked a little awkward. "They will do their best for everyone. This evacuation is on a scale like no other. We simply don't have the resources."

Charles softened his stance. "My men here need to get to Cherbourg and retreat with their unit. I will stay in France as long as possible to search for my family."

The marine looked at him. "You do realise you might not make it out? The enemy is already attacking along the coast. They have moved like lightning, their forces unstoppable."

He stopped short of shrugging his shoulders. He explained they would leave soon and were merely mopping up stragglers and taking out enemy scouts.

Captain Hayward wished Sergeant Butcher and Corporal Heinz all the best for the future, however long that may be. Both soldiers insisted they could stay with him, but he said they had to return and would fight another day to avenge the atrocities of this war. The formalities went out the window, and both men hugged the captain. Lieutenant Hazewater made no comment. He understood this was a grave time for all and that dark days lay ahead.

The sun was slowly setting. Captain Hayward remounted and galloped towards Mont Saint-Michel. The Lieutenant had told him that this had been a destination from Paris for civilians, although the French coast was vast. Rumours were circulating that Jersey was being used as a staging post for Britain. He would wait there first before moving on to Saint-Malo.

The French countryside was in full bloom. The fields carried a sweet freshness as the summer drew to an end. The birds and insects still seemed happy to occupy their day with normality. He questioned how Mother Nature had not sent a storm to destroy this abomination. He was a churchgoing man but questioned the ideal around such an uprising. Had the Devil gained a foothold on the land and was now taking the souls he so desired?

When he thought about his family, his heart sank. He didn't know what he would do without them. His hand swept over the revolver. In fairness, he did know.

That night, he rested in a small barn with livestock hanging around, looking unmanaged and a little lost. In the morning, he found a stream to wash and drink from. He had a little food with him and scoffed it down for energy, forgetting its staleness.

He then made sure the horse drank and petted it as it did so. He appreciated that the animal had saved his life on many occasions.

Together, they arrived outside the causeway leading to Mont Saint-Michel. It was tidal, and he remembered reading as a boy that the sea could come in faster than a galloping horse. A slight sea mist swept across the mudflats. Tufts of grass swayed, catching the eye of the captain and his horse. He looked over at Mont Saint-Michel. It was an enchanting abbey and town. He wished his family were with him now. He also hoped they had made it to a port on the coast.

He turned the horse and moved towards the abbey. Coming towards him was a small group of riders in an aggressive formation. Once close enough, they relaxed their stance. They could see he was a British soldier.

"Monsieur! Monsieur! We need your assistance. The enemy is arriving, and we must hold the causeway until the tide comes in."

Charles looked on, but his heart and mind were in another place.

"My wife and children, I must find them."

"We have accepted many British families into the abbey, and many have left for Jersey and Britain. They could very well be in there."

Charles looked up to the skies. He had no idea whether they would say anything to gain support in this dark hour, but the castle had to be defended, so he agreed to help.

"How long until the tide comes in?"

"We have half an hour."

In the distance, a long limb emerged on a sand dune. It raised itself and sniffed the air, then let out a bellowing croaking sound.

A small hill was to the left of the causeway, and Northern riders slowly started to appear. Priests arrived on the other side with drone cavalry.

"Shock troopers," called out one of the soldiers.

Captain Hayward turned to the men.

"May God have mercy on our souls," the captain calmly said.

They numbered fifteen. Charles looked at this small band of broken men. Some were older than his father; others were barely older than his son. They did not have an officer with them, which probably meant the castle had few defenders.

"Time is against us here. They must not reach the castle. We must stop them,"

More long limbs came to the front and were joined by wolves. Captain Hayward shook his head, then looked away momentarily and smiled. This was just madness. What had happened to Europe and its people? Why so much death? He looked at the picture of Rebecca and the children and placed it back in his tunic.

"Stay close to me, men. Let them come onto the causeway. We'll charge them and then retreat. Just maybe this will give us enough time."

The men and young boys lined their horses together, almost four abreast. Charles could see one of the young lads shaking. He made sure he made eye contact and winked. The boy smiled.

"Wait for the whites of their eyes and listen to my command."

He withdrew his sword.

They could hear the priests' laughter as the Northern riders and drone cavalry entered the causeway. The wolves, with their long limbs, began to cross the mudflats.

"Wait, wait...Charge!"

The enemy was tightly packed coming forward and was not expecting an assault. Charles had put the grown men alongside him, and in the second row, the younger lads followed with spears. The attack caught the Northern riders off guard and broke their lines. Charles saw his wife and children in his mind's eye. It gave him the strength he needed as he faced death. The horses gathered speed, and they met the enemy head-on. His sword connected with a drone cavalryman as he came forward. He swiftly brought the blade around again to slice at a Northern rider. The ferociousness of his attack inspired the others, and they fought like wounded lions. They were outnumbered but kept on fighting. Tragically, they were being picked off one by one, but no one wanted to retreat. It was a fight to the death.

On seeing a small boy lying on the track, Charles let out a call to the heavens. He grappled with two drone cavalrymen, pushing one off the causeway and taking the head off the other. He shouted for the men to retreat, but there were only four of them left.

Charles grabbed the ailing boy's body and remounted his horse. Something smacked into his back. The pain was intense, but his adrenaline carried him on.

They retreated towards the abbey whilst being pursued. However, Fortune was on their side that day as the tidal prediction had been slightly out. The sea was starting to come in. The speed of the water filling the mudflats meant the creatures were caught in two minds on what to do. Some of them had already pressed far out onto the flats, while others tried to access the edge of the track. The priests started to push them forward, but the causeway was congested.

The gate opened as the defenders rode in and were shut swiftly after that. A Gatling gun had been mounted at the front gate. It had taken a lifetime to get it working, but when it did kick in, it had the desired effect, easily cutting down the oncoming forces. Their tightly compacted formation was their downfall. The priests amongst them ordered the retreat as the water started to swell around their horses' hooves. Those who were left behind soon got into difficulty and were swept away by the incoming tide.

Charles gave the boy to a group of women who had rushed out to greet them. They had all been wounded during the battle. The lad had been struck on the arm and leg with a spear and was losing a lot of blood. The women took him away to seek medical advice. This is when Charles fell to his knees. He brought his arm behind his back and touched the site of the pain. When he brought it back, his hand was soaked with blood. The pain was agonising and caused him to go slightly giddy before falling forward a little and then collapsing onto the ground. A retired British doctor in the abbey helping with the sick and wounded. Captain Hayward was brought to him, and he began working on the wound. For now, the abbey was safe.

Captain Hayward opened his eyes briefly. The pain was excruciating.

"I must get to the coast. My wife and children are coming from Paris...I must find them."

He was delirious from the pain and soon blacked out. When he came around, he saw a man with a grey beard looking at him.

"Don't fret, I'm a doctor. Well, I used to be."

Charles asked about the boy and was told he was doing fine.

"Doctor, I must get back to the coastal ports, my family. They were coming through the catacombs in Paris—"

He was interrupted before he could finish his sentence.

"I'm dreadfully sorry to hear about your family, Captain, but I'm afraid we're at sea, returning to Great Britain."

With that, he pulled back the curtains to the side of the room to reveal open water and waves breaking against each other. The captain began to cry. It hurt his back to do so. He then tried to raise himself but could barely move.

"How long have I been out?"

The doctor came to his side.

"You were in and out of consciousness for a week. We had to leave for Jersey, and now we're on our way back to Britain."

The captain wiped his face.

"Where's my uniform?"

The doctor looked concerned. He paused to think about what the captain was after.

"I've taken the bullets out of your revolver for now. Please don't do anything stupid. Your family could be in Britain already or making their way home."

The captain sighed. The doctor could be right. Maybe they had reached a coastal port and found a ship back home. He thought about how he could have done things differently; he also thought about all the other families now suffering the same worries as him.

"My men were in Cherbourg. Have you any news of that port?"

"I'm afraid I know very little. We were cut off in the end."

The doctor told him he would let him rest before visiting him later.

Chapter 31

Nazar watched over Calais as his forces raided the city. Ships and boats were leaving altogether. It was the same story across the whole of the French coastline.

A drone general came forward.

"Your Highness, what shall we do with all the prisoners?"

Nazar looked at his wife riding towards them and then turned to look at his drone general.

"Kill some and feed them to the flesh-eaters and long-limbs. We will need some as slaves for our new order. Cities have to be built, and so do temples."

He then let out a raucous laugh, followed by a question. "Did we get Benedict?"

The general lowered his head.

"We do not know, sire."

Nazar looked displeased but the arrival of Oksana calmed him.

She approached him, dragging a bag accompanied by a large wolf at her side. She then showed her husband the contents of the bag. Inside was a collection of heads. She proclaimed them to belong to the great generals of Europe. They laughed, embraced each other, and then gazed at the smoke rising over Calais.

The high priestess swept back her long black hair. Her beauty was captivating.

"What about all the people that have escaped to Britain?"

Nazar crumpled up his face.

"The Empire will fall."

Printed in Dunstable, United Kingdom